THIS
IS
NOT
OVER

ALSO BY HOLLY BROWN

A Necessary End

Don't Try to Find Me

THIS
IS
NOT
OVER

HOLLY BROWN

WILLIAM MORROW

An Imprint of HarperCollinsPublishers

THIS IS NOT OVER. Copyright © 2017 by Holly Brown. All rights reserved. Printed in the United States of America. No part of this book may be used or reproduced in any manner whatsoever without written permission except in the case of brief quotations embodied in critical articles and reviews. For information address HarperCollins Publishers, 195 Broadway, New York, NY 10007.

HarperCollins books may be purchased for educational, business, or sales promotional use. For information please e-mail the Special Markets Department at SPsales@harpercollins.com.

FIRST EDITION

Designed by Chris Welch

Library of Congress Cataloging-in-Publication Data has been applied for.

ISBN 978-0-06-245683-0 (paperback)

ISBN 978-0-06-265959-0 (library edition)

17 18 19 20 21   OV/RRD   10 9 8 7 6 5 4 3 2 1

ACKNOWLEDGMENTS

Thank you so much to everyone who's believed in me: the Harper/Morrow team led by my incomparable editor, Carrie Feron, and supported by the wonderful Nicole Fischer; my godsend of an agent, Elisabeth Weed; and the family and friends who've never wavered through so many books, published and unpublished. We did it again, Darrend! I'm so fortunate to have you by my side.

Thanks are also due to my "host," who shall remain nameless. Sometimes inspiration comes from the most unlikely of places, and I am so grateful for that.

THIS
IS
NOT
OVER

1

Dawn

Please note: It is April 23, 2014. You'll have your deposit within
seven business days, just like it says on Getaway.com. I've put
through a refund to your credit card for the full amount, minus
$200 to replace the sheets. I couldn't get the stain out despite
professional laundering and bleaching, and it was rather large
(gray, about the size and shape of a typical house cat, though
the house rental didn't allow pets). That's neither here nor there.
At any rate, I already told you about this.
　Miranda

That's it, the entire e-mail. No *Dear Dawn* or *I'm sorry you had to
stalk me to get your deposit* or *Sincerely* or *All the best*. Just *Miranda*.
And does she really think I don't know today's date?

　I haven't felt anger like this in I don't know how long. No, I know
how long. Since before Rob. He's the antidote for all my inadequa-

cies. I'm good enough because I have him in my life. Because I'm the woman he loves. I'm *that* woman now.

Stop reading. Stop rereading.

But I can't.

I'm sitting at my battle-scarred kitchen table, staring at the screen of my five-year-old laptop in my one-bedroom apartment in a rapidly gentrifying neighborhood in Oakland (soon we'll be priced out), and I've been struck dumb. A stain the size and shape of a house cat? Like my husband and I are, collectively, Pigpen from *Peanuts*, and we leave a cloud of ash in our wake?

I'm an honorable (enough) person, and for sure Rob is. If we'd ruined Miranda's sheets, we would've owned up to it. I would've contacted her myself, apologized profusely, and said, "Take my deposit, please." No, I would have bleached the sheets, and if that hadn't worked, I would have run out to the nearest Target in a state of abject mortification and bought a new set (because those were not $200 sheets, I promise you that). Then one or the other of us, Rob or myself—whoever had left the ejaculate or the powder or whatever state (solid, liquid, or gas)—would have sought medical attention immediately, because WTF?

But that sequence of events never took place, because there's no way the stain is real. This woman, this Miranda, is trying to scam us out of our $200, half the amount of the security deposit. She's stealing from me, from us.

That's neither here nor there.

She's a thief and a liar, and she's trying to make me feel like I'm filthy, literally. Like I'm beneath her. Sure, she owns an ocean-view house in Santa Monica, and I own nothing, but that doesn't give her the right to . . .

Breathe, Dawn. WWRD—What Would Rob Do?

He'd let it go, because life is too short for grudges. But then, he's never been wronged, not in any way that matters.

I already told you about this.

Another lie.

What gets me is that she's so undeserving of that gorgeous house she doesn't even need to live in. It's an extra, a spare. I wonder about the opulence of her first home, if that's her second. How does a person like her get a setup like that? Where's the justice in this world? I bet she doesn't even appreciate her good fortune. I would, if it were mine.

I should be studying. This semester's been brutal, and I'm closing in on graduation. My good fortune is in being with Rob, someone who supports me in finally finishing my college degree. It's not every man who insists that his wife devote herself exclusively to her studies. I am incredibly, insanely, painfully lucky.

But I'm so pissed—both about Miranda's actions and about the snotty, deceitful tone she used to justify them—that I can't concentrate. Miranda stole my husband's hard-earned money, and how can I just let that go? Not to mention she's stealing my time and my energy. She's hijacking my emotions. I'm a slave to my outrage.

It's not only about the $200 (which I could most definitely use); it's the principle. She's trying to shame me, to make me think I did something wrong, something dirty, in order to buy herself what? A dinner? A pair of cashmere socks? That's after we paid her usurious price for a rental that was, admittedly, beautiful, but with no add-ons. No sweet surprises. Not like in Monterey, where we discovered a bidet and two free member passes to the aquarium. We went every day just to stare at the jellyfish, getting lost in their hypnotic undulations, imagining what it would be like to go through life with your own attached parachute, knowing you can never crash.

Monterey was my favorite getaway with Rob, because there was something about that house rental that allowed us to inhabit another life completely for those five days. I could envision a future where Rob and I are members of the aquarium ourselves, regular visitors with our kids, a boy and a girl (twins?) who stand agog as thousands of sardines swim in their circles like a silvery carousel.

It might sound shallow, but I'm pretty confident that Rob and I will have attractive children. Rob's handsome, and I've often heard that I'm beautiful, in an old-school, Christie Brinkley way (blue eyes, big toothy smile, no one suspects that I've been dyeing my long blond hair since I was a teenager).

The truth is, I don't feel beautiful, or even pretty, because I'm barely five-foot-one and at thirty years old, I still have the temperamental skin of a teenager: always at least one pimple, usually more, plus the brown dots that are the slowly healing legacy of pimples past. I'm constantly trying out new skincare products—no, not just products, entire systems. I start with great optimism ("I think I see something! I'm smoother and more supple!"), only to have my skin reassert itself with a vengeance. When people look at me admiringly, I feel like I'm putting one over on them.

Hopefully, our kids will inherit Rob's complexion, among other things.

But back to Miranda, the matter at hand. It's probably unfair to compare her Santa Monica rental to the Monterey house. I'll compare it instead to the one in Mendocino, a pleasant median: with a hot tub perched on a sea bluff, the kitchen sans the Vitamix that was shown in one of the pictures (but not promised in the text so I couldn't officially complain), the mattress that sagged slightly in the center, and the dun-colored days despite being outside the parameters of fog season.

Miranda's house still loses. Six hundred dollars a night and we had to go searching through cabinets to find replacement lightbulbs. Not to mention how loud the dishwasher was, and the hairline crack in the living room ceiling, and the absence of mini-shampoos or bodywashes. I felt her stinginess at every turn. A quarter inch of olive oil left in the bottle, grocery store brand. No spice rack, only salt, pepper, and thyme. How did thyme make the cut? How about some basil, or oregano? Red pepper flakes, for shit's sake?

When Rob and I get away, I'm after five-star accommodations, but in a house rather than a hotel so I can marinate in that lifestyle for a little while. It's the adult version of playing dress-up. I dislike when hosts meet us at the house because then I'm reminded it's theirs, and I have a visual to go with that knowledge. But that's only happened once. Normally, rich people do it like Miranda does, with minimal contact: key in a lockbox, call in an emergency.

Burned-out lightbulbs, lack of basic cooking supplies, and cracks in plaster remind me of my real everyday, where things need replacing and fixing and sometimes you run out. Vacations are for abundance. While Rob and I are away, money is never an object, and that's the biggest break from real life. I even have a different wardrobe for vacation (slinky cocktail dresses for which I scour consignment shops, and stiletto heels instead of wedges), and I start using Crest Whitestrips a month out so I can wear the red lipstick that's too much for everyday.

I'm reborn in those houses. They scrub me clean of all the debris from my past. I'm Dawn 2.0. Because the true American dream is that you don't have to be who you were, you're not where you grew up, you're not defined by the family you left behind or the family that left you behind way before that.

Getaway.com has never let me down before. I read through all the reviews thoroughly before I book. I pay special attention to the three-star ones, which seems to be as low as anyone will ever go,

2

Miranda

Beware of your "host"

THREE STARS

I wouldn't have left a review at all, if I didn't feel it was my civic duty to warn others. Sure, there were small issues with the house itself (burned-out bulbs, a light switch that didn't work at all, no toiletries provided, a poorly stocked kitchen in terms of cooking oil, condiments, etc., and also from the kitchen, a more obscured ocean view than it appeared in the pictures—things that shouldn't have been going on given the equivalently priced rentals). But I wouldn't be mentioning any of that if it wasn't for what happened after we left.

I was checking the "pending transactions" on my credit card to see when my security deposit would be returned. I e-mailed the host, Miranda, to inquire about the delay. Miranda didn't respond to my first e-mail, and her reply to my second was a curt "Just keep checking, it'll show up."

I wrote again a few days later to politely nudge her. I got an extremely unfriendly e-mail that accused me of leaving a stain that was "rather large (gray, about the size and shape of a typical house cat, though the house rental didn't allow pets)." Because of that, she said she was deducting half our security deposit (Getaway.com won't let me say the amount, but you can do the math).

WHAT????!!!! She's accusing me of smuggling in a bedraggled cat? My husband and I are clean people, and we're not blind. We would have seen a stain on the sheet. We've never left such a stain on sheets in our entire lives. Gray? Really? And impervious to bleaching? It all seemed pretty crazy to me—like she's just finding a way to keep our deposit, maybe as retaliation for me asking about it? I don't know. All I know is that the sheets we slept on were not worth the money she kept. Maybe she's confusing the dollar amount with the thread count.

But the kicker was when she said at the end of her e-mail, "I already told you about this," which she absolutely did not.

This struck me as extremely shady. I know that other people have had different experiences (there are lots of four- and five-star reviews for this property, which is why we booked it to start with). But I thought we should share our experience and you can factor it into your decision of where to book.

I cannot believe what I'm seeing. I am a certified hospitable person. I open my home to people, and I let them call me with any problems or questions, at any time. And they do. The kind of people who pay $600 a night for a two-bedroom beach house often have "problems." I answer their calls while I'm in the middle of dinner. I answer their calls when I'm in the dressing room at Barneys. I answer as I'm in my bed, about to drift off to sleep. I tell them, "Second drawer on the left," or "No, that's vegetarian. For pure vegan, try Golden Mean, or Viva La Vegan."

I do my best to be a thoughtful, good person. I volunteer. I let cars merge in front of me on the L.A. freeways during rush hour with a friendly hand wave. I treat people decently—family and friends and guests and strangers—unlike some people who shall go nameless in their reviews.

I know who D.T. is, of course. She's darkened my inbox enough over the past week. Dawn Thiebold actually wrote me FIVE times to ask about her security deposit, sometimes leading with, "Don't know if you got my last e-mail . . ." and signing off with a perky "Thanks!" and in between came the badgering. If she can afford to stay at my rental, then she can afford to wait until the transaction posts to her credit card, within seven business days as promised.

I don't have much tolerance for people who live beyond their means and then act entitled. She had to change a lightbulb? She was denied her constitutional right to condiments? There was a partially obscured view from the kitchen? She fails to mention that it's "obscured" by a gorgeous purple jacaranda tree in full spring bloom. The living room view is completely unobstructed, as noted in every other review, but not in hers. She doesn't highlight a single thing she likes.

I am a little touchy about the rental, I know that. It was my parents' home in their later years, and I can still see the contentment they felt as they surveyed that ocean panorama. Now my father's gone, and my mother's in her assisted living community, requiring more assistance every day as the dementia worsens, and I never feel like I'm doing enough for her, no matter how many flowers

I bring or how much tidying up I do or how often I tell her she's a fantastic mom and I love her. More and more often, she barely registers my presence. It's a terrible thing, being invisible to your own mother.

I try not to take it personally. It's the inexorable aging process; it's a disease, getting old. No love is strong enough to overcome biology. But I can't help but feel that it should be, that it is for some other family, some other mother with some other daughter.

My brother, George, says it's the same during his infrequent visits. He lives in Idaho with his family, so he doesn't have to concern himself with her decline. He doesn't have to watch it, day by excruciating day. He doesn't have to see her falter and disappear.

He also doesn't have to handle any of the arrangements. I'm the power of attorney, it all falls to me. "It's not like you work," he once told me. As if it's not work to deal with all the guests, being hospitable and available, ensuring that no one's broken anything or stolen anything or left, say, cat-sized stains on sheets. My father had left the Santa Monica house to both George and me, but I bought him out, just so I wouldn't have to feel the resentment of doing everything and then giving him his cut. So that it would be all my work, and all my profit. I convinced Larry that it was a good investment, and one that I would manage exclusively. He didn't know there was a hidden catch. He doesn't need to. Marriages work best with a "don't ask, don't tell" policy, on a bedrock of "what you don't know won't hurt you."

Eva's coming tomorrow, but I always pre-clean the Beverly Hills house. Today, it's with some extra fervor, courtesy of Dawn and her review. I scrub the granite countertops and every stainless steel appliance until I can practically see my reflection. Or perhaps that's my angry aura.

I've never been very comfortable with anger. It's important to keep it at bay. Cleaning helps. In this case, it's going to take more than just one room. Fortunately, I've got four thousand square feet.

I love this house. Well, I used to, when I could still see it. Now, it's just backdrop, the set against which my life with Larry plays out. We've been here for almost twenty-five years, since Thad was three. I remember when the Realtor first showed it to us: a four-bedroom Spanish villa, just blocks from Rodeo Drive. The feeling was so warm—taupe and burnt orange, the variegated walnut wood floors with matching beamed ceilings, the rounded doorways and fireplaces. Thad was tearing through here, letting out excited yelps. He thought he was home. I wanted it, badly, but Larry was barely past residency back then. Maybe I was still reeling a little from what had happened during the residency and thought more penance was due; we didn't yet deserve such a bounty. But Larry disagreed, and his parents were willing to give us the down payment. He was sure that despite everything, the world should (and would) be good to us.

If you saw only this house—high ceilings, ornate mosaic tiling, terra-cotta interior courtyard, Olympic-sized pool—you would think that it had been.

I move into the living room, though dusting isn't nearly as satisfying as a vociferous spray and wipe. I should probably do one of the bathrooms. The master bathroom, maybe. I could clean the expanse of the shower, with its four showerheads.

I'd dressed to visit my mother, in the silk blouse she used to like when she still cared about what I wore, and I strip it off. I pull my shoulder-length ash-blond hair into a ponytail, trying not to see myself as I am: middle-aged verging on old, gaining flab in the midsection despite swimming and strengthening my core four times a week, in the plunge bra that Larry likes, when he remembers to look. Fifty-seven isn't so old.

How old is Dawn? Young, I imagine, from the cadence in her e-mails and her review.

That review. I spritz the marble wall and wipe with such ferocity that I begin to fear carpal tunnel.

What if she costs me future bookings? I've got guests for the rest of April and May, but summer is prime time, and now is when people book for summer. If I lose that income . . .

Dawn has no idea what she's doing to me. Or maybe she does. Maybe she's just that rotten.

No, I simply need to make it clear to her that she's wrong, that this was all a misunderstanding, and she'll be reasonable. She'll take the review down. Most people aren't rotten, they're confused. Like Thad.

What galls me about the review is that it makes me look dishonest, when that's the last thing I am. Not that I reveal everything to everyone. I'm circumspect, even with Larry. But I would never play fast and loose with someone's security deposit.

I might not have been bubbling over in my e-mail responses, I don't use exclamation points or (God forbid) emojis, but I told her what she needed to know: The security deposit would be returned within the specified time frame. They always are.

I left a voicemail to tell her about the sheets. I know that I did. Could I have left it on the wrong phone number? Hard to imagine making a mistake like that, but then, it was a hectic time. I was concerned by what I'd seen on Thad's Twitter feed, not to mention his Instagram, and he didn't return my calls, not for days.

Maybe I wasn't so pleasant in that phone message, because I was peeved to discover the sheets. On the very rare occasions when guests have left damage in the past, they've informed me. They've apologized. We've worked it out together. When people are honest, I generally don't even opt to charge them. But Dawn slips out the back door and then harasses me about her deposit, as if those sheets could escape my notice. It was like someone had come into my late father's home and taken a dump in his bed (though the stain wasn't feces, because human waste can be bleached out. I raised a child, I know this from experience). I still don't know what caused that gray stain. I don't want to know. But Dawn must.

Even if I give her the benefit of the doubt and say she really wasn't aware, she should have been chastened once I called her attention to it. Instead, she came out swinging. She's the "shady" one, not me.

Or she could just be young and in need of some correction. I'll write to her, we'll clear all this up, she'll delete her review, and that will be that. No harm done. I can forgive most anything; I know that from experience, too.

3

Dawn

I'm shocked that you didn't address your issue with me first but instead chose to post a scathing review. Now people will be worried about their security deposit when they don't need to be. Look at my other reviews. No one else has had any problem with me. On the contrary, they rave about my hospitality.

I don't know why you didn't receive my voicemail. I did leave one. I was surprised that you didn't call or e-mail me to discuss the situation. Honestly, I was surprised you hadn't initially called the stain to my attention, as people are usually cognizant of the damage they do. Because I didn't hear from you, I assumed that meant you were fine with me handling it on my own by subtracting from your security deposit.

You suggest in your review that I'm a liar. I can assure you I am not, and have never been accused of that before. I've also never had a situation like this.

I'd like to ask you to take down your review, as it is full of misleading information. I depend on reviews for my business, and
false ones are harmful as well as hurtful.

Thank you,

Miranda

I usually like this taqueria. It's not authentic, not at all, but it's got
happy primary-colored walls touting its non-GMO goodness. It's
the kind of place Rob and I will go when we have bambinos of our
own because it's affordable, and the high chairs and booster seats
are plentiful, and the salsa bar isn't just wiped down with some
germ-saturated rag every fifteen minutes but routinely spritzed with
spray cleanser.

Today, though, everything's on my nerves. We couldn't get a
booth, and the table right next to us features a hyperactive bespat-
tered toddler. The harried mom keeps giving us apologetic smiles,
and I smile back because she seems to be doing the best she can to
catch the items he's knocking over. She's just a woman, after all, not
a multiarmed creature from Greek mythology, but still, I wish their
food was to-go.

Rob's doing his best to understand me, but he just doesn't get
this Miranda thing. His face is full of affectionate mirth, with the
barest tinge of bemusement. "You're cute when you're worked up,"
he says. In the four years we've been together, I've tried not to get
worked up in his presence. I let his mellowness waft over me; I wear
it like a security blanket.

He chews his burrito an extra-long time, contemplatively. The
mastication has a damage control vibe. He wants to talk me down.

WWRD? He'd have let this go already. I hate that I can't.

It's like Miranda's e-mails are calculated to push every one of my
buttons. But how could that be? She doesn't even know me.

I catch the frazzled mom stealing an appreciative glance at Rob. I don't blame her. I still look at him that way myself. Sandy hair, green eyes, thin build, in a button-down and jeans. She's got no ring on, so either she has no husband of her own or what she has isn't necessarily worth telling the world about, and she surely wouldn't mind one like Rob.

Her instincts are spot on. A Rob type would always be faithful, ever true; you'd have to get sick of him. And if you did, if you broke his heart, he'd still never go negative in a custody battle; he'd always respect the primacy of the mother, while being the world's greatest dad, who tickles and jokes and teaches all while deriving effortless delight.

Not that we're ever going to break up. I love Rob, a lot. He's not perfect, which works for me. I could never be with a man of all smooth planes. But he keeps his sharp edges well concealed, and no woman in a taqueria would ever suspect.

"She's not a communications major, like you," Rob finally says. "She probably doesn't know how she's coming across."

I thought that after a full minute's delay, he would have come up with some magical solution and all these feelings I'm having would evaporate. But he's trying, and that counts for a lot.

"She sounds really full of herself," he adds, "which is annoying."

"Absolutely."

"Her punishment is being her. She spends her time looking down on people, so she'll never be happy. But you will."

It's ironic that his remark comes as I am staring dispiritedly at my carnitas taco, unable to take another bite. I can feel a new pimple forming on my cheek, under the surface. It's not just a pimple, it's a cyst. Those hurt. I blame Miranda.

No, I blame me for letting Miranda get under my skin, literally.

I can't tell Rob that during class today, I was formulating and discarding different responses to her e-mail. They were mostly variations on "Why do you think you're so much better than me, you old cooze?" I can't imagine talking down to someone the way she talks down to me. My parents never talked like that. But then, they were train wrecks, and my dad barely spoke to me at all. Mom's the one thing I've successfully let go.

Rob hit the nail on the head, though. Miranda does sound abominably sure of herself. She almost had me convinced that the stain is real, and that she had left me a voicemail. But I know neither of those things is true. If there's anything that's going to piss me off, it's forcing me to question my reality. I've done enough of that in my life.

She was "shocked" I hadn't discussed my issues with her first. Shocked I didn't think she was the cat's meow like every other person who'd ever stayed in her house. Shocked I didn't know I'd ruined her sheets. How has her old heart withstood so much shock?

She's accusing me of writing a false and misleading review. But she's the one who's offered no proof of her claim. Where's the picture of this supposed stain?

She is a liar. And her biggest lie is that she isn't.

"Why does it matter, though?" Rob asks. "Why does she matter?"

"Because you don't treat people the way she's treating us."

"So then don't treat people like that. That's all you can do, right? You control yourself. You don't control her."

"Someone needs to teach her a lesson. Don't you think?"

I want very much to hear his answer—it feels like a litmus test somehow—but he's saved by the salsa. I catch it in my peripheral vision, but it's too late to move out of the way. It's the red stuff, no verde here, and it splashes onto my leg. The toddler's mother is beside herself, apologizing profusely. "We're going to go now," she tells me. "We'll get out of your hair."

"That's okay," I say. I dip a napkin in a cup of water and rub at my thigh. "He's a little boy. It happens."

"More stains," Rob says, grinning. "We can't seem to get away from them."

"Let's say, for the sake of argument, that there was a gray stain. What could have possibly left it?" I'm trying not to be distracted by the mother, who's inadvertently banging me in the head with her bulging diaper bag as she tries to gather everything on her table into piles while subduing the toddler at the same time. He's got white-blond hair, crew-cut style, and the sailboat graphic on his shirt is mottled by salsa, as if there's been an onboard massacre.

"Don't worry," Rob says to the boy's mom. "Leave it all. We'll throw everything out for you. Just get the little guy home. He seems tired."

"He is!" She sends Rob a grateful smile. "Thank you so much! Enjoy your night!" She glances at me. "And again, I'm so sorry."

"Not a problem," I say, because it shouldn't be. I know what I should feel; now I just have to get there.

Let Miranda go. If I could do it with my mother, Miranda should be easy.

But then, I've never let go of what my father did.

4

Miranda

I received your e-mail. While I understand your concern that my review might damage your business, I did not hear you in any way addressing my issues. What I heard was a stream of "you're wrong" and "me me me."

I was not trying to be scathing in my review; I was being honest. Getaway.com is a community and its members have to look out for one another by posting their honest experiences.

My honest experience with you has not been good. The reason I didn't choose to address the issue about the sheets with you first is because I did not find you trustworthy. To wit:

1. You told me to "keep checking" my credit card statement for my refund, which seemed to indicate that I would be receiving the deposit in full.

2. You had ample opportunity to mention the sheets in our

e-mails but you didn't. And you still haven't provided any
photographic evidence of the supposed stain.

3. I always receive my e-mails, voicemails, and texts, yet I've
never had any messages from you in any form warning me
that you'd be deducting $200.

All of these things together gave me the impression you
were not acting in good faith. Our subsequent communication
has not altered that impression. For example, you didn't take
responsibility or apologize for anything; you just asked me to
take the review down.

The fact that there are no other three-star reviews doesn't
mean everyone has had positive dealings with you. Maybe the
people who were dissatisfied don't like to write reviews. Maybe
you're just in the habit of trying to bully people into taking their
reviews down, and making them question their reality. Sorry it
hasn't worked this time.

Dawn

Me me me. You sure have got me pegged.

If she could see me now, pulling into the circular drive of the
cancer center where my husband is a chief radiation oncologist,
where he saves people's lives, as I deliver a homemade lunch to keep
him going in that mission, she'd have to eat her words.

Larry is off to the side of the sliding glass entrance doors, a scowl
on his face as he stares at his phone. I'm not surprised to see that
expression. I knew it was a bad day when I received his text this
morning: *What are you having for lunch?* It's how he tells me that it's
ten A.M. and already a rough one, and he could use my cooking;
he'd like to see my face.

I give the horn a jolly little beep, and he looks up and over, the irritation melting away. I love that I still have that effect on him after

all these years. I work at our marriage every day, so he won't have to. It's our division of labor, and it's a fair one.

He's not a handsome man, Larry, but then, I've never been a beautiful woman. I've always liked his features, that they're large but not cartoonishly so; they're trustworthy. I have a trustworthy face, too, the one you pick on a busy street to ask where the nearest something or other is, but my features are all on the small side. I draw outside of my natural lip line and fill it in with a bright color, lest my lips disappear. Maximizing my eyes is no picnic either. Every decade, my makeup routine gets ten minutes longer.

But you do what you have to. You run to the store after you get your husband's ten A.M. text and you make quinoa with wild salmon and asparagus and you drive it to him and it's all worth it when he opens the passenger side door and gives you that smile that says you're helping to turn it all around for him, you're making his day exponentially better, because what's a lifelong partnership for if not that?

He eases down into the passenger seat, still trim after all these years. He accepts the container with an appreciative glance inside. "You didn't go to any trouble, right?" he asks. "You were already making this for yourself?"

We're not really supposed to linger here in the drive, it's for pickups and drop-offs only, but I've pulled way up and the security guard knows Larry and me. He'd never shoo us along. I've made sure we're not blocking anyone. Unlike Dawn, I'm conscious of my impact on others.

She's clearly not about to take back her review. She's determined to see herself as the wronged party. It's a joke, but I can't afford to laugh. I'm genuinely afraid.

What if potential renters believe her? What if her vicious words somehow cancel out the other twenty-seven raves and they stop booking with me? Sometimes nastiness is more compelling than the truth.

The stakes are high, in ways Dawn couldn't even begin to understand. It's not just about me, or about Thad. It's about the ripple effect outward—the harm Thad could do to other people. He's well over eighteen, so I'm not legally liable anymore, but I'm still morally liable. I will be for the rest of my life. That's what motherhood means.

I try to push down the rising panic. I tell myself it's not life or death, but I can never convince myself. Not where Thad is concerned. There's no way to forget the overdoses, the ambulance rides, the fear.

I see people walking in and out of the glass oncology palace, their backs hunched with exhaustion or too upright, like they're using every bit of strength to maintain the rigidity of hope. Some are weak with chemo, in wheelchairs or leaning on their loved ones for support. I do what I can to ease their suffering, which is to keep Larry's stress as low as possible so he can give them the best possible care, a fighting chance.

I wish I could stop fearing that review, but I know how potent lies can be.

Larry kisses my cheek. "Thank you," he says tenderly. "The salmon looks fantastic. So do you, by the way."

I give his hand a squeeze. Such competent hands. "Fortunately, I happened to be making your favorite today."

"I could use it." He looks out the window briefly, and I know better than to ask. He prefers to complain about the system—the medical oncologists who need to be more honest with patients and their families and stop prescribing treatments that will only prolong discomfort and not lives because of their own egos, because they view death as failure, because they get higher reimbursement for more treatment than for honest conversations—rather than tell me about the specific losses he faces every day. It hurts him to watch good people die. He doesn't have to say it; I can see it.

Radiation oncologists don't get to know their patients as intimately as medical oncologists do. Larry spends a lot of time doing treatment planning (viewing simulations, consulting with other physicians) and less direct time with the patients. But he carries their prognoses; he carries their sorrows, even if he can't name them as such. Governed by confidentiality, he isn't allowed to name them at all. No patient names, no identifying details, but sometimes, he can't hold it all in. Sometimes, he slips. That's when I have to hold him up.

"What's going on with you?" he asks.

I tell him about my trip to the market, about the price of wild salmon, about the new robe I bought for my mother. "She used to have such good taste," I say. He reaches out and touches my shoulder. He gets it; he understands erasure, bit by bit.

This is not the time to be petty and it's certainly not the place, but Dawn keeps intruding on my thoughts. She's like Thad, like all of her generation—unable to slow down and take another's perspective, unwilling to say she's wrong and reverse course. Life is all about reversing course based on new information. But Thad hasn't had to learn that, has he? He's been too busy teaching me.

I will not tell Larry about Dawn. I will not dignify her with that. Her name will not pass my husband's lips, because she is not worthy.

If she's not worthy of my husband's breath, why is she worthy of my brain waves? I don't like thinking of the answer to that question. I don't like admitting that I have the available bandwidth and he doesn't.

It's more than that, though. Dawn really could hurt me with that review and, by extension, she could hurt Thad. I'm a mama bear. No matter how old he is, he's still my cub.

Then there's that tone of hers. That supercilious, hyperprofessional tone, as if she, Dawn, were the reasonable one, instead of the person who's defending her untenable position. She thinks she should be able to evade responsibility for the damage she's wrought. Well, I have news for her. We all have to pay.

I shouldn't respond to her last sally. I shouldn't waste another second, another keystroke, on her.

Yet I can't help but worry that people won't see through her. Her little shtick about wanting to do her civic duty to protect the community (from me!) could persuade some people. There are plenty of other rentals to choose from in Santa Monica, despite the fact that, technically, the city ordinance only allows long-term rentals of thirty days or more. It's a crowded marketplace, and I've never had any trouble standing out, in the best way. With Dawn's review, I could be standing out for all the wrong reasons. I haven't had any queries about availability since it's been up.

If Dawn won't remove it, then I'll have to write a response on the site. We'll go head to head, and I'll have to convince potential renters that of the two of us, I'm the one to be trusted. That shouldn't be too hard, since I'm the one with all those five-star reviews. I've been vetted.

Maybe I should try just one more e-mail to Dawn to see if common sense can prevail? Not just common sense, but common decency. Dawn and her husband did the damage, now they need to suck it up, instead of doing more damage, this time to my business.

That's a good line, I might want to use that.

It's not like it's just about me. Dawn could not be more wrong about that. As if to prove my point, just then I get a text from Thad saying, *Got the money, thanks.*

I don't want Larry to see it, and thankfully, he doesn't even cast a glance.

He made his position clear more than two years ago. He won't even consider contact with Thad until Thad's gone to a rehab and then a sober living environment for at least six months, and if there is contact, it will have to be entirely facilitated by professionals to, in Larry's words, "minimize the possibility of manipulation."

Larry is not a cold man. He's become that way where Thad is concerned. I don't possess that ability. I'm a mother, and a woman, and it's not sexist to say that matters. I've tried plenty of Nar-Anon meetings to stop what they call the enabling, but I can't change my most fundamental aspects. I've failed Nar-Anon like Thad's failed Narcotics Anonymous. What mother isn't, on some level, addicted to a child in trouble?

Still, I know I shouldn't have given him that money, not without placing some conditions. Clean drug tests through a reputable facility, for example. Is there such a facility in Tucson? Why is he even in Tucson? He won't answer me directly about much, and that's no exception. I can only try to deduce his motivations from his Twitter feed. He has hard-partying friends there. Artists, he calls them; "tweakers," in common vernacular. I never thought the word "tweaker" would be a regular part of my vocabulary, but nasty surprises are part of life.

Reversing course; it's what we all need to do sometimes. I'm doing Dawn a favor to teach her that now, while she's still young.

5

Dawn

Dawn,

I apologize for the misunderstanding. Apparently, you didn't understand in my previous e-mails that you owed money for the sheets. I did leave a voicemail, but that's neither here nor there. I also should have taken a photo. As I mentioned, I've never been in a situation like this before, and it didn't occur to me that my integrity would be in question. It never has been before.

Maybe it wasn't you who stained the sheets. Maybe it was your husband, and you didn't know. Sometimes we overlook things. Life is busy, you were in a rush to check out. I believe that you honestly did not know about the damage.

But now that you do know, I'd ask that you stop doing further damage, to my business. Your review is based on miscommunication and inaccuracies. It is tantamount to character assassination, as it paints me as someone who would steal a security deposit.

My husband is a doctor. I do volunteer work. I have almost all five-star reviews on my property because I treat people well. That is my life.

This is your chance to treat people well, because now that you know better, you cannot in good conscience leave your review up.

Please call if you'd like to discuss this further. Then we can hear each other's tones, and that will reduce the possibility of additional miscommunication. I still feel we can come to some workable solution, and that you can at least amend the review.

Thank you for reading, for being reasonable, and for staying at my house,

Miranda

We all have our reasons, and our justifications. When she thanks me for being reasonable, she's really saying that I should come over to her side. We were just talking in class about implied judgment and the authorial voice, so I know what I'm talking about.

She's a terrible communicator. She's not in control of her message at all. I could almost feel bad for her, if she wasn't such a self-righteous, condescending bitch.

I apologize for the misunderstanding.

It's pretty much like saying she's sorry I feel that way. I see through her. I *read* through her. But I need to stop replaying her words in my head. Let her go, Dawn.

"Are you listening?" Salina asks as we tromp across campus. I nod; I got the gist. She was dumped again. No, "dumped" would mean there was some commitment to begin with, and that's not really the case when you meet through Tinder. When your love life is orchestrated by GPS, you only get a certain latitude for complaining.

"I know, it sucks."

"He didn't even spell my name right."

"No one spells your name right."

She tilts her head slightly in acknowledgment. "True." Her hair gleams auburn in the sunlight. I've always thought Salina is way prettier than she—or the world—gives her credit for, but then, I tend to overestimate the attractiveness of people with perfect skin. It's celestial, that skin of hers.

"Sorry," a scrawny undergrad says, after he accidentally side-swipes me. I don't know what it is with twenty-year-olds, why they can't navigate around moving obstacles, i.e., people. He probably thinks the campus is a video game and he's lost his control paddle. Or whatever they use for video games. I wouldn't know. I'm a sentient being, inhabiting the actual world.

Miranda's making me irritable. It's my last semester. I have a ton to do, and a future to worry about. I don't have time for her bullshit.

Salina stops at the fountain, balancing one leg on its circular lip. It's turned off (budget cuts, most likely). She leans over and adjusts her complicated gladiator-style sandals. She's in a spaghetti-strap dress with no bra. "I just don't get it," she says.

"It could be your vibe." I'm trying to phrase it as delicately as I can.

"My vibe?" One eyebrow lifts, as if in warning.

"You want to be taken seriously, right?"

She looks horrified. "Hell, no!" She's twenty-four. Sometimes I feel that six-year gulf in our ages acutely. But it's not just age; it's lifestyle. She's out partying and hooking up; she shows up for class in last night's eye makeup and an oversized hoodie belonging to a man whose name she may or may not remember, one who definitely can't spell hers.

My husband is a doctor.

Shut up, Miranda.

Salina and I sit down on the fountain and survey the campus. It's concrete, utilitarian, and aggressively geometric: circular fountain, square quad, rectangular buildings. No climbing ivy or hallowed halls at this state school branch. The only nod to aesthetics is this fountain, with its central brass mermaid holding a pile of books, water burbling out of her mouth like a blow job gone wrong. It's surrounded by the campus's only expanse of lawn. Students are sunning themselves in the grass. There's a mix of youngest (straight from high school), young (transfers from other community colleges, like Salina), and older (returning students, like me). I could have gotten my degree online, but Rob said I should have the "full college experience." He loved Pepperdine. Yet this is a far cry from the cliffs of Malibu.

Salina sighs. "I just keep thinking, what's the point?"

"The point of what?"

"Of it all."

Pseudo-existential thoughts inspired by Tinder—was that what Rob meant about the college experience?

This is your chance to treat people well, because now that you know better, you cannot in good conscience leave your review up.

She's so myopic that she thinks the only good I can do is the good I can do for her. As if I'd actually call and hear her brandish her presumed superiority in real time.

There's no workable solution here, Miranda.

It occurs to me—and I allow myself a private smile at the thought—that I've gotten under her skin as much as she's gotten under mine. (My cyst has been throbbing intermittently throughout the day, pulsing like a beating heart.) Otherwise, she wouldn't have written again, asking me to reconsider.

So the rich can have their gated communities, but thanks to social media, thanks to Getaway.com, they can't be protected entirely from the proletariat. We can get at them.

"I've got to go in a few minutes," Salina says. "I'm late for the dermatologist."

"You go to a dermatologist?" I can't conceal my surprise. I thought skin like hers was born, not made.

"A cosmetic dermatologist. I get lasered." Her tone is matter-of-fact.

"What's your skin like when it's not lasered?"

"More like yours." That same matter-of-fact tone, but I feel myself blushing. "You know, not too bad, but not like this." She gestures to her own visage.

I've stopped visiting dermatologists on my insurance plan. They all overdo or underdo; they prescribe oral antibiotics for life, or some stupid topical cream that does nothing. But cosmetic dermatologists and lasers—that sounds like heaven. "How much is it?" I ask.

"Five hundred dollars a treatment. It works best in a series of six. Then you get them every six months as maintenance. I'm in debt for about three grand but it's totally worth it."

I try in vain to find a single pore on her face. Just one. It can't be done. I practically moan with yearning. But $500 a treatment? A series of six, plus maintenance?

There's no way I can afford things like out-of-pocket dermatology, not when I'm in school and Rob's supporting me. Not when he's working with his dad at the store he'll someday inherit, but shouldn't. I've hinted that engraving is perched on the ledge of obsolescence. It is most definitely not a growth industry. You can't upsell. You can't get someone to buy two engraved watches, or silver platters, or whatever. He should be in sales. He could make a fortune, with his looks and personality.

But I don't get to push him, not when he's been so good to me, not when he's told me no, no, you can't get a part-time job, focus on your degree. I wanted to contribute to the household, maybe move into a nicer apartment, but Rob insisted. I've never felt so taken care of, not even when I was a kid, especially not then. My father was such a lousy provider, financially, emotionally, you name it, and my mother needed me to buffer her from his indifference and his affairs. She needed me to look after her. I never climbed into her bed when I was afraid or crying; she crawled into mine, seeking comfort. I never felt safe, or secure. The next eviction was always looming. Neither of my parents had really wanted a child, though you could argue that my mother made the best of it: she took what she could. Eventually, my dad joined her.

But Rob is a giver. He's the one who planned our first getaway, a surprise rental in Napa. It was a magical weekend, so much more than I thought I deserved, and I told him that we couldn't repeat it, we couldn't afford to. He must have seen how much I love a getaway, the chance to be someone else for a while, my future self, and he said as long as we only do it a few times a year, it's okay. He says I'm worth it. No one's ever thought so before.

With him paying for everything, I've gotten the best grades of my life. I work hard, because it's for both of us. Yet here I am, in my last semester, with no clear idea of a career. I'm afraid I'll let him down, that I'll prove to be a bad investment, and the fear completely overshadows any sense of pride or accomplishment.

Maybe I am having the true college experience, because I don't want it to end. I don't want to be thrust out into the real world.

"Rob wouldn't let you spend money on your face?" Salina asks.

She's trying to sound sympathetic but I hear it: the implied judgment, the authorial voice. She likes Rob, because you can't help but like Rob, but she's been a little suspicious of him ever since I told her that he wanted me to take some time off right after college and get pregnant. He does make a compelling argument: If I have our kids first, then I won't be established yet in my career; I won't have to step away when I'm gaining some momentum. I could just start fresh when the kid is, say, two or three.

Salina called that "retrograde." She's got that amorphous Beyoncé-flavored feminism ("Woman on top, bitches!") that has no clear tenets. In my case, it neglects one crucial fact: At the rate I'm going, I could use another two or three years to figure out what I want to be when I grow up.

Yet somehow, my IUD is still firmly in place.

"I don't need Rob's permission," I say, "for anything." That's not how we work. "It just wouldn't be responsible, that's all. Three thousand dollars for my face, when he's the one working. When we might start trying to get pregnant soon."

"Responsible? That's about as sexy as being taken seriously."

"Our sex life is fine." At the look that crosses her face, I amend. "It's good. It's hot."

She doesn't try to contain her incredulity as she swings her bag over her shoulder. "I should get to my appointment. See you."

As she sashays off, I flash back to Miranda. I hear her accusing me of character assassination and exhorting me to be reasonable. Has anything truly great ever happened to a reasonable woman? I think not.

6

Miranda

Dear Miranda,

    I've chosen not to call you because I didn't want to be condescended to live. It's bad enough by e-mail.

    I'm standing by my review. The only amending I would do is to add an additional warning: Future guests should beware that if they put up an unbiased review, they'll be hounded by their former "host."

    You still haven't given me a genuine apology, or attempted to address my grievance by any financial means (for example, a partial or full refund). It seems we're at an impasse.

    Dawn

An impasse that can be solved by a cash infusion, if I'm reading her correctly?

I underestimated this girl. This is a shakedown, pure and simple.

I don't know why I didn't recognize it sooner. I suppose it's because I try to see the best in people, and I assume they do the same. Call it my Anne Frank streak. It's why it never occurred to me to take a picture of that stain.

I've been sitting in my car in front of the Santa Monica house for the past fifteen minutes, mulling and fuming. I need to calm down and weigh out my options. Anger is not among them.

I could report her to Getaway.com. Maybe I could get her review removed that way. They wouldn't want to sanction blackmail, after all. I'm a long-standing, valued member of their community. I've been posting my rental on their site practically since its inception.

But as I reread the e-mail, I see that it's brilliantly constructed, with built-in plausible deniability. There's no direct threat, no quid pro quo offered; it says right there that she's not going to change her review in my favor. "Miranda just inferred that she could buy me off," she could tell them. "I'm not for sale!"

See, brilliant.

Or I'm giving her entirely too much credit.

Let's say it's not a ransom note. Let's say she composed this in a minute flat, and it never crossed her mind that she was opening the door to a cash offer. Let's say she's innocent. I could give her the $200 back. I could say that she doesn't feel she did the damage and that I don't have photographic proof, so she can have her money and we'll call it even. All I ask is that she amend the review to show I'm an honest and reasonable person. Or better yet, delete it altogether.

It would be a draw. No, a win-win.

It's only $200. That's a good value, for losing that review. I still haven't had any inquiries since it's been up. It's not unheard of for me to go three days without a booking, but not even a single question? She's definitely hurting my business, and I can't afford a dry spell. I need continuous cash flow.

One could argue that if she accepts the money, I'm the winner. I'll have proven that she's not about protecting the unsuspecting community from a rapacious landlord but about avoiding responsibility.

I want to know that she knows that. I want her to cry uncle. My gut is telling me that there is nothing innocent about this girl.

As with terrorists, I can't let Dawn win, can't let her have the perception of winning. I'll accept only a complete and unconditional surrender: that review comes down before any payment is rendered.

She claims that I've shown myself to be untrustworthy—well, right back at her.

She's giving me a way out, I have to focus on that. This is good. I need to see this as good.

What if she turns down the $200, what if she tries for more?

Then I can report her to Getaway.com. They'll have to see her for what she is.

If she just turns me down, though, then she's won. She'll think she's exposed me, and that I was lying about the stain the whole time.

Why does it matter what she thinks? I don't know her, she doesn't know me.

Yet I've come to hate her.

That's crazy. I don't hate people. I was raised by parents who told me that hate is for people who can't find love, who can't locate their compassion. I believe that.

Give her the money, get rid of the review, and return to my life. It's a good life. I mean, look around. Look at this house.

I do, I look up at it. I don't hate people, and I love this house. Part of why I break the ordinance in order to rent it only for short stays is because I have a fantasy of moving in here, for a little while at least. A trial period, even. I've mentioned to Larry that it wouldn't be such a bad commute to the oncology center. But he says he would never be happy surrounded by what he calls, derisively, "the creative types."

I like the creative types. I like the pace. I like that people walk here. I like the beach and the pier. When I need to clear my brain, I still like to ride the Ferris wheel, just like I did when I was little, a controlled spiral out over that expanse of ocean.

I love this house not just because it's beautiful or close to the beach. I love it for what it meant to my father in his later years, how it transformed him, and my parents as a couple. My father was a workaholic, much like Larry, and in this house, he learned to relax. He became a Santa Monica man—with a favorite café where he'd read his newspaper, and a bicycle built for two that he'd ride with my mother along the path to Venice Beach, and the smoothies he'd make after long, meandering trips through the farmers' market, discovering combinations like star fruit and jicama. He and my mother had always been companionable, with few conflicts, but in Santa Monica, they rediscovered each other. They would touch casually, effortlessly, thoughtlessly. His hand on her back, a stray kiss on the cheek. They had this whole new tactile vocabulary, and you could tell they enjoyed speaking it. Those last five years of his life, of their lives together, were glorious.

I have a fantasy that the house will have the same effect on Larry, that he and I will someday experience the same renaissance as my parents. But he doesn't see what I see, not yet.

I wish I were a creative type myself, frankly. The closest I come to it is with the flowers that I arrange and bring into the house before each check-in. Dawn never commented on that, did she, on the explosion of lilies and snapdragons and one central rose in the foyer?

No, of course not; I'm the condiment-withholding, deposit-stealing monster.

I pick up my latest bouquet and carry it toward the house. It's a two-bedroom white-shingled Craftsman, with a white picket fence and a Meyer lemon tree in the front yard. There's a large deck with an ocean view. There's lots of light wood throughout—the floors, the kitchen island, and even the fireplace—creating an airy feeling that's not hippie-beachy but is summery all the same. The master bedroom and the living room both have ocean views, too. The sofas are sky blue, the furniture white, and the throw rugs white edged with blue. This house was where my parents found joy in what could aptly be called their golden years, and I can still feel it, like a friendly haunting.

Ordinarily, that is. Today, I'm looking around critically. I see the little scuffs on doorframes and the floor, the marks left by my short-term tenants. This is my home, and they troop through, these in-grates, and they evaluate. Mostly favorably, but there have been others over the years who needed to be told that their reviews were inaccurate and inappropriate, that if their vacation experience failed to match the beauty of this house, it's their fault, and not the home's. Dawn is the first person to refuse to take down her review. Perhaps she's not refusing at all, but inviting an opening bid.

If this were just about me, if it were only a matter of fewer shopping trips to Barneys, then I would ignore her altogether. But I have to think about Thad, same as I have every day for the past twenty-seven years. Once you're a mother, it's never just about you.

I fill a vase with water at the kitchen sink. Sunlight pours in through the large window, and between the beautiful purple flowers of the jacaranda, I can see the ocean just fine, thank you.

7

Dawn

We can agree to disagree. Remove your review, and I'll refund your $200.

I'm surprised that Miranda is texting. I'd assumed she was one of those old people who used e-mail exclusively. So she does have my correct phone number after all. That means that I should have received the voicemail she supposedly left.

Liar.

What about pain and suffering? I text back.

One laser treatment and I can probably let all of this go. No matter what Miranda thinks, I am reasonable. And self-interested, like everyone else. The community will have to fend for itself. Besides, I'm sure that Miranda has learned her lesson, and she won't mess with people's security deposits without photographic evidence again.

I know that one laser treatment isn't ideal, but it's something. It's a start.

What does that mean?

Now she's going to play dumb.

I mean, $200 covers the sheets, but it doesn't cover everything.

What's everything?

All the aggravation. All the time I spent writing my review, and e-mailing back and forth with you. All the wasted energy.

Ditto.

I'm not the one who started it.

Yes, you did. You left the stain.

I DID NOT LEAVE THE STAIN!

Do not yell at me.

Are you wasting my time again?

I'm trying to resolve this. I'm trying to be the bigger person.

There it is. That's the Miranda I've come to know and love.

Are you being sarcastic?

Obvi.

This is why I dislike texting.

Then why did you text?

What do you want from me, Dawn?

I want you to make things right.

That's what I'm trying to do.

With $200? That's what you think this is about?

What is it about then?

Apologize, sincerely. And change that first numeral.

You want more than $200?

I deserve more. I told you, pain and suffering. And an apology. Not the bullshit kind.

My apology was not bs.

"Sorry for the misunderstanding"?

That was sincere.

You're sorry that I misunderstood you? That's more like an accusation.

I'm sorry that I was not clearer. How's that?

Now you're being sarcastic.

No, I'm not. You don't know me.

You don't know me.

Let's stop this. Right now.

Ball's in your court.

I apologized.

For not being clearer.

Yes.

Not good enough.

I'm not giving you more than $200. That wouldn't be fair.

Where's the pic?

Of the sheets?

No, of the Sistine Chapel.

Enough sarcasm.

I'm not a child. Don't correct me.

I didn't take a photo. I've never needed one before.

So you've done this to other people before?

You're taking my words out of context. I told you, I didn't hear back from you. I thought you were okay with being charged for the damage, until I read the review.

Now you know I'm not okay. I want a refund.

I'm offering you a refund.

Of more than $200.

Then that's not a refund. That's blood money.

What the fuck are you talking about?

Classy.

I'm breathing heavily. If she were right in front of me, I might become the old Dawn, the one who had to scrap, who had to learn to protect herself because no one was going to do it for her.

I'm not that girl anymore. I'm not.

I'm Rob's wife. He's never seen that side of me. I extinguished it when I married him. Expunged that girl, like a story that should never have been written. It's better this way. I am.

It feels dangerous, these exchanges with Miranda. It's like a séance, summoning forth who I used to be, and I have to admit, sometimes I feel like I've missed her.

You think you're so classy, I type, *the doctor's wife, stealing people's money? I would never do that. NEVER.*

I've never so much as shoplifted a lipstick, and I grew up without. I knew true temptation, and I resisted it, every time. What hardship has Miranda known? There's nothing worse than someone who has so much but needs just a little bit more. There's nothing uglier than greed.

This was a mistake. You're completely unreasonable.

You're a snotty bitch.

This is over.

This is not over.

8

Miranda

Owner's response to "Beware of your 'host'":

I'm a reasonable person. Just ask any of the people who've previously stayed at my home. Please read all my other, glowing reviews. If this reviewer had contacted me directly instead of posting a review, everything could have been easily resolved.

The view from the kitchen window is spectacular. The only "obstruction" is a gorgeous purple flowering jacaranda tree. The kitchen is fully stocked. I'm not sure why the reviewer didn't get mini-toiletries. They're always provided, and they're from Gilchrist & Soames. This may have been an oversight on the part of the house cleaner. I've already mentioned it to her. The light switches are all in working order. There are plenty of extra lightbulbs in the pantry. I'm sorry that the reviewer had to change her own. Again, it must have been an oversight.

I'm also sorry that the reviewer didn't notice the stain she'd left. I don't know what it was, or why it didn't come out after bleaching. I did have to buy new sheets (600 thread count Perielle, with a retail value that Getaway.com will not allow me to state but you can find out easily enough). I subtracted the amount I paid from the damage deposit. I informed the reviewer by voicemail that I was going to do so. Because I never heard back, I assumed that she was okay with paying for her damage. I'm sorry she never received the message.

I've apologized repeatedly to the reviewer for any miscommunication but have only received hostility in return. I try to be a good host, and generally, I succeed. Again, please see all my other reviews.

Some people want to find fault; they want to hate. That seems to be the case here. (Please see D.T.'s other reviews, like the one where she complains about the Mendocino weather, as if the host could have controlled that variable.) Unfortunately, some people can't be pleased.

I heave a sigh of relief as I press the Save button.

Dawn's had her say, I've had mine. Let the renters decide who's more credible.

I'm late for my visit with my mother. I know she won't actually remember the time I told her I'd be there, but I don't like to be late for anything. I respect other people's time, just as she did.

She was always five minutes early, while my father was chronically late, his face blotchy and red (with embarrassment, I'm sure). But she never shamed him. She stood up for him. She wouldn't let George or myself say a bad word about our father, even if he failed to show up for a school play or a family dinner. "He's the hardest worker you'll ever meet," she told us, and if anyone felt shame then,

9

Dawn

Don't forget to talk to the doc, OK?

Love you.

So much.

"You'll feel a slight pinch," Dr. Kroy says. I breathe in sharply; it was more than slight. But equal to her pinch is the pressure of Rob's trio of texts. "You okay up there?"

"Fine," I say. I've always had a hard time with pelvic exams. I have a ridiculously sensitive cervix, and even when they use the smallest speculum they've got, it still hurts. Rob wonders if it's in my mind, a psychosomatic thing. It rankles, that word, "psycho."

Dr. Kroy pulls off her plastic gloves as she emerges from between my legs. It's always funny, that moment when the gynecologist pops up, like you've just given birth to her. I sit up on the table and huddle protectively beneath my pink paper gown. Always pink. Now *that's* retrograde.

The counters of the exam room are vulva pink, and the light is less than flattering. I always feel self-conscious about my skin in rooms like this, though I know Dr. Kroy sees real cysts, on ovaries and cervixes; she's not going to be freaked out by the ones on my face.

Besides, she's a sweet person. A motherly type, even though I'd guess she's not that much older than me. She's probably in her early forties, with clear (if a little crepey) skin and curly brown hair caught up in a bun. I bet growing up, she tucked all her dolls into bed and knew, without question, that she'd have babies someday. Me, I thought no way. Until I hit twenty-five. Then I couldn't settle fast enough.

No, that's not the right way to put it. Rob's a catch.

Some people can't be pleased.

Fuck Miranda. Referencing my Mendocino review was just low. I didn't blame the owners for the bad weather, but Miranda made it sound like I had, and what are the odds anyone will do any cross-referencing?

"So now that the fun stuff is out of the way," Dr. Kroy says with a smile, "what else did you want to talk to me about?" She gestures toward the form I filled out upon check-in, where I indicated I had questions and/or concerns. Then she perches on the pink rolling stool, which signals we're in for a heart-to-heart.

"Rob and I might want to start trying soon," I say. It seems unnecessary to add "for a baby" but it also seems weird not to add it. I mean, why is it a given that "trying" means "baby"? There's a lot in life worth trying for.

Dr. Kroy's smile broadens. I guess the only trying anyone ever talks to her about is of the procreative variety.

If you try, you can fail. That's the risk. Everyone will know it's me. Isn't it always the woman's fault? It would be too fitting, me being barren.

Even if I succeed at getting pregnant, I could miscarry. That would be failing to carry the baby to term. Or I could fail at parenthood. It happens. Just look at all the wreckage out there.

"Are there any tests we should run first?" I ask. "To make sure I'm ready physically?" From my hopeful tone, you'd think I want my OB to put the kibosh on my fertility plans.

She shakes her head. "Nope. We'd just take your Mirena out and you're good to go."

"What about the herpes?"

"Herpes wouldn't stop you from conceiving or increase the odds of miscarriage. Once you are pregnant, we'd put you on acyclovir a few weeks before you're due to make sure there are no lesions when the baby's exiting the birth canal. But herpes doesn't put you at higher risk for any complications. Odds are you'd have an entirely normal pregnancy and an entirely healthy baby."

"Odds are," I echo weakly. I wish I could smile as easily as she's doing. I wish she'd been my mother. If I'd received this kind of reassurance throughout my life, I'd know how to metabolize it now. "I won't have a mom in the delivery room with me."

Don't know where that came from.

Her expression turns sympathetic. "Did your mom pass away?"

I shake my head, but I don't elaborate.

"It can activate old wounds," she says. "When you're thinking about having a baby, you start thinking about being a baby. What it's like to be a parent, what it's like to be a child. It's scary stuff."

"But you think I can do it?"

"You're in good health. You're thin. You don't smoke."

That wasn't what I meant, but okay.

"Are there infertility issues in your family?"

"Not that I know of."

"Any history of miscarriages?"

"I don't know."

"How old was your mother when she had you?"

I've been trying to fake the middle class for so long, but it's the little things that out me. "Fifteen." My mother is forty-five now. She might even be younger than Dr. Kroy. "How long do you think it would take for me to conceive?"

"That's hard to say. Some people get pregnant the same month they take the IUD out; for others, their cycle has to regulate."

"On average, how long would it take for someone with my health history?"

She cocks her head. "Are you asking because you want it to be sooner, or later?"

"Rob wants sooner."

"So you need to figure out what *you* want." She's still wearing that sympathetic expression, which is a little annoying, because this is a happy conversation. This is about what I want, and what I can have, because I'm thin and I don't smoke and I have a husband who loves me. It's not like when I got diagnosed with herpes and I had to go back into the past. Who did I sleep with, who did I infect, who infected me. This is about the future. My happy future. "It's a ten-minute appointment to get the IUD out. Why don't you keep it in for now, and just call me when you're ready?"

I stare down at my hands for a long minute, thinking of Rob and the disappointment he'll feel, how to tell him that I just can't give him what he wants, not yet, and then, slowly, I nod.

10

Miranda

How dare you? You don't know me. How dare you say that some
people need to find fault, some people need to hate, some
people can't be pleased. Look in the mirror, you self-righteous
cunt. Volunteer work is for people who don't have a job because
they mooch off their doctor husbands. It's for people with time
on their hands, and no purpose, and a need to think they're
better than other people. I bet you call them "the less fortunate."

Maybe you're fortunate in some ways, but not really, because
you're still you. You're full of yourself, and sure of yourself, and
that's a very dangerous combination.

You think the best thing you can be is "reasonable"? Then I
feel sorry for you.

The only other person who's ever spewed such hatred in my direction is Thad, and he was on something when he did it, I know that.
He didn't mean what he said. He couldn't have.

Maybe Dawn's an addict, too. These sound like the ravings of someone who's chemically uninhibited, who's abandoned all self-control.

If it is substance-induced, though, it's not really about self-control. Addiction is a disease. It's a medical condition, and one of its characteristics is that people revert to their basest selves. They do unimaginable things because they're drunk or high, or because they're coming down, or because they're in agony chasing their next fix.

Desperate people are capable of ugly things. This, I've learned.

She lives in Oakland. That's one of the most dangerous cities in America. It's also, paradoxically, red-hot according to the *L.A. Times* real estate section. Apparently, the home prices in some neighborhoods rival San Francisco, across the bay. I don't know what neighborhood she's in. It could be one that's riddled by crack and meth and whatever hybrid has come down the pike. *She* could be riddled.

Oakland's only six or seven hours away from here. She knows my full name. She could probably find our address without too much difficulty, the Internet being what it is.

I look over at Larry, sleeping soundly beside me. He doesn't know anything about Dawn, and if I told him, he'd tell me to go back to sleep, the house alarm is set. He's always believed himself inviolate, untouchable. He'd say, "She wrote a review on a website and you're terrified of her?" But it's not the review. It's her tenacity. This should have ended already, yet she just keeps coming at me.

I put my hand to my breast. I can't remember the last time my heart pounded like this, and that must be what she wants.

I don't know anything about her, not really. I don't know about any of my guests. There are no background checks. They send inquiries, and if they can provide the 50 percent deposit up front, I book them. In my house. In my dead father's house. It's never once occurred to me how unsafe that is. I suppose I've felt somewhat inviolate myself, except where Thad is concerned. There, I'm nothing but vulnerable.

I think of the people who are at the house right now, a young couple with a child. For a second, I feel relief, as if a child is somehow prophylactic, or proof of decency. But no, plenty of lousy people are parents. Plenty of lousy people are children.

This isn't me. I don't think things like this. I don't think the worst of people. Dawn's wrong; I don't teach poor kids how to read or feed the hungry in order to feel superior. I don't do it because I'm rudderless.

No, she didn't say rudderless. She said purposeless.

The hell with her.

I don't think things like that either. That's gutter talk.

It's three A.M., and I'm wide-awake. This is not my normal state of mind; these are not my true thoughts. I'm not myself.

I sit up, and while it's too dark to really see, what with the blackout curtains, I take in the room and everything in it perfectly. It must be memory, not sight. I did pick out everything in here: all of it heavy wood, hand-carved, the iron accents also forged by hand. Not very imaginative, I recognize now. A Spanish villa, with Spanish hacienda furniture, and drapes and bedding in the colors of a flamenco dancer, all red and black.

It's not like the bedroom displays lack of taste, or lack of expense. Just lack of imagination. Besides, I was grieving. Thad was seventeen, and I had to face the boy he was. The man he might be. The man I hoped he wouldn't be, and now he is.

No, he's still a work in progress. He's like unfinished furniture. He needs to be sanded down and lacquered properly. The problem is, who'll finish him now? It's too late for me. Parents have their chance, and if they leave work undone, then it's for the world to complete.

This bed is the one thing Larry chose. I insisted that it match the style of the other furniture, and he was fine with that. Size was all that mattered to him. He wanted a California king.

I objected at the time. I said it was like being marooned on separate sides of an island, it felt that large to me. I was trying to get across in imagery what I couldn't bring myself to say: You'll be too far away; we'll barely be able to reach each other. But he'd just laughed and said, "Doesn't everyone want a private island?" He was teasing and said we should name it. Laranda. Mirly. I pretended to laugh, but I felt like crying. It felt like the end of something to me, but there was no explaining that.

I still grope for him sometimes, like I used to, but the distance seems too big to traverse. I can't help thinking he doesn't want me to traverse it, why else get this bed? It's not like we were always on top of each other in our old king; we had plenty of space. Why did he need more? There aren't many things that feel worth waking him up for when he's on the other side of an island. I can't help feeling that he wants me to bear my burdens alone.

We still have sex every Sunday morning, regular as yoga, and it provides the same sense of release. I'm more limber afterward, and if I've had an orgasm, then there's that. I like that he still seems to want me, that there've been no performance issues despite his age, and that he often still gives me a bracing slap on the butt as he gets up to shower. It feels personal.

No, there's no sense in waking him up when I can't tell him about Dawn. He'll say that if it's stressing me out so much, this rental business, then we should just get rid of the Santa Monica house. Oakland isn't the only place real estate is on an upswing.

Larry would tell me we could make a good profit and take some more vacations. "Buy our own island, for real," he'd joke. The thing about Larry is that he likes parity. He likes to give, and then get. We could afford more vacations now; we could afford a third home. But he likes to frame things as inducements: You do this, we can have this. You sell the house, we'll have more time together. Why not just have everything now, because we have only this one life, because we have only one son and we don't even see him, by Larry's edict?

I can't give up the Santa Monica house, not when Thad depends on it.

The cash infusions aren't only for him. They're for the good of society. He's a tick, and I voluntarily offer myself, I let him suck my blood, so that he won't have to do what so many other addicts do. So he won't break into houses or deal drugs or sell himself, so he won't spread the misery around. I'll be his host, and others will be spared.

His host. Funny, I'd never thought of it in those terms.

It all started when Thad was fourteen. That's when I was first aware something was wrong, so his use probably began months, possibly years, before. It was a blow to me on many levels, just one of which was that I'd always considered myself a tuned-in mom. Some would say hypervigilant; Thad used the term "suffocating." I'd say devoted. He was my primary job, and I'm a hard worker.

I've gone over and over this in my mind, with much guilt and self-recrimination and fervent wishes for a time machine, and I've reached the conclusion that I missed the signs and symptoms because they weren't actually much of a departure from Thad's normal behavior. He'd been displaying mood swings his entire childhood. Anger and aggression? Check. He was never violent toward people, thank God, but when he was mad, he'd yell without regard for who was around. Sometimes he almost seemed to take delight in humiliating me in public with my failure to control him. There were times when he smashed whatever object was within reach, remorselessly.

Let me amend that: He did have some regard for who was around. He never acted that way in front of his father. I still don't really understand why Larry had this impact—it wasn't like he ever laid a hand on Thad—but there was a respect, a reverence even, that was entirely absent from Thad's attitude toward me.

I like to think that while I took the brunt in bad times, I also had more good times with Thad than Larry did. Life is not a contest, I realize, and perhaps it's uncharitable of me to tabulate. But I feel like there has to be some additional benefit for my troubles. I remember sharing laughter with Thad, and, occasionally, confidences. That is, sometimes Thad would reveal his true heart—the boy who loved his friends, wanted to create art, cared what happened to his family, and was bewildered by the outbursts that seized him with such regularity.

So it wasn't until he lost his appetite and about fifteen pounds in less than a month that I suspected something was truly wrong. I took him to the pediatrician, who did a physical and ran a bunch of tests but couldn't find any cause.

Now I realize that it was practically malpractice for a pediatrician to know so little about such obvious signs of methamphetamine abuse. The addiction was progressing on its dangerous course through my little boy, and I was depending on Dr. Paolini to arrest that course. Instead, he sent us on our way with a recommendation that I make Thad protein shakes and bring him back if the weight loss continued. Larry trusted Dr. Paolini (they'd played golf together) so I felt like I had to also. I overruled my parental instincts, the first in a series of mistakes.

The eye twitching appeared next. Dr. Paolini said that tics were a sign of stress. I was to put less pressure on Thad academically and "give him a little more breathing room." The good doctor had formed an impression that I was what's now called a helicopter parent. Thad seconded this new recommendation, enthusiastically.

Dr. Paolini gave Thad's addiction space in which to flourish. More time with friends, less time doing homework, reduced supervision—it's a teenage addict's dream. Thad's pediatrician was his first enabler.

I remember knocking on Thad's door (he now spent more time with his door closed, invoking Dr. Paolini as justification) and hearing his frenzied "Wait a minute, wait a minute!" When he yanked the door open, he was beaming. He ushered me into his room and showed me what he'd been building. It was an art installation made out of items from his childhood. A sort of Tower of Babel had been constructed from Tinkertoys, Legos, and action figures. Most of them had been affixed haphazardly, with glue in long dried rivulets. "I call it *Toy Chest*," he said, with a pride that I thought misplaced.

"It's good," I told him weakly.

"You're such a phony." His gaze and tone were equally savage. "That's what this piece is about."

"About phony parents?"

"About loss of innocence. About corruption. About the ways people chip away at kids—you chip away—one Lego at a time."

I said, "I'm glad to see you're enjoying yourself," and withdrew from his room, closing the door behind me. I leaned against it, breathing heavily. For years, he'd viewed me with increasing scorn, and I couldn't pinpoint why. There was one clear theme: I was wrong, all the time. I was a bad mother who didn't give him what he needed. What did he need? I couldn't figure it out. He couldn't—or didn't want to—tell me. We were caught in a vicious cycle. I believe he must have wanted to escape it as much as I did, but neither of us could find a way out. We didn't have the words.

It was awful, feeling so inept, so nervous, around your own son. But I didn't realize that the worst was still to come. Meth addiction manages to be both insidious and rapid. The protein shakes actually worked enough that the weight loss stabilized, but what I would later recognize as repetitious behavior (a key symptom) continued. Thad kept building onto his art project until it took up half his room. And it was a large room. It was like a monster living alongside him, the monster of my failure. Now I know that the frequent trips from his old playroom to his bedroom were meth-induced hyperactivity. He had to keep moving.

I'm ashamed to say that I never saw his dilated pupils. He didn't even wear sunglasses; we just didn't look into each other's eyes. I never noticed any body odor, though I've since learned that he probably had a smell akin to cat urine, the same one meth labs have. He was most likely emitting a stench through his sweat, through his pores, but I was keeping my distance.

Ultimately, there was no hiding the tooth decay. I took him to the dentist twice a year—no matter what enmity existed between us, I was always on top of necessary appointments—and the dentist was shocked by the degradation. Unlike Dr. Paolini, he was aware immediately of the cause. He called me into his office for a private talk, something that had never happened before, and told me, bluntly, that Thad had "meth mouth. Early stages, but it'll move fast." He asked what kind of help I'd already tried to give Thad.

I was mortified. If I admitted I hadn't realized what was happening, he would have thought I was a negligent parent. "He won't see any of the therapists I've found for him," I said. It wasn't a complete lie. We had tried therapy in the past, and he was either silent or spun webs of lies about his father and me. I couldn't imagine we'd have a different outcome even if I'd known about the meth.

My God, meth. That wasn't even in my lexicon. Speed. My son was doing speed. I didn't even know how that was administered. Did he shoot it up? If I looked at his arms, would I find scabby track marks? I hadn't even thought to look. I *was* a negligent mother, the last thing I would have ever expected to be.

I was suddenly furious. Larry's a doctor. He should have detected this. If he ever paid any attention to his son, he would have. I wasn't going to let him get away with this workaholic/absentee father bit anymore. Things were going to change. They had to.

"A therapist isn't enough," the dentist said. "He needs a program. Inpatient is probably your best bet. Something immersive. He's a tough kid."

I was suffused with gratitude. Even the dentist could see that I was up against a lot. My failures were understandable, predictable even, as Thad was no ordinary child.

"The good thing is," he continued, "you've got control now. You can force him into a program whether he wants to go or not. Once they turn eighteen, you lose your edge." I had the sudden feeling he was speaking from personal experience. "So do all you can, now. Get him in ASAP."

The urgency in his exhortation brought tears to my eyes. I did something completely unlike myself: I reached across the desk and grabbed his hand in mine. "Thank you," I said. "Thank you so much."

He nodded and looked away, uncomfortable with my touch but too kind to draw back. "Before he goes, bring him back for a fluoride treatment."

Thad knew something was up during the car ride. I wondered if he was high right then. I was so naïve. I thought it was just a high and a low. I wasn't yet cognizant of the stages of meth intoxication: the rush, the high, the binge, the tweaking, and the crash, each with its own distinctive characteristics that I would come to know well, through painful experience. Once I knew to look, it was all I could see. It was unmissable. His rapid speech and interruptions meant he was high, while his hyperactivity was indicative of a binge. Oversleeping meant he was crashing.

I knew that our family had to change, profoundly, and family was my domain. So this was my problem, more than anyone else's, and I hadn't a clue how to begin to solve it.

I still don't. The phrase "knowledge is power" doesn't apply to the parent of a substance abuser.

Strange that I can even feel afraid of someone like Dawn when the worst-case scenario has been happening for thirteen years now. No, not quite the worst. Thad might be using, but he's still alive.

And I still have a sense of self-preservation. That vitriolic e-mail from Dawn was a none-too-veiled threat. She's warning me that I'll get mine. She's not stupid enough to say it directly, but people can read between the lines. Getaway.com must have a department that protects the safety of its customers. I can send them the e-mail, file some sort of report, and then Dawn can be thrown off the site, out of the community, and all her reviews will be deleted. That could solve all my problems.

Unless Dawn is truly nuts. She seems to care about her participation in the community, and if I take it away from her, there's no telling what she'd do. I could be unleashing something awful.

These are three A.M. thoughts. No one cares that much about being on some website. No one would drive six hours to take vengeance on a stranger.

But better safe than sorry. I'll deal with Getaway.com, and not with Dawn herself. Better not to respond, to let her feel she's had the last word. Yes, that's the safest thing.

11

Dawn

I am in receipt of your hateful e-mail. I reiterate: You don't know me. Nothing you say is remotely true, but then, consider the source. You need manners, and class. But I don't blame you. I blame your parents.

Rob's licking my nipples. He thinks I like that, when really, it makes me feel like I'm a saucer of milk and he's a cat.

Someday, when we have our baby, I will be a saucer of milk.

Did I just shudder? That's okay, Rob mistook it for pleasure.

He's not forcing me to have his baby, contrary to what Salina might think. I chose him because I wanted to have his baby. Well, I wanted to have someone's. I was seeing babies everywhere, as if for the first time, and wanting to wear one around my torso in a little sling, and to stroke the downy hair, and to love and be loved, unconditionally. What I never thought I'd do, what I never thought

I'd want, because I had no example to follow—I suddenly wanted it, badly. My biological clock was set to go off at precisely the age of twenty-five.

But now that motherhood is staring me in the face, I find myself blinking. Dr. Kroy made it sound like it's frightening even for normal people, the ones with role models.

I put my hands in Rob's silky hair and lift his head. "I'm sorry," I say with a smile. "I'm kind of preoccupied."

"You have a lot of schoolwork?"

I should say yes. That would obviously be the more respectable answer. But I want an honest marriage, one in which I'm accepted fully, cysts and all. "I got another e-mail from Miranda."

A shooting star of exasperation crosses his face before he nods, once again full of understanding. "What'd she say?"

I tell him. He already knows what I wrote to her. I showed him before I sent it, and he laughed and said, "Well, okay then." I like to think that what he meant was *I'd never send it, but I like that you're ballsy; I like that you're you.*

He also knows that Getaway.com won't let me rewrite my review to include quotes from Miranda's e-mails, the ones that expose her for the elitist prig she is. I'd have to delete my current review and write a whole new one, and it would go through the same approval process as the first, and the woman I spoke to on the phone (after being on purgatorial hold for more than ten minutes) advised me that "ad hominem attacks wouldn't be permitted."

Like she even knows what "ad hominem" means. She's probably reading it from a script. I bet whoever wrote the script didn't even know what it was. It's the kind of verbiage that when placed before "attacks" confers faux legitimacy.

It's not like the Getaway.com rep even knows what it is I want to say. *I* don't yet know what I want to say. But my problem is that the longer the review is, the harder it will be to maintain the interest of the reader and to be taken seriously. So I won't be able to supply the full context; I'll have to synthesize my dealings with Miranda into something relatively pithy, and then she'll get to respond to the new review, and of course, she'll point out all the supposed holes in my story and make it sound like I'm spinning things in my favor, which, in fact, is what I'll be doing. It's what we're all doing, all the time.

"By now," Rob says, "you must have expected Miranda to say those things. It sounds just like her, only more concentrated."

"Sure, but it's still obnoxious." It still stings. My parents are classless. I'm supposed to be the fruit that rolled far from the tree, all the way to San Francisco. Well, Oakland. I couldn't afford San Francisco.

"It's meant to be obnoxious. It's meant to bug you."

He's right. Miranda's hit a bull's-eye, and she's done it by being entirely predictable.

"That pisses me off more," I say.

"You're pissed off at me?"

"No, no. She's got me pissed off at myself. For being bugged. For giving her what she wants."

"So stop giving her what she wants."

It's that old joke: "Doc, it hurts when I do this." "So stop doing it." It comes so easily to Rob—not doing the things that hurt. I feel like some kind of freak. Is it the way he's looking at me, or am I just imagining that? Nothing's felt okay since Miranda got in my head.

So stop letting her in your head, that's what Rob would say, like a punch line.

He reaches over and strokes my cheek. I don't like when he touches the skin of my face. I'm always thinking of the bumps he might be feeling, and about the oils on the pads of his fingers, how he might be causing a new pimple right this second. It sucks the eroticism right out of the room.

I've never told him that before, because I don't want him to feel constrained. He should be able to touch his wife wherever he's moved to do so. So I guess I'm not 100 percent honest with him all the time. I need to look out for him, too. It's not like I'm alone in this marriage.

"Time to forget," he says softly, "about Miranda," and then he leans in and kisses me, his tongue gentle and probing. He ratchets up the intensity, and I mirror him, but without much feeling. Well, without much sensual feeling. No, that's not true either. Anger is a sensual feeling. There are few things more visceral, really.

I don't know who I'm angry at anymore—him, or her, or me. He's the only one who I know with certainty doesn't deserve to be on the list.

I think he can tell I'm not into it, but he's still pushing me. Do I play along with him, fake it, for lack of a better term, in the hopes that I'll start to authentically feel? And what if I don't? I don't like to stop things once we're far down the road; it seems rude. Then I'm stuck playacting, and I prefer not to do that. Not with my husband. With previous boyfriends, sure, but Rob and I are different.

A blow job, maybe? No, it's a Tuesday night. Who gives blow jobs after they've been working hard all day? On a weekend, I'd finish him off like that. Hand job, that says weeknight.

He's kissing me, and I'm kissing him back. There's reciprocity, but not mutuality. He's driving the car, I'm along for the ride. This is the kind of foreplay Salina was imagining when I told her my sex life was fine.

I pull back, just a little, and I'm not sure what I'm going to say. He's breathing heavily, about to proceed to the next level, to go down on me, maybe, since the tit kissing was such a bust earlier (no pun intended).

"You okay?" His voice is a little rough with desire, and I do like when he sounds like that.

"I'm just—still preoccupied."

"Stop thinking. Start doing." That's not the sandpaper of desire I'm hearing, it's full-on irritation.

He's right to be annoyed. I've let Miranda take up residence in my mind, so much so that I'm talking to Rob about her when we should be having sex.

Then it comes to me: I'm avoiding sex with my husband, and I'm using Miranda to do it.

That is so messed up that I pretty much leap on top of him, mounting him like a stag. We will have sex tonight. I've got no choice, really.

12

Miranda

I'm visiting Grandma later. Is there anything you want me to tell her?

Anything at all?

Maybe just send her your love?

I texted Thad hours ago. His lack of response hurts—not on my behalf, but on hers. Through all his problems, my mother consistently showed him unconditional love. For his part, Thad was always respectful to his grandmother, even kind. When I observed them together, it was with pleasure, but not always without envy.

I flip over my phone for a quick check, just in case I missed his return text. Normally when I'm with people, I turn off my cell, but with my mother, I place it facedown. That makes me sad, realizing that she's in another, somehow lesser category of personhood. But as if to reinforce this, she's not even looking at me, or at my phone. Today she remembered I'm her daughter but she's shown no interest in engaging with me. That might be worse than being forgotten entirely.

It's a pretty day, though, and a lovely garden. There's lots of purple and white, lavender and daisies and hydrangea, in hedge-lined beds. If you walk the path of stepping-stones, you arrive at a fountain. Though my mother is actually in decent health physically, she opts to walk as little as possible. She never glances at the nearby birdbath and its colorful inhabitants.

My mind wanders a lot when I visit my mother. I feel guilty about that, I know I should focus and keep the conversation going, but sometimes I think, What's the point? She vacillates between not knowing who I am and not caring. But at least today she's calm.

She's getting state-of-the-art care, has a whole treatment team, and still, calm is the best I can hope for. Her psychiatrist says that in addition to the dementia, she's showing signs of "agitated de-pression." I've Googled that term, and there's so little agreement as to what it means that it's practically colloquial. I'm a doctor's wife, I don't need colloquial. I like medical terminology, a definite diagnosis, so I can find out about all the best treatments. Or Larry can.

"Agitated depression" seems to be a catchall for the fact that some days, in addition to seeming confused, she's surly about being confused. Sometimes she's actually aggressive. My formerly mild-mannered mother, once a faultless paragon of class, physically at-tacked another resident last month. I was called, she was sedated, and they've added a benzodiazepine to her medication regimen since. I know benzodiazepines are highly addictive, but I didn't even protest. I was just glad they didn't toss her out, the way the rehabs used to do with Thad.

They're called residents, but really, they're patients. My mother started out vibrant when she moved here after my father's death. She was grieving, of course, but she was in her own apartment, in independent living, making friends, joining clubs, taking classes. Then she rapidly worked her way down the chain: from independent living to assisted living to skilled nursing, and finally, to rehabilitative (though it doesn't take Google to realize that she's not being rehabilitated, and the word "living" was dropped along the way). This is the final stop. Well, not the final. Death would be final, but she's never leaving here, and she's never improving either.

They take good care of her. She's always neatly dressed, her thinning silver hair glossy and brushed, and her face, which appears to lose muscle tone each day, is clean of all food particles even now, when I'm here right after lunch.

Sometimes I wish I could catch the staff doing something wrong. I wish they were failing to administer her medication, that they weren't encouraging her to exercise her mind and body, and then I could say, "Aha, she could be doing better! I just need to find her the right place, the right care!" I could go into a flurry of research and advocacy, and there would be hope. We could change her prognosis. But by all accounts and observation, the care is excellent. It's my mother who's sinking. She's the *Titanic* and they keep her decks swabbed.

I remember when she first arrived. She was living on her own for the first time in close to fifty years. Heartbroken over my father, but so game, so willing, so participatory. I once found her in a common area doing Wii bowling. She gardened. She was in two different book clubs, fiction and nonfiction. She took a class in postimpressionism and another in Thai cooking. She was learning Italian, and how to meditate. Ironically, so much of it was to stave off the memory issues that hadn't revealed themselves, and now look where she is, despite all that brain exercise. Despite a life lived with kindness, decency, selflessness, and above all, love. So much love. This was a good woman. She must still be, somewhere inside.

Yet here she sits, practically inanimate, in the center of an English garden with the daughter she's tolerating with an amiable enough expression because it's one thirty and she had a benzodiazepine just after lunch. I time my visits to coincide with her most recent dose. The idea of her suddenly screaming and attacking me—it's too much to bear. Best to be proactive.

There's no chance of me relaxing today. I haven't heard back from Dawn and, given how provocative my last e-mail was, it's particularly disconcerting. The Dawn I've come to know wouldn't take a shot across her bow without responding. And if she's not responding by e-mail or by text, then it may be by some other mechanism. Oakland isn't such a long drive.

Why did I write back? What was I hoping to accomplish? I kept thinking how Dawn should end our correspondence, stop the madness, but why can't I?

Maybe she already has. Her silence says she's done with me.

Why do I feel the oddest sort of disappointment at that thought?

I just have to hope that I successfully countered all her accusations in my rebuttal on Getaway.com. People shouldn't take her seriously once they read what I have to say. I'm the one backed by twenty-seven positive reviews; she has no one to recommend her. Please, let the reservations pour in. I have a son to support.

It never occurred to me before that his age is the precise number of positive reviews. That has to be a good omen.

I just need to know Dawn hasn't ruined me. One new booking, that's all I ask.

I hear an incoming text: *Moving again. My roommate was using. Bad scene.*

I can't help but think of the parallels that exist between Thad and my mother. They both suffer from progressive diseases. Neither of them can manage a job. They rely on others to meet their basic needs. She has no hope of rehabilitation, and in my darkest moments, I don't think Thad does either.

He's about to ask me for money, I can feel it.

With Grandma right now, I text back. *We'll talk later.*

Tell her I love her.

I will.

I've got a lead on a new place. Just need help with the deposit.

Later.

You want me to be in a sober living environment, right?

My whole being brightens as I tell him, *If you move into a sober living house, I'm happy to pay for that.*

That was one of Larry's prerequisites for allowing Thad back into our lives. It wouldn't be immediate, the reentry, but this could be a great first step. Soon I'd be able to stop all this cloak-and-dagger nonsense, and Dawn's review wouldn't matter anymore. Not that Larry would want me to pay for it, but what he doesn't know won't hurt him.

"It's Thad," I tell my mother when I finally catch her eye. "He sends his love." I'd call her look quizzical if it contained any curiosity.

I'm going to be living with a guy who's two years clean.

My stomach tightens. *I meant an official sober living house. Not just a house with a sober person in it.*

I hate those places. I hate 12 step. So preachy. But I am clean, Mom. I swear it.

Even a broken clock is right twice a day. Even an addict could be telling the truth.

Will you help me? Please?

I look at my mother, who is looking down, never at me, and I think of Thad's tweet from yesterday (*amped in the Amphitheater #bringyourfriends*), and even a cursory Google will tell you that the Amphitheater neighborhood in Tucson is full of drugs, crime, and vacant buildings, and tears prick my eyes because he knows I check his Twitter feed and he doesn't care because he doesn't have to, because he knows I'm a slave to the fear that hitting bottom will mean death and the hope that this time he'll change, and his father's cut him off and I never will, I'll always say the same thing eventually, he'll wear me down and so I might as well just say it from the start, I might as well say it now . . .

Yes, I'll help.

13

Dawn

Entry-Level Marketing and Communications Specialist

Wildwood Marketing specializes in marketing campaigns and promotions for small and medium commercial businesses. We've been named one of the Top 500 Places to Work in the San Francisco Bay Area! If you have an exceptional work ethic, high leadership ability, and are looking for advancement, then we're looking for you!

Our unique cross-training program incorporates:

- Sales & customer service
- Marketing presentations
- Acquiring new customers on behalf of our clients
- Advertising, communication & public relations!

Public Relations Assistant

Do you share a passion for storytelling? Our mission is to help brands shape an authentic narrative that reflects their values and engages audiences. Here at R2T4, we develop audience-focused campaigns that are insightful, creative, and impactful. If you're an influencer, we're looking for you.

Responsibilities Include:

- Data entry
- Electronic and physical filing
- Event planning
- Proofreading
- Formatting various documents
- Managing social media posts

Marketing Coordinator/Event Planner

We are a new and upcoming winery, and we are looking for dedicated and hardworking individuals to join our family. You would be a member of a team of professional, dedicated employees managing internal and external marketing efforts.

Job Duties & Responsibilities:

- Coordinate events, meetings, and trade shows
- Provide administrative support to each member of the marketing team
- Maintain e-mail lists
- Track customer complaints
- Assist in collating marketing materials

Professor Myerson enters the classroom, not a minute too soon. I was getting more and more discouraged with each job listing. If you subtract the stapling, somehow every job listing boils down to sell, sell, sell. Is that all communication is good for?

When I first enrolled at the college, I spoke with an academic adviser ("call me Mark"). I knew I wanted a degree, and to stop working in retail, but beyond that, it was all pretty fuzzy. Mark asked a lot of pertinent-sounding questions, listened carefully to my answers, stroked his patchy beard contemplatively, and then declared, with an appealing level of certainty, "You should be a communications major." He said it would give me the broadest base from which to find a career, and that it was an obvious match for my skills. Much later, I learned that he was Salina's adviser, too, and he'd told her exactly the same thing.

The irony is, he'd accidentally pegged me. I began to like school for the first time in my life. The Art of Communication, Argumentation and Debate, Persuasive Communication, Principles of Interviewing, Gender in the Media . . . it sounds cheesy, but I felt like I was finally finding a voice that people could respect. I got so caught up in learning that I managed to forget my real goal—to rise above where I'd been, to pass—and now here I am, bumping up against the uncomfortable truth that life is ultimately mercenary.

I am, too. Because in theory, it'd be great to raise awareness for an organization whose mission I believed in, like a hospital, university, charity, or other nonprofit, but there's no money in that. The money is in the private sector, in helping companies brand themselves (pardon me, develop authentic narratives). If I ever want a house like Miranda's, do I have to sell, sell, sell . . . my soul?

It's probably not as stark as that, but I definitely need to decide what I really want, and fast. I don't have the time to flounder like a twenty-two-year-old. Whatever path I choose, it has to be right. I'm about to get my degree, which is supposed to be an achievement in itself, and I've never felt so behind the curve.

As Professor Myerson scribbles across the whiteboard, my mind returns once again to Miranda. She's become a welcome refuge from real life. It's harder than I would have imagined, not answering her last e-mail. I tell myself I'm taking the high road, and that she's left with nothing but her own petty nastiness. But even Rob said how full of herself she is. She's probably thinking that she's silenced me, put me in my place, and she believes that place is about ten rungs beneath her.

I shouldn't care what she thinks. She's the worst of the entitled rich. It's not a category I've had much contact with throughout my life, but we all know they exist. If reality television has taught us anything, it's that.

Let it go. If *Frozen* has taught us anything, it's that. The cold never bothered me anyway.

Not true. I mind the cold, and I mind hunger, and I've had enough of both in my life. Has Miranda experienced either? I know Rob hasn't, no matter how sound his advice is.

I can't focus during class. That's aggravating, since it's my favorite one, Ethics and Law in Communication, and Professor Myerson is my favorite teacher. We parse case studies and learn the precepts of the profession but also look within ourselves to see how they jibe with our own morality and integrity. Somehow, it manages to be theoretical yet personal, all at once. Usually, when I'm in the classroom, I'm so stimulated that I nearly tingle; I'm that engaged and alive.

Don't get me wrong. Professor Myerson does not turn me on. He's in his fifties, and you can tell he's never been what anyone would call handsome. While he might find me attractive in some objective sense, I don't feel like he's attracted to me either. (And I'm alert for that, because throughout my life, it's been my bread and butter. But I don't want to get by that way anymore.)

"Dawn, stay behind a minute," Professor Myerson says. The rest of the class files out. The whiteboard attests to the hyperkinetic nature of his teaching; arrows abound. "Were you bored by *Baltimore Sun v. Ehrlich*, or was it me?" Busted. But he smiles, his teeth the color of pale urine. The light is harsh in here. I instinctively wonder if the fluorescence is voiding my concealer.

"I've just got a lot on my mind."

"Final semester blues?"

"Is that a thing?"

"It is now." He smiles again, with what I hope is an avuncular sort of kindness. "Today's class notwithstanding, you're one of my best students. You're sharp, and you've got a real flair for analysis."

My heart sinks. I'm remembering that saying: Smart women want to be told they're beautiful; beautiful women want to be told they're smart. I push my hair back, deliberately bringing my encircled ring finger into prominence.

"I just wanted to see how the job hunt is going," he says, and I drop my hand, embarrassed to have misjudged him.

"Lately," I say, "I've been feeling kind of lost."

"Lost in what way?"

"I don't know what I want to be when I grow up."

He laughs, then his face stills as he sees I wasn't making a joke. "You're what, twenty-five?"

"Thirty."

"Thirty's young. With the state of Social Security, you've got forty years of work ahead of you, easy. What's another six months? What's a year?"

"Or I could just pop out a baby or two."

This time, he doesn't laugh, though I might have been kidding, I'm not sure. "Stop by during office hours. We can kick around some ideas, see if I've got any contacts who might be able to help."

I thank him, but he must be able to see that I'm still worried.

He reaches out and pats my arm. His touch is awkward and re-freshingly devoid of sexual nuance. "You'll figure it out soon enough. You'll know where you're headed."

As I scuttle out of the room, I'm unsettled, and I don't know why. My favorite professor thinks highly of me; he's willing to brainstorm and maybe he'll even introduce me to some potential employers; and he's right, I have forty years of work before me. What *is* another six months? Or a year?

My heart thrums, and I run down the flight of stairs and out onto the concrete slab that is our quad. I just want to go home. But not to my boxy apartment, and certainly not back to Eureka, five hours north of here. Whatever happens, I'm never going back to that life. To those people (one of whom is the old me).

I should call Rob. He can always take a break and talk to me. That's one advantage of him being in a dying business with his father. Even if he has engraving to do, there's never much urgency. Oh, sure, sometimes people need things in time for their anniver-sary or their graduation, but mostly, there's plenty of time. Rob is a saunterer. I've never seen him run, I realize, not in the whole time I've known him.

But I'm running. I want to get away from Professor Myerson and his yellowing teeth and his reassurances that there's more than enough time. That's the lie of all lies. There's never enough. Scarcity. That's what I understand better than anyone.

Meanwhile, Miranda has two houses. Two fucking houses! I bet that one in Santa Monica cost more than a million, so her real home must cost two million, maybe even three or four. She doesn't know shit about going without, though as old as she is, she must know something about running out of time.

Is she actually old, though? She could have gone to boarding schools where they taught her to write like a hoity-toity bitch. Maybe she was raised with money, and then married money. Maybe she's young and gorgeous and gold digging, with some decrepit doctor husband.

I go into the student union with its semicircle corral of Chick-fil-A, Pizza Hut, Taco Bell, and Panda Express, a throng of lacquered tables in the center. I sit down and whip out my laptop.

The adrenaline is pumping, the anger is back, and I'm relieved by it, I really am. It's like an old, cherished friend, the kind who means well but still fucks your boyfriend.

I sic her on Miranda. I know Miranda's last name, of course I do, she was my host. I Google Miranda Feldt, Santa Monica. Google helpfully puts a line through "Santa Monica," and I have my results. Miranda Feldt, wife of Lawrence Feldt, radiation oncologist at Beth Aaron Oncology Center, one of the most prestigious in the greater Los Angeles area. Their website is a glossy brochure, highlighting an impressive new glass building, state-of-the-art this and state-of-the-art that. They offer complementary therapies—massage and meditation and "energy work" in what looks like a spa environment.

I stare at Lawrence's picture, and I have to admit, he looks like a guy who could kick cancer's ass. He's not good-looking (his features manage to be bloated yet too defined, like he's a charcoal sketch come to life), but he drips confidence and competence. Nothing about him screams "dick," exactly, except for his wife.

So she didn't lie about her husband's position, and she didn't lie about her volunteer work either. She's on a bunch of boards, all so disparate that it's the equivalent of trying to look well-rounded on a college application.

I bet she is old, though. Because young women aren't on boards, are they? Plus, no photo is readily available. No social media profiles have popped up.

Next page of results: She's a big donor to Fielding Academy, a prep school with its own crest, of all ridiculous things. It's L.A., not London. Her son went there. Thaddeus Feldt. I'm not sure there's ever been a more pretentious name.

I see a picture of Miranda, Lawrence, and Thaddeus at his graduation from Fielding Academy. Miranda looks like she's in her forties, though I'd guess that a good rule of thumb for rich women in L.A. is that whatever age they look, add at least five years. The picture is from nine years ago.

She's in this little bolero jacket suit that is more obviously expensive than it is attractive, and that fits my overall impression of her. She's of average weight, with blond hair in a neat little bob and features that are nothing special. She's squinting into the sun as she smiles, making her eyes disappear completely. There's a pinched quality to her face and her posture, though it's presumably a happy day.

I think of what Rob said. Wait, did he say it, or is it just something I've heard him say so much that I'm transposing? Regardless, it's this: Her punishment is being her. Karma is not something that happens to us; it's who we are. It's having to live with ourselves.

But Miranda has it good, whether she realizes it or not. In fact, if she doesn't realize it, then it's even more bothersome. Her husband saves lives, just like she said. She can give her time to whatever causes she chooses. She can spend her days lunching and buying ugly well-made clothes.

Then there's Thaddeus, her strapping son. His arms are draped around his parents, and you can just tell how close-knit they are. They probably had family dinners every night and weekly game nights. He's tall and kind of hot, in a Joaquin Phoenix meets Justin Theroux way. The Fielding Academy site helpfully informs me that he was headed for UC Santa Barbara, a college that's way better than mine. By now, he's graduated. He's well on his way to being rich himself, or he's already there. He may have his own business, using his charisma and his parents' seed money.

I could Google and see if I'm right about that, but I feel like it might inflame me too much.

Besides, I already have enough here that I can use.

14

Miranda

Rothko never painted like this. #artallnighter

I saw Thad's tweet when I should have been deep in slumber, and then after seeing it, there was no way I could get to sleep. Despite what he told me yesterday, he's using again. Of course he is. He says it spurs his creativity, and I know it spurs both of our insomnia.

Didn't Rothko commit suicide?

Larry's sleeping peacefully beside me. He's the one who decided to cut Thad off completely, but he never seems worried about the consequences of that. Take action, never look back. That's his style. I wish it could become mine. It's his personality, reinforced by his chosen career. In his branch of medicine, you have to make decisions based on the information available at the time, and all your options may be substandard, and sometimes the patient dies. His approach to Thad seems no different.

I remember the day more than two years ago when he said it was time to take action. I asked him, "But what if Thad dies?" and was met with a stare that said, *That's his prognosis, isn't it?* Patients die. Addicts die.

We were at the kitchen table, hammering out the details. It was a Sunday morning, when we would normally have been having sex, but Thad hadn't come home the previous night. He wasn't following any of the conditions of moving back into our house, he was clearly using meth, and he was stealing from me (though I didn't tell Larry that part).

"This is over," Larry told me. His eyes were hooded. He wasn't used to sleepless nights, and he was angry about it. Thad was keeping him from giving his all to the patients.

Lox and bagels were sitting in front of us, untouched. Larry had picked them up that morning as if this were a breakfast meeting. But we were both drinking coffee, copiously.

"We have to help him," I said, but my voice faltered. "Otherwise . . ."

"Otherwise what? He'll keep using? He's never stopped. We can't do anything for him. At this point, it's every man for himself."

"What does that mean?" I asked, fearfully.

"That we're cutting him loose. We're cutting him off. He can go to rehab, or not. I'm not making any more arrangements for him, getting him into any more facilities so that he can get kicked out or walk out. I'm not paying for one more thing. I don't care where the hell he goes."

I took another long drink of coffee. "I care."

"Well, you'll need to work on that. On detaching."

"If we give him an ultimatum, he'll say no. You know how he is."

"I'm not talking about ultimatums. It's different this time. I've divested myself from the outcome," he said. "Here's what we do.

We tell him that we're cutting him off. He's fully responsible for himself now. If he decides to go to rehab, he finds one himself and he finds a way to pay for it himself, and while he completes it, we're going to have no contact with him. Zero. From rehab, he goes to a sober living house. Once he's been there for six months, clean, with the negative drug tests to prove it, we'll consider allowing him back into our lives."

"You want him to do all that with no guarantee that we're ever going to let him back into our lives?" I was stunned. I thought that Larry would insist on rehab again, but I never thought . . .

"This is over," he repeated. "As far as I'm concerned, Thad is dead to me. Whether he can be resurrected, that's up to him."

Neither of us spoke for long, fraught minutes. "This seems cruel," I said.

"Cruel is what he's done to himself, the ways he's squandered his life and all the advantages we've given him. Cruel is what he's done to us. Turnabout is fair play."

"It's not fair play. He's our son. He's got a disease."

The look in his eyes told me he wasn't buying that old line. "The only reason I've put up with this shit as long as I have is because he was my son."

"He's not anymore?"

Larry didn't need to answer.

"He's not dead to me," I said.

"Suit yourself. Feel what you want. But we need to present a united front. No contact until he's done rehab and then sober living."

"I can't be united in that."

"What do you want to do? The same old thing we've been doing? I'm tired of this merry-go-round. Aren't you?"

Of course I was. But I couldn't kill my son off, not in my own mind, not even for self-preservation, which is what I'm convinced Larry was doing. Thad's addiction was destroying Larry in ways that he wouldn't speak out loud, and I'd stopped talking about the ways it was destroying me.

"Okay," I finally said, "but you can't say that to him about being dead to you. You keep that to yourself. We stick to the facts: rehab, and then sober living for six months, and then we talk again."

"Rehab, then sober living for six months, and then we'll see."

It went as I knew it would: the three of us in the living room that night, Larry calmly explaining what was going to happen, me standing by silently, and Thad furious, with me more than Larry. "You're really cutting me off?" Thad spat out, glaring at me. "When I haven't even been using, I just stayed out with friends?"

"We have no choice," I said. "We hope that you'll use this as a catalyst to—"

He turned on his heel, picking up the trash bags full of his possessions that Larry and I had gathered. He was headed out the front door, to who knew where. But I cared. Larry might not have, but I'm no Larry.

"Keys," Larry said, approaching Thad, hand outstretched. I tensed, fearing some sort of physical confrontation, but Thad didn't even look directly at Larry, he just pulled the keys from the ring. Then he was gone.

I tried to hold the line. I really did. I knew all the reasons I should, with all the supporting lingo: the enabling had to stop, and the tough love needed to begin. Everyone at Nar-Anon said Larry's approach was the best.

But then I got a call from the hospital. Thad had overdosed, again. "It's more of Thad's manipulation," Larry said. He took my phone and texted Thad: *Now are you ready to get help?* The answer:

No rehab. I'll go to meetings on my own. And I need rent. It was the only time I ever saw Larry out of control physically. He threw the phone across the room.

Larry thought Thad needed to hit bottom. I thought—I continue to think—that for Thad, the only bottom is death. It's not a chance I can take.

At the time, my father had recently died. I couldn't lose another family member; I wouldn't. And the Santa Monica plan—it was like it came from Dad himself, like he was my guardian angel. The house, an income stream, just fell into my lap, at the time I most needed it. Larry agreed that it made sense to buy George out, and there I was, in business.

It was almost too easy. The Santa Monica house was mine to oversee, and Larry never asked questions. So after I told him what I was charging per night, which was $150 less than the real price, I never had to lie to his face again. It stopped seeming like a betrayal at all. Larry had his job, and I had mine. Two of them: the rental and Thad. They're both my business, one scaffolding the other.

Thad has remained dead to Larry. I don't even say his name. I can't imagine what would happen if I told Larry that I've been bringing in more money than I let him believe and transferring the surplus to Thad. That's not just a lie of omission. That's true betrayal.

But I couldn't kill off my son. He'd have to understand that, wouldn't he?

I can't help but notice that I haven't heard from Dawn, or from any potential renters. I find myself wanting to write to her and say, *Are you alive?* I've gotten so used to thinking that no communication might mean death, because of Thad.

Having a child is supposed to change the whole way you think, but I never expected to wake up each day checking my son's social media to confirm his continued existence. I tell myself this, by way of reassurance: no dead man has ever tweeted.

But Dawn is not my child. No news from her is good news for me.

I tell myself that, but the tense feeling in my stomach persists. I actually can't wait for dawn to come. The real dawn, that is. Daylight. Because it really does feel the darkest right now.

Then something amazing happens.

I was just thinking about Grandma, how she used to bake those Purim cookies with me. You know the ones with the apricot and the prunes in the middle? I'm too tired to spell them.

He's tired. Not crashing, just tired. Maybe he really was simply inspired to paint. It actually was an art all-nighter, not a meth binge. Stranger things have happened.

Hamentashen, I text back. *She always said you were a great helper.*

How was she yesterday? Any better?

She knew who I was. But she wasn't saying much.

I miss her.

I miss her, too.

And I miss you.

I let out a choked noise, then I clamp my hand to my mouth. I don't want to wake Larry. What would he say if he knew Thad and I were in touch?

My boy misses me. I've already given him the money he asked for, and yet, he's texted me, out of nowhere. He has no ulterior motive and here he is, being loving, when I most need that.

I miss you, too, I tell him. More than he could ever know.

15

Dawn

This is an open letter to the city of Santa Monica. As one of the landlords here, I know I speak for many when I say please, PLEASE, crack down on all the people who are violating the ordinance against short-term rentals. Take a quick look at Getaway.com. There are so many listings allowing stays of less than thirty days that you wouldn't even think Santa Monica has an ordinance. I have tenants who I've caught subleasing my unit for long weekends. How are people allowed to just flout the rules like this?

It's because there's practically no enforcement. The city attorney's office says they only prosecute the cases that are referred to them. Right now, they don't have a single case pending! They say they don't have the manpower to go out and find these people since the listings don't contain exact addresses.

That's their excuse? Just because something's hard doesn't mean it's not worth doing. The citizens need to start applying some pressure to City Hall if we want to keep Santa Monica special. Are you with me?

Sincerely,

Arnold F. Giraldo

I am definitely with you, Mr. Giraldo.

The funny thing is, I liked Santa Monica—the city proper—the most. More than Mendocino for sure, or Santa Barbara, or even Monterey. I liked the people, the way you could hesitate on the street, looking the tiniest bit lost, and they'd ask if you needed anything. I liked the pedicabs to Venice Beach and back, and I liked the buskers at Third Street Promenade, especially the handsome, floppy-haired one who played electric violin to an instrumental soundtrack and rendered pop music poignant, and the pier, and the beach itself, so clean and beautiful.

But Miranda's house . . . I would never admit this in my review, it would make me sound nuts, but I felt like that house didn't like me. Like in a cheesy horror movie: "Something wanted me out." Like it was inhabited by a not-so-friendly ghost. Or like I was possessed by one.

There's no other explanation for my behavior that trip. Normally, Getaway Dawn is the best Dawn there is. She's the most relaxed, and happy, and sexual. She hasn't a care in the world, because (the illusion of) money is buffering her from the irritants of life.

The Santa Monica trip was full of highs and lows, in what I came to realize was actually a very consistent pattern: Outside of the house, I was Getaway Dawn. Inside the house—beautiful as it was, another thing I didn't want to admit in my review—I was someone else. I was critical of Rob, and buttoned-up sexually. I felt . . .

watched. I felt judged. I kept going to the window and looking out, half expecting to find people on the street, peering in, their noses scrunched in distaste. Now I think it was the house itself, the spirit of Miranda.

Again, how else to explain the way I treated Rob? Everything he did, inside that house, struck me as wrong. Worse, he seemed boring. Our conversation was like a limp dick, and our sex was just as uninspired.

On the second day, after visiting a farmers' market full of produce so gorgeous it was nearly pyrotechnic, I decided to cook us lunch. It seemed very vacationy, indulgent, as I only cook dinner at home. Breakfast and lunch are cereal and leftovers, respectively.

We had this amazing peach puree from the farmers' market, and Rob mixed it with champagne as I gazed at the bounty of vegetables spread out over the center island. I was so sure it would be a good trip for us, the best yet.

Rob has a tendency to propose toasts, and normally, I like that about him. He's trying to make ordinary things an event. I guess it's in keeping with his commemorative line of work.

So we were at the kitchen island and he handed me a Bellini and lifted his own. He started talking—rambling, really—about how far I'd come, and how I'm going to graduate soon, and how proud he is of me, and how he's so happy he could make it possible, and at first, it was sweet, but then it started to turn. I felt like he was really toasting himself. I set down my glass, and I went to the sink, ostensibly to wash the vegetables. I hoped he'd pick up my cue and *stop fucking talking already,* but he kept going.

I couldn't take it anymore: "I'm not a stray you rescued!" My ferocity startled me as well as him.

He set his glass down and came up behind me, snaking his arms around my waist, and I wanted to tell him to get off me, which is not at all like me, not at all like us, so I stifled myself. But it was surprisingly hard.

"What's wrong?" he asked.

"I can barely see the ocean through that tree!" I said tearfully.

"No, really, what's wrong?"

I didn't know then. I really thought it might be the promise of a full view that was then obstructed. A promise that's never delivered on is a lie, isn't it?

Now I know: It was the house. It was Miranda, and her miasmic negative energy.

I forced myself to lean back into Rob so that we could breathe together. Then I said, "Let's go out for lunch." We were on vacation; money was no object; we could even waste this rainbow of produce, if we so chose. Something in me sensed that we needed to leave that house to be at all okay.

I could tell he disapproved of that idea, of the potential waste, and normally I would, too. (Ultimately we didn't waste it, I made dinner later, which didn't feel vacationy but like a chore.) Rob agreed, reluctantly. We got out of the house for a while, and the day turned around. Until dinner, that is.

Every time we were in that house, it seemed like I was the one scrunching my nose at him, finding fault, and on the last night there, he snapped. "Quit being such a bitch for six hundred dollars a night. Be a bitch at home, if you need to." I was stunned. He'd never called me a bitch before. Now that I think of it, he didn't *exactly* call me a bitch then, but that's how it felt. He wasn't done either. "I do all this for you," he said, and there was an undercurrent, an undertow, of resentment that I'd never heard, never even suspected, before. He was the one who'd insisted we could afford the getaways, and that I shouldn't work until after graduation, even though a big part of me wanted to work, to contribute, to never be dependent like my own mother had been.

I hissed at him, "Don't you ever call me a bitch again, asshole!" and he stormed out of the house.

It was the first time I was alone in that house, and I felt like it was laughing at me, like it wanted this to happen.

All of this seems so crazy that I couldn't even identify it at the time. But now, with all this shit with Miranda—it seems almost, well, plausible. Possible, at least. Houses have personalities, right? They have the personalities of their owners. Miranda's malevolence seeped into the walls and the floorboards, and into me.

So maybe when she charged me for that stain, my reaction wasn't entirely about the stain, but also about the experience. We were unhappy in that house, Rob and me. We gave Miranda $2,400 to inhabit her funhouse—a hall of mirrors, distorting us and our relationship into a grotesquerie. Then to add insult to injury, she stole another $200.

After Rob took off that final night, I couldn't stay there by myself. I was too frightened. I walked the beach and eventually found him. "Great minds think alike," he started to say, with a pained smile, and then we were holding each other tight. I think he was frightened, too, and we found a relieved communion underneath the lifeguard station. Our sex was fevered, and I was so glad we were going home the next day. I wanted to never think of that house again, or that trip, but then Miranda did what she did, and how could I just let it go? Really, after everything?

And now I've been vindicated. Miss Self-Righteous Upstanding Citizen has been routinely violating the rental code of Santa Monica, where she's on the board of the Homeowners Association. She attends regular meetings (her name is all over the minutes, which are available online), and meanwhile, she's lining her pockets with short-term rentals. This proves she's a hypocrite, as well as a thief, a liar, and a snotty rich bitch extraordinaire.

I e-mailed the city attorney's office, including a link to Miranda's listing on Getaway.com along with the supporting proof that she rented to me for four nights. They'll shut down her little operation.

There she was, pretending to be so ethical. Telling me about all the good she does in the world, all her volunteer work, as if her character were above reproach. Ha!

I'm thinking all this as I lie in Rob's arms, trying to fall asleep. "Wouldn't it be amazing if there was a baby inside you, right now?" he asks dreamily.

"The IUD is like ninety-nine point nine percent effective."

"We could be the point one percent."

When I came home from Dr. Kroy's with my IUD intact, I was hoping he would recognize that as a kind of answer.

It's not only that I don't feel ready to try for a baby. I feel sure that it just can't work out for me. Either I won't be able to get pregnant, or I'll have a miscarriage, or the baby I'll produce will have some terrible defect, like taking after one or both of my parents. Dr. Kroy says that I'm in good shape, but some part of me doesn't believe her. I think that we have to pay for our past sins somehow, and this seems the most likely time for the bill to come due. It's even called a due date.

"Let's defy the odds," Rob says, slithering down my body. When he goes down on me lately, it's always a means to an end. It's foreplay, not the main event. Now he's fantasizing that the main event could lead to a baby.

Much as I thought I wanted one when Rob and I first got married, nothing could be less erotic to me right now than evoking a baby. Long before him, I used to say that squalling, screaming parasites are the best birth control. If teenagers had to fuck to a soundtrack of needy infants, that condom would be on so fast the cock would have rug burn.

"I'm pretty tired," I tell him, stilling his hand on my pajama bottoms.

He rests his face against my hip bone and stares up at me, appearing oddly cherubic with his steady gaze under those thick lashes. "I can wake you up."

"I need to sleep. It's been an exhausting day."

"Let me guess. You turned her in." He sounds none too pleased, but that could be spillover from his failed seduction.

"She was breaking the law."

"It's not like it's a real law. It's a don't-remove-this-tag-from-your-mattress law."

"People should not be renting her house." It's like he's forgotten what happened there. Doesn't he get that I'm doing this for us, and for the other couples who shouldn't be subjected to the same situation?

He sighs. "Let's not talk about this."

"You brought it up." He was the one inviting Miranda into our bed this time. I shift my weight, and he takes the hint, moving from between my legs.

"Are we okay?" he asks as he resettles on his pillow.

I don't look at him as I adjust the sheet. Just the word "sheet" . . . How do I get Miranda out once and for all? Hopefully, that e-mail will do it. I've given the city of Santa Monica conclusive proof, so it's in their hands now. This is not exactly reassuring, seeing as they've never prosecuted anyone under the ordinance. She could get off with a warning. They could see her swanky address and decide not to mess with a doctor's wife. She could be laughing at me right now, at my feeble attempt at justice.

"Yes," I say, twining my fingers in Rob's hair, "we're okay."

"We can do better than that," Rob says with a grin as he assumes the muff-diving position once again. This time, I know better than to protest.

I do something that always works in a pinch. I remember the others. The bad boys that got away, for good reason. I shouldn't do it but sometimes I have to.

Because it turns me on. Because I want to be turned on. Because I want to have the most cataclysmic orgasm, the kind that obliterates stained sheets and babies and poverty and failure and injustice and an uncertain future.

I lie back and scream.

16

Miranda

It's not like Rothko in terms of the subject matter; it's how I layer the color.

Rothko was one of those dark painters, right? All somber blues and browns.

Suicidal blues and browns is what I mean, but I'm just happy that Thad is still talking to me. For the past few days, we've been engaged in a running conversation, spanning hours, a connection of our hearts and minds. It's been unprecedented and wonderful. I never knew texting could be so beautiful.

There used to be a Rothko collection at MOCA. You should go.

Let's go together someday, I text back.

I'm thinking ahead. If we keep talking like this, maybe I can convince him that he should move into a sober living house and start taking the drug tests. If he's clean anyway, why not prove it to his father? I'll remind him that Larry is a scientist, and they like their data. Suck it up for six months, Thad, and I'll do my darnedest to convince Larry to let you through our front door. We'll be a family again.

I spy Violet walking toward me along the beach path. *I've got to go. Talk later?*

It takes a few beats for him to respond, and I think, Oh, no, I've lost him again. But then he tells me: *Yeah, talk later.*

I smile as I turn off my phone and greet Violet. She takes the seat opposite me. I'm in high spirits, and I hope it shows.

Violet's never asked me to lunch before. She let me pick the spot, one of my favorite restaurants alongside the beach, with white shutters and blue awnings. Similar to my parents' home décor, I just realized. A tandem bike cruises by, with a fit mom and dad towing a child behind. It's vacation mode over here, all the time, which is why I love Santa Monica. It's probably why Larry is so unmoved by it. He vacations only under duress.

Violet's eyes scan the beach in front of us—the original muscle beach, where a skinny Asian kid is doing pull-ups, the ocean a cerulean blur in the distance—and when they light on me again, the pupils are meth-jumpy.

"Is anything wrong?" I ask.

She adjusts the brim of her floppy hat. It looks like it's macramé. She's got beach style while I'm in an Hermès scarf. Her hair is light brown and flyaway, hanging to the middle of her back. It's a young woman's style, with an old woman's thinning hair. Not old—mature. She's my age.

"I'm uncomfortable with what I have to say." She touches the hat again, as if it's a talisman that gives her strength.

We're not friends, just friendly. We've known each other since I took over my mother's seat on the board of the Homeowners Association. Everyone loved my mother, including Violet. They wouldn't even recognize her now. My mother was effervescent, where I'm reserved. She was sparkling wine, I'm pinot.

I don't really have friends anymore, only friendly acquaintances. My social world shrank as Thad's problems grew. I was more consumed with him yet less able to speak about him. It hurt to hear about their children's achievements, so that made me feel mean and spiteful, and then when we got to Thad, it killed me to hear their pity, their false reassurances: "He'll get better soon, it's just a phase." Sometimes they didn't know what to say at all, which I preferred but they didn't, so as many friendships drifted into acquaintanceship at their hands as at mine.

My social world reminds me of a science project Thad did in elementary school. It was one he loved because it incorporated art. He made concentric circles out of wire, a sun at the center, and the trick was placing the different planets with the correct proximities. He was most into painting the Styrofoam balls perfectly, so I had to coach him through the placement. I'd say, "No, Saturn doesn't go there; Pluto is the farthest."

Now every friend I've ever had is Pluto, and it's not even a planet anymore.

Mostly, that's okay. I was surprised to find how little I missed them as they moved outward, concentric circle by circle, through drift and design. It was probably because I still had my mother, and we used to be so similar that I could tell her little and she'd know everything. But I try not to think about the encroaching loneliness. Dwelling never helps.

Violet takes a deep breath, like she's about to say something important. "I found out that you've been renting your home out for less than the requisite thirty days." She brushes her hair back from her face, keeping her eyes on the table. "Don't ask me how I know.

But you need to stop or you're at risk of being prosecuted by the city attorney."

I stare at her, flabbergasted. Prosecuted! I'd be humiliated. Larry would be horrified.

I suppose I shouldn't be this shocked. I should have prepared for this possibility. But everyone knows that the city attorney doesn't even investigate these sorts of cases, let alone prosecute them.

Someone brought this to Violet's attention. Someone who's been lying low, waiting to strike. A viper with the initials D.T.

"Who gave you this information?" I say.

"I can't answer that."

"I deserve to know my accuser."

She gives me a strange look. I'm behaving strangely, in other words. I take a deep breath myself, recomposing. Dawn can't make a fool of me; only I can do that.

"I have a well-connected friend," Violet finally says. "She wants to protect the reputation of the Association, so she passed this information along to me. She's no 'accuser.'"

"But someone must have called in a tip. I need to know who it is in order to properly defend myself." There, that sounded better.

"My friend didn't give me a name, and I couldn't give one to you even if I knew it. Listen to me. I'm doing you a favor." Her eyes bear down on mine. "They have your listing from Getaway.com. They have your address, confirmed, on a rental agreement."

"A rental agreement between me and who?"

"I told you, I don't know."

"But I know. I've been set up. By someone who's vindictive. She's out of her mind. Doesn't that matter?"

Violet looks at me like she's just discovered I've been living a double life, like she doesn't know me at all.

I want to tell her that she doesn't, in fact, really know me, or my situation. She doesn't know why I need the money from the short-term rentals. She doesn't know that I tried to comply with the ordinance in the beginning, to find tenants for thirty days at a pop, but it didn't work out. Long-term renters didn't want to pay what the house is worth, whereas the nightly rent is in line with my financial needs. Besides, I couldn't give up my parents' home for a month or more at a time. It was the site of their greatest joy. I couldn't let someone live in it and deny me access for so long. I like visiting each week, usually more often. It brings me a sense of well-being and peace that I can't seem to find anywhere else, not even in my own home.

What I don't like is letting Larry think the profits are less than they are so I can skim off the top for Thad; I don't like the dishonesty. But these are not choices. They're necessities. Does Violet have any idea what that's like, living over a barrel?

Don't panic. Just stay calm.

I can afford to lose the rental now that Thad is talking to me like a real person. He's going to agree to a sober living house, and then none of this will matter, not in the slightest.

Except that I'm even more afraid. Now that Thad's being sweet, there's more to lose. What if he still doesn't want to go to sober living next month, and I can't subsidize him any longer? He'll go back to the Thad I've been used to, the one I can only follow on Twitter.

I need that money. It's an insurance policy.

Can Violet even fathom what it's like to feel this way about your own child?

I would never attempt to tell her, not with the way she's looking at me.

"I'm not the only one doing this," I say. "Do you know how many listings there are on Getaway.com for Santa Monica rentals? Not to mention the other websites?"

She looks startled. Perhaps I was supposed to be chastened, apologetic. Grateful. Small, that's what she was hoping for. I'm supposed to grovel at her feet.

Any sympathy in her face is gone; I'm left with disdain. "I used to tell my son that just because everyone's jumping off a bridge, he doesn't have to," she says.

That seemed pointed. *Does* she know about Thad?

Dawn's got me paranoid. Or maybe she's got me seeing clearly for the first time. Violet looks almost happy. Superior. She must have had it out for me for a while. An expression like that, it doesn't materialize from nowhere. Her house is nice, but it's at least ten blocks from the beach, and not nearly as beautiful as my parents', and it's her only one. She couldn't rent it out if she wanted to.

"This might go without saying," she says, "but it would be best if you resigned from the Association."

"And then when I do, when I can no longer besmirch the Association's honor, your friend will turn me in?" I say.

She seems surprised, and a little hurt. "Of course not. This is between us. All the city attorney wants is for you to comply with the ordinance. Prosecuting you wouldn't help anyone."

I don't know what to believe anymore. I'm not sure how to construe Violet and her "friendly" warning. She could have come here with the best of intentions, and then thought I'm the one who turned on her.

What I do know is this: the rumors will swirl, and my reputation as well as my livelihood will be destroyed. Dawn has scored a direct hit.

"It's not what people think," I say.

"It never is." Violet's smile is spiked with pity. Right now, that's probably the best I can hope for.

Dawn can't get away with this, except she already has.

17

Dawn

5-Star Home, Best Location

Gorgeous Two-Bedroom in the Heart of Santa Monica!

Luxury Beachfront Townhome

Oceanview Penthouse

Family Beach House, with All the Trimmings

Your Own Spanish Villa

Santa Monica Stunner!

I scan and scroll. Miranda's listing isn't on page one, where it used to be.

Not on page two either. Or three. Now I'm into the listings that are $700 and $800 a night, so . . . mission accomplished. I've vanquished her from Getaway.com, which is the most important thing. That house is out of circulation. Miranda is a host no more.

I keep hoping that something will mark the turning point for me, that I'll find the measure of satisfaction I need to stop this ugly obsession with Miranda. I realize that's what it is, and that it's unhealthy for me, and for my marriage. Last night with Rob was just off, there's no other way to put it. It's the worst thing in the world, to be self-aware but without self-control.

I want to be as good a person as Rob is—not only doing the right thing, but wanting to do the right thing. Sometimes I can't help but think that he's had a much easier road to becoming that person, with loving parents and a comfortable childhood and a private Christian college. He's been surrounded by goodness and light.

Stop making excuses for yourself, Dawn. You're surrounded by light now, too. Just be better.

Why is it so hard to be better?

Because Miranda has been provoking me, goading me, dragging me back into the darkness.

But she's not on Getaway.com now. It's over. Done. I've finished it.

I stare at the laptop screen and tell myself that I've won. I force myself into a kind of pleasure, though it begins to evaporate almost instantly, like a melting snowflake. I don't trust it.

I have a long history of not trusting happiness. On my wedding day, I stood in front of the bathroom mirror for what seemed like ages (with dimmed lighting, of course—I always install dimmers in rental units, no landlord ever minds). Soon, I'd drive myself over to the Sheraton where Rob and I were to be married in one of the smaller banquet halls, not even a hall really, more of a meeting room where they'd hold corporate conferences for a hundred people or fewer and look at PowerPoints and munch crudités. But beggars can't be choosers, and I didn't have many guests to invite, and Rob's family was paying because, well, just because; that's always the best answer where my family is concerned. I'm looking at myself in the bathroom mirror, already in my wedding dress, a $99 David's Bridal special, but for once I think I look beautiful. I tell myself, "This is how it all starts. This is happiness."

I'd felt ecstasy before—hell, I'd done plenty of ecstasy—and I'd been sorta happy before, but on my wedding day, I felt a happiness that was pure and clean and true. I was that bride who's full of hope. Later, when I danced in Rob's arms to our first song ("I Will Follow You into the Dark" by Death Cab for Cutie), I felt actual joy. The joy of more joy to come. If not fulfillment, exactly, then the strong promise of it.

But in the bathroom mirror beforehand, putting on the finishing touches for my big day, I was just plain happy, and it felt weird as shit. I kept squinting at my reflection, and fortunately, the light was too dim and my makeup too expertly applied to see any blemishes. All I saw was a woman who looked exactly right, and felt precisely what she was supposed to feel. Sure, I wasn't supposed to be alone. I was supposed to have a gaggle of girlfriends sipping champagne and exclaiming over me; I was supposed to have my mother. But I don't like all that noise, and I didn't need it that day, not to be happy. To be poised on the cliff of joy.

But it creeped me out a little. No, not a little. A lot. This joy precipice. This joy fault line (since we are talking about the Bay Area). The only thing scarier than wanting is getting. Because after the getting can come the losing.

"Is anyone sitting here?" It's a male voice, flirty in that languid twentysomething way. That's the problem with trying to get anything serious done in the student union. They think I'm younger than I am, and they're too young themselves to glance at ring fingers before they speak.

I keep my eyes on my laptop screen, providing no encouragement. "No," I say.

"Cool." I look up only when I hear the chair scraping away from my table to his.

Then it hits me: Getaway.com is just one site. Miranda could have migrated to another. She could think the oversight is lax in Santa Monica (which it obviously is, or the city attorney wouldn't rely on whistleblowers like myself). She could think I'm too stupid to find her and report her again. She probably changed the text of her ad, or priced it higher or lower to throw me off the scent.

Speaking of scents, the Chick-fil-A is especially pungent right now. It makes my stomach lurch in protest. You'd think that lardy Taco Bell would overtake it, but no, Chick-fil-A is the winner in a nostril assault contest. It's not even eleven A.M., people.

I lift my coffee cup to my nose and breathe deeply, the way you do at a department store between sniffs of different perfumes. It cleanses my olfactory palate.

Going through the other sites will take a long time, since their search engines are all slightly different. But I don't mind. What else am I going to do, look at job listings?

Grim determination is strangely enjoyable. I like being dogged. I like knowing that I can't be beaten, that I won't be beaten, not even by someone with money, i.e., power. Miranda's not going to squash or silence me.

"Hey!" I didn't see Salina coming. "What are you working on?"

She cranes her neck to see my laptop. "Planning another vacation? Rob is too good to you."

"Not till the fall, at least," I say. "I'm just daydreaming."

Salina wilts into the chair opposite me. Tall, skinny girls can do that. If this were the 1920s, she'd make the most of a fainting couch. Her skin looks amazing, as always. I'd kill for laser treatments. "How's it going with the job search?"

"Great."

She doesn't even catch the sarcasm as she grins broadly and leans in. "I think I met him."

I lean in, too. "The One?"

"Please. But he is the one in a million. He's a fucking unicorn. Seriously, his dick's as big as the horn." She spreads her hands absurdly wide.

"Ick. I don't want someone to puncture my small intestine."

"Trust me, it's worth the risk." She flutters her eyes in a pantomime of orgasmic delight. "We've seen each other twice, and we've fucked ten times. Ten! I'm telling you, I believe now."

"In unicorns?"

"In unicorns, in God, in the oneness of the universe." She rummages around in her bag. "I'll show you."

"I'm a married woman. I can't look at your dick pics."

"I was going to show you his *face*. Give me a little credit." She continues her search. "Shit. I lost my phone again. I should go retrace my steps." She can't even muster annoyance; she's too buoyed by the unicorn.

I can't remember the last time I was so properly fucked that life's cares couldn't touch me. It's rare in married women. A properly fucked wife is a unicorn.

No, that's not true. I have orgasms practically every time Rob and I have sex. Salina is in an unsustainable phase. What I envy is that she can know that and still enjoy the experience to the fullest. She's not going to try to turn her unicorn into something he's not. She won't try to put a bridle on him. She's not going to romanticize him into The One.

I get it now, this whole Miranda thing, why I can shut down her listing and still feel less than sated. It's because even if I look at every site and find her rental on none of them, there are things I can never know.

Miranda might not realize I'm behind it; she might not care. Maybe she was starting to think a rental property was more trouble than it was worth, having to deal with people like me. She might even think that I did her a favor. It's not like she needs the money.

I've got no resolution. No satisfaction. It's sex without orgasm.

Miranda's left me with blue balls.

18

Miranda

How are you going to fleece people out of their security deposits now? Ha ha, fleece, sheets, get it?

Oh, I get it. It's not enough for you to screw up my business, my life. You want to rub my nose in it. You want to be sure I know it was you, as if it could have been anyone else.

How can a virtual stranger gloat about the destruction of an-other? She must be pure evil.

I don't think I've ever felt this kind of rage before. I'm shaking with it. I'm parked in front of my mother's senior living community, but there's no way I can go inside, not in this condition. With my luck, this would be one of her more alert days, when she picks up on and synthesizes what's in the air around her. I can't bear to be the cause of her agitation. I can't run the risk.

I'll just drop the flowers off at the front desk and say something's come up. An emergency. It's not like she anticipates my visits. She won't miss me.

The sun through my windshield is blinding, painfully so. I rest my head on the steering wheel, trying to block it out. All of it.

I must have done something for it to have come to this. We're not just bystanders to disaster. We have to be contributors. Because if we're complicit in some way, we also have some power. I can't bear the alternative.

It's part of why I subsidize Thad. Because I created him, through what I did or didn't do, through action or inaction. I said something wrong, many somethings; more likely, I failed to say anything of value. My love wasn't enough. But I can correct that. Thad and I have texted ten times so far this morning.

But right now, I'm furious with myself.

Larry might know what to do about the rental, and about Dawn, but I can't pick his brain, not after my lies of omission. He doesn't know about the Santa Monica ordinance, and he certainly wouldn't approve of me violating it for years. If I tried to explain why, I'd only expose the extent of premeditation, damaging our trust irrevocably.

I need a new plan, that's all. I can do this. Larry isn't the only one with brains in this family.

I can't kick out the current guests. Where would they go? By the time I parted ways with Violet, I let her think she'd put the fear of God into me. She would never suspect that I'd honor the next two weeks' worth of reservations.

It's risky, but I need some buffer money until I decide my next move. I need to have enough to pay Thad's rent for the next few months. I can't cut him off cold turkey. He'd panic, and that would send him right back to drugs, if he's ever left them. He says he has. *You have to trust me,* he texted this morning. *I'm clean.*

I want to trust him, so badly, yet I have to wonder. Is it possible that all this talk is because somehow, through some junkie sixth sense, he can see that his money is in peril?

No, that's ridiculous.

He's clean, and I have to come clean. We finally have something in common.

But how can I come clean? Larry's mother had an affair, and he's never forgiven her. He says it's not about the affair per se; it's about the dishonesty, about her lack of character. He would never forgive or see me the same way again. Even if he didn't divorce me, I'd have to live every day knowing that in his eyes, I'd been soiled, permanently.

"Hello?" I say. I recognize the number. It's one I called earlier today, relieved to get the voicemail.

"This is Claire Turner. You canceled my reservation for next month?"

"I did. I'm so sorry. I hope I properly conveyed that in the message."

"You did. You properly *conveyed* it." Her tone is pointed. No one understands a family emergency anymore? It wasn't a lie. My family is on the verge of crisis. "Now what am I supposed to do? All the good rentals are taken."

"I'm sure that's not true. I refunded you in full."

"Yes, but now in order to get something equally nice, we have to spend more money. That's how it works when you wait until the last minute. Not that we did wait until the last minute."

I can't worry about Claire Turner right now, and her vacation in jeopardy. "I've already apologized, and issued a refund."

"That's not good enough. You should give us the difference in what we're going to have to spend now."

"If you read the contract at Getaway.com, I'm not liable for any—"

"This is about decency! It's about treating people how you'd want to be treated. We've been planning this vacation for months. My children were looking forward to staying by the beach. Do you want to break the news to them?"

At another time, I might have paid her the difference, just to avoid the confrontation. "I'm very sorry. I wish there was something I could do for you."

"That's not good enough."

She sounds like a young mother. I've been there myself. "Things happen in life that we're not expecting, and that we're not prepared for. It's good to get practice at rolling with them. I hope that you're fortunate enough that this is the worst setback you ever experience. I truly do."

"How dare you patronize me!"

I look toward the building that houses my degenerating mother, the one who barely remembers me on a good day. "Good luck to you." As she continues to sputter, I disconnect the call.

The hell with her. With all of them.

As a fireball hurtles upward through my body, I make my last call. It's to the one reservation that's come in since Dawn posted her review, and I'm ready for what he's about to say. In fact, some small part of me relishes it.

"My wife told me not to book with you. That you'd say there's a green stain on the couch in the shape of an antelope, and you'll need to keep the whole deposit."

"Yes," I say. "That sounds just like me."

"I'll be sure to note that response in my review."

I feel an unexpected freedom. There are no more reviews. No more hospitality. Nothing some stranger can take away from me. I'm not submitting myself for anyone's approval anymore. "You do that," I say, and *click*.

19

Dawn

Hi, Professor Myerson. I just sent you a LinkedIn request. Could you please approve me ASAP? I can use all the contacts I can get. Thanks!

    Dawn

"Dawnie," my mother says. She throws her arms around my neck, and I can feel her small body wrack with sobs.

I reach to hug her back, because it's the only human thing to do, but I'm reeling. I haven't seen my mother since my wedding day, and we've spoken only once in that time. How did she even find me?

The only thing I can think of is that my address was on my wedding invitation. Rob and I have lived here for our entire relationship. It's a depressing thought, actually. But my mother wouldn't actually save the invitation in its envelope with my return address, would she? She's neither sentimental nor organized enough for that.

These are not the right thoughts, I know. I should be asking her what's wrong, what I can do to help, but I just want her off me. I learned better than to throw my arms around her when I've been distraught. She'd crumble whether it was my heartache or hers; my heartache would become hers, but not in any way that could help me. She'd subsume my pain.

I realized early on that she could handle nothing. She'd wane at the slightest criticism. If I confronted her on a parenting failure (and really, she was a disaster as a mother), she would dissolve into tears and self-recrimination. "You're right, you're right, I'm the worst," she'd weep. I would have had to be a sadist to keep on with it. So I'd wind up taking care of her, telling her it wasn't really that bad, but it was. She was messy, distracted, self-involved, ignorant of things that mattered, forgetful in ways both public and private (I can't even count how many times I sat outside buildings waiting for her to drive up in the clunker of the moment). Her affection was absentminded, like she was petting a dog because she liked the feel of fur, not because she loved the dog.

It's inaccurate to say that she was self-absorbed. She was other-absorbed, and that other was her husband and never her child. They got together when she was a child herself, and she had me at fifteen. My father was seven years older, which was actionable in California, but her parents were eager to foist her on him. I guess she'd been a wild child, and they were too old to deal with it since she was an accidental change-of-life baby. So they signed her away and I was born in wedlock, just barely. They were in love. Well, she was utterly, irrevocably, unrelentingly, destructively in love with him.

He must be dead. That's the only reason she would be here, clinging to me.

I release her and look into her ravaged face. She's short like me, but sickly-skinny underneath a very faded denim jacket that might actually be from the eighties. She's got my blue eyes, and her hair is shoulder-length and crunchy-dry, a sort of sandy/wheaty color with darker streaks, a dye job gone wrong or gone too long. Her skin is ruddy, with pockmarks from acne, plus deeply grooved wrinkles.

I thought I'd never see her again, and I was good with that.

"He's dead, isn't he?" I say. She nods and then bursts into a fresh round of tears. I think she's going to grab me again and I involuntarily step back.

Rob steps forward, into the breach, and she hurls herself at him. Her crying takes on an even more hysterical, performative quality, though I know her grief is real. No one could be more bereft, more lost, than my mother without my father.

Ironically, he was just about the least dependable person around. His work ethic was nonexistent. He was fired from job after job as a laborer for being late or lazy or both. After a while, all he could get was temporary assignments from Manpower, and even those were few and far between. He often didn't come home, and it was pretty obvious he was screwing around. When he was there, he was emotionally absent, staring at the TV, barely talking to either of us. But Mom said constantly, "He's my rock." She meant it as a compliment, not in a can't-get-blood-from-a-stone sort of way.

I'm not thinking any of this consciously, but it's all there when I look at her. Rob's face is suffused with compassion, and I should be grateful. She's helpless in the best of circumstances, and someone has to be there for her.

If she'd called to tell me the news, I would have jumped in the car and gone to her; then all of this emotional upheaval would be confined to Eureka. But she has no right to cross my threshold in her hour of need after being MIA for the past three years. She's assuming we'll take her in, put her up, as if she's the child and I'm the mother, just like always.

She mismanaged her entire life, and now she's alone, with no means of support. While I pity her, I can't just forget that her choices cost me my childhood. When she saw my father wasn't holding jobs, she should have gotten one herself, but instead, she chose to believe he would pull it together soon. Her delusion meant we were constantly broke, sometimes hungry, and often evicted. She looked to me for reassurance: that not only was I okay, but she would be okay, too. Practically every year, I was the new girl in a poor school. She has no idea what that's like; she was too fragile to be told. Besides, I don't know how many times she asked, "How was your day?" and then rambled over my answer.

Her life was chaos, and she made that mine, and then she sought absolution. I gave it to her, again and again, because I felt sorry for her. Because I thought she was my father's unwitting victim. Because she didn't know any other way. Because she was the one parent who seemed to love me. Always because. But during those three years of no contact, I realized that it hadn't been real love at all. I'd been used, and it's not going to happen again.

"Was it sudden?" I ask my mom. What I mean is, *Did you have time to make arrangements? Was there life insurance? Are you about to get kicked out of your apartment?*

"Very sudden," she says. "A massive heart attack. He was barely fifty." She just keeps clutching Rob, a man to hold her aloft, the story of her life.

It occurs to me that I've just learned my father is dead. I should have some sort of emotional reaction to this news.

Is this what shock feels like? Or is it possible that I truly don't care? If the shoe was on the other foot—if my father had gotten the news of my death—I don't think he would have given two shits. One, maybe, but definitely not two.

That recognition makes me a little sad. So I guess that's something.

Finally, the embrace between Rob and my mother comes to an end, and we all gravitate toward the couch. It's the same couch we've had since I moved in, a white Jennifer Convertible that we bought new. The springs have become uncomfortable with time, but it does turn into a bed, and I know that my mother will be sleeping on it for one night at least. It's too late to send her back to Eureka.

"He was gone before the ambulance arrived," she says, closing her eyes, tears leaking out and down her cheeks. "I pounded on his chest and I blew into his mouth. I don't know if I did it right. I just tried to do what I saw on TV."

"I'm sure you did all you could," Rob says.

Her eyes are still closed. "I never thought it would happen like this, that I'd have to leave him."

"He left you, Mom." That's what dying is.

"No, I mean, I had to leave his . . . body."

"You left his body in Eureka without making arrangements?"

"I can't afford to have him buried. Isn't that awful?" Now she looks right at me. "He'll be a ward of the state."

"A ward of the state is an orphan," I say. "He's a fifty-two-year-old man." Who died without a penny to his name. Who surely doesn't have life insurance, or a wife who's capable of handling his remains.

I last saw them three years ago, when they were an hour and a half late to my wedding. They missed the ceremony and got tipsy at the reception. My father tried to feel up a bridesmaid, and my mother cried in the bathroom.

They never called to apologize for the scene. They never called at all, in fact. The next Mother's Day, Rob encouraged me to reach out and bury the hatchet. "They don't know there even is a hatchet," I told him. "They think that's normal behavior." He said I should be the bigger person. It seemed like a low bar, but okay.

So I called. My mother asked a generic question like "How's marriage treating you?" half listening to the answer before she went on about her usual struggles with rent and bills and my father. I endured fifteen minutes of this and then she came up for air, saying, "Well, I'll let you go." She already had, years before. After that phone call, I let her go. There was no point in saying that I wouldn't be calling again. It seemed like a safe assumption that if I didn't reach out, then I would never talk to them again. I didn't figure on a moment like this.

"We'll deal with all of it tomorrow," Rob says. "You don't need to worry. We'll figure out what needs to be done."

I hope he's just being comforting, that he's not actually considering footing the bill. A life of irresponsibility, so much so that they can't even afford a funeral, should not be rewarded with a bailout. But I can't say that in front of my mother. I don't want to kick her when she's down; I just don't feel like it's my job to pick her back up. Not anymore.

"We'll make up the couch for you," he tells her. "Have you eaten?"

I watch my sweet husband make her a plate of our leftover pasta, the pasta that I'd put into a container for his lunch tomorrow, and I'm thinking she doesn't deserve it. She hasn't earned the food out of our mouths.

I don't want to tell Rob I feel this way. He's displaying the characteristics of a good father, but I'm not feeling like I'd be much of a mother. I haven't seen it done, and I don't want to practice now, not like this.

20

Miranda

Thad, is everything okay?

Just text that one word, "okay." Even "OK" is okay.

Eva is due soon, but I can't help myself. I'm cleaning madly—not just my usual pre-cleaning/straightening, but a full scrubbing of the quartz countertops. My phone is lying close by, and I check often, in case the incoming text fails to ping. Ping, Thad, ping.

I haven't been worrying whether he's alive. I haven't even been checking his social media. For the first time in I don't know how long, I didn't need to. I had genuine contact with my son. How indescribably sweet it's been.

But now I have a much more familiar feeling.

For the past few years, money has been my leverage. Thad might ignore me much of the month, but not in that last week, not just before rent's due. I've often feared that if I turned off the green faucet, he'd have no reason to ever communicate with me. And I needed that scant amount of communication, that paltry recognition that I'm his mother, not just a follower of his Twitter feed.

This last week, though, I've been a different kind of junkie, craving just one more hit, one more text. I want him to tell me about his art, the show that he's working toward, the all-nighter he's just pulled. I lap up his pipe-dreamy nonsense. Just keep talking—well, texting. Stay live, and real.

Last night, he signed off that he loves me. And today . . . radio silence.

The more I think about it, the more out of character (and ominous) it all seems. Was that him saying good-bye? Has all this correspondence been a prelude to his final act?

I toss my sponge in the sink and grab my phone, checking Twitter and Instagram. Nothing since yesterday.

Thad, please answer.

I'm getting worried.

Thad wouldn't kill himself. That's not who he is. He's overdosed before, but they've always been accidental.

Haven't they?

Yesterday afternoon, he seemed nearly jubilant. High on life, that's what I decided to think. He was so sure that his ship was coming in, that his new work was the best he'd ever done. He said a gallery owner was interested.

He could have been just plain high. Once he crashed . . .

Thad wouldn't commit suicide. He's not the type. As Larry once said, Thad's always had "curiously high self-regard for someone who's accomplished so little." But that's when Thad was much younger. What if it's finally caught up with him, the sense of failure?

I grab my phone and begin to text madly, a flurry of support:

I love you.

I'm so proud of all the new work you're doing.

I'm sure it's wonderful.

He hasn't Instagrammed it, or sent me pictures. But that doesn't mean he hasn't been doing art. That doesn't mean he's been on something.

It's my fault. I should have asked him to send me a picture. Generally, I'm relieved not to see it. Because what I've seen makes no sense to me at all. It looks like graffiti, what you'd see on a wall and think that the neighborhood's gone to hell. Strange, thuggish cartoon figures, and oversized letters spelling out words like "ghettology." He says he's "subverting the dominant paradigm." How am I supposed to respond to that?

He used to hate when I said I didn't quite get his art, that I'm not the target audience. He hated when I said I was sure it was good, if you like that sort of thing.

I shouldn't have sent that last text, the *I'm sure it's wonderful.* I can't afford any missteps. The truth is, as much as I've loved hearing from him these past days, it's been terrifying, too. I've been texting on eggshells. If all I do is read his tweets, then I can't inflame him. I can't lose what I don't have.

He must be using again. He might have overdosed, accidentally or on purpose. I need to do something, I can't just sit here texting all day.

I hear Eva deactivating the alarm system from the foyer. When I appear in the living room, she looks up, surprised. I'm rarely home when she arrives. It makes me uncomfortable to be present while someone cleans my house; I feel lazy and critical all at once.

"I'm just leaving, Eva," I say, shoving the cell phone into my purse and passing her on my way to the front door.

"Have a great day!" she calls after me.

Once in the car, I know just where to go.

As I drive, I tell myself that Thad will be okay, he always is. How many times have I made myself crazy, imagining him lying dead in some filthy drug lair, and then he Instagrams a picture of himself at a Burger King? This will be just like that.

I still don't know what I'm going to do after the final two rentals are done. I suppose I could go to management companies and see if they could get me a steady supply of thirty-day renters, though I despise the idea of them walking through my parents' house, with their beady appraising eyes. After they take their cut, what would be left for Thad?

Larry makes more than enough money to subsidize Thad. He could take care of ten grown children, if he wanted to, easily. But there's no way he would, and if lump sums began disappearing from our joint account, he would notice sooner or later. He'd follow the trail, and I'd be sunk. Our marriage would be over.

Miranda and Larry, engraved, embroidered, emblazoned, written in the sky (he did that for our twenty-fifth anniversary)—what would I be, solo? An aged divorcée, a castoff. I'd be wealthy, since there was no prenup, but it wouldn't matter, or rather, it would only matter to the lowest of the low, the bottom-feeders, the young men living off their cougars. You see them everywhere in this town, and the women often look proud, and I'm embarrassed for them. They have no idea how the world views them. But then, to be that blind—maybe they're the lucky ones. If I had to start dating, it would be on my own merits, fair market value, and I shudder to think what that would be.

Besides, I love Larry. He's tender toward me, and I toward him. We still snuggle on the couch and eat popcorn while we watch movies. We might not go into tedious detail about our days, but the curiosity is there. The concern is there. It's never left.

Can I convince Larry that I never knew about the ordinance?

Would I be able to lie right to his face? I don't trust my acting abilities, while I trust his discernment.

I push open my car door and stride up the steps to the police station. It's a small building, quaint, almost like a one-room schoolhouse. I tell myself they're going to be friendly inside.

At first, that's how it is. I sit across the desk from a pleasant uniformed officer in his early thirties. "Slow news day," I say with a smile, casting my eye around the room. He laughs generously. The acoustics of the room are somewhat intimidating, seeing as there are five desks nearby occupied by other officers, none of them with witnesses, or whatever it is I am.

"How can I help you, Mrs. Feldt?" Officer Llewellyn says. He's almost handsome, in an army regulation sort of way, but with a long, slightly crooked nose. I see by the picture on his desk that he's a family man, with a sunny wife and three kids. He makes good eye contact, seems sincere and interested and sympathetic. This is going well already.

"My son is in Tucson, and he might be in trouble. I'd like the local police to do a welfare check."

"Is he of age?"

"Yes, he's twenty-seven."

"Have you called the Tucson police already?"

"No. I don't have my son's address."

Officer Llewellyn cocks his head, almost imperceptibly. I feel myself flush, a mother not knowing her own son's address.

"I thought that if I just called them, they'd say they couldn't help me without an address. But if the LAPD asked them, they would manage to do something more. Maybe they could track him by the GPS on his phone?"

I smile in my most maternal, trustworthy way. I could be this officer's mother. He needs to remember that. How would he want his own mother treated in a situation like this?

"When did you last hear from your son?"

"Last night." I see the look in his eyes: *You don't have your son's address yet you're alarmed that you haven't heard from him in twelve hours?* But I won't be deterred. "I need a welfare check. I've had them done before." I remember how angry Thad was to have the police sniffing around. He yelled, "Do you want to get me arrested?" Then as now, better arrested than dead.

Officer Llewellyn asks, "Under what circumstances did you get the other welfare checks done?"

"When I was concerned for his welfare."

"Because . . . ?"

I flush more deeply. "Because he's a drug addict who's overdosed three times before." I haven't said those words aloud in so long, yet the shame feels like yesterday. This man must be thinking that it's my fault, in some way, shape, or form, and I agree with him.

"You know a welfare check is just a knock on the door and a walk around the premises if there's no answer?" It's my turn to nod. "If he's inside and he's overdosed, I don't imagine he'd answer the door." I notice that one of the other officers at a nearby desk is glancing over, as if he wants to catch Officer Llewellyn's eye. But my officer is fixed firmly on me. He doesn't think I'm a joke, just naïve. Or maybe pathetic. The junkie's well-dressed mother prevailing on police resources might be an old story.

"Maybe if they really pounded on the door, it could wake him up," I say, but he's shaking his head. There's kindness in it, as if he doesn't want me to embarrass myself further.

"It's not something I can do. I call other police departments when it's a serious matter, and I'm sorry, but this doesn't qualify. I'd advise you to call them yourself, on the nonemergency line."

My eyes fill with tears. Crying in public . . . my mother would be horrified. He hands me a tissue from the box on his desk. "He hasn't answered my texts all day."

"I imagine that's very frightening, given his history."

"We've been talking more lately, and last night, he told me he loves me." I'm nearly whispering by the end.

"Sounds like a good talk."

A last talk. "Are you sure there's nothing you can do?" If I'm going to cry, I might as well try to get mileage out of it.

"The odds are, he's fine."

"He says he's been clean."

"Maybe he has been. Maybe he is. Maybe his phone died. Maybe a lot of things. Don't leap ahead, that's my advice to you."

As an officer, he's probably seen a lot of things himself. It's good advice, the same advice they would give me at Nar-Anon. Often good advice is the hardest to follow.

"Is there anything else I can help you with?"

I'm sure he doesn't expect me to answer that. It's a polite kiss-off. But since I'm here . . .

"Actually," I say, "you might be able to help me with this one."

"Yeah?" He smiles, like he's delighted to have the opportunity. His mother raised him well.

"There's a woman named Dawn Thiebold," I begin. As I describe her behavior—including the last e-mail where she called me the C-word and basically threatened me—I feel more confident that Thad is fine, and that I was meant to come here to talk about Dawn. To stop her.

I'm sure I'm not her first victim. Women as relentless and as cunning as she is, women unable to take responsibility for their own actions and pay the price, they must strike again and again. Yes, that's what it is. She's a bully, and everyone knows that if you stand up to a bully, they back down. They find another target.

Not that I want her finding another target. I want to shut her down, same as she shut down my rental. That means scaring her, and the best way to do that is with the law, which must be on my side in a case like this. After all, harassment is a crime.

Officer Llewellyn listens with patience and concern as I explain it all, right up to Dawn sabotaging me with the Homeowners Association.

"How did she do that?" he asks. It's the first time he's interrupted my recitation.

I have to tread lightly. I hadn't thought this through, and now I hope that the officers here don't know or care about Santa Monica ordinances. The last thing I need is for this complaint to expose my own violation, minor as it is. I didn't harass or threaten anyone; no one's been harmed by my actions. On the contrary, I've given people a beautiful place to spend a few days or a week. I've been a good host to many, even to Dawn herself.

"She made those same false accusations to the Association," I say, thinking on my feet.

"About you keeping her deposit when she claims that she didn't actually stain your sheets?" Several officers look over, and this time, it's less oblique, more overt. There's no question what they think of me. They're glad that Llewellyn got the crazy old broad. Is this a police station or a frat house?

"I know it sounds ridiculous," I say, lowering my voice. "It is ridiculous, and petty. She's trying to ruin my life over something that she did." I reach into my purse for my phone. "I have all her e-mails, and the texts, too. It might take me a minute to find them all, but I can show you, I can prove—"

"I'm just trying to clarify so I can see if it meets the definition of civil harassment. If it qualifies as stalking, or abuse, or a credible threat of violence. Is that the case here, do you think?" His tone is neutral, but his intent is clear. He thinks the answer is no. He wants me to be the one to say it, to disqualify myself.

I stop scrolling on my cell. I have the sinking feeling that he's not interested anyway. I thought that if he couldn't help me with Thad, the very least he could do was help with Dawn. Together, we could have turned this visit to the station into something useful. I feel a surge of disappointment. I misjudged Officer Llewellyn. "She's contacted me repeatedly," I say, looking down. "She's trying to scare me." I feel like I'm going to cry again, and I know it won't do any good. I've been humiliated enough, to no purpose.

"Show me the e-mails," he says, like he's taking pity on me. "If she makes any sort of direct threat, I'll see what I can do."

"She's too smart to be direct! But it's in her tone. Here." I slide him the phone after finding the most recent e-mail. I wanted to delete that filth immediately, but I knew, on some level, that I shouldn't. It could be evidence.

He scans the lines. "It's definitely hostile, I'll give you that." I brighten slightly. Maybe this hasn't been a waste after all. "You said she lives hours away. Has she come anywhere near you, or threatened to?"

I lean in, needing him to look into my eyes. His mother's eyes. This is a good boy. He's the son that I should have had. He wants to help me. He just thinks his hands are tied. "You're talking about a subjective standard. I find her texts and e-mails abusive and threatening. I offered to refund her $200. What more does she want? Why is she still in contact with me? Why is she baiting me with that text about the fleece sheets, ha ha? Wouldn't you find it unnerving?"

"She needs a hobby, that's for sure." He looks at his desk. He hasn't looked at the other officers, not once, no matter how they try to catch his eye. He wants to do the right thing here. "You need to give me more, okay? This is the most aggressive of the e-mails, correct?" He holds up the phone, and I nod. "She writes to you, what, once a day?"

"No, not that often."

"The kind of harassment we see—sometimes we're talking about a hundred contacts a day. We're talking about explicit threats. Often we're talking about women whose husbands were beating on them for years, who have reason to fear for their safety. They need protection."

He's lecturing me, I realize. He's telling me that I'm wasting his valuable time. Well, I happen to think he's been wasting mine. I snatch my phone back.

"Based on what you've got here," he says in summation, "it doesn't qualify for a restraining order, especially with the distance, and that's the first step in harassment cases. Establishing the restraining order, and then when they violate it, they can be prosecuted."

"There should be some consequence for this behavior. She goes to buy a house, or apply for a job, and they see what kind of person she is. I want this to touch her in some way."

"That's not how it works. You don't get to put black spots on her record. This isn't about retaliation." His face has changed; he thinks he misjudged me.

"It's about my personal safety."

He shakes his head slowly, a little sadly. "She'll have her own side of this, you realize. The e-mails and texts you sent her are going to be part of it, too. You haven't shown me any of those."

"I have nothing to hide. You can see everything."

He shakes his head again, like he doesn't want me incriminating myself. "I don't understand why the Homeowners Association took her seriously enough to throw you out."

"I wasn't thrown out. I was asked to resign. It was a courtesy."

Does he know about the ordinance? Is this entrapment?

No, he wouldn't do that.

He's not trying to figure me out anymore; he believes me. I've been trying to get him to see me as his mother, but instead, he thinks I'm my mother, that I'm losing my faculties.

"In Santa Monica," he says gently, "rentals are for thirty days or longer." I feel my face growing hot. "You're going to be okay. Things like this, people like Dawn—they flare up, and they flare out. She's going to forget about you soon. Geography is your best protection. She might be trying to scare you, but she's not going to hurt you."

He can't know that, any more than I can.

"Just between us, I've always thought it's a stupid ordinance." He smiles at me. "All you need to do is mark that woman as 'spam.' Everything she sends you goes straight to spam. Don't let her take up any more of your thoughts, okay?" When I don't answer, he says, "I can show you how to block her on your phone. That should take care of your problem."

I feel like crying (for the third time, this isn't me at all), and he can see it. He doesn't want to make his mother cry. So he keeps talking. "Just don't engage her anymore. She gets nothing back from you, there's nothing to fuel her fire. She burns out, like I said. So where are you headed after this? Do you have a friend you can call?"

He's a good man, and he's telling me that Dawn gets to take away my income and my reputation and my peace of mind, and there will be no retribution. There will be no protection. The law will do nothing unless she crosses more lines. I'm a sitting duck.

That's with a sympathetic officer. Imagine what I would have gotten with that oaf at the next desk.

"Do you work?" Officer Llewellyn asks me. I shake my head. "Volunteer?"

"A little."

"Good." He smiles. "Keeping busy is good."

So this is how he sees me. As a woman who's so bored that she's scaring herself, that she's making mountains out of molehills, credible threats out of nothing. He thinks I just need something to do.

He's not entirely wrong, though. I'm barely a mother anymore, and I'm not really a daughter, I'm a flower delivery service, and I'm not a host anymore, Dawn's seen to that, and I'm not yet a landlord, not that I've ever wanted to be one, and soon I won't be a board member, and I haven't volunteered in weeks.

So I guess I'm just a wife. A wife with a secret, and a big problem.

I thank Officer Llewellyn and wander out into the sun, dazed. As I sleepwalk toward my car, I trip on the legs of a homeless man. He snarls at me, "Watch it," as if I'm the one who's not supposed to be here. He's living a block from the police station, without fear, and if they won't even move him along, if they let him feel like he owns the sidewalk, then I never had a chance of them calling the Tucson police about Thad, let alone pursuing a woman hundreds of miles away.

I'm truly on my own.

21

Dawn

Hey, Salina.

    Hey, girl.

    I can't come to class today. Take notes for me?

    Def. Hot date with Rob?

    It's my dad.

    Gross.

    No, I mean, he died.

    Shit! So sorry.

    I have to go to Eureka.

    Soooo sorry.

    Yeah, I know.

    How are u?

    Fine. I barely knew the guy.

    But still.

    I have to help my mom. She's a mess.

Make sure Rob takes care of u.

He always does.

"Morning," my mother says wanly. She's standing in the doorway of my kitchen in a long T-shirt and nothing else (except, hopefully, underwear). It's not like I think her scrawny frame would hold any appeal for my husband, but still. She's a widow now.

Even though Rob and I sprung for bright-colored curtains, it hardly remedies the dinginess of the kitchen. The walls are gray with tons of tiny holes like an ear piercer's run amok; the linoleum has a pattern of faded yellow diamonds with an overlay of ineradicable grunge; the oven is the color of an old avocado; the refrigerator moans constantly. It pains me to realize that this place isn't much nicer than the ones I lived in with my parents. But since it's located in the Temescal neighborhood, just a few blocks from Telegraph Avenue with its wine bars and cheese shops, it costs five times what an apartment of similar size and quality would in Eureka.

But my mother wouldn't know that. Seeing through her bloodshot eyes, I feel like I haven't come so far after all.

As she colt-legs forward to take a seat across from me at the kitchen table, I slam my laptop screen shut. I couldn't even begin to explain why I have a picture of Miranda, Larry, and Thaddeus up on my screen—to her, or to myself.

I know where Miranda lives. I figured it out on Zillow. The Feldts bought their house twenty-five years ago, in Beverly Hills. It cost a million and a half then, so it's got to be worth way more now. Funny how you can have all that money, and the Internet offers you no protection at all. I don't just know her neighborhood; I know her exact address.

Between my mother at one pole and Miranda at the other, I find that I'm scanning my kitchen with far greater distaste than usual.

"I have to tell you something," my mother says. "It's about your father."

I listen for the words I've been wishing for my whole life: *Your father is not actually, biologically, yours.*

"I wouldn't tell you this if it wasn't going to come out anyway."

Way to embrace truthfulness, Mom.

"Your father and I weren't legally married."

"But you have his name. I had his name." I was thrilled to shed it but it feels oddly as if my mother is taking something away from me.

"We went down to the courthouse to get married," she continues, pushing a strand of hair back from her face so it can join the great unwashed masses, "and we found out my parents had signed the wrong form. Your father said we didn't need some piece of paper to prove we were meant for each other, definitely nothing signed by my parents." She stops, tears welling in her eyes. She actually thinks it's a romantic tale.

I'm illegitimate. A bastard, or whatever the female equivalent is. What would Rob's perfect parents think about this? For years, his mother's been making a valiant effort to think I'm good enough for him.

My mother's been lying to me for thirty years. She would have lied for another thirty, if it wasn't "going to come out anyway."

"We were in love," she says, in her defense. "You know how we were."

"That I do."

"Don't be like that, Dawnie." She reaches a limp hand across the tabletop in my general direction, as if she doesn't actually want it to make contact with me; she's content with proximity, the illusion of connection.

"So you changed your name to his?"

She shakes her head. "I just used it. I signed everything that way, and you know what? No one ever checks. I guess now, with computers, they could find it out quickly, but back then, all you had to do was say it. I became Wendy Xavier. I figured that it would be true soon enough, that we would be man and wife. Common-law man and wife, since we were spending our whole lives together. And you know what else is funny?"

"No, I really don't."

"What's funny is that your dad did the same thing I did! He made himself an Xavier, without any help from the courts. He wasn't born that way."

Generations full of fraud. How adorable. Babies having babies. Free love. Call yourself something, make it so.

I want to throw up. "Are you my real mother?" I ask.

"Now that's not funny."

"So why's it going to come out now?"

"Because California has no common-law marriage. I'm scared to find out how I'm going to get his body now. It belongs to me, Dawn, after all these years. All I've been through."

Does she mean the other women, or his breathtaking level of disregard for her emotional and physical well-being, or his abject failure to provide while he left her with all the household and child-rearing responsibilities? Is it all of that, or is there some other reason she left his body, unclaimed, back in Eureka, other than she didn't have a marriage certificate or money?

"Good morning." Rob swoops into the room, placing his hand on my shoulder. I look upward, at his freshly shaven chin. He asks my mother, "Could I borrow Dawn for a minute?" as if she should have any say in the matter.

I follow him into the bedroom, shutting the door behind us. It's all white in here: the canopy bed, the comforter, the end tables, no

TV. Not a hint of color, not even on the throw pillows. Life, in here, is pristine. That's why it's so galling that Miranda would accuse me of staining anything. I've tried so hard to get clean after what my father did to me.

"Did you overhear my mother's big confession?" I say. "She never legally married my father, and there's no common-law marriage in California. She might not even be able to claim the body. Can you believe her?"

"She's grieving."

"What does that have to do with anything? This was years ago! She couldn't even manage to get married right."

"I feel sorry for her, that's all. She was old school, relying on your dad completely. She just wasn't very competent."

"I spent my whole childhood feeling sorry for her. Enough is enough." When he doesn't respond, I add, "Old-school moms were very competent. They worked. In the home. What was she doing?"

He comes toward me, arms outstretched.

"No, I'm okay. I don't need a hug. I need her out, ASAP."

He drops his arms. "ASAP might be a while. We can't just send her back."

"You make it sound like we're deporting her."

"I just mean, she's got no job. We have to help her."

"She should have gotten a job years ago. Now she has no choice. Necessity is the mother of invention."

"If she's never worked, how's she going to start now? Her husband just died. She's got to be depressed."

Laziness is not a disability. Sucking at life is not a disability, and it's not a get-out-of-jail-free card. It's not a mooch-off-your-grown-daughter card. But I'm not about to say any of that. Rob's full of compassion toward her, and he wants me to feel the same. "What do you think we should do?"

"Well, first, we need to get your dad. I did some quick research. If we don't claim his body, they're going to cremate him."

"That doesn't sound so bad." Fire and brimstone, a day of reckoning. That doesn't sound so bad at all.

"He's your father, Dawn."

For Rob, it's simple: You don't leave your dad to be burned up. For me, it's simple, too: Yes, you do, if you had that kind of dad. The gulf between our life experiences is rearing its head, prominently. But Rob thinks neglect is the whole story when it comes to my father. I was too ashamed to tell him the truth; I didn't want him to see me in that light. I've tried so hard to forget any of it ever happened—to forget that I was just the sort of girl something like that would happen to.

"You've been working your ass off to support us while I finish school," I say. It never occurred to me until just then that I've been mooching. Like mother, like daughter. But I'm going to earn it all back soon enough. I'm going to outearn Rob. Professor Myerson recognizes my potential, and he sees loads of students. "We don't have extra cash lying around for a funeral." Not the gift money from the wedding. Not our savings. Not for that man.

"It's not the funeral I'm talking about; it's the burial. It's having a final resting place for him, someplace your mother can visit. Someplace you can visit."

"Is this about religion?" I say. "Because you know I don't believe like you do." I thought he'd accepted that about me. "I wasn't raised in a church like you were."

"This is about doing what's right for your family. We have savings for important things like this."

I can't get him to see what I see, not without telling him what my father did. He doesn't see my mother as I do either: a woman who didn't need to choose her husband over everything else in life.

She didn't need to choose him over solvency, or happiness, or her only child. It's her fault—what my father did, what I *let* him do—all in the name of protecting her. It's her fault, even though she never knew about it.

My mother's lost, all right, but it shouldn't be my job to find her. When I've been lost, she never came looking.

Now that she's shown up here, I'm stuck with a terrible choice. I can allow my husband to think badly of me for not wanting to take care of my mother and bury my father, or I can tell him the truth and he can think badly of me for another reason. I'll be dirty in his eyes, the same as I was in my own for so long.

It's a terrible choice, all right, but an easy one.

22

Miranda

Sorry for being MIA. I was on an art binge.

To use that word so casually . . . Is he just torturing me? There's only one kind of binge as far as I'm concerned, and he must know that. He has to know that I've been on edge the past two days. Going from all that contact to nothing made me understand what withdrawal symptoms must be like. The Tucson police were as unhelpful as I'd feared, and while I tried to listen to Officer Llewellyn's advice about staying busy and assuming Thad's fine, my nerves were jangling nonstop.

I dig my toes deeper into the sand. It's nine A.M., and I managed only a few hours of fitful sleep last night. I imagine Thad's been awake just as long, bingeing.

There are plenty of people running and biking along the path, but I've got the sand to myself. Blue skies, blue water, as far as the eye can see. I wish I could enjoy it. I wish I could believe that art's the reason he disappeared.

I'm glad to hear from you, I choose my words with care, but I have to tell you, it's been rough on me.

What has?

Not hearing from you.

I have a life, too.

I've tried to give him so much, and yet he feels he owes me nothing. If I insist on more, I could end up back where I was, checking his whereabouts on social media.

Just a text, that's all I'm asking. It can just say "OK."

And if I'm not okay? Do you want me to lie?

Have you been using again?

I knew it. I knew you didn't really believe me.

Tread lightly.

I'm sorry. You said yourself you've been MIA. That used to mean you were using.

I told you, I was making art.

I'm glad you were.

No answer for minutes.

I'm sorry, Thad. I don't want to go back to the way things were.

I'm moving forward, one way or another.

Tell me about your new work.

You really want to hear?

Of course.

I'm working on a series. These huge canvases, like painting inside a subway tunnel.

Has he painted inside a subway tunnel? I've wondered before if he's done actual graffiti. Tagging, I believe it's called. I like to think not, same as I like to think he hasn't stolen from strangers or prostituted himself.

The problem is, I have to squat.

What does that mean?

I can't exactly work on 20 foot canvases in my apartment.

So where do you work?

In an abandoned warehouse.

Is that safe?

Probably not. But what's the alternative?

He wants me to be the one to say it: rent a workspace. Then he can say that he can't afford it, and I can say . . .

Hopefully, you'll get your gallery show soon.

There are a lot of steps between here and there. Paint ain't cheap, and I need a whole lot of it. I need to hope no one fucks up my shit just for fun. I'm painting by candlelight so no one sees the light from outside.

He's cursing again, though he knows I don't like that. While he's not asking directly, my heart sinks anyway. I'm feeling like I've been had, yet again.

Why don't you give me your address? Maybe I can send you some art supplies.

You don't know what I need.

I can send you a gift certificate to an art supply store.

Email it.

He doesn't want me to know where he lives. He doesn't trust me. *He* doesn't trust *me.* I'd laugh out loud if I weren't on the verge of tears.

I want to believe that he hasn't been bingeing on meth, just art, and that he isn't angling for more money, and he's not really hiding his address.

Trust but verify. That's why I want his address. So that next time he goes MIA, as he put it, I'll at least be able to enlist the police properly. I could even fly out there myself. I haven't laid eyes on my son in going on three years, and I ache to see him.

The reason I do so many allnighters is because I don't want my canvases there at prime squat time without me.

Maybe it's safer to paint during the day, though.

Probably. But I can't leave them unguarded.

I want to believe he's just making conversation. But he knows that his safety is paramount, as far as I'm concerned. He's asking for more money, without asking.

Fortunately or unfortunately, because of the Santa Monica house situation, I really can't help him. I'm already paying one rent for him; I can't pay two.

At any other time, I might have been tempted. As it is, I've put myself on the hook for a gift certificate for art supplies, and I didn't get the information I was fishing for.

I probably would have paid for a workspace even though I know it's a classic enabler move. He should get a job and pay for it himself. But I would have thought, What if he just needs a hand(out) right now and then he'll get his gallery show and become self-supporting? I would have had to argue myself down, because a parent's natural state is one of gullibility; we want to believe in the goodness of our children.

But now I don't have that battle, so I tell him I'll e-mail him a gift certificate, and he says thanks, he should get back to work. I notice that he doesn't sign off with love this time.

I stare out at the ocean, the rise and the fall, the crest and the crash. I take a deep breath and remind myself that I just got good news. The best news. Thad is okay.

Now I have to get down to business.

"Hi, Vi!" I cringe a little, hearing my own false happy voice. "Just leaving you this voicemail because I didn't get a response to my text, the one where I told you that I'd canceled all my reservations for the house and taken down the ad?" The upward lilt at the end of the sentence—does it make me sound like I'm lying? I am lying, after all. Do all liars spend their lives worrying like this? If so, why do they do it? The truth would be so much less stressful, in most cases.

"I'll be turning in my resignation to the board. I know you're right, it's the best thing to do, but I'm really going to miss everyone." I'll wait to hear from her before I submit it. Maybe she'll have mercy and tell me that I shouldn't go through with it.

"Call or text back, okay? I want to make sure that this hasn't damaged our friendship. That's the most important thing. I wasn't myself the day we met for lunch. There's so much going on with my mother, with her—condition, it's deteriorating rapidly." Only a slight overstatement, she is deteriorating, absolutely, and "rapid" is a relative term. "I apologize if I didn't handle the information you provided as graciously as I should have. I really appreciate you bringing it to me. You were looking out for me"—well, for the board—"and I can see that now, so clearly. Thank you, Vi. Let's talk soon, okay? Again, thanks. Enjoy this beautiful day."

My fingers tighten on the straps of my sandals. It is a beautiful day, flawless as my diamond engagement ring. I walk back toward the Santa Monica house, seeing my first pedestrian of the day, a toned woman in some sort of unitard walking a Bernese mountain dog. "Good morning!" she sings out, and I try to respond with equal enthusiasm. That's only polite.

I'm across the street from my house, and I notice that there's a tricycle on the front lawn. I told my guests in no uncertain terms that they could not leave anything around, anywhere. I can't afford to have anyone turning me in when I'm this close to being law-abiding again.

Normally, I try not to issue too many rules to my houseguests; I want my home to feel like their home during their stay. But you give these people an inch, they take a mile.

Glaring at the tricycle, I reach for my phone. "Hi, Tracy," I say, my voice overlaid with thick syrup to mask the irritation. "It's Miranda. I just wanted to check and see how your stay is going so far. Also, a quick reminder. The house is going on the market soon, and the Realtors might want to give potential buyers a quick look-see, just from the outside, so it's VERY IMPORTANT that you keep the perimeter entirely picked up. No toys on the lawn, for example, nothing like that. I hope this isn't too much of a hardship." I don't need their review, the listing is already down, and I'm doing them a favor by not having canceled their reservation at all. My voice sharpens. "Thank you."

The living room shades are up, but I see no movement in the house. They must all be sleeping in. I also told them not to leave lights on when they're out. I need as few signs of habitation as possible. Fortunately, there's no driveway to park in as the entire house is boxed in by the white picket fence. I stare at the tricycle, on its side beneath the auspices of the Meyer lemon tree. What are these people, animals?

I push open the gate—it is my gate, after all—and pick up the tricycle, carrying it around to the back of the tree where it won't be visible to a casual observer on the street. They're lucky I don't just take it. Teach them a lesson about where they leave their personal belongings. Santa Monica is beautiful, but it's not Mayberry.

I quickly exit the yard and return to my car. I tell myself I've got every right to be here. I'm just delivering a bunch of dahlias to the sweet elderly neighbor couple. They're actually younger than my parents, but retired. They're very spry. It occurs to me that I'm fast approaching the age where "spry" would be a compliment.

They know I rent the house out. They've never said boo about it, though it's possible they aren't aware of the ordinance. This isn't the first time I'm bringing Harriet flowers, but it is the first time I'm doing it with an ulterior motive, and that deepens the pit in my stomach.

I don't know who I am anymore. I'm spying on my guests, I'm leaving them snippy voicemails and moving their children's toys, I'm bribing my neighbors to keep my secret.

Dawn is destroying me. Not just taking away my rental income, but making me behave like another person, like someone sneaky and underhanded. She's remaking me in her image, and I won't have it. I'm a good person.

I walk up to Harriet's house and I leave the flowers on the doorstep. No note, no request, just an anonymous gift. She might think they're from Calvin, a bit of spontaneous romance after all their years together. My father used to do that for my mother sometimes after they moved to Santa Monica. He discovered his sentimental side, the happiness he derived from hers. He learned what it meant to be fully present.

I flash on an image: playing hide-and-seek with George, me in my father's closet, breathing in the smell of him since I so rarely got to take him in given his long work hours, my foot kicking something surprising, discovering my father had a hiding place of his own . . .

Where did that even come from? I'm under too much stress, that's what it is. It's been so long since Larry and I have had a vacation. Clearly, I need one.

I feel the tears threatening, and I hurry back to my car. After the guests leave, this is over. I live honestly. I will not be Dawn, in her gutter in Oakland. Water finds its own level.

That was my mother's expression. Rest in peace, Mommy.

She's not dead! She's still in there, somewhere. I need to try harder to draw her out. I'll read her the books she used to love, and we'll watch her old favorite movies. I'll bring photo albums. I've gotten complacent, but there's work to be done. I'm going to bring her back to me, and she'll help me recover myself.

I'm about to start my car when I notice a Mercedes SUV is tooling by, ever so slowly. The driver is a middle-aged man, and he seems to be looking carefully at each house. I think he slows even further in front of mine, but I could be imagining it. He doesn't stop.

Someone from the city attorney's office? No, Vi was supposed to have taken care of that. But she was also supposed to have answered my texts. Would someone from the city attorney's office drive a Mercedes SUV, anyway? He could. This is Santa Monica.

Or it could be someone else, unrelated. Someone Dawn sent? Is she somewhere nearby?

A shiver goes through me. I wouldn't know Dawn if I saw her. She could have been that woman with the Bernese mountain dog, who did seem awfully eager to make eye contact during a simple "Good morning" exchange.

Officer Llewellyn says geography is my greatest protection, and that Dawn's going to burn out soon, and I hope he's right. But I should know what she looks like, just in case.

I punch her name into my phone. There she is, the only Dawn Thiebold to pop up. I didn't even need to add the "Oakland." She's on Facebook, Twitter, and something called LinkedIn. I'm exhorted to log in to find out what she "shares with her friends." No, thank you. I am definitely not her friend.

Even her enemies can find out that she is currently a communications major at a lowly state school, that she used to work for Target and PetSmart, that she's married, and that she's beautiful.

I wouldn't have guessed that last part. She doesn't have a beautiful girl's name, that's for sure. A communications major, please! She'll go far with that. Especially when you consider her distinguished resume.

Her husband must have money. So she can afford to go back to college at the only school that would let someone like her in, and they can go on expensive long weekends where she mistreats other people's possessions and then thinks she doesn't have to pay for it. That's what beautiful women do, right? They expect things to be handed to them, and to get off scot-free.

I've worked hard for everything I have, including Larry. Particularly Larry. He was eyeing more beautiful girls when we got together—the Dawn Thiebolds of the world—but none of them would have made a better wife.

Would one of them have made a better mother?

I try to shake that thought off. This isn't about me, what I have or have not been, where I've succeeded or failed. It's about Dawn and her egregious behavior.

I was Phi Beta Kappa at Scripps College, the Bryn Mawr of the West. Not that she would have heard of either of those fine schools. Someone like her would never even consider a women's college, never value the community and camaraderie that only an all-female environment can provide. A woman who looks like her needs male attention at all times. The most beautiful are the most insecure. They require constant tending, like roses, and are just as thorny.

The woman with the Bernese mountain dog is already coming back this way. Maybe a dog like that can't run very far. At least I know now that she's not Dawn. She's nowhere near as attractive.

I don't want to spend my time looking over my shoulder. Not for the city attorney, and certainly not for Dawn.

One good thing about seeing her picture is that she doesn't seem quite as threatening. How scary could a toothpaste commercial model be?

Officer Llewellyn said to do nothing except block her. But I feel like he's wrong about that. It's slinking away, showing fear. With bullies, you need to go right at them.

I start typing.

I stare for an extra minute, which is an eon in text time. Nothing in it is untrue. The threat is purely implied.

She has a husband. She has a LinkedIn profile. She has things to lose. This will resonate.

I will be free of Dawn Thiebold.

23

Dawn

The police have advised me to block you. All further
communications should cease.

   Miranda

There's some old movie, with some old mobster, and he says with
his heavy New York accent something like, "Every time I try to get
out, they pull me back in."

That's Miranda, pulling me back in when I really was starting to
let go.

She's been to see the police about me? Unbelievable! She's the
one who stole my security deposit! She's the one who was cheating
the system in Santa Monica! She's the one bothering me, time and
again. I try to get out and she pulls me back in.

What does this even mean? Am I in real trouble? Am I going to get some kind of official document, or a visit from an officer, or am I just supposed to take the word of a liar like her?

I haven't done anything wrong. I wrote a review to warn other potential consumers, and I turned her in for violating the law, and *she's* the one talking to the police? I didn't even know there was entitlement on this scale. There ought to be a new word for it. Something longer, like "onomatopoeia."

As if I need this on top of a dead father, a needy mother, a stalled job search, and an imminent graduation. I'm at a rest area en route to Eureka to see my father's body, and the only consolation is that my mother is not in the car with us. She's been chugging along in front, sending up smoke signals in her maroon Ford Escort with one mismatched door. Now she's in the bathroom, and I'm watching a toy poodle watering the base of a tree. I know how you feel, oak.

It's been silent between Rob and me for the past hour. We're at a stalemate, a tense "agree to disagree" where my father is concerned. Rob still feels like a burial is the right thing to do—the only "humane" thing to do—and that's only one letter off from "human," and I feel like if I play this whole thing wrong, he'll think I'm half a person.

I spy him exiting the restroom, and I move away, around the building, where he can't see me. I'm actually running away from my own husband. This is what it's come to.

I'll go with my mother to view the body, then we'll go to her apartment where I'll make her tea and tuck her in for the night, and Rob and I will drive back home. If he wants to be generous with our money, we can help her out with next month's rent. That's a better use of the cash anyway. For the living, not the dead. Rob will have to see that, won't he?

Just the thought of Eureka makes my skin crawl. Nothing good ever happened to me there. It was a geographic accident, as much as I was a biological one, and I want to get back to the Bay Area, where I really belong.

I'm missing Professor Myerson's class today, which I resent. My mother shouldn't have shown up at my door, dragging me into this, dragging me back. Every time I try to get out . . .

Behind the building, there are two little girls running around, one with long braids, the other with her amber-colored hair loose and strands getting caught in her mouth, both in blowing summery dresses, their high-pitched squeals lost to the wind, but their joy unmistakable. If Rob and I have one, then we're having two, at least. Then they'll never be alone in the world.

". . . cooties!" I can make out that one word, and I smile. I didn't think "cooties" would stand the test of time.

When one little girl tackles the other, and they begin to roll around, and the tackled yells out, "Mooooommmm!" and said mom appears, looking harried, I decide it's my cue to return to the car. I round the building and see that my mother is in Rob's arms, sobbing again. I want to not mind; I want to be as effortlessly compassionate as Rob is.

I stand nearby but within her line of sight, should she raise her head, and finally, she does. She looks at me and wipes her eyes. "Sorry. We can hit the road again."

"You have nothing to apologize for," Rob says, and my eyes widen. He thinks he gets to absolve my mother, the woman who has never truly acknowledged the million things she, in fact, should be sorry for. Instead, she always does what she was just doing: She cries, she looks pathetic, she invites pity. Weakness is her justification, always. I used to fall for her tricks, but that's over. Still, I can't be upset with Rob; he's just being a good guy.

"We should go," I say, "if we want to get to the morgue before it closes."

My mother nods bravely, a little girl afraid of monsters but willing to try sleeping without a night-light, and I get in the driver's side of our car. Rob glances at me in surprise; he tends to be the default driver. As soon as he's in the passenger seat, I peel out. "Don't you want to wait for your mom?" he asks. I don't answer. "I got you this." He places a Snickers on my thigh. "You barely ate any breakfast."

"Thanks." I smile, immediately feeling guilty for my momentary annoyance with him. He knows that I only allow myself Snickers on road trips, and cheesy celeb magazines on plane rides. He knows me. He loves what he knows.

I'm in the fast lane, eager to get some distance between my mother and me. Rob keeps glancing back, looking for her car. He probably thinks we should ride her ass to make sure she's okay, but he's being way too cautious. If her car breaks down, she'll text me. Highways go both ways.

I see her whizzing up, dodging cars in other lanes, and then she cuts in front of me at what must be ninety miles an hour. I catch a quick glimpse of her face—she's enjoying herself, showing the world what a Ford Escort with a mismatched door can really do—and I have to laugh at Rob's obvious surprise. He doesn't know this side of my mother, that she can be reckless as well as weepy.

This is the mother who woke me up from a dead sleep when I was nine years old so that we could sit in the car on a stakeout in front of some woman's house and she could make me her confidante. My father never showed up there, which probably just meant she had the wrong woman, but it was a fool's errand anyway. No matter what he did, she would stay with him till death did them part, and it finally has. I'm not about to cry for either one of them.

"I think we should be ready to stay the night," Rob says. "Your mom doesn't seem like she should be alone yet."

"I'll ask Aunt Tanya to stay with her." Aunt Tanya lives in Eureka, too, but one of the nice parts.

He watches my mother's slightly weaving bumper. "It's going to be a lot for her, just seeing the body. They were together a long time. If my father . . ." He can't even finish the sentence. His parents go to the gym together four times a week, and wear pedometers to count their steps, and never put butter on anything, ever. They are united in trying to thwart mortality at every turn. "We should spend the night, and consider maybe bringing her back to stay with us for a while."

"Stay in our apartment? For a while?" I infuse each word with maximal incredulity. "On our couch?" He can't have forgotten that we have a one-bedroom apartment.

"Not a long while. Once she has a job, she could rent a room somewhere close. Hayward, maybe, or San Leandro. She'd be near family, you know? That's important, after a loss like hers." I've noticed he keeps referring to it as a loss, rather than a death. As far as I'm concerned, it's just death.

"My mom is better off making minimum wage in Eureka, where rents are cheap, than in the Bay Area near us."

"Maybe you're right," he says, but I can tell he thinks he is. "You know, this could be an opportunity for reconciliation. No matter what she's done or hasn't done, she's still your mother."

No, she's not.

If my father hadn't died, she wouldn't have tried to fix our relationship. That's not what she's here for. She wants to use me, and I'm not going to let that happen. Rob's too quick to smudge out my past.

Besides, I can't focus on any of that when I'm some sort of fugitive from justice. I bet Miranda's got the police on her side already.

She lives in Beverly Hills with her doctor husband, and she probably showed up at the precinct in a mink stole or something.

Rob and I should be talking about Miranda's e-mail right now, making a game plan. An impending visit from the police is a lot more pressing than my father's death. But he thought I should have put the Miranda stuff to bed a long time ago, and I don't want to see the look on his face when he learns about this latest turn of events.

Better not to mention it until there's really something to mention. After all, I didn't break the law, she did.

I turn on the radio and hum along to the first song I know. Rob and I don't talk until we're pulling into the hospital parking lot.

"I'll go in first," he says. "I'll get everything arranged, and then come back out for you and your mom."

He stops by my mother's Escort in the adjacent space. She rolls her window down by hand. I leave my windows up so I don't have to hear them, though I see by his gestures that he's turned his graciousness on her, full-force, a fire hose of solicitude.

I stare straight ahead. I'm not going to her car. If she wants to talk, she'll have to come over here. Rob is doing enough caretaking for both of us. It's probably what she wished she'd gotten from my father all those years, but then again, if she had, she might have gone looking for some other jerk. My dad's formula of 80 percent callousness/20 percent love worked like a charm. It might have even been more like 90/10.

I play Candy Crush on my phone until Rob gets back, and my mother doesn't leave her car until Rob opens the door for her. He's keeping up a running monologue as we walk into the hospital and take the elevator down to the basement. "We have to decide by tomorrow what we're going to do. They gave me a list of funeral homes we could use if we go that route. If they cremate him, you can still pick up the ashes for $450"—the distaste on Rob's face is evident—"so that's an option. But we have time, that's my point, a little more time, and that's good because . . ." I tune him out.

The morgue attendant is waiting for us in hospital scrubs and a white lab coat, an expression of perma-sympathy on his broad face. The morgue is just a numbered room, like any other.

The attendant escorts us inside, his voice a soothing drone. The room is a little cold but not frigid, with white linoleum floors and pale mint walls, and there are those stacked steel drawers that I've seen on *Law & Order* and *CSI*. There's a wall of fans humming faintly. On a stainless steel cart in the center of the room with a sheet over it is what must be my father's body. I'm filled with the fear that I'll feel nothing when I see him, or that I'll be overtaken once again with the slow-burning anger I've tried to outrun. Every time I try to get out . . .

The attendant is asking a question, I can tell by his intonation if not by the actual words, so I nod. I'm as ready as I'll ever be. My mother is leaning against Rob, and I'm standing on my own, moving forward, somehow. The sheet is drawn back, and there he is, looking pretty much as he did three years ago. His pallor wasn't healthy then, he had a certain greenish cast at my wedding, but then, he was drinking heavily. He doesn't look peaceful, exactly, but he's not tormented either.

He should have suffered more.

I hear my mother wailing, and Rob is holding her up, but all I can do is stare. So this is death. A lot like life, isn't it? At least at this stage, a day into the whole thing. That's my father, formerly good-looking, increasingly jowly, his hair long and a little greasy in defiance of his receding hairline. That's him, passed out. Sleeping. No, dead.

It's good to have the confirmation. This is over. He's over.

We're back in the parking lot, and I'm in some sort of fugue state, the state of trying not to remember. All that indifference for all those years, and then when he finally noticed me, when he finally paid attention, it was so much worse.

Rob has gotten my mother buckled into the passenger seat of her car. He literally kneeled beside her and pinned her in with the safety harness, and I assume he'll be driving her home. I'm milling around, seeing all the people entering and exiting, an ambulance pulling up into its bay. I may be shaking, just a little.

Rob grabs me to him, hard, and I know that he wants me to feel the right something. I'm full of some chemical I've never felt before. It's not adrenaline; it's itchy, and antsy. I want to dispel it, so I say the first thing that comes to me.

"Burn him up," I tell Rob. He pushes me away from him, just as hard as he pulled me in a minute before, and it's involuntary, I know. It's uncontrolled repulsion.

He takes my arm and leads me away, to the pavement in front of the hospital. He doesn't want my mother to hear the rest of this conversation.

"Burn him up," I say again, as if I like his horror. Translation: This is me. Go ahead and leave if you want to.

But I don't want him to. Oh, God, I don't want that.

"You're in shock."

I feel like I'm on a slalom, I can't stop sliding down. "Let the state pay for it, and then we'll pay the four hundred or whatever, and I'll spring for a little urn so my mother can keep him with her always."

"This isn't you. For the past twenty-four hours, you haven't been yourself. Let's go get something to eat, then we'll sleep on it. No decisions until tomorrow. That seems like a good rule."

"I don't want to stay in their apartment. I want to get as far away as I can, as fast as I can. We need to go home."

But Rob doesn't understand, and I can't tell him.

"We can't always do what we want," he says carefully. "Sometimes we have to take care of other people."

"It's my job to take care of her?" I quit that a long time ago.

"Unless you think she should burn in hell, too."

"You're putting words in my mouth."

But there's no explaining further, so I let him take control. I let him pick up food that no one eats, and I let him fawn over my mother, and I let him lay out a makeshift bed on my mother's grungy living room floor amid the thrift store furniture, and I let him spoon me in the darkness. I try to fall asleep to the sound of the kitchen faucet dripping and my mother's keening behind her closed bedroom door. It's as if she wants to throw herself on a funeral pyre. I'd always assumed that to be the misogynistic practice of a patriarchal culture; I'd never before thought of that as a custom that benefits the widow, a form of euthanasia.

"What if our kids disappoint you?" Rob says into the darkness.

So he still thinks kids are an inevitability. He hasn't changed his mind about me based on what he's witnessed today. That's good news. The problem is, lately I've been changing my mind about them. Instead of seeming like future kids, they seem more like hypothetical ones.

I married Rob to have babies. What'll happen if I decide against them? Will I still want Rob? Will he still want me?

"What if our kids aren't who you want them to be?" he continues. "Will you turn your back on them so completely you don't even care if they're dead, if they rest in earth or burn to ash?"

"No kid could ever be as disappointing as my parents."

"Say they manage to be. Let's say they let you down again and again. They appear to have no redeeming qualities."

"I'll try to love them," I say, "no matter what."

"You'll *try*?"

He's scared, that's what this is all about, and I can't blame him for that. From his perspective, I've been frighteningly cold where my dad's death is concerned, cold as his body on the slab. "I'll love them," I tell Rob, "because I'll choose to. Every day."

"It's not about choice. It's not an act of willpower. You love your kids because you can't help it. You can't do anything else."

"Why do you assume that love is going to come so easily to you, no matter what kind of people they turn out to be? That's pretty arrogant."

"It's *arrogant* to assume that I'm going to love my kids?"

"Under all conditions, in every circumstance, yes."

"It's what parents do."

We are so very far apart. "You're a good son, with good parents. Your family has never been tested. So if you face adversity with our kids, you might be the one to crumble. You might be the one to question God: 'Why did you give me these rotten kids, when I'm such an awesome person?' But me, I'll handle it, like I've handled everything."

He's quiet. "That was mean."

"You get to question my bona fides as a potential parent but I can't question yours? It's supposed to be a given that you'll be amazing and I'm suspect?"

"I never thought you were suspect."

"Before today."

He's quiet again. We both know what that means.

My mother renews her sobbing, and it occurs to me that she conveniently stopped during my conversation with Rob.

"We have to leave tomorrow," I say. It's a matter of survival. "I'll call to check in on her, and maybe we'll drive back up some other weekend, but I will not be her mother." Not ever again.

"Let's wait and see how she is tomorrow—"

"And you're not going to be her father."

In this third silence, I'm seized by terror. I can't lose him. I cannot go backward. He's my future. I knew that the first time we met. Well, within a few dates. Stable but not boring. Attractive but we weren't ripping each other's clothes off. Our relationship was an orderly progression. He was healthy, in mind and body, and I'd be healthy, too, by extension, and through example.

So I give in. "Before we leave, we'll make all the arrangements. We'll get my dad buried."

He's surprised, and then delighted. Is it because he's won? No, Rob's not like that. "Are you sure?"

I say yes, because I have to.

He pulls me to him. Relief radiates off him, like the rays in a child's drawing of a sun. I feel the warmth of it, and I focus on that. He loves me; he doesn't want me to have any regrets someday; he knows what's right.

For the sake of my marriage, and my husband's good opinion of me, I will acquiesce to the burial of my father.

I'll insist on the cheapest burial possible, without a funeral or any sort of service. If my mother wants add-ons, she'll pay herself. But the burial—why fight anymore? It is, after all, Rob's money.

My stomach is churning. I tell myself it's the scent of whatever's rotting in my mother's garbage. But I can't help feeling that I'm conning my husband. I'm letting him believe that he's turned me around in my thinking, that I'm something other than I am.

It makes me feel, for the first time, like I'm in a sham of a marriage. And yet, I'm desperate to preserve it.

24

Miranda

It is with great regret that I must resign from the Homeowners Association. I've been privileged to serve, and I continue to love our community as much as ever. Sadly, personal commitments have interfered with my ability to give it the attention that it deserves. I consider you all friends as well as colleagues. Please don't hesitate to be in touch in the future, and I hope to see you around Santa Monica soon.

Sincerely,

Miranda Feldt

That's one unpleasant task taken care of. I might as well face the other, which promises to be far worse.

It's late, and I'm at the kitchen table, in the room farthest from our bedroom, where Larry is relaxing. Thad has ignored my requests all day for us to talk on the phone, and the several voicemails I've left. I'll have to use his preferred medium.

I'm going to bed soon. Could I call you now, please?

What's up?

Let's talk. I want to hear your voice.

Let's just text. I'm in the middle of some stuff.

It's occurred to me that he texts because he doesn't want me to hear his voice. If I did, I could tell immediately if he's been using. It's not just the timbre, but the cadences. It's all of it. Within seconds, I'd know.

I'd really like to actually talk. If you're busy now, then call me later. I'll stay up.

You're acting weird. What's up?

He's digging in his heels. He always had a stubborn streak. The more I push for a phone call, the more he'll insist on texting. He can outlast me. He always has.

I need him to hear my voice, to know how sorry I am that I can't give him more money. I didn't want it to be this way.

The Nar-Anon people would tell me that I have no reason to apologize; the end of enabling is good for everyone involved. But they're not the ones with something to lose in this situation. I don't want him to disappear again. He's already been much less available over the past couple of days, ever since I didn't take the bait about the studio space. Not unpleasant, just slower to text back, and less chatty when he does. But it could be a coincidence. He could be on another art binge.

I detest that word.

Did you see the paintings I posted on Instagram?

I did, but I don't know what to say about them. Art is for uplift, and his work . . . it's gutter. There's just no beauty in it. I wonder if that's how he's subverting the dominant paradigm, forcing people to look at something so distorted and ugly.

I haven't seen them yet.

Look now. I'll wait.

Am I imagining the note of challenge?

Do you like them?

Very much.

What do you like about them?

The size. And the emotion of them. They're very emotional.

You don't really like what I do. You never have.

He's picking a fight. He's obviously in a rotten mood. It's the wrong time to tell him about the money.

I like that you like it. I appreciate that you have the urge to create.

Text silence. I've offended him.

I'm getting that show, you know.

That's fantastic! I'm so proud of you!

I didn't get it yet. I need the time and the space to paint. 24 hours a day.

This again. He's trying to force me into paying for a workspace so he can produce all that ugliness. I flash on the installation that took over his room in high school, the Tinkertoys accusing me of . . . what? I still don't even know.

Any kindness, any engagement of late, has all been in service of this, of getting me to fork over more money.

Well, he needs to know there won't be any more money.

This has to be done, for his own good, and for mine. Dawn has inadvertently done me a favor. Such irony. I should text her: *You only made me stronger. I'm a better mother now.*

Stay strong, right now.

I need to tell you something, and you won't like it.

I already want to take it back. This isn't the time to tell him about the money, not when we're both so prickly. Yet some kamikaze part of me wants to see where I really stand with Thad.

What?

I said, what?

Forget it, we'll talk about it some other time.

Tell me now. I don't need your manipulation.

Is he kidding?

Tell me now.

I'm sorry, but I can't give you any more loans. After this month, there's no more money.

Did Dad lose his job?

No.

But there's no more money? You guys are bankrupt? That sounds like bullshit.

There's no more money for you.

Why's that?

Because after this month, the fund is dry.

I did my research earlier today into the Santa Monica rental market, looking up comparable houses to mine, and there's no way around it: With a lease of six months or a year, I'll make less money; I won't be able to siphon off much without arousing Larry's suspicion. If I do thirty-day rentals, there's no guarantee I can get a tenant each month. Whichever way I go, I won't be able to help Thad as I have been. A few hundred here or there, sure, but that's all. Anything more and Larry might figure it all out. My marriage would be in jeopardy.

I can't explain all that to Thad, not by text. That kind of story requires nuance, and human emotion, and personal connection. Thad doesn't want any of that with me. He wants my money.

I can feel where this is heading. I cut him off financially, and he'll cut me off emotionally. This could be the last contact I have with my son.

No, that's not going to happen. We've made such progress. He told me he loves me.

Thad, talk to me.

I don't know what you want me to say.

Say you understand.

I understand. You don't believe in me.

That's not it. My circumstances have changed, that's all, and I just can't afford it.

So I'm expendable.

No. This is why I wanted to talk to you, so you could really hear me.

You don't want to help me, that's what I hear.

You're wrong. I haven't been helping you, I've been enabling you.

Fucking NA speak.

Don't curse at me, please.

Of all the moments for you to turn your back on me, you pick now. That's fucking great. Your timing is impeccable.

What do you mean?

I'm on the verge of something, Mother. Something big. And all I need is a little help. And then your circumstances change. WHAT THE FUCK, MOTHER!

He's in shock, that's all. Anger is a natural part of that. He'll calm down. He doesn't mean what he's saying right now. He loves me, he told me so.

I'm still here to give you moral support. I do believe in you, and your talent.

Bullshit.

It is bullshit, but suddenly, I'm tired of being cursed at. I'm tired of being cursed with this son of mine.

It's time to stand on your own feet, Thad. That's what's good for you.

I need to devote myself exclusively to my art.

To his meth, he means.

No. I saw his canvas. It was enormous, just like he said. Trust but verify. I saw the photo. I verified.

Why don't you get a part-time job so you can still work on your art at night, or on the weekends?

No response, for more than a minute.

In the past, I've urged him to get a full-time job—no, not just a job, a career—so this is a change for me. I hope he sees that.

I'm making art. That's my job.

Then you need two jobs.

I can't believe this. I've been confiding in you, and you turn around and cut me off. Just like Dad.

Money isn't what you need. You need to be able to take care of yourself, without relying on anyone. You need life skills.

That's rehab talk. I'm not an addict. I'm an artist. I need time and space and materials. I need parents who believe in me. ONE parent who believes in me, at least.

I'm sorry. I want you to have everything. But you need to earn it.

You never believed in my talent.

He's not wrong. I don't see any skill or vision. I see mess. I see the complete absence of discipline. He wears his sloth like a badge of courage, as an identity. He's an artist, he can't live like regular people. I see Legos glued haphazardly while on a meth binge. I see him blaming others—namely, me. He's still that same boy. He hasn't grown up.

I'm to blame, at least in part. But which parts?

I think you need training. Go to art school.

Art school? My art is about the school of life. It's about experience.

You make drug art.

It's inspired by the street.

Then go live on the street.

I'm surprised by myself. Yes, he pushed me, but I should model restraint. I'm still a role model.

I'm sorry, I didn't mean that.

I think you did. That's what you want to happen.

No, I want you to get a job and support yourself.

You want me to hit rock bottom. It's all that NA poison.

This has nothing to do with NA.

I'm clean, Mother. I have been for weeks.

For weeks. He just plucks time periods out of the air.

I'm glad to hear that.

You'll pay for art school?

I didn't say that. But I can't stop myself. *If you stay clean for six months, we can talk about art school.*

What am I saying? Larry wouldn't go for that. After six months, he wouldn't even consider speaking to Thad, let alone paying for art school.

But it's a promise I'll never have to honor. Because in my heart, I know that Thad won't be able to do it.

I'm already halfway there.

So now it's been three months, not mere weeks. He'll say anything. Tears fill my eyes. Because I want to believe him, and every lie he's ever spun.

You need to go somewhere for regular drug tests. I need to verify.

You never trust me.

I wish he was joking. I wish he had the self-awareness for that.

Trust but verify.

I'm your son.

Oh, I know. I never, not for one minute, forget.

Did you hear me, Mother? I'm your son! Look what you're doing to me. You have tons of money, and you don't want me to have any of it. You want me to suffer.

This is no good for you. You're a grown man, begging for money.

You try to manipulate me. To control me with your money.

It's laughable, the suggestion that I control anything, least of all Thad.

You did it just this conversation. You say your circumstances have changed, you have no money for me, you're so sorry, and then you tell me if I'm clean for six months, you'll pay for art school.

I said we'd talk about me paying for art school.

See?

You're twisting my words.

You're the one who's getting it twisted. You always have.

I want you in my life. I want us to talk on the phone. I want us to have a relationship. I'm your mother, not your banker.

You're abandoning me when I need you. I'm talking to a gallery owner about my latest paintings. I need to finish the series. You can't do this now. Just give me two more months.

Two more months, he says, but it'll never end. I'll just be kicking the can down the road. In two months, it'll be two more. I know that. He knows I know.

No. I'm sorry, but no.

I need that money. I have to finish the paintings.

I want you to finish your paintings. Get a job during the day, paint at night.

It doesn't work that way.

It'll have to. I'm sorry, Thad.

I wait one minute, two, three. When I can wait no longer, I sign off (*I love you*) and walk upstairs, slowly. He's done with me, but I fear his night is just beginning.

I take a long, hot shower, trying to scrub off our interaction. I want to forget, and I want to believe. It's a terrible hinterland.

Once I'm wrapped in a robe, my skin still pink from heat, I crawl into bed next to Larry. He's reading *The Economist*, glasses perched low on his nose like pince-nez. I move toward him, until I'm clinging to him like a vine.

Earlier, he went on a diatribe about the colleague I don't even know by name; I just know him as The Ignoramus. I hear about every bad medical decision The Ignoramus has ever made, that he should be thrown out of the profession before he can do any more damage to any more lives. I can only hope it's out of Larry's system for the night. I can't listen to anger, not even the righteous kind.

"Hey," he says, surprised that I'm on his side of the bed, "what's going on?" He pets the shoulder of my robe. I see softness in his face and love in his eyes.

I squeeze my own eyes shut, and I take a leap of faith. I say a name far more unmentionable than The Ignoramus's. I have to know where I stand with Larry, too.

His body tenses, and when he speaks, his voice is equally tight. "You talked to Thad?" He's no longer petting me.

"No. I just read his Twitter."

"His *Twitter*?" This isn't what I need, a reminder of how scathing Larry can be. It confirms my fear of how quickly he could harden toward me.

I feel the proximity to the third rail of our marriage. Since everything started with Dawn, I entertained a small hope: that I was overestimating my betrayal (really, it was just a series of lapses, a mother's inability to give up on her son) and underestimating Larry's love for me.

But if I can't even say Thad's name without Larry doing a pretty good impression of rigor mortis, then it's as bad as I feared.

No Thad and no talk about the residency. Those are Larry's rules, and I'll have to abide by them.

25

Dawn

California Code of Civil Procedure Section 527.6:

(b) For the purposes of this section:

(1) "Course of conduct" is a pattern of conduct composed of a series of acts over a period of time, however short, evidencing a continuity of purpose, including following or stalking an individual, making harassing telephone calls to an individual, or sending harassing correspondence to an individual by any means, including, but not limited to, the use of public or private mails, interoffice mail, facsimile, or computer email. Constitutionally protected activity is not included within the meaning of "course of conduct."

(2) "Credible threat of violence" is a knowing and willful statement or course of conduct that would place a reasonable

person in fear for his or her safety, or the safety of his or her
immediate family, and that serves no legitimate purpose.

(3) "Harassment" is unlawful violence, a credible threat of violence, or a knowing and willful course of conduct directed at
a specific person that seriously alarms, annoys, or harasses the
person, and that serves no legitimate purpose. The course of
conduct must be such as would cause a reasonable person to
suffer substantial emotional distress, and must actually cause
substantial emotional distress to the petitioner.

There's plenty of coastal beauty between Eureka and Oakland, but
we don't have time to see any of it. We're taking the inland route,
101 all the way, baby. I want the quickest way back home, to our
real lives. I don't belong in Eureka. I never did.

As Rob drives, he keeps shooting glances in my direction, asking
if I'm okay. I don't know what to tell him.

The truth is, I'm more than okay with my father no longer walk-
ing this earth. What I'm not okay with is feeling like I had to give
Rob what he wanted, that we had to use our wedding money to
bury my father, lest my husband find me inhuman. That hurts. But
I tell myself that it's my own fault for keeping the truth from him.
How can he be compassionate about what he doesn't know?

We made the arrangements first thing this morning, and then we
got the hell out.

I didn't tell my mother this, but my father's headstone will be a
granite pet marker I ordered online. It saved us a little cash and felt
oddly appropriate, like a final in-joke that I'll share with no one. It's
not like we needed much room on the stone, since it will only have
his name and the dates of his birth and death. No "loving husband
and father" needed; no listing of his accomplishments. Rob and I

also saved money by skipping the embalming. There will be no funeral, no open casket. I've seen dear old Dad for the last time, and I'm more than okay with that, too.

It's the cheapest casket on the cheapest plot of the cheapest cemetery within a twenty-mile radius. Even so, it all came to nearly $3,000. When Rob put down our credit card, I felt like screaming. Of course my mother didn't offer to chip in. She stood five feet away, sniveling, as if none of it had anything to do with her.

I woke up this morning on the floor of my parents' apartment, sunlight flooding through the bay windows of the Victorian that's reminiscent of every residence of my childhood. The houses were always shabby, in deep disrepair, but my mother thought that a turret and a gable could camouflage any ills. We weren't disadvantaged as long as we lived in a Queen Anne or an Eastlake or a Colonial Revival. Victorian architecture has many subsets, and they're all represented in Eureka, which has perhaps dozens of historical districts, too many to be maintained. So my mother picked the right locale for perpetual downward mobility.

Eureka is not without its charms. Tourism is one of its top industries, now that lumber has mostly died. Old Town is quaint and cute, and there's a waterfront boardwalk on Humboldt Bay. Hiking among the nearby redwoods is a pretty spectacular experience. You feel so small, but in the best way.

Growing up, I felt small in the worst ways. It's stupid to blame Eureka, or anywhere, for that. The first years of your life are all about your parents, and the environment they create. Eureka didn't render me irrelevant; my parents did.

I wasn't much to look at through childhood, but early puberty did some heavy lifting. When I was twelve, I underwent a hormonal surge. My hair grew long and glossy, and practically overnight, I was wearing a C-cup bra. The acne didn't kick in until I was almost fourteen, so looks-wise, it was an enchanted age for me.

Early development has its drawbacks, especially with negligent parents. I didn't have the brain to go along with my body. I was hungry for attention, and older guys were happy to provide it, for a price. They'd ply me with alcohol, and I'd have sex with them, sometimes with condoms, sometimes bareback. It was all out of my control, and I didn't necessarily mind. If I kept carrying on like that, I thought an adult would have to step in. My parents would have to save me.

I'd been labeled as a slut the second my tits came in, so in school I felt doomed where female friends were concerned. It was a self-fulfilling prophecy, a vicious cycle: the more I slept with guys, the more alienated I was from girls, and the more I needed male attention. They were using me, but they were all I had.

That's the moment when I most needed a parent. I couldn't find my way out of that conundrum without guidance. But my mother kept talking about how nice it was that I was popular, and that she knew I'd make good decisions. It was a total cop-out, especially since she never asked any questions. I was a thirteen-year-old being picked up by a carful of sixteen-year-old boys, and she'd yell "Have fun" as I sailed out the door.

I was lucky I didn't get pregnant, or HIV. I remember that painful itching when I was fifteen, the furtive scratching, the fear of looking down, the hope that it would just go away on its own. Herpes turned out to be a wake-up call. I met a sweet gynecologist at Planned Parenthood who realized that I was being taken advantage of, that my body didn't feel like my own but a commodity that I could barter to stave off loneliness and inconsequence. She set me up with a counselor who gave me the full battery of STD tests and a whole lot of kindness. She told me I was worth something, and I'd been waiting my whole life to hear that from someone with no ulterior motive.

I stopped having indiscriminate sex, and I joined a few clubs ("prosocial activities," the counselor called it), and I even developed a few friendships with females, but my troubles with men were far from over. My father saw to that.

But Rob doesn't know that chapter, since I've tried to rip it out of the book. He does know that as soon as I graduated high school, I got out of Eureka. Ten miles out, to be precise, to oppressively progressive Arcata, where I spent a few semesters at Humboldt State. It's the marijuana-growing center of the universe, and had all the harder drugs anyone could ever want, which you could pretty much take in full view of cops without fear. It was free drugs and free love, a hippie utopia. The grassy plaza in the town center reeked of patchouli and the body odor of the homeless. It was bordered by cafés, restaurants, and stores. There were festivals that went by various names but were all paeans to public nudity. In my Intro to Feminism class, I drew the conclusion that the power lay in keeping my clothes on (my professor disagreed, and gave me a C+). I dropped out and moved to the San Francisco Bay Area, a place I'd long dreamed of but never actually been.

My bad-boy complex persisted, but I'd grown up some. I knew better how to string them along, how to hold their interest, how to keep any need for love and affection to myself, and how to leave sooner. The first time I knew for sure that they'd cheated or lied, I was done.

Any dime-a-dozen therapist would say that I was playing out my daddy issues. They'd probably be right, much as I hate being a cliché. But we're all cliché sometimes, or clichés wouldn't exist.

"Are you sure you're really okay?" Rob asks.

He's a good man, and I've found my place. Eureka is not going to pull me back into its clutches. I smile at him. "I am now."

"If you need anything, you know I'm always here for you, right? You know that?"

"It's the thing I'm surest of."

We smile at each other, and when he turns back to the road, I suddenly think, I should tell him. But how can I tell him now, when he's smiling at me like that?

The police have advised me to block you. All further communications should cease.

This morning, I did plenty of online searching, looking up information about harassment, cease and desist orders, anything I could think of, leapfrogging from one site to the next, until I was satisfied that Miranda is full of shit. Again.

But if she isn't, if she can somehow convince people that I pose a credible threat of violence, or that I've annoyed and alarmed her to no purpose . . . I don't want to even think about what that would do to Rob's opinion of me, which is already under siege.

I was going to drop it, I really was, but I can't possibly let it go now. Every time I try to get out, someone pulls me back in. My dead father, my mother, Miranda. It never ends, does it?

I'll have to be cagier in the future. I can't go right at Miranda; I'll have to zigzag. Now that she's armed me with the statute, I know just what to avoid.

I glance at Rob, who appears to be in his driving zone, and then I know exactly where to go.

His Twitter handle is @theRealThadFeldt. What an asshole. Like anyone would pose as Thad Feldt, like he's that important. He's clearly got his mother's ego.

Four hundred twenty-nine followers. Now he's got 430.

I'm not sure what I'm looking for, exactly, but I feel like the real

Thad Feldt could come in handy. Between every parent and child, there's something dark and secret. All I have to do is find the chink in Miranda's armor, and exploit the weakness, untraceably.

He is a weakness, all right. Miranda's son is a #loser. A twenty-seven-year-old living in Tucson with no job, Instagramming his art, talking about some big break that you can just tell will never happen, and making veiled and not-so-veiled references to drug binges that he says "jump-start his creativity." He dropped out of UC Santa Barbara, and he acts like that gives him street cred or something.

Because—get this—he makes graffiti. He has these enormous canvases and he basically tags them with puffy letters and jacked-up cartoon characters. From his tweets, it sounds like he's squatting in abandoned buildings, or that could just be where he does his lame art. He might sleep somewhere else, with someone else, because he is actually pretty good-looking, though too skinny for my taste.

I cannot believe that holier-than-thou, pillar-of-the-community Miranda has a son this degenerate. It's too perfect. I might not even need to punish her for her prissy little attitude; the world's already doing it for me. Even though I'm just finishing college at thirty, Thad makes me feel like an overachiever.

I get a Facebook friend request, and I'm startled to see that it's Thad. It's intrusive, somehow, an unauthorized cross-pollination. I was following him on Twitter, but now he's followed me to Facebook. For some reason, the migration feels a little menacing. But I've never entirely minded that feeling.

I could just ignore him. It's not like I want to be friends with Miranda's son. But he could be useful as a "friend."

I accept. Within seconds, he's made contact.

Who are you, beautiful? Why are you following me?

I know your mother, unfortunately.

I like your art.

Cool. I like your face.

I'm married.

I can still like your face, can't I?

What's the point? I live in California. You're in Arizona.

I grew up there. In Cali.

Where?

L.A.

I knew he wouldn't say Beverly Hills. He probably pretends he's straight outta Compton.

Dawn's a great name. A new day, every day.

Thanks.

Not like Thad. What's a Thad?

A phony douche bag, maybe?

You look like dawn. All bright and clean. A fresh start.

Ha ha. If he only knew his mother had accused me of staining her sheets.

I've got to go. Good talking to you, Thad.

Talk again?

In your dreams.

"Who was that?" Rob says.

"Salina," I say. "Another heartbreak."

We exchange smiles, a brief moment of solidarity built on our presumed superiority. We drive on.

26

Miranda

I'm sorry about how we left things.

I never meant to control you.

I've made a lot of mistakes, I know that.

I want the best for you.

How's your work going? I'd love to see more!

Thank goodness all this is by text. I could choke on my own disingenuousness. Calling his art "work," using an exclamation point at the end . . . next thing it'll be smiley-face emojis.

Thad's ignored my texts for the past day, and I can't avoid the realization that he doesn't have to get in touch ever again, now that there's no money in it. I try to tell myself that he's consumed by his art. A few hours ago, he Instagrammed a new painting that looked a lot like the last one, only with slightly different colors, but maybe that's what artists do, that's why it's a series. He's working, that's all. He'll be back in touch soon.

Unless I've sent him over the edge, and now he's on a binge. I shouldn't have delivered the news so callously. I punched him in the gut, and you should never do that to an addict.

If the devil himself had designed a drug, it would be crystal meth. It's cheap, and Thad can smoke it (he always hated needles), and it's even more potent when smoked (what a bonus). It increases dopamine, which brings on a pleasure so intense that nothing else in life can compete, and changes his brain so that he's slower and dumber and less capable of resisting. He's a hamster on a wheel.

I find myself playing a familiar game. It's called "Was It Then?" I run through Thad memories and wonder which was the fork in the road, the missed opportunity, the time when he could have become an upstanding citizen, if only I'd made the right choice.

When I chose to use formula rather than to breast-feed because it seemed more sanitary and less invasive . . .

Was it then?

When I let him cry it out in his crib, rather than comforting him. I thought it was a victory that he stopped crying altogether, that I'd made him a little man.

Was it then?

When he started having tantrums that lasted not minutes but hours, screaming and kicking with such ferocity that I sewed a version of a toddler straitjacket so that he couldn't harm himself, and I'd sit outside his room with a pillow over my head, crying and helpless, and I told Dr. Paolini something's wrong, it has to be wrong, and even though a mother knows better, I allowed him to pooh-pooh me and say it was just a phase, and I left Thad alone with all those big feelings, all that fury, and that phase went on for not months but years.

Was it then?

When he delighted in art projects, even as a young child, and

I bought him all the supplies, and I dutifully hung his creations on the refrigerator, but I was so busy, I made myself so busy with housework and cooking and volunteering and clubs, because even then, he scared me. I didn't tell anyone that, not even Larry. I was so ashamed. But those were moments when I could have sat down beside him and drawn pictures myself. They would have been awful, I'm no artist, but the time spent . . . the time I failed to spend . . .

Was it then?

When he asked Larry to do father-son activities with him, sometimes Larry would, but not nearly as often as Thad wanted. I didn't push Larry because, deep down, I was jealous. What about mother-son activities? Those happened all the time. Me chauffeuring him here, and buying for him there, and arranging for him to be with his friends, and eating dinner with him while Larry was still at work, me questioning, Thad giving short answers. It's a painful thing, being found so uninteresting. I didn't know what made Larry so intriguing to Thad, except that Larry was unavailable, and I was right there, all the time.

Larry worked longer hours once Thad came along. By necessity or choice? Coincidence or avoidance? Did Larry dislike fatherhood, or did he dislike being Thad's father? I can't say, can't know, because he wouldn't share that, any more than I'd share my jealousy. Some things can't be spoken.

Was it then?

When Thad was eleven, he came home smelling of alcohol. I dismissed it. Where would Thad have gotten alcohol? I'd picked him up and dropped him off at a friend's house, and I knew those parents well. They were home, and they were supervising. There would be no open bar at the Schultzes'. So he went upstairs and went to bed, after he pecked me on the cheek.

He never pecked me on the cheek. He must have been rubbing

my nose in his bad behavior. Or the boy who never cried was crying out for help.

Was it then?

He didn't like to do anything organized. No sports or clubs. Not even art lessons; just art, on his own.

If Thad had played soccer or baseball or basketball, even if he'd been a benchwarmer, or if he'd been on the debate team or the chess team, even third-string, I know Larry would have shown up for the games, the matches, the meets. Larry wanted to be a spectator; he wanted to cheer. That was the father he'd planned to be.

If I'd encouraged Thad—no, insisted—that he participate in some after-school activity, anything to make him feel even temporarily like a winner, or get a job, something to limit his free time, idle hands and all that . . .

Was it then?

I spied without having the backbone to do anything with the information I gathered. I told myself I was monitoring, but I never had the guts to confront. He had condoms when he was thirteen. I counted them so I'd at least know if he was using them. There was a bong in his closet. Over time, it was gathering dust. I never found the paraphernalia of anything more serious, and I told myself that he'd experimented, and he was finished now.

Was it then?

After the dentist visit—my first encounter but far from my last with the term "meth mouth"—I returned home full of fear and self-loathing. I'd been in denial, I was a bad mother, and I couldn't avoid the truth anymore. When I saw Larry, I wept in his arms. I had failed our son.

Larry held me. He said we would get through it, together. What he really meant was that he was taking over, thank you very much, and a big part of me was relieved.

Larry said that Thad didn't need a drug program; he needed structure. He needed consequences. We could provide that. He felt that the dentist was well-meaning but alarmist in his inpatient recommendation. What does a dentist know about rehab, anyway? We could handle this. I was to be the presiding corporal to Larry's general.

Larry seemed as sure as the dentist had. And I didn't live with the dentist. So I went along with Larry's plan.

I was the one who had to implement the consequences Larry devised. But after hours of Thad's yowling and diatribes, I'd start to wobble and, eventually, buckle. Not all the time, but enough to encourage Thad. To make him think he could win if he persisted.

There were many little betrayals of Larry along the way, before the big ones. Larry gave a consequence that I thought was too punitive, one that I knew I wouldn't be able to follow through on, and instead of speaking up, I would invalidate it. I'd sneak Thad his favorite food, or let him out of his grounding early. He would spin such glorious stories, perhaps as a reward, all about the things he was going to do with his future, and what he'd realized about the perils of drug use. "They don't make me creative," he would say, "they just trick me into thinking I am. I'm smarter than the drugs now, Mom."

All the while, what I was really doing was trying to make him love me. If I released him from prison, if I granted him early parole, wouldn't he have to love me?

I like to think he believed those things while he was saying them, that they were his own hopes for himself. He wanted to be smarter than the drugs, and he knew I wanted that for him, so he said it like it was true. I was the receptacle for all his wishful thinking.

All that wasted time, with me trying to do what I obviously couldn't, substituting one denial for another, while Thad's progressive disease progressed.

Was it then?

I finally told Larry that the plan wasn't working, that Thad was getting worse. Larry went into research mode, finding the best adolescent treatment facility he could.

Thad began attending intensive outpatient treatment five days a week, where he surprised us all with his seeming compliance and two months of clean urine tests. Then came the overdose, and that awful ambulance ride where I revisited every mistake I'd ever made and prayed for another chance. Thad spent a few hours in the ER, followed by a week in the psychiatric hospital. We were told he might be bipolar, it was hard to make a definitive diagnosis until Thad had been clean for a while.

We said he had been clean for a while, we'd seen the test results; the psychiatrist said that Thad had confessed to his continued use throughout the program. "He was tricking the test," he said, "maybe using someone else's urine."

Someone else's urine. The words every parent dreams of hearing.

Thad's confession may or may not have been true, but it got him kicked out of the intensive outpatient treatment program. They told us that his needs exceeded their capacity. Join the club.

We tried three different inpatient rehabs. He never lasted more than six weeks. At the first, he physically attacked another boy while on a meth bender (the rehab didn't know how he'd gotten the meth). He was ejected from his next rehab after he started a fire while trying to turn cleaning supplies into meth. Then there was the locked facility in Utah where we paid out of pocket and were told he had "incited the other boys to riot." When Larry hung up, he went silent with rage. Then he finally said, in a voice so caustic I felt burned by it, "So Thad's got leadership skills that we never suspected."

Home again.

Was it then?

Thad begged us to let him stay for good. He said that sending him away was only making him worse, and indeed, it did seem so. He now had acne, and open sores, and his teeth were worse from the clenching of his jaw. The dental work cost thousands.

I can't know if it really was the meth fueling him, if he was that out of control or if those were calculated risks, exit strategies. Larry felt sure that it was the latter. He'd lost his patience with making calls to colleagues, and with Thad's willful decision to remain an addict. That's how Larry saw it, no matter how many books I left lying around that said Thad was in the grip of an insidious disease. Larry felt that Thad was choosing to destroy his own life, and ours.

Thad did stay home, because Larry had given up on finding a new placement, and he went back into an outpatient program, one with such low standards that no one could be denied treatment. There were dirty drug tests, and sneaking out, and stealing from us.

Someday, we privately reassured ourselves, he would be eighteen. Then the world would give him his consequences, and he would have to learn, finally. We would no longer be responsible.

He was, after all, still attending his "treatment" program. At least those were three hours each weekday when I knew he wasn't using.

We told ourselves we'd tried everything. But was it true?

Was it then?

Strangely, Thad was showing up for school and getting good grades. He claimed the meth helped because he was able to stay up all night and study; I didn't even bother contradicting him anymore. He said that he was going to go to college, and when he did, he'd leave all this behind him, like meth was child's play. It was a facsimile of opening up to me, and even if he was spewing nonsense, I was happy just to have that much connection with him.

Then I learned that he was dealing drugs. I was crushed. I'd thought he'd confined his problems to our home, but to think that he was leading other kids, other families, down this same path was devastating.

I did something I'm not proud of, something I would certainly never admit to Larry, something that may have planted the seeds for what was to come: I started to give Thad money again. Yes, I knew it would support his habit, but I couldn't stomach the alternative.

Was it then?

I told myself it could have been much worse. He really was going to school, and he would be accepted to college. His skin had cleared up, and while he was still thin, he wasn't malnourished. The surliness and the rages had abated. He was a functional addict, and there are plenty who aren't. He seemed to be keeping it under control. Was it what I wanted for him? Of course not. But it was the best I could do.

Larry had stopped attending family sessions, and he didn't ask about the results of the drug tests. Once again, Thad was my domain.

I hadn't given up. I was just trying a different approach. It was one that I wouldn't talk about at Nar-Anon meetings, and eventually, I stopped attending those altogether. I did reading into the harm reduction approach, and that seemed more attainable than total abstinence. But I knew that Twelve Step was all or nothing, black and white. They'd never approve of what I was embracing, which was the lesser evil. Fighting to put Thad into one more rehab wasn't going to get him to college. Thousands of people go to rehab and they overdose anyway. Some of them die.

When he was accepted into UC Santa Barbara, perhaps on the

strength of a personal essay on overcoming drug addiction, he was obviously excited. He was seeking pleasure in something outside of meth. There was good reason for optimism.

Only he went away and started to binge and tweak and there was the hospitalization for the seizure and another overdose . . . was it then?

Or is it now?

I just told him I'm cutting him off. I didn't use those words, but that's what he heard. If I stick with that, it could be what he needs to really get himself together, once and for all. Or this could be the thing that causes him to feel hopeless and use, perhaps in large amounts. He could overdose again, and this time, he might not wake up.

I don't know which way to go now, same as I didn't know all those other times. There's no road map to follow. I try to tell myself that he's responsible for his own actions, but I also know that meth has stunted his development; it's short-circuited his brain. He's stalled at the age he first started using seriously. That means he's got the judgment and impulse control of a twelve-year-old, if that. And I've abandoned him.

Nar-Anon would say that every day is an opportunity. Thad's still alive, so I did something right. Where there's life, there's hope.

I have to believe that.

27

Dawn

I'm so alone, I can't stand it.
  I think about him all the time.
  All I do is cry.
  I can't stay here.
  Dawn, is your phone working?
  Call me soon.
  Text me, all right?
  Can I see his body again?

You're not supposed to leave your widowed mother hanging, I know that. But her woe-is-me shit is draining. Yes, she just lost her husband, but I lost my father, too. She hasn't once asked how I'm doing, or what it means to me.

Not that I want to discuss it with her, or with anyone, but that's not the point. The point is, my own mother hasn't asked. Instead, she's decided to make up for all the years of minimal (and then no) contact with a daily barrage of texts and phone calls, bemoaning her wretched state. Every hour, I text back: *I know, Mom. I'm sorry.* Despite Rob's hopeful take, there's no opportunity for rebuilding a relationship with her, since she still doesn't seem to realize I exist as a separate person; she only wants someone to look after her, same as always.

Rob thinks I should be doing more. He's stopped saying it, but I can see it in his eyes. He's right, I should want to do more. But I want to do less. I want to text back once a day, max, and tell her to pull herself up by her bootstraps and get the job she should have gotten years ago. It was pretty crappy of her not to have worked when she had a husband who couldn't keep the family above the poverty line, and a young daughter who couldn't always be sure there would be food on her plate and a roof over her head. Her failure to step up was a big part of the nightmare that was to follow when I was sixteen. But, as Miranda would say, that's neither here nor there.

Mom knows she can't see the body. We've been over this. Does Hallmark make a "He wasn't embalmed" card?

"Dawn, are you here?" Professor Myerson gives me a sympathetic smile. There's a bit of crust protruding from his nose. We're sitting closer than I'd like in his office, but that's because it's a tiny box. Probably not much bigger than Dad's casket.

"Sorry. I'm listening. It's just—my mom is kind of needy these days."

"That's understandable. How long were your parents together?"

"A long time." It's the last thing I want to talk about. Rob's been trying to get me to talk about my feelings, and when that doesn't work, he wants me to empathize with my mom. The harder he tries, the more I want to point out how self-absorbed she is. The buildup of these texts just proves it. If she thinks I'm going to invite her to live with me, after all she's done—no, all she *hasn't* done—over the years, then she hasn't just lost him, she's lost it.

You can tell Professor Myerson's age by how much paper is in this office. There are stacks piled high, nearly tipping, like Leaning Towers of Pisa. I don't know how he can stand the claustrophobia of the place.

Another ping. "Go ahead," he says. "Answer her."

There's no getting around it. I don't want Professor Myerson thinking I'm heartless.

I'm in a meeting. Call Aunt Tanya. Go to the grief group.

I found her a grief group that meets through the local hospice. It's pay-what-you-can-afford, which, in her case, means free.

"What was I saying?" he asks.

You were giving me a canned speech about how many different professions I could pursue with a communications degree. "I think you were talking about how I could go into teaching."

"Right, right. That's just one of many avenues. Really, it's limit-less. What do you like doing?"

"I like writing. I'd like to be intellectually stimulated while doing some good in the world. I don't want to do direct sales or customer service, and nothing where they use the word 'branding.' I want to make decent money."

He screws up his face in concentration, and I realize that the combination might be as elusive as I'd feared. "So nonprofits are out. Sales and marketing jobs are out. No advertising." He taps his pencil. "This is a tough one, Dawn."

"I thought you said it was limitless."

"You've narrowed the parameters significantly, that's all. It can be done. All problems can be solved."

He gets an incoming call that he seems relieved to take. He steps into the hall, leaving me alone with my qualms and, a second later, with my mother.

I just don't think I can stay here much longer.

If she'd tried to reenter my life under other circumstances (or best of all, with no particular circumstances, just because she missed me), it would be different. But I can't hold my arms open to her, not like this.

I wish Rob was her son. He's just a way better person than I am. Since my dad died, I'm reminded of that all the time. Rob's responses are the right ones to have; mine are wrong, wrong, wrong. That makes sense, since his life experiences have been pure, and I was corrupted. But I just have to fake my way through and hope he doesn't find out.

After a while, it dawns on me that Professor Myerson isn't coming back. I feel a bit spurned, that he didn't even think to say good-bye, but maybe he had to go to class. He could have finished his call and realized he was late. Or maybe I'm just asking too much of the world, and of him.

I haven't heard anything from the Oakland or the L.A. Police Departments, so I guess I'm in the clear. A small part of me hopes they show up at my door. Then I can make sure they know just what kind of woman Miranda is. After all, she's the one who committed a crime.

I debate whether to call the city attorney's office to follow up on my complaint, but if Miranda found out, could that be construed as harassment?

I won't contact the city attorney or Miranda again. I don't need to. There are other ways to get to someone. For one thing, I have her address. And then there's Thad.

He texted me hours ago, though I have no idea how he got my cell number. All he said was *Hey, beautiful.*

I start with Twitter; he goes to Facebook. I friend him; now he's texting on my cell. This is a guy who ups the ante, a real boundary breacher.

I should tell him to lose my number. No, I shouldn't respond at all.

But no one's pursued me in so long. It's been ages since anyone plucked this particular string inside of me. I can feel its twang, all through my body.

What IS a Thad, anyway?

28

Miranda

Property management fees are one consideration when deciding which company you should hire, but they should not be the only consideration. Sometimes unusually low fees are a sign of poor-quality services. Remember, a management company is safeguarding one of your most important assets!

There can be some variety in the fees and in the fee structure, but they will usually involve some or all of the following: management fee, vacancy fee, setup fee, leasing fee, advertising fee, lease renewal fees, reserve fund fee, maintenance fees, eviction fees, unpaid invoice fee, bill payment fee . . .

"Can I get you anything? Some more tea?" The waitress is young and blond, exuding immense good health if not actual beauty.

She's caught me rubbing my eyes as I take a break from the read-

ing on my phone. I find a smile for her. "Thank you. More tea would
be lovely."

I'm not a tourist, but I've always liked this hotel bar with its deep
beige-and-brown-upholstered chairs and the view overlooking the
pier. Today, though, I'm preoccupied. Thad hasn't texted me but
he has been tweeting incessantly, nonsensically. He's using again,
I know it.

But I need to ignore my heavy heart and decide what to do with
the Santa Monica house. Maybe it's time to make a radical case to
Larry. That house was so good for my parents' marriage; it might
be able to work its magic on ours, too. We're not broken, but that
doesn't mean we couldn't use a renovation. Larry just turned sixty-
one. He could start reducing his hours in anticipation of retirement.
We could even split our time between the two houses.

I haven't heard from Dawn since I sent her that warning from the
police. She finally heard me. It's over. So what happened with her
was a blessing in disguise, a wake-up call, an opportunity.

Hi, Mom.

See? Everything's looking up. My natural optimism has been
tested through all the years of Thad's addiction, but it's never been
extinguished. God doesn't give you more than you can handle; it's
always darkest just before the—

I'll have to scratch that expression from my lexicon.

I'm so glad to hear from you, Thad!

The exclamation point was genuine that time.

I have to tell you something, and you're not going to like it.

He's using my words against me. My newly buoyant heart plum-
mets again.

I don't think it's fair that you just cut me off.

We've been over this.

You said your circumstances changed, and the funds dried up. Is that still true?

Now my heart is racing. I could tell him I don't know; I could say that there might be some money, somewhere. But he's been using, and I need to stop enabling. I need to hold the line.

Yes, it's still true.

Does Dad know?

Know what?

That you're cutting me off.

Larry thinks I cut him off years ago. Thad knows that. This is going nowhere good.

Yes, he knows.

I'm going to text him to confirm.

I thought the worst he would do was ignore me.

I'm going to tell him what you're doing to me. That you've been paying my rent, and now, when I'm on the verge of something big, you're screwing me.

He's using, that's the only explanation. Otherwise, there's no way he would make this kind of a threat.

Are you sure your circumstances have changed?

This is Thad, lucid. This is extortion.

My son's a terrorist. There's no other word for it, really. I never admitted it before, but he's been my terrorist for years. Terrorists control through fear; they narrow your life choices; they are merciless.

In this case, he wins. My shoulders sag as I text back:

They might not have changed. What do you want?

Two months of rent and a workspace. Art supplies, too, that'd be good.

Two months, and that's it. No more.

Two months is all I need. I'll get that show, and then I'll be set. Thanks, Mom. You won't be sorry. You'll see.

I can't even manage a response.

I want you to come to the show. It'll sell out, I know it will, and I'll fly you out to see it.

Is he lying? Is he deluded? Does he really want me there, or is he trying to put a balm over blackmail? I don't know what's just happened. My mind is reeling. He's a monster, and he might not even know it.

I love you, Mom. We'll talk soon.

For the first time, I hope not.

29

Dawn

If you could be anywhere right now, where would you be?

A fascinating hypothetical, Thaddeus, but the answer will have to wait.

I know where I wouldn't be, though: dinner with the in-laws.

Even though I call Rob's parents Mom and Dad, at their insistence, none of us are fooled. Someday I might really feel like a Thiebold, but I'm reminded, every time I see them, that it's not today.

Their home is in Elmwood, just a few blocks over from the engraving store on College Avenue, and typical of the neighborhood, it's a large brown-shingled Craftsman. Some people have replaced the brown shingles with white stucco or other facades. There are some A-frames and Mission styles and Victorians interspersed, but regardless of make and model, all the houses are uniformly well-maintained (these are not my mother's Victorians). Every other car is a Prius. While these houses are worth millions now, "Mom" and

"Dad" bought theirs more than forty years ago. This is the family's primary asset, especially since the store is shedding value fast.

Tonight, "Mom" slaved over a vegan dish with quinoa and root vegetables, while "Dad" clucks over it appreciatively. "Dad" is rail-thin and ruddy-faced, with a neat ring of ear-level gray hair. "Mom" carries just a little extra around her midsection despite all the power walking and the quinoa. Her hair is close-cropped and almost black, accentuating her green eyes (Rob's eyes). She's at that age where attractiveness is about the suggestion of past prettiness, and she's pulling that off. They both wear a lot of REI wicking fibers, and North Face on top of it. They're forever stripping off fleece zip-ups.

They're happy people, is the thing. Well matched. They found their mates as teenagers, just looked across the high school cafeteria, and bam.

I've seen them get testy with each other on a few rare occasions. But somehow, that only makes their union more impressive. They get annoyed, and then they hug it out, and they do it without a lick of shame.

Rob's allowed to get in a mood, and no one holds it against him. But I don't feel like I can do that. For one thing, my moods are way darker than Rob's. For another, I catch "Mom" looking at me sometimes like I'm a diamond ring that needs formal appraisal. She's not convinced I'm real.

And she's right, I'm not real around them. I'm not myself. I'm the self that I imagine they'd want for their son. I never used to perform that self for Rob. But since my father died, it's different. Now I have to prove I'm human.

"Dad" and Rob are talking about new marketing strategies and how to make an engraving shop "go viral." I bite my tongue. No one is asking for my opinion. If I offered it, I'd only be marked further as an outsider. Thiebolds are relentlessly optimistic. They're convinced that mom-and-pop engraving can be resurrected; all they need is to set up a Twitter account, and voilà.

Finally, the conversation runs its course, and "Mom" takes over. "How *are* you, Dawn?" Her head is cocked in condolence. She's asking how I'm coping with my grief, which is supposed to be profound.

"I'm okay." I avert my eyes to indicate that I'm barely holding back the floodgates, and that there should be no further inquiries, unless she wants this family dinner to turn into a deluge.

"Losing a parent so young," "Dad" muses, pausing between bites. "You just don't expect that. You can't prepare."

I glance at Rob, who is following the conversation with an unsettling avidity. "No," I say, "you can't prepare." Unless the parent in question was dead to you for years. Unless he was never really alive where you were concerned, until he needed you and used you and threw you away.

But "Mom" and "Dad" would never understand that. I don't think Rob could either. It's unfathomable to the real Thiebolds. I look around this comfortable house where he grew up—with "Mom's" needlepoint of BLESS THIS HOME on the wall and "Dad's" woodwork on the end tables and family portraits in the curio cabinet and sturdy Shaker furniture that may have been passed down through the generations—and I have no right to expect him to get it.

It's why I've never told him what my father did, what I did, though a few times this past week, it's been on the tip of my tongue. Just do it, Dawn, you married a kind man, one with compassion to spare. Tell him, and he'll say how brave you are, what a survivor. He'll only love you more.

I excuse myself to the bathroom, and I see all three Thiebolds exchange a look. They're assuming that I'm so upset I need a moment, and they approve of that.

I pull my phone from the front pocket of my jeans and sit down on the already-closed lid of the toilet seat. Rob is their son, no question. He doesn't just put the seat down, but the lid, too, religiously.

I shouldn't be doing this. I shouldn't be texting another man from my in-laws' bathroom when they think I'm having a good cry. When I've already been feeling like I'm too different from Rob, and he's too good for me.

But Thad isn't.

I'd be in Monterey, I tell him.

How family-friendly.

Fuck you.

Sorry, I'm in a shit mood. I can't paint.

Why not?

Too tired. Kind of down.

Down about what?

Do you ever feel like the world is passing you by?

Sometimes.

Like you've wasted so much time, and you might as well quit while you're behind.

He's ridiculous. He's a maudlin poseur. I have a great husband one room over, and a plate half-full of quinoa, and in-laws who care about me, probably more than my own parents did (which, admittedly, is no massive feat, like overtaking a slug in a footrace).

I'm ashamed to be in here feeling what I do. Which is exhilaration.

I don't quit, I say.

It's a lie. I quit college the first time around. I've quit relationships. But I don't have to tell Thad the truth, and that's part of the thrill. He's no one to me. He's someone to Miranda, and that's another part of the thrill. Plus, he's in Arizona, so I've got a buffer zone.

I wonder what he'd say if he knew that I just spent two hours earlier today destroying his mother's online reputation. She made it easy. All I had to do was use her own words, which doesn't violate any statutes.

Some shit you need to quit, he texts.

Like drugs?

It's the first time I've directly mentioned what is so obviously on display in his tweets: That he's got some sort of drug problem. Sometimes he's romanticizing it, as if it gives his art integrity; sometimes he's touting that he's got a certain number of days clean; sometimes he's talking gibberish like he's high. He is one confused puppy.

We've all got our demons is his answer.

What's yours, exactly?

Meth. And I like pills. Weed does nothing for me. Heroin puts me to sleep.

I've never tried meth.

You shouldn't (unless you like multiple orgasms while skydiving).

I'm pretty sure the opportunity won't present itself. Meth doesn't seem like a social drug that's passed around at a party, like a joint or lines of coke. Not that I party anymore.

You should only say yes if you're a certain kind of person, he continues.

What kind of person is that?

The kind who has things they can bear to lose. Like everything.

I want to ask him more but I've been gone a little while, and my face isn't remotely blotchy. My eyes aren't red. If anything, the color is high on my cheeks, like I've just been having a very good time, not a weepfest over my dead father.

To be continued . . .

I flush the toilet as a backup cover story and head toward the dining room. It's a shoes-off house, which means no one can hear you coming unless they're listening hard, and the Thiebolds are absorbed in hushed conversation. I pad through the kitchen and am nearing the curved doorway of the dining room when some intuition makes me stop in my tracks. Furball inches over to me from her food bowl, her flab swishing. She's twenty pounds if she's an ounce, the repository for all the Thiebolds' self-denial. They probably feed her all the cupcakes that they wish they could eat themselves, displacement as love.

But she's warm, and she's sweet, and her fur whispers against my bare ankle in a way that feels oddly supportive. She's the Thiebold I'm most at home with, if you don't count Rob.

Whom I can hear talking about me from the other room, his tone worried and respectful. " . . . doesn't seem to be feeling it yet. It's going to sink in soon, and I feel like she might fall apart. I don't know how to help her."

"You just stay close, that's all. Close enough for her to lean on you," "Dad" tells him.

"When Grandpa died, I was in shock for a little while. Maybe that's what's happening for her." This from "Mom."

I think I hear Rob sigh. "She didn't even want to bury him. Is that normal?"

My cheeks flush. I never thought Rob would question it so explicitly, out loud. To his parents, of all people. He must know that I've been on my best behavior, that I've wanted to be a daughter-in-law they could be proud of. I feel like he's just outed me.

"It doesn't sound normal to me," "Dad" says. Somehow it hurts more, coming from "Dad." Mothers are supposed to be critical of their daughters-in-law, guarding their territory, wanting to maintain primacy in their sons' lives. "But what do I know? I engrave for a living."

"She was probably worried about the money," "Mom" says. "She didn't want to spend your money. I still can't believe her parents didn't set anything aside, or have any life insurance."

She's being sympathetic, but I feel like my whole body is baking in a kiln. She called it "your money," as in Rob's. She still doesn't think of it as ours, mine and Rob's.

"She gets stressed out about money," Rob concedes, but he doesn't sound sure. He's doubting me. To his parents.

"She should be stressed about it. She doesn't earn any." Who is this "Dad"? Does he always talk this way behind my back? "No more fancy vacations for a while."

"They're just long weekends," Rob says. "They mean a lot to Dawn. I don't want to take them away from her." Way to throw me under the bus. "It's probably because of how she grew up."

So he's told them that, too? I've said as little as possible about my upbringing.

He can never know what happened when I was sixteen. Never. Because then they'll know. If they think I'm defective now, imagine what they'd say then.

But they're not the ones questioning me; Rob is.

"The next time she wants to go away, I'll tell her no," Rob adds. "It's not a good use of my money."

"My money"? That's how he sees it?

Plus, I never suggest the getaways, he does! Sure, I'm always enthusiastic, but I would never bring them up first. I'm too self-conscious about not working, even though that's his doing. I wanted to work.

He's making me sound like some kind of gold digger. He's the one who always told me that he wanted to take care of me, in all ways. He told me I was worth it. Was he bullshitting me then, or is he bullshitting his parents now?

I'm floored. I always thought Rob was the straightest shooter, honest to a fault, and entirely trustworthy. That's the husband I knew, and wanted.

"Is she going to Eureka again soon?" "Mom" asks.

"I think she should, but no, she's not planning to."

"Every family is different," she answers. She's defending me, but she's insulting me, too, via my family. "I do feel for her mother, though. Losing your husband of so many years. I can't even imagine." I can picture her shuddering as she squeezes "Dad's" hand.

"That's weird, too," Rob says. "He wasn't actually her husband. They didn't manage to really get married, if you can believe that. They messed up the paperwork." The three of them share a soft chuckle.

Rob knew I was embarrassed to find out my parents weren't married, and yet he used that factoid like a bit of comic relief. I never thought he would share my private business so cavalierly, like his true loyalty, his affiliation, is to his normal parents and not to his abnormal wife from her laughably substandard family.

I can't bear to hear any more. I move forward, and Furball lets out an aggrieved meow, like I've defected. I reach down and stroke her just for a second before I make my reappearance.

"Hey, you," Rob says, a little too warmly, like someone who's not sure how much has been overheard. He knows he has something to hide.

All I can hope is that he's honest with me later about what's been said. I won't confront him; I want him to come clean on his own. If he apologizes and says he won't do it again, I can forgive. I'll try to forget.

I'm subdued for the rest of dinner and dessert. They're probably chalking it up to grief, but really, I can't stand to talk to any of them. I don't even want to look at them. My eyes are on my plate, and the table, and then, finally, gratefully, the door.

"Mom" gives me a good-bye hug en route, which tips me off. Usually, they both see us out, with long and equivalent embraces in the foyer, and "Mom" always releases me at the precise second that "Dad" releases Rob, and vice versa. But tonight, it's a solo act from "Dad."

"I have something for you," he says, reaching into his pocket and proffering a folded check. "To defray the cost of the funeral expenses."

Rob takes the check, but he doesn't open it. "Thank you." His tone is solemn, reverential.

I fight to find the right tone, the same one as Rob's. No, I should sound even more grateful. My voice should quiver with emotion. He's coming through when my parents didn't, proving that he is my family.

I can't tell him that there will be no funeral, that my father didn't live the kind of life that requires memorializing. I should feel grateful toward the Thiebolds, same as I should feel sad about my dad and sorry for my mom.

But I don't feel any of those things, because I'm not normal. Even my husband said so, and he doesn't know the half of it.

"Dad's" words from earlier ring in my ears. Beneath all his choreographed hugs and his kind expression and his amiable demeanor and tonight's check is the truth. They're not my real family, and they never will be.

They're trying to accept me and make me feel welcome. The check is here, in Rob's hand, and "Dad" is looking at me expectantly. They can't help what they think, deep down, and what they feel, any more than I can.

Despite good intentions, the whole gesture feels condescending and humiliating. It's how I felt when they offered—no, insisted—on paying for the wedding. I would have preferred city hall or a Vegas elopement, but they wouldn't hear of it. Rob and I couldn't deny their largesse. The Thiebolds had enough friends in attendance to stock both sides of the aisle.

The check "Dad" is holding underscores that I'm the white trash who's married into their solid upper-middle-class family. Yet it's not that solid, not really. Yes, this house is lovely, it's a true home, but their affluence is a facade. "Dad" probably thinks I don't know that the family business is in trouble. Maybe he denies it to himself, or even to "Mom." But Rob tells me everything (or so I thought, until tonight), so I know that despite this trophy presentation, their business is dying every day.

True generosity would be giving Rob a life raft so he could push off. "Dad" needs to absolve his son of the responsibility to go down with the ship, with his family. Let him move on with his life, find a real career, with a future, one that will support the next generation. Our baby, if we have one.

Did I say "if"? When. I meant "when."

Rob is too loyal to his family; he won't just walk away. He needs to be set free.

To do so would be the most generous act of all, but "Dad" is incapable of it. Whether he's too selfish or blind, I don't know. So the Thiebolds aren't so perfect after all.

That should make me feel more like one of them, but I've never felt like less.

30

Miranda

#streetart #banksy #vibing #artallnighter

It's a night of favorites (Larry's, not mine): roast chicken and vegetables, a Diane von Furstenberg wrap dress, the unpronounceable
perfume from Barneys that's colored pale lilac yet scented like lilies.
We eat in the dining room rather than the kitchen, our place set-
tings perpendicular so that we occupy the same general region of
the twelve-person table. The chicken is on a heavy silver serving
platter, a wedding gift thirty-six years ago.

Larry smiles at me fondly. "What's the special occasion?" he asks,
and I smile back, opting to treat his question as if it's rhetorical. He
sees through me, I can feel it. I'm sweating, but I tell myself that
only makes the tang of the French lilies more pronounced. I'm all
the more irresistible.

Who am I kidding, I've always been resistible. I'm no Dawn. I bet she doesn't even need to cook when she's trying to put one over on her husband; she can just shake that long hair and flash that smile. My wiles are of another sort entirely.

I put some chicken on Larry's plate, leaning over just so, giving him a glimpse of my décolletage.

Don't think of Dawn; don't think of Thad. Focus on Larry, on the task at hand. I arrange the vegetables around the chicken, making sure he has a little of everything.

"To what do I owe my good fortune?" he tries again. He's not going to let me off the hook; he's too smart for that. I'm not going to be able to pull this off.

"I've been so busy lately," I answer, "that I've been neglecting you." I avoid his eyes as I prepare my own plate. Then I reposition my dress in order to sit down without any wardrobe malfunctions. I can't bring up the Santa Monica house too soon; I need him to finish his glass of Syrah first. There has to be a respectable distance between his question about my motives and the actual lie.

I'm going to lie to my husband, flagrantly.

I don't want to, but Thad has taken away all my choices.

The fact that he could do this to me when we'd briefly grown closer, when I had hopes that there was more closeness to come . . . "heartbroken" is too mild a word.

That's neither here nor there. I have to do what I have to do. That's what parenthood is. That's what life is.

I hope Dawn gets hers, that's all I can say. She pushed over the first domino, and my whole life's toppling. I hope she's somewhere right now, suffering.

Did I really just think that?

I take it back. I'm not this venomous person. She's young and foolish and needs to do some growing up, that's all. All I'm wishing is that her growing pains have a little extra emphasis on the pain.

Focus on Larry, that's all I can do.

I force a smile. "How's the chicken?"

"Perfect, as usual." He smiles back, briefly, before he powers through more of the bird. He's a robust eater, and he likes to eat first, talk later. I'm pleased when he takes a long swallow of Syrah.

I sip daintily. I need to keep my wits about me.

"I'm going to look through old pictures tonight," I say. "I want to find some good ones of my family from when I was growing up. Pictures of all of us at Mammoth, that kind of thing. Some visuals might help."

He swallows, Adam's apple wobbling. "Help with what?"

"With my mother's memory."

"That's optimistic." What he means is, it's not going to work.

"There are studies that say stimulation can prolong the early stages."

"She's not in an early stage, sweetie. I just don't want you to get your hopes up."

I set my fork down and say, quietly, "What's so wrong with getting your hopes up? It beats the alternative, doesn't it?"

"Sometimes it keeps you tilting at windmills, until you're crazy as Don Quixote."

I wonder if he's thinking of Thad. I wonder if he knows, about everything. If he's chalking it up to me being crazy. His wife, the windmill tilter.

That's probably the most favorable interpretation: not guilty, by reason of insanity.

He munches silently for a few minutes. I'm too tense to eat, but I do a pantomime of raising my fork to my lips, with a small morsel on the tines.

"You can find a study for anything," he says.

"Hmm?"

"Those studies that show you can delay the disease progression by looking at home movies. I bet there are studies that show the opposite." He drains his Syrah and looks right at me. "I don't have a study to support this, not at hand, but it seems to me that trying to stimulate her memory could have some unintended consequences."

"Like?"

"Like she understands that that's her, and that's her family, but she can't recall anything. It's like knowing you used to be someone, and you're not anymore. You'll be reminding her what she's lost." He sees the expression on my face, the hurt. He reaches for my hand. "I just want you to be prepared. Forewarned is forearmed. You're a tender heart, my love. It's one of your best qualities, and one of the most dangerous."

I nod. Sometimes I wish he could love one of my ideas, instantly, without reservation. But I do know he loves me. His heart isn't tender, exactly, but it's in the right place.

"Talk to her doctor," he says. "See what he thinks first."

"She," I say. "Dr. Wallace is a woman."

"Even better." He grins. "Female doctors often work harder and think longer." Then he polishes off the last of his sweet potatoes and a final bit of chicken. "Bring her some of this food."

"Dr. Wallace?"

"No, your mother. It's her recipe, isn't it?"

I did tell him that, once upon a time. I don't even know why, it just flew out of my mouth, something to make him love my food a little more, to create domestic continuity, maybe. It was a white lie, nothing like what I'm about to say. I make a noncommittal noise that can be taken as assent. Then I pour him another glass of wine.

He's used to finishing first. As I nurse my food, he tells me about his day at work: the consultations, the politics, and the collegial disagreements. He really lights up while talking about The Ignora-

mus's encouraging a patient to do more treatment when that patient should be advised to begin hospice. It occurs to me that he's
doing this with an almost discomfiting amount of relish, like he
enjoys sitting in judgment of The Ignoramus more than sitting in
compassion for the poor patient whose life (and death) is being im-
pacted. As if he's forgotten that he wasn't always so perfect himself.

My discomfort right now isn't really about the residency. It isn't
about Larry at all. He made his mistakes a long time ago, while
mine just go on and on. They say it's not the crime, it's the cover-up,
and his crime may have been worse but he was honest. This is about
my sins, not his.

Over apricot torte and coffee, when Larry has had two and a half
glasses of wine, I decide it's time. Let the deception begin.

"You know I've been so busy lately," I say. "I haven't even been
cooking proper meals for us, like the one we had tonight. Between
volunteering, my mother, and the rental house, it's hard to keep up."

"You manage beautifully." He's beaming at me in the candlelight.
He's going to try to have sex tonight.

"I'm thinking it's time to cut back on my commitments. I could
rent the house out on a longer-term basis. A three-month lease,
maybe. Then I wouldn't be fielding questions all the time, and
having to get ready for the next guest. Dealing with money. Returning security deposits. It's surprisingly time-consuming."

"Is it?" He swirls the wine in his glass.

"I do most of it while you're at work, but still, we get calls on the
weekends sometimes. Remember that call about the plumbing at
three A.M.?"

He furrows his brow, trying to recall the imaginary emergency.

"So I think it's time. I want to focus on other things. It's just not
rewarding anymore, being a host. I want to be a landlord. I mean,
we can be landlords." I'm trying to sound light about it all, as if

it's no big deal. Meanwhile, my insides are corkscrewed. "I'll visit a property management company and let you know how it goes."

"Then they'll take a percentage?"

"Yes, but they'll negotiate higher rents, too." I think of the extensive list of fees that are possible. If I chose a company with fewer fees but let Larry believe there were more, I could skim some off the top. Or if I told him I was using a company and then didn't . . . More lies equals more possibilities. The corkscrew tightens. I don't want to live like this, but I see no way out.

Larry does not look happy. "You said we make more money with the long weekend rentals. We can charge a lot more per night than if someone has a lease."

My stomach manages to tense one more revolution. Right now, I could be murdering my marriage. Right this instant.

But what can I do except continue? Commit to the big lie. "I don't want to stress you out, but the house needs foundation work. That can be expensive. Tens of thousands, possibly."

"How long have you known this?" I'm surprised by how cold he sounds, as if he thinks I've been keeping this from him. If he only knew.

"I'm telling you as soon as I found out."

"So you want to get in a long-term tenant *and* hire a property management company—both of which mean we'll make less money—at the same time we have to put tens of thousands into a new foundation? What kind of sense does that make?"

"It's not just about money. It's about time and energy. My time and energy."

"I can appreciate that, but Jesus. Tens of thousands?"

I plunge ahead. "I don't have enough in the Santa Monica account to cover foundation work. I'd have to take it from our regular accounts." And funnel it into the secret account, the one with the siphoned money, from which I transfuse Thad. Two months, that was our agreement. Maybe he'll honor it. Maybe he'll get that show, or better yet, he'll go six months clean and Larry will get on board with art school. Thirty thousand dollars will be a good buffer, and then who knows?

Larry's watching me appraisingly. It's not that he thinks I'm lying; it's that he doesn't trust my judgment. He feels like he needs to step in. It's similar to raising Thad. Larry is hands-off until he decides that I'm out of my depth and his services are required.

He'd never say that. But that was the feeling I had, then as now. In both cases, he's probably right. I have let things get out of hand. Thad used my love for him against me, and when that stopped working, he resorted to the ultimate threat and I caved. Larry would die before he caved.

"If you don't want to rent the house anymore, maybe it's time to sell it. The market's booming." Seeing my panicked face, he says, "I know you're attached to that house, but it's worth considering."

"It's more than just an attachment."

"We need to weigh out the emotional and the rational here. But not tonight. Not on the heels of this fantastic meal, with you looking like a million bucks in that dress." Yes, he does want sex. I could not be less desirous if I tried. "Let's table this for the time being. You'll get the estimates for the foundation work. Afterward, we'll visit the property with a Realtor and see if it's a good idea to do the work first or just put it on the market."

"You're talking like it's a done deal," I say, "like we're definitely going to sell. How long have you been thinking about this?"

"Nothing's decided." He takes my hand and kisses it. "Eva can do all the dishes tomorrow."

He starts to lead me up the stairs. All I can think of is what's ahead of me, tomorrow and the day after that. I'm going to have to broaden the lie: get the highest estimates I can for the fake foundation work from disreputable companies, and find a Realtor to say that property values will be even higher in a year, or two, or better yet, five. Then there will be no plausible deniability. Larry will know I created this whole elaborate scheme in order to deceive him.

That's if he finds out. I need to keep that from happening, at all costs.

"I'll be upstairs in a second," I tell him. "I just need to turn all the lights off."

I go to the kitchen and flip the switch, and that's when I notice that the lights outside are on, the pool illuminated azure. I don't actually remember turning them on, which sends a shiver through me, given my mother's condition.

Could all the stress I'm under activate my family's predisposition? It's a cruel irony that my mother was the one to get dementia after she spent all those years acting as Daddy's memory. It was a joke between George and me that even when my father was home, he wasn't all there. He spaced out sometimes in midsentence. Fortunately, Daddy's forgetfulness turned around. Once he was retired and in Santa Monica, his memory was fine.

I'm about to turn the outside floodlights off, but something makes me pause. I step outside and scan. At first glance, everything's in order. Then I look more closely at the pool to see what's floating there. I move closer.

It's a drowned rat. Or it could be a mouse, I'm terrible with rodent identification. It's a skill that I've, thankfully, never had to master.

Just my luck. Manuel isn't due to service the pool for a few days. I marshal the energy to go outside and grab the net, steeling myself.

Dead rodents. Is that an omen?

31

Dawn

Whatcha doing, beautiful?

I've got a new painting on Instagram.

One selfie, that's all I ask.

The secret to Thad's interest—the secret to most men, patheti-cally enough—is responding to every third contact. One to three, that's the magic ratio. When I do respond, it's often with a nonan-swer. I flirt. I deflect. I obfuscate. He begs for more.

While I've spilled a few discreet nuggets, he knows little about me and how I spend my day. I withhold and he pursues. It's a simple formula that I employed with great success from ages nineteen to twenty-five. Then I met Rob and decided I could trust and open up. Look how that's turning out.

It's clear by now that Rob isn't going to confess to me about his conversation with his parents. He might not even think he did anything wrong. Maybe he didn't. He can't help it if he thinks I'm some kind of freak.

Thad, however, thinks I'm perfect.

It helps that he barely knows me. By revealing so little, I don't feel like I'm betraying Rob. If anything, Rob's the one who's betrayed me, dissecting me with his parents like a frog in biology class.

Three texts from Thad, so it's time to give him something.

Some of us have more important things to do than selfies.

You can be a bitch, you know that?

I'm definitely not going to respond to that.

But I kind of like bitches. I was raised by one. She made me what I am today.

It's the first time he's referenced Miranda. I've got to answer.

And what are you?

I'm a charming fuckup. Haven't you figured that out by now?

How did she make you?

I don't think I got a hug from her until the day she sent me away to rehab.

Aw, poor little rich boy. Mommy never hugged him. She just gave him everything. But he hasn't yet told me that he was raised in Beverly Hills. He's still pretending to be a starving artist.

Did rehab work?

I wouldn't give her the satisfaction.

Do you have a dad?

Sure. Did you?

It seems pointed, the past tense. I wonder if he Googled me, if he knows about my father dying. The one thing my mother paid for in all of this was an obituary. It was full of misspellings and falsehoods about what a great man he was, and a loving father ("survived by his beautiful daughter Dawn Thiebold").

No, I answer, *I don't have a dad.*

Sorry. Or not?

Not.

I'm telling him too much. Stay a woman of mystery, a trench coat disappearing into the mist, and you'll never get hurt. They'll never touch you.

That was my mistake with Rob. I became real.

32

Miranda

Bengal Construction

62 reviews

1 STAR

Make sure you do your homework before you hire a contractor, especially for foundation repair. Don't rely on the contractor to tell you what to do, especially when that contractor is Bengal.

We've had to file a formal complaint with the Better Business Bureau and the Contractors State License Board . . .

1 STAR

I had three companies give me estimates. This was the only one who said I needed significant repairs, to the tune of $25K. These guys should be put out of business. No, they should be run out of town on a rail.

1 STAR

Frank came to my house and said I needed a new foundation when other companies said I just needed some beams added for stability. I was quoted $60,000 for a job that ended up costing $9,000. Frank gave me an estimate after five minutes, and he was looking at something on his cell phone for half that time. No measurements, nothing. Wouldn't call them again, ever.

2 STARS

They called me back fast, I'll give them that, and they were polite. The work, though, was a disaster. They were never on time, they left trash everywhere, and they did different work than in the contract! I wouldn't have known if I hadn't asked for pictures. Then I had to ask for a refund of the difference between what they said they'd do and what they did. They gave it to me, which is why I gave them that second star.

Sometimes people surprise you with their character and integrity. There you are, standing before them, begging to be ripped off, saying things like, "I just don't know anything about foundations! I don't even know where my crawl space is!" and they refuse to take the bait.

And sometimes people disappoint you with their character and integrity. Frank from Bengal Construction has the face and mannerisms of a classic shyster. I was sure that he would be the one to give me an extravagant estimate. But instead, he tells me, "Your foundation's pretty much fine, just a few spiderweb cracks. I can come back in a couple of years and check again, but for now, I'd say you've got no problems."

My eyes widen. I almost want to laugh—me, with no problems?—but something else must cross my face instead, and I must have surprised him right back, because his eyebrows hoist and he adds, "This is good news, missus."

He can't even remember my name, which was one of the knocks on him in the reviews I read. His company had the worst Yelps of any in the greater Los Angeles area, and that's saying something. In a metropolis as sprawling as this one, Frank and Bengal Construction have screwed people end to end, from East L.A. to Culver City.

I chose the three most disreputable companies I could find to give me estimates on foundation work. With the way my luck is going, the next two will have similar attacks of conscience.

I can't go home empty-handed. If I have to, I'll work my way down the list. Someone will be willing to screw me. This is Los Angeles, after all, home to Hollywood, land of a million rationalizations and creative interpretations. One man's spiderweb crack is another's gold mine.

It's been a disappointing day, all told. Earlier, I went to my mother's facility and met with Dr. Wallace. I need to keep moving, to keep busy, so I won't think about Thad's threat, and how close I'm dancing to the edge of my marriage, to the end of life as I know it.

I was just hoping for some good news, that I'd be told I can impact something (in this case, someone) in a positive way. Dr. Wallace gave me a gentle smile and said, "Your presence is enough. So many family members stop coming over time, but you're still so consistent. That's what she needs."

Dr. Wallace doesn't know how I've struggled to stay consistent, how many visits I've wanted to blow off since they don't seem to matter to my mother anyway. "I want to help bring her back," I said. I need to do something, doesn't anyone understand that? Progress instead of progression—that could be my slogan. I should float it at a Nar-Anon meeting and see if there are any takers.

"Lewy body dementia is a little different than Alzheimer's or Parkinson's," Dr. Wallace replied. "Stop me if you've heard this before.

Her short-term memory is not as affected as it would be if she had Alzheimer's. But her fluctuations in attention, concentration, and awareness—well, you know how those can happen suddenly. It seems like you're going to have a good visit, and then she's agitated. There are the hallucinations, and the delusions. She talks to your father often, as if he's right there."

I was startled. I've never seen that, and no one has mentioned it before. "Does she ever talk to me when I'm not here?"

"Not that I'm aware of, but that doesn't mean it doesn't happen. You could ask the nurses."

As if I need to expose myself to further humiliation.

"My point is, she's unpredictable. The photo albums could be agitating to her, or soothing, but it can turn on a dime. They could trigger a delusion or a hallucination. Then we'd have to medicate her further. We want to keep her calm without having to resort to neuroleptics because those can have all sorts of unpleasant side effects for someone with LBD."

LBD. Little black dress. Or a warpath deterioration that robs you of all that you were and all that you loved.

"The best thing you can do is keep coming. And take her on walks, as much as she's willing."

"She's not very willing."

"Then just keep coming. You're doing all you can."

She meant this to be comforting. But being told that you're powerless is never actually a comfort. I never could embrace Step One. Neither could Thad.

When it comes to him, I truly am powerless. I have to submit to his tyranny, and meanwhile, he sends me texts about the paintings he's working on, as if all is normal. I respond, through gritted teeth, fearing that if I don't, he'll retaliate through Larry, or he'll use more drugs. He'll harm me or he'll harm himself. He's holding me hostage.

Something's changed inside of me since the blackmail. I can tell myself that this isn't the real Thad, it's his addiction. I can say it's not about me, it's about the drugs. But I can no longer manage to believe. Not every addict would blackmail his own mother. I never heard a story like this at Nar-Anon.

This isn't only about drugs. It's about who Thad is, and who I am, and what he feels about me, all of which is devastating and angering in equal measure. I'm used to dealing with devastation where Thad is concerned, but the anger . . . I don't know what to do with that. It's an electric current running through me all the time now.

Just keep moving, it's all I can do. Keep busy, like the officer said.

"Thanks, Frank," I say, reaching out to shake his hand. "I appreciate your time."

He starts to walk away, and then seems to think better of it. "A word to the wise," he says. "You need to Google yourself."

"What?"

"You seem like a nice lady to me, someone I'd like to do business with, but what I read on the way over here . . ." He shakes his head, like it's not to be spoken out loud. "Google yourself, you'll see what I'm talking about."

Wait a minute. *He* wouldn't want to work with *me*? Frank of Bengal Construction with its D- grade from the Better Business Bureau and innumerable one-star Yelp reviews was scared off by my Google results. Whatever he found was so bad that he decided to swindle someone else.

"What did it say, on the Web?" I ask.

"It's about your rental."

Of course. Dawn. Just because she hasn't contacted me, that doesn't mean I'm safe. I should have known she'd see through my baseless police threat, that someone like her would simply find other means to torture me.

Oh my God. The lights I didn't remember leaving on outside, the mouse in my pool. No, not a mouse. A rat. Brownish-gray, the same color as the stain she left on my sheets. Dawn was in my house, or someone else was, at her behest. A woman as beautiful as her could easily have henchmen.

No, it can't be. No one would do that. It was just bad luck, for the mouse and for me. It was a random act of God.

Since Frank's being honest and happens to be standing in front of me, I go ahead and ask him. "Do you know if Beverly Hills has a rat problem?"

Frank thinks I'm nuts, that's plain to see. He's probably reconsidering his original estimate of zero. A woman this insane would have replaced her whole house, subbasement to roof.

"I'm no expert," he disclaims, and then he goes on to tell me how it's common knowledge that rats have been living it up in Beverly Hills since the drought of the late nineties sent them scrambling. He distinguishes between black rats, which live in attics and trees and move like ballerinas, and Norwegian rats, which are grayish-brown, big and lumpy and slow. He tells me that I don't need to be worried about them carrying disease, that's for crowded urban spaces like tenements; no, in Beverly Hills it's about chomping through power lines, and if that hasn't happened, if my electricity is still humming, then I've got no problems. He loves that phrase, it seems.

So a Norwegian rat decided to take a dip in my pool, that's all. Beverly Hills is apparently teeming with them, though I've never seen one before. It's merely poor timing that I'm having my first sighting now. It wasn't Dawn or one of her henchmen. It wasn't someone sending me a message. It was a fluke, that's all.

I thank Frank again. Maybe I'll even give him his first good Yelp review.

He smiles as he tips his head to one side, a gesture of false modesty. See, classic shyster. But even shysters can come through for you sometimes.

I don't have time to Google myself because the next estimator is pulling up in his truck right now, DUNLEAVY CONSTRUCTION emblazoned on the side.

Even if she had nothing to do with that rat, Dawn's soiled so much more than just my sheets. She's tainted the Santa Monica house. This place felt inviolate to me, which sounds odd given that I was opening it up to strangers. But I'd never had a real issue before Dawn, and in fact, all the e-mails from satisfied customers, the positive reviews, and the praise had validated my sense that the last home my parents ever shared was a truly wonderful place.

I miss checking my e-mail for inquiries about the house. I liked reading the palpable desire of strangers, and after their stays, their effusive words. Now, I just keep hearing Dawn's nastiness in my head, and her petty complaints. I can't help but think of the partially obstructed view from the kitchen. I look at the bed and I can still see that stain, which is presently morphing into the dead Norwegian rat.

Wait a minute . . .

In my original e-mail, I called it a cat-shaped stain. She's correcting me, telling me it's the shape of a large rat. Even if rats are now indigenous to Beverly Hills, there's no way it was a coincidence.

As I wait for Dunleavy to emerge from the crawl space, I leave a voicemail for Officer Llewellyn. I explain the cat/rat shape. He'll have to take me seriously now. I wish I'd thought to save the corpse. It just hadn't occurred to me that vermin would be evidence.

Should I Google myself now? I've never thought to do it before. I have limited social media presence. That's for young people, people like Thad, not for women my age. It just seems desperate to me when sixty-year-olds are posting selfies. Just that word, "selfie," makes me cringe. You take pictures of people you love, and you with them; you don't just photograph yourself. We used to call behavior like that narcissism.

Dunleavy emerges, and he says that it's not just a matter of repair work; we're looking at total foundation replacement. He tells me to brace myself, and then gives me the estimate I'd been hoping for: $35K. Now all I need is to convince Larry that we can't sell the house this way, any home inspector would tell the potential buyer and it would queer the deal, so we'll need to repair it. Besides, we can't sell it anyway because I'm too sentimentally attached. No, because we can recoup the $35K and far more if we just hang on to the house longer. Another five years, and during that time, I would detach. I would work toward letting go. I would become more rational, more like Larry.

Thirty-five thousand will buy me at least a year of helping Thad. During that time, I can try to convince him to give rehab another go. He can be magically transformed into a better person. He'll do regular drug tests, and if they come back clean, he can rebuild his relationship with Larry. We could pay for art school, and Thad could parlay that into a job. He could give up this long-standing myth of exceptionalism and hunker down and work. It'll buy me a year, and that's as far out as I can afford to fantasize.

A year is a long time. Anything could happen. This isn't over yet.

33

Dawn

Hi. What should we do for dinner tonight?
  I can cook.
  Are you sure? We could go out.
  I'll cook. You don't need to spend your money.
  Okay, see you soon.
  See you.

Hey, Thad. Where were we?
  You were about to tell me something about your mom.
  Oh, yeah. She keeps bugging me.
  I know that drill.
  Since my dad died, she keeps hinting that she should move in with me.
  I bet your husband loves that idea.
  He likes it a lot better than I do.
  That's fucked up.

It is fucked up. I should want to help her.

No. I mean it's fucked up that he cares about your mom more than he cares about what you want.

He's just being a good person.

To her, maybe, but what about you?

I don't want to talk about Rob.

Awesome, I don't either. I want to talk about you.

I'm not a very good person.

Bullshit.

My mom needs help, and I don't want to give it.

What goes around comes around, Dawn. It's just karma.

You believe in karma?

When it comes to parents and kids I do. You take good care of your kids, they'll take good care of you. You mess your kids up, they'll mess you up right back.

My mom's already a mess.

Exactly. Karma.

There's something whacked in your logic, but honestly, I can't figure out what it is.

We all started out good and pure, right? If we're not anymore, it's because of what was done to us, probably by our parents.

But at what point are we responsible for our own lives, and our own choices, and we can't blame anyone else?

How old are you?

30.

You've got 5 years to go. I've got 8.

Sometimes I just get so mad. I feel like I can't really have kids because of her. Like I wouldn't know what to do with them.

You can do whatever you want.

Sure, we all can.

No. You, Dawn Thiebold, can do whatever you want. In a world full

of shitty false people, you are amazing. There should be more of you.
Make more.

I've actually got tears in my eyes. Who would have thought Thad
could have that effect?

I feel bad now, that I misjudged him. I assumed he was a loser.
I mean, I know he doesn't have a job, and I don't get his art. But
then, I don't get art, period. I've gone to museums and it all just
leaves me cold. I don't know how people can stand in front of a
painting for more than thirty seconds, even if it is beautiful. Because I can recognize beauty, and appreciate it, but then you move
on, you know?

Thad's got this warped worldview, but there's truth in it. Plus, he
makes me laugh. We've never even talked on the phone, yet there's
an intimacy to the way we relate. I answer all his texts now.

I can't fully explain his allure, and I don't have to, since no one
knows we're even in contact. All I know is that I'm not some Eliza
Doolittle type to Thad. He's not trying to elevate me. He gets me,
and likes what he gets.

It could just be that I'm hungry for male attention. There was a
time when I could count on always having a guy on the string, even
two or three of them, but that seems like forever ago.

Rob's always given me plenty of attention, but lately, it's felt more
like scrutiny. Ever since that dinner with his parents, I catch him
studying me, like he's trying to figure out how I can be so cold
about my dead father and my live mother. It makes me want to
hide. There are things he can't know, things that I can never tell.
Our conversations have become depressingly superficial, and the
distance between us is growing. I'm afraid of what could happen if
we continue this way. I just never saw it coming.

I met Rob more than four years ago, when I was an assistant
manager at Target. I was due to go back to college the following se-

mester, with a plan to work all day, go to school at night, and study whenever I could fit it in. I was entirely independent, relying on no one, with no one to rely on me. Then one day, I glanced down the frozen food aisle, and there he was, reading the nutritional information on an entrée for one. A good sign, as far as his singlehood was concerned, though not the sexiest male behavior. It was—I'd soon learn—classically Rob.

The Target customer base doubled as my dating pool. I liked to approach attractive men and offer assistance. Sometimes I did it when they looked genuinely confused, but that wasn't the case with Rob.

I was learning to distinguish between men who were attractive and men I was attracted to. In my late teens and early twenties, good sex was worth the drama. The two were proportional: The greater the drama, the better the sex. I liked a roller coaster, and I could spot one at a hundred paces. Love? Who needed that? I just needed the upper hand. Hard-to-get was my playbook.

But then something changed. I started noticing babies. And families. I started wanting something I'd never wanted before: a real home, one that was stable and loving. The men I was attracted to could provide multiple orgasms, but they couldn't provide that.

At the same time, I'd been reading a rash of articles by regretful women in their thirties and forties. Some had gone on to have babies without mates; some were just plain alone. All of them had the same advice: settle in your twenties, when the odds are good, before the goods are odd. In your twenties, they opined, you're not too set in your ways, and neither are the men. You can meld. You can grow, together. Settle when you're marketable, with ripe, juicy ovaries. Settle before the men are irreparably damaged. Settle without desperation. Settle now.

While there was plenty of backlash—women who offered alternative stories of finding their great love at, say, forty-three, or ones who just found the very notion of settling to be antifeminist—I was persuaded. I decided that it was time to set the table for the family I was going to have.

Enter Rob, stage left, the undeniably good-looking, neatly dressed reader of ingredient lists. I asked if he needed help, and he dug around to find some inane question, and we were off and running. I'd found someone patient, kind, and reliable, from a good family. He gave back rubs and foot massages. He was a better-than-average cunnilinguist. What more could I ask for?

I felt so fortunate to have Rob, given my family history and my relationship history. That he could know all about both and still choose me—that was thrilling in itself. Sure, I left out a few details, but I was sure they would never be salient again. He proposed within the year, and not only marriage; he also proposed that I move in with him and give up my job so I could focus on school.

To any outsider, there was no settling involved. A lot of the time, I didn't even think I was doing it. But there was a niggling thought beneath it all that I didn't find Rob fascinating, in mind or body. He didn't entirely capture my imagination. He was just so knowable.

I was relieved when he did anything unpredictable. I wanted to fuck him senseless the first time his temper flared. It was a road rage incident. We'd been sideswiped, a near-collision, and he tailed the guy home, all the way to San Leandro. Rob was taller, and the other guy was more muscular, a roughneck type, but Rob was furious. He slammed the guy against the car door. "That's my wife in there!" he shouted. "You don't *ever* fucking do something like that with my wife in the car!" The guy started nodding, agreeing, he wouldn't ever fucking do it again, and Rob was shaking with adrenaline when he climbed back into the driver's seat. I was shaking, too, with desire. I'd been with men who'd gotten into fights before, sometimes nominally to defend my honor, but they were looking for any excuse to burn off some testosterone. It didn't mean anything. But Rob was different. He was actually looking out for me, and he was capable of badassery.

It registered that he could turn that rage on me someday. But that just added to the excitement.

I do sometimes think that I could have settled richer. If I'd relaxed my requirements about the person being attractive and in my age ballpark, I know I could have married up, fiscally. Someone would have been happy to have me as his trophy wife.

But that's a level of compromise that I wasn't capable of at age twenty-five. Would I be capable at thirty-five, or forty? Hopefully, I won't find out. Rob and I will be long past the rough patch we're in now, my parents will once again become irrelevant, and I'll get over this weird ambivalence I'm having about kids. We'll be a family, with two children at least, living in a beautiful house that Rob will buy with his great new job after extricating himself from the family business and that I will supplement with my income as a successful . . . something or other. We won't need getaways in rental homes. I won't pretend to have anyone else's life. We won't want anything but what we have.

34

Miranda

Bewarethisrental.com:

I originally posted this review on Getaway.com. The landlord, Miranda Feldt, has since taken down her listing, so I'm reposting it here. People can draw their own conclusions.

Beware of your "host"

THREE STARS

I wouldn't have left a review at all, if I didn't feel it was my civic duty to warn others. Sure, there were small issues with the house itself . . .

Déjà vu washes over me. This is how it all began, the step-by-step destruction of my life. If not for Dawn, Thad wouldn't be blackmailing me now. I wouldn't wake up in cold sweats for fear that my husband is going to find me out. I wouldn't be the liar I am now.

Dawn's thorough, I have to give her that. Hers is a thoroughly reprehensible hatchet job. Google me, and she's commandeered the whole first page of search results.

If it hadn't been for Frank, I wouldn't even have known this was going on. Maybe it would have been better that way. Because I'm not sure there's a thing I can do about her lies.

I've lost all credibility with Officer Llewellyn. When I told him about the rat, he went silent for thirty seconds, at least, and then he asked, "Did you block her like I told you to?" I said that I haven't, but I haven't actually needed to. She's too smart to contact me directly. He asked if I had an alarm system; when I said yes, he told me to set it, whether I was home or not. "That'll give you peace of mind," he said. My tax dollars at work.

Since Dawn has stopped contacting me, she's skirted the harassment laws. I know that Officer Llewellyn won't see her online smear campaign as a credible threat of violence.

But it is violent, what she's done to me. It's a direct attack. She's managed to find every disreputable site with graphics upscale enough to pass for reputable. So at a quick glance, when the page of Google results materializes, I appear to be the equivalent of a vacation rental slumlord. Bewarethisrental.com has no rebuttal feature. Others are free to add their own experiences with me, but I have no forum to respond. It's a free-for-all, and I'm a landlord piñata. The fact that I was a host and not a landlord seems to matter not a whit.

There's a website where Dawn posted our entire correspondence rather than just her skewed distillation, or rather, it's what she purports to be our entire correspondence. She's even included our text exchange. I don't have the heart to do a line-by-line, but I'm sure she must have done some creative editing. What about her calling me a self-righteous c—? Where's her mocking text about who I'll fleece next?

Her shakedown attempt reads like I was the one trying to buy her off, as if I'm the unsavory character. I'm sure I never invoked Larry's profession. She must have searched me online and found that out herself. By now, that would be far down on the list, supplanted by all her trash.

I'm also sure I never said, *You need manners, and class. But I don't blame you. I blame your parents.* I wouldn't resort to such a low blow.

She acts like she's the philanthropist and I'm an entitled name-dropper, an elitist snob rather than who I really am.

Not that I'm clear on who I am these days. She's got me tense and paranoid, and I'm having to do things that I never would have considered. I'm embroiled in a double life, all because of her, and I fear she's not done yet.

There's no mention of the rat she left in my pool, now is there?

If anyone from the Homeowners Association decided to look me up, they'd know that I'd been breaking the ordinance, and that my resignation wasn't just about being too busy to serve.

If the city attorney's office finally gets their act together, could they be pressured to prosecute me retroactively? It's possible I haven't even dodged that bullet completely. Dawn wants this to follow me. She's out to ruin me.

I feel like I'm in the midst of pure evil, and I don't know how to begin to combat that. But somehow, I have to find the strength.

I try to locate phone numbers for the websites. If I can just talk to the right person, go up the supervisory chain, I can appeal to their sense of decency. I've always been good with people if I can speak to them, live. Obviously, e-mail and text are not my forte.

Since there are no phone numbers, I have no choice but to write.

I do my best to explain that Dawn's actions are malicious, and potentially actionable, and that the websites won't want to get mixed up in this. I respectfully request that they take Dawn's post down.

But I have little hope. Not just because those websites display no sense of decency, but because I have no confidence in my ability to express myself. Dawn has robbed me of that, too. It can't be an accident that there's no place for rebuttal; that's a deliberate choice the websites are making. They're for the Dawns of the world, and whether those people are lying or not is of no concern or consequence. The First Amendment protects them, and Dawn, too.

I could consult an attorney regarding defamation of character, but I couldn't go ahead with a lawsuit, not without telling Larry. Maybe just a threatening letter would be enough. I wouldn't need to tell Larry I'd done that; there's enough in my rental earnings to cover one letter. But my Thad fund is going to run dry quickly if I don't get cash for the fake foundation work.

I have the estimate but I haven't been able to approach Larry about it yet. He came home from work obviously upset, saying little. I surmised that a patient was dying, because that makes him quiet whereas hospital politics makes him loud. I'm embarrassed to admit it, but I was relieved. I didn't want to encounter any more pressure about calling Realtors.

When did my life become Watergate, one giant cover-up with a million tiny moving parts? I'm not a duplicitous person. This isn't in my nature, and it's certainly not how I was raised. My mother would be horrified if she knew. It's the first time I've ever been grateful that she isn't capable of higher cognitive functioning.

Because I'm not actually this person, Dawn has the advantage. She knows how to play the game. Her conscience might not make a peep, whereas mine protests at every turn.

After dinner, I tell Larry that I'm going out with a friend for a drink, and he says that if I'm late, I should go in the guest room; he doesn't want his sleep disturbed. It's another sign of his internal tumult, but I know he doesn't want me to pry. A good meal is the best I can do for him, and I've already done that. He pecks me on the cheek. "Have fun," he says.

Nar-Anon is many things, but fun is not among them. The last meeting I attended was years ago. Yet I feel myself being drawn in again—to the promise that there are steps forward, that it works if you work it, that you're only as sick as your secrets. I'm also drawn to the people, my brethren. They'll understand, intimately, the moral quandaries and compromises that beset the family of an addict. They wouldn't judge. They might even have a suggestion I haven't thought of for extricating myself.

I have to do something. Life works if you work it.

It's the same church basement. Same dim lighting, and rows of folding chairs, and a table with coffee and pastries. I recognize some of the faces. Our addicts have us all stuck in a time warp. There's the woman whose daughter is a bit younger than Thad, the one who clutched my arms and told me urgently that I had to keep coming back, that I had to try at least six different meetings before deciding whether this was going to help. She pegged me as a flight risk immediately. Ultimately, I did run away. I couldn't stand the thought of being a lifer, and yet, here I am.

I don't know how they arrived at this number, six, but it gets repeated often. There's a lot of repetition to the Twelve Step experience, so many sayings and slogans, and I suppose predictability is a comfort in the face of addiction's unpredictability. I don't know what my son will do, of what he's capable, but I know to end the phrases "progress" with "not perfection" and "let go" with "let God." I can anticipate that much.

Then there's the fellowship. These people get it. Rich, poor, black, white, Latino, there are no divisions, only collective pain. They're tired, yet they're hanging on, and they have a smile for the newcomers, always. It's like everyone is thinking that it has to turn out well for someone, that, say, one out of ten loved ones will make recovery stick, and of course, they'd like to be the one, but they'd celebrate if it's you, too. We're all just pulling for someone on the team.

I make sure that I'm a little late, so that I can avoid the pregame small talk. I slip into a seat, smiling around like a bee flitting from one flower to another, not landing on any one person for long. I catch the tail end of the Serenity Prayer. Then the leader welcomes newcomers, and I say my name and that I'm not entirely new but I haven't been there for a while. There's a warm, enveloping chorus. I'm as close to a newcomer as they have here tonight.

Then people start sharing their stories, heartbreaks, disappointments, and lessons. So many mistakes, but they all boil down to two, really. There's enabling—giving to the addict, instead of trying to "be" for the addict. Then there's codependency—focusing on how others feel instead of how you feel, not speaking up, bottling, keeping their secrets, being furtive with your own emotions. You're likely falling into enabling or codependency by forgetting the three C's—that you didn't Cause it, you don't Control it, and you can't Cure it.

Sure, I'm making all those mistakes, but what's the way out, really? Admitting I'm powerless? That's where it fell apart for me last time. I feel like that admission would be the end of me. If I'm powerless, I'll give up. I'll lie in bed until I mummify.

They're telling me that I need to stop focusing on Thad's survival, and begin to focus on my own. But I'm already doing that. The $35K isn't really for him; it's to save myself.

I need to open up to someone, somewhere. I'm as sick as my secrets, and that's pretty sick.

36

Miranda

Inspired by a new lady #beauteousmaximus

In the end, I left the estimate on Larry's dresser like a coward. It was after he'd already fallen asleep, so he discovered it this morning. When he asks me if I've gotten any others, I say yes, that was the best of them. He shakes his head with something like disgust, and I tell myself that it's not directed at me, it's at these thieving contractors. Only I know they're not the true thieves, I am. I have to hope he doesn't figure that out.

I watch him fasten his cuff links. He's the only man I know who still wears them, and somehow, that makes me ache with tenderness for him. What did he ever do to deserve to be married to me, to be lied to like this? Nothing, unless you count the residency, and I'm fairly certain he doesn't.

He kisses me on the cheek and says we'll talk later and make a game plan for the house. He folds the estimate carefully in half, then in thirds, placing it in his wallet. I'm filled with fear. What if he doesn't believe me? What if he shows it to someone and they tell him that they've got a great foundation guy he should call?

I sink back under the covers, though I know I won't sleep. I didn't, all night long. I was at such loose ends that I forgot Larry's request to sleep in the other room, but my entrance into bed didn't rouse him; that's the advantage of the California king. Despite the darkness, I kept seeing the outline of that paper on the dresser, thinking that it's not too late, I can still take it back. Throw it away. I hadn't yet passed the point of no return. Prostrate myself before Larry, tell him I'm just a mother, that's all, I couldn't abandon my son, but I'm finally ready.

I'm still choking on the e-mail I wrote to Dawn. I think it was the right move, the only move, really. Swallow my pride, and think in terms of outcomes. I want to cleanse my online presence, and that's entirely in Dawn's hands. The websites responded to my inquiries with form letters sprinkled with legal jargon, just enough to say that basically, they have the right to defame whomever they want.

It's not only about the posts. Even if Dawn doesn't take them down, we need to reach détente. I don't want to look over my shoulder anymore. No more rats in my pool, literally or figuratively. I want this over. Four hundred dollars is a small price to pay.

I reach one hand out from beneath the covers, groping hopefully for my phone, pulling it under. In the dim cave formed, I do my obligatory checks. Nope, no communication from Dawn. The posts are still up. No texts from Thad.

It appears he's been awake all night, tweeting. Is "a new lady" code for a new drug? Maybe it's not meth this time. Maybe it's "Molly." I just read about a bunch of college kids who were admitted to the hospital after a bad batch of MDMA. One of them nearly died. I have to hope they'll learn their lesson. Nearly dying was never lesson enough for Thad.

He didn't contact me at all yesterday, and I was relieved. I didn't contact him, and I don't plan to. I'm fine with just being a follower for the moment.

It's the first time I've played this particular game of chicken. I've always needed to reach out, to confirm that not only is he alive but he's still accessible, to confirm that he's not so angry as to write me off for good. I've feared his anger since he was a child. But these days, that's not my biggest fear. I suppose that's refreshing, an old dog like me being able to develop a new fear.

37

Dawn

Entry-Level Public Relations Marketing Assistant

Our company does marketing/PR work for the world's most re-
nowned nonprofits to reduce poverty. We are looking for creative,
collaborative individuals who enjoy working with fundraising teams
and want to know their work is meaningful . . .

Starting Salary: $35,000

Public Affairs & Media Relations Specialist

The Public Affairs and Media Relations Specialist supports, orga-
nizes, and publicizes the company-wide philanthropic program delivery . . .

Comprehensive benefits package. Salary range $32,000–
$40,000 DOE

Coordinator of Donor Relations

The Coordinator of Donor Relations provides support to the Director, and coordinates activities to increase the engagement and participation of donors and prospective donors, including fundraising activities, direct mail appeals, and special events . . .

Starting salary commensurate with experience.

"It's not too late," Rob tells me, "to go see your mom." His hand is already on the front door. It seems like this is how we communicate lately, in a series of parting remarks.

I'm standing in the kitchen doorway, still in my pajamas. For a second, I consider biting the bullet, just getting in the car and driving to Eureka so I can get back in Rob's good graces, but some structural beam inside me holds. I shouldn't be out of his good graces. He shouldn't be sitting in judgment of me. People grieve in their own ways, and in my case, that means that every time I remember that my father's dead, I feel relief. This could be a just world after all.

"Aunt Tanya's spending a lot of time with Mom," I say, "and she's doing better." That's my assumption anyway. Her texts have dwindled significantly.

It's only fair that my mother becomes Aunt Tanya's problem. My aunt lives right there in Eureka; she has a comfortable middle-class life, works part-time, and has no children. She can afford to adopt my mother.

The last time I saw Aunt Tanya was at my wedding, and I noticed two things: she looked ten years younger than my mother, though she's actually five years older, and her face didn't move much. I'm guessing those two facts were related, that she's Botoxed to the hilt, but she was the member of my family I was least embarrassed to introduce to Rob's parents.

"I've got a lot to do this weekend," I say. "With finals and applying for jobs." I hate that I still feel the need to explain myself, to justify why I don't want to spent the weekend in the hellhole of my youth. If Thad can understand it, why can't Rob?

He barely nods, his disappointment palpable. "I'm going to work late tonight," he says. "My dad's out sick, and it's the busy season." I wonder if this is punishment for my refusal to go to Eureka. When he first mentioned a possible trip earlier this week, I thought he intended to go with me, but maybe he always meant for me to be on my own.

Once he's gone, I throw myself into my senior project, working nonstop for hours, glad to think of nothing else. When I turn my phone back on, I'm surprised to see that it's almost seven P.M. The shop closes at five, and he's never been this late. He hasn't texted me all day. If he were anyone else, I might think he was the one with something to hide.

I can't believe Rob is unplugging from this marriage. If anyone should be pissed, it's me. He's the one who betrayed me in that conversation with his parents. He doesn't know that I overheard, but you'd think he'd have some conscience about allowing them to believe I'm a gold digger.

Could he actually believe I am a gold digger? I look around at our nearly squalid apartment. Fuck him.

There are twelve texts from Thad.

I skipped lunch, and the refrigerator is nearly empty. I think of texting Rob to tell him that I'm about to order a pizza, but don't. He can fend for himself.

After I call the pizzeria, I settle onto the couch and turn on the TV. I've earned some mindless celebrity trash, and *TMZ* obliges. I hear the sound of an incoming text. It's Thad. I smile, but I don't respond immediately. Keep him waiting, and wanting.

I eat my pizza on the couch as *TMZ* becomes *Entertainment Tonight*. When the phone rings, I answer without looking. It's got to be Rob, finally. I've never bothered with discriminating ringtones.

"Hey," says a resonant baritone. Not the male voice I expected to hear, and not the one I expected Thad to have, that's for sure. He could sing opera.

He's just upped the ante. For all he knows, Rob is right here beside me.

"Hey," I say, my voice softened by gratitude. I hadn't even realized I didn't want to be alone.

"Can you talk?"

"For a little while."

"I was about to text you and then I thought I'd take a chance. See if you'd answer."

Ah, so he's testing me. "I almost didn't answer."

"Because of your husband?"

"Because of you."

He laughs. He likes being slighted. I wonder if Miranda instilled that in him. "You sound different than I thought you would," he says. "Better, actually."

"You do, too. Actually."

"If you thought I'd sound like shit, why did you pick up?"

"If you thought I'd sound like shit, why did you call?"

Another laugh. It's deep, and knowing, like he's always in on the joke. Sexy, like his voice. "Because I knew you'd put me in a good mood."

"What's wrong?"

He sighs, a touch dramatically. I don't mind, I could use a show. I turn off the television. "You know I'm trying hard to get away from my old patterns. Not using meth, or whatever else I get my hands on. Trying to do my art from a pure place. But it's not just that. I'm trying not to be who I used to be with girls. Women, I mean," he amends, like he's anticipating my objection. "I don't want to just screw them and go home, or send them home. I want to wait for someone who matters." The briefest of pauses. "Who matters a little. I'm not talking about marriage or anything. But it's hard, waiting. It's hard being alone. Sex helps with that for a night. Well, a couple of hours. I don't like waking up next to anyone."

I've always found it irresistible, men wrestling with their demons. There was one, a rich tool named Aston, who made me a part of the fight. He would call me—like Thad is doing now—and tell me about his yearnings, how hard he was trying not to cheat, but he'd never been with one person for so long (the first time he said this, we'd been together three months), and somehow, I felt for him. I also felt turned on. He needed my help. He needed me to become someone else, just for a little while, someone new. He needed me to be good enough (well, bad enough) to keep him from straying. For a while, I was. For too long, probably.

It's uncomfortable, getting horny with someone other than Rob. It's wrong, I mean. But I want to help Thad. I want to help him get through the night. It's like I'm programmed, on autopilot.

"Did you and Rob have sex today?" he asks.

"No."

"Are you going to have sex with him tonight?"

"I don't know." Probably not. I can fuck angry, but Rob's like a woman: sex is an outgrowth of intimacy.

"I love that picture you sent me. You're so beautiful, Dawn." His voice is growing syrupy. He can see me in his arms right now, and I can see it, too.

Rob and I are down to once a week, and we don't talk about sex, we never really have. It's something to be done, not to be imagined, and I miss this—stoking the fire, knowing it'll blaze later.

I need to stop. I shouldn't be talking this way. Listening this way. I've been cheated on, yes, but I don't cheat.

"I'm married," I say.

"If I had a dollar for every text where you wrote that." I can hear him smiling. His body is stretched out languidly, a rubber band waiting to be snapped. One of the things I used to love most about sex with Aston was the contrast: the slack, and the tension. He was a master of that.

"Admit it," he says. "You're into me, at least a little."

I don't answer, which he probably takes as a yes. I should stop this right now. Hang up. Rob could be back any minute.

"I was with someone last week," Thad continues. "I kept my eyes closed so I could turn her into you. My tongue was in her pussy, and I imagined your taste. Salty-sweet." His hand is on his cock, I know it is.

I won't allow my hand to move. I'm not a cheater, and Rob could be driving up right now. But I am wet.

"I don't even need to come," he tells me, "I just want you to."

"Bullshit."

"I'm not saying I wouldn't come after, but first, I do you. Head to toe, every part of you." He moans.

He keeps talking, telling me where he's licking and kneading and how my body responds, and then it does respond, involuntarily. I shudder to a stop, without having moved. He did it all.

But I don't make a sound. I won't give him the satisfaction.

Only he must sense what's happened, because he gets his anyway. In growls and snarls and yelps, like a dog whose chain has just been cut. I've never heard a man come like that.

"Dawn," he says, again and again.

I'm silent, staring at the door. I came on my couch with a man who's not my husband, when I knew Rob could return any minute and find me. That's part of what made it so hot.

"Where are you?" he says. "I want to see it in my mind. The exact spot where I made you come."

"You didn't 'make' me anything." I'm suddenly furious, though I keep my voice low. Rob could be walking up the building stairs right now.

"I could feel it, Dawn, even if I couldn't hear it. I know you couldn't let it out with Rob around. How far away is he? The next room? On the other side of the bed?"

"It's eight o'clock, asshole. We're not in bed."

"Why are you so pissed?"

"Because you used me. And I'm telling you, I did not come. I didn't get anything out of that. It was all about you, and not me, and don't ever pretend otherwise."

He's quiet for a minute. "I'm sorry. I never meant to use you. I wanted to be close to you. I thought you'd like it."

"I didn't like it. You don't respect me. You don't respect my marriage."

"You're right about the marriage part. Sorry to break this to you, but there's no way that guy is satisfying you if you're texting me all the time."

"You're texting me all the time!"

"I can be an asshole, that part's true. I just, I don't know, I feel like there's this connection between us."

That connection, insanely enough, is his mother. But he couldn't know that. Could he? Could this whole thing be a way for him to get back at his mother?

I know he dislikes Miranda. He hasn't said that much, but it's pretty obvious.

"Am I wrong?" he asks. Pleads, really. "If I'm wrong, if there's nothing here, I'll stop texting. I won't call you again. Is that what you want?"

"I don't know what I want." But I know I don't want him to go away. I just can't tell him that, not right now.

"I'm sensitive to rejection, is the thing. My mom"—it's hard to believe we're going to talk about his mother less than five minutes after near-simultaneous orgasm—"she messed me up. She was all up in my business, but cold. She could give a lecture, but fuck if she knew how to give a hug."

The hug thing again. I'm guessing he's learned that the way to draw women in is to play the bad boy who, deep down, is just wounded and hurt, who needs a good woman to love him. I'm more susceptible to that ruse than most, because I think it might actually be true. We're made bad by our bad parents. So who did it to me, really, my father or my mother?

The funny thing is, I'm most drawn in because of who Thad's mother is. Because Thad holds the key to Miranda, and Miranda holds the key to something that I can't yet understand.

"I should go," he says.

"You get what you want and you hang up?"

"You mean you don't want me to go?"

He's a tricky son of a bitch. Ha ha, son of a bitch. He really is. "No, you should go."

"I wasn't trying to use you, Dawn. I feel like I'm falling for you."

"Don't."

"Like that's ever worked. Do you know how many times I touched hot stoves growing up?"

I laugh. "You warned me you're an idiot."

"An asshole. I never said idiot. But I'm a fool for you."

"You're corny, that's for sure."

"Can I call you again sometime?"

"Let me think about it."

But I already know my answer, and I'm pretty sure he does, too.

38

Miranda

Kimberly Zhou was born in Hong Kong and speaks eight languages fluently. She is able to bring international flair (and international buyers) to the Westside real estate market, with an emphasis on the beach neighborhoods. In the past three years, she has broken records in Long Beach, Pacific Palisades, Marina del Rey, and Venice. She plans to break more.

It's been on the tip of my tongue all morning, my confession, but I look at Larry and I remember his rigid body beside me the night I said Thad's name and I just can't bring myself to speak.

Confess, and I subvert Thad's blackmail. I take away his power.

Confess, and Thad will likely have destroyed my marriage.

I tell myself that addiction has recalibrated Thad's moral compass, that he's not entirely to blame, that he's not trying to destroy me, he's just trying to meet his own needs, rapaciously. But in his increasingly sporadic texts to me and his much more consistent tweets to the world, he sounds so upbeat. His conscience isn't eating at him at all; he's completely fine with what he's done. Maybe he's even happy with it. He's turned the tables on his manipulative mother, and secured himself double rent. This is as enterprising as Thad gets.

The word that comes to mind is "soulless." And if that's true, then the world isn't what I thought it was. If Thad can do this, then there must be no bounds for someone like Dawn.

I'm torn up by betrayal, anger, and fear, yet I'm doing my best to keep up appearances. Right now, I've got a frozen smile on my face as I tour the Santa Monica house with Larry and Kimberly Zhou, the Realtor who came highly recommended by Larry's colleague. She's petite and lovely. She doesn't walk so much as levitate; her steps are that light. She plays it up, in silver ballet flats and a diaphanous dress. Her hair is black and absurdly lustrous, cut in an asymmetrical bob with the straightest bangs I've ever seen. She must get her hair cut every three days to maintain it.

Her personality is just as blunt. "I don't blow smoke," she says repeatedly, and presumably the end of that sentence, left unspoken, is "up your ass." Even though I'd dislike any Realtor at this moment, I especially dislike this one. She hasn't said a kind word about the house yet, just a series of "mm-hms" and the occasional "you'll want to put some money into upgrading this." Her proprietary air suggests she knows she's got the job as our sales agent, it's just a matter of whether she wants to accept.

Larry likes her, I can tell. He's amused by her go-getter affectations.

She pulls back the curtain on the tub in the back bathroom, a move that seems inappropriate to me, too intimate, as if she's saying she thinks we might be hiding the body in there. Given her demeanor, I suspect she'd sell a house where a murder had recently occurred, qualm-free; she would just want to make sure she represented both the seller and the buyer for double the commission.

I fight the urge to yank the curtain back into place, but then my eyes follow hers to a ring of dirt in the white tub.

Kimberly raises an eyebrow. "That's not permanent, is it?"

"No," I say. "The cleaners must have missed that."

There's no way they missed that. They might have forgotten to put out toiletries before, but they would never commit an oversight this egregious.

It has to be Dawn. This is the answer to my groveling e-mail: "You want a stain, I'll give you a stain." The war is raging on.

She's saying she can get to me, whenever she wants. After all, she's entered both my houses, in a week's time. Or someone has, at her request. I'm not safe, not at all.

I can only pray that I'm wrong. My mind searches for alternate explanations. For example, the cleaners could have been less thorough than usual because they knew it would be their last time working for me. It could be another fluke, like the dead rat that's indigenous to Beverly Hills.

But I don't believe it about the rat, and I certainly don't believe it about this ring. Two "coincidences" makes a pattern, even if I can't get Officer Llewellyn to see it. I imagine his eye roll to the colleague at the next desk if I call him about this one.

Is part of Dawn's scheme to rob me of all confidence and credibility? Has anyone ever been so diabolical?

"Have those cleaners come back out and take care of what they missed the first time around," Larry says. He sounds irate, and it takes me a second to realize it's at me, not at the cleaners. He clearly thought I should have done a walk-through myself before

Kimberly arrived. I'm supposed to take care of everything in our lives, no grime left behind. "You coming?"

I give him a sharp look that he fails to notice; his focus is on Kimberly. I trail behind them. She's got a suggestion about adding some wainscoting, though we can talk more about that later. Larry is lapping at her feet.

I feel faint as I walk behind them down the stairs. We're headed for the back door, and I know she'll have problems with the yard. It's just a rectangle of grass. My parents wanted as little upkeep as possible, and despite my love of gardening, I can't bear to change an inch. I can still hear my dad when he realized that you can't get a teenager to mow a lawn anymore, "not even for twenty bucks," and I remember how we all shared a laugh at his incredulity, and he pinched my mother on what he called her "keister," and she swatted him with a dishrag, still laughing. Landscaping would feel like a betrayal of that idyllic scene.

But I've got bigger problems than the lawn. We approach the back door, next to the laundry room, and I see muddy footprints across the linoleum. The footprints are large, men's. They must have been made by someone Dawn is manipulating, or paying.

Paying might be worse for me. A mercenary might have no limits as to what he's willing to do.

Just a few minutes ago I was mocking Kimberly about representing a house where a murder had happened. Now I'm worried that I'll be the victim.

I'm blowing this out of proportion. A rat, some footprints, a tub ring—it's not like it equals . . .

This all started with some sheets and $200. I've already refunded her double. Anyone else would have dropped this long ago. Dawn really must be nuts, capable of anything.

"If you hadn't already laid those cleaners off," Larry says, "I would tell you to fire them immediately." He yanks open the back door.

Kimberly is rattling off more ideas about the cheapest way to improve the yard, ASAP. "It absolutely can't stay like that," she says, "but maybe we can get away with just buying a play structure. That could mean we're cultivating parents with young children, which has its advantages and disadvantages, especially since it's only a two-bedroom. Let me think on it more."

We return to the living room and Kimberly delivers her findings. "I want this listing," she says. "Someone will pay top dollar for it, I'll see to that. But I won't blow smoke." She thinks we need to stage the house—"this nautical thing is not doing you any favors"—which she'll pay for, but we'll also need to do some renovations, which we'd need to cover ourselves. "I'll tell you exactly which types of fixtures, enamels, trims, et cetera. You'll want to follow my recommendations exactly."

"Why's that?" I ask. My social graces are gone by this point.

"Because with the Santa Monica tech boom and the right upgrades, we can get four and a half million for this house."

Larry shoots me a glance of barely concealed pleasure. That would be an improbably huge profit—almost triple what my parents paid in the span of ten years.

Larry turns back to Kimberly with his poker face. "And how do we know you're the one for the job?"

Kimberly pulls out her portfolio: glossy pictures of houses she's sold, and the listings of nearby comps, highlighting the records she's broken. Larry grills her for a little while but it feels purely de rigueur. He's already sold, and he's convinced that she'll do the same for whoever comes in the front door.

"You're on a walk street, and location is everything," she says. "Plus, the house is gorgeous. The views are spectacular." Her voice is affectless. She seems unaware that it's the first compliment she's paid to the property she's declaring to be worth more than four million dollars. It occurs to me that this could be a strategy on her part. We expect Realtors to fawn all over us, the customer is always right, blah blah. She's playing hard to get. Based on Larry's expression, it's working.

Now she's explaining what a genius marketer she is, all the different themed open houses she's done, the creativity she'll bring, the catering, the high-end staging, all on her dime. "I haven't broken any records yet in Santa Monica, and I want to. I think this is the house to do it."

"We'd like that, too." Larry grins at her.

"The views are the star, but," she warns, "the improvements have to be made. A $100K investment will net you half a million. We'll have a bidding war, I guarantee it."

"Four million plus a bidding war?" I can't contain my skepticism. The hubris of young people—the Kimberlys, the Dawns, the Thads—is revolting.

"We price it at four million, or just under, and we'll end up where we want to be. Trust me, I know what I'm doing."

"There's something I should mention," Larry says, and it has a sound like he's putting on the brakes. I look at him hopefully. "The house needs a new foundation. To the tune of thirty-five thousand."

"Well, that will need to be taken care of before we sell, absolutely. We need to do it fast, just like the rest of the renovations. We want this on the market during the summer months, July at the absolute latest. We want the option of families, and kids start school in August."

Larry takes the foundation estimate out of his wallet. I feel stricken. I didn't expect him to actually bring it here, to hand it over to another woman. It's like he's just felt her up right in front of me.

As Kimberly scans the paper, she adopts a look of overblown horror. "You cannot go with these people. Where did you ever find them?" She might as well have asked if I got a degree from Moron University.

This is how she talks to a potential customer? I look at Larry, expecting him to be offended, but instead he just says, quietly, "Miranda found them." Like I've embarrassed him. Like he's losing faith in my judgment by the second. Instead, he trusts Kimberly, whom he met a half hour ago, the woman least likely to understand a sentimental attachment.

"They came recommended," I say.

Kimberly shakes her head. "Good thing I came along. I have my own guys. They'll give you a great deal, plus they'll work fast. You might not need as much work as you think." She holds the estimate back out to Larry, as if it's dripping with blood. "These guys are notorious for upselling. You might need a minor repair, and they'll tell you it's a total replacement, like they did here."

That's what I was counting on.

My face flushes. How long until Larry's onto me?

I won't just sit and wait. I flash on the tub, and the muddy footsteps. Dawn's taken this battle straight to my door and beyond the threshold, literally. It's time to stop playing defense.

"Would you excuse us for a moment?" I say, implying that Kimberly should step out.

"Of course." She doesn't budge from our couch. She's staggeringly impudent, that's the only word for it. Well, there's another. Bitch. This is an entitled bitch. She's gotten everything she's ever wanted. I do not want her to have this listing, especially if it's worth four million and change.

Larry follows me into the kitchen and I commence whispering. Whispering, in *my* home! Because she's planted on our couch like an azalea bush, like she's the native.

"I don't trust her," I tell Larry. "She's too young, for one thing."

"That's in the plus column, in my book. She's full of energy. It's amazing, her success in such a short time."

"We didn't see her failures. The houses she overpriced and couldn't sell."

"You saw the link I sent you, right? I did my research. What do you take me for?"

I'm not sure if that was a dig about the foundation work estimate or not. I choose to think not.

"Who recommended her," I ask, "Peter?" He nods. "I'm pretty sure he's sleeping with her. She's just his type." Peter's conquests are legendary. His wife is a mousy old thing who stayed home raising their children, and the criteria for his girlfriends are that they're pre-thirty and ambitious.

Larry waves a hand dismissively, but he doesn't actually deny it. "She knows her stuff. She's got a vision, and a hell of an impressive track record already. Let's go with her."

"We haven't decided we're going with anyone. Have we?"

He squinches his face. It's clear that we—as in, he—have already decided.

No more defense. I'm going to need to go on the offensive, if I want to save all I have.

Nice hasn't gotten me anywhere in life. I don't have the respect of my son or my husband. I'm dealing with people who are capable of anything, and I have to be, too. They're soulless; I'll be heartless. After all, Thad's already ripped mine clean out of my chest.

39

Dawn

Thanks for the refund. Better late than never, I guess. And while I appre-
ciate your epiphany, I'm standing by my reviews. You did what you did,
and you can't undo it now. We all have to sit with the consequences of
our actions, no matter the size of our bank accounts or our houses or who
we married.

I delete everything after "actions" and send the text. It's not
nearly as satisfying as I would have hoped. Sure, I'm an irritant, a
pebble in Miranda's shoe, but we're still worlds apart. For example,
I'm about to go fishing in the bathtub drain with an unspooled wire
hanger, and she's got people for tasks like this. No review I post can
change that.

But she's also got Thad. And, in my way, so do I. It's just a question of what to do with him.

After a few probes with the metal formerly known as a hanger, I remove the dangling hair clot and carry it over to the trash can. This cannot seriously be my life.

Sure, I do most household tasks since Rob works more hours than I attend class, and he brings home the bacon; it's only fair. But he should be able to wipe up Doritos crumbs, and his own urine from the rim of the toilet. I feel like he's on some passive-aggressive trip. He got home after ten on Saturday night, claimed he had lots of engraving to do, and he didn't send a single text, day or night. He was probably waiting on one from me, something sweet, telling him I couldn't wait to see him. Well, I'm not feeling so sweet lately.

I don't even get what his problem is. Is it that I have my own mind and feelings and past, and I won't jump at his every suggestion? Why is he so eager to get me out of town to visit my mother anyway? It would be the ultimate irony if my straight-arrow husband had someone on the side.

No, despite everything, I know he wouldn't do that. It's just that something's changed between us, and I don't know if it's him or me. My dad's death is killing my marriage.

Another text from Thad, saying nothing. Well, he's saying something. He's saying, "Waah, I'm insecure."

What part of "don't call me, I'll call you" does he not understand?

Still, it's harder than I would have expected to ignore him. I don't miss Rob, exactly, but I do kind of miss Thad.

I take a quick shower, get dressed, and head for campus. Professor Myerson told me to stop by his office before class, and some part of me is sure it's bad news. I feel the hot breath of graduation on my neck.

If finally getting my bachelor's degree doesn't create a sense of pride and excitement, would having a baby? What if it didn't? Sometimes having a child just seems like Russian roulette. You could get

Rob, or you could get Thad. You could have a bullet lodged in your brain for years on end. Years without end.

I wait outside Professor Myerson's door while he finishes up with another student. My phone pings another incoming text.

Don't freeze me out, Dawn.

Oh, shut up.

Real mature.

Like it's real mature to say "real mature."

This is what you do, Dawn. It's your m.o. You get too close, and then you disappear. You don't want anyone to really know you. I'm not going to let you get away with it.

You don't know me, or my m.o.

Exactly my point.

This is pointless.

I don't want to be clever with you. Let me in.

No. Stay out. Where's my skull and crossbones emoji?

Does your husband let you get away with this shit? Is that why you stay with him?

I'm not going to answer that. I shouldn't have answered him at all.

See, now you're going to run away. You're too good for that.

See, he really doesn't know me at all.

Finally, Professor Myerson ushers me into his office. If possible, there seems to be even more paper and less space than last time.

"I've been thinking about your conundrum," he says, "and I think I've got something for you."

It's the last thing I expected to hear. In our previous meeting, he slipped out the back door rather than continue our conversation. Not that this broom closet has a back door. This office does not engender hope, frankly. It reminds me how third-tier my school really is.

"I can get you an interview with a VP at Whaley-Barnum." He's practically oozing self-satisfaction.

"The pharmaceutical company?" I tell him I want an ethical job that pays and he comes up with Big Pharma?

He nods, still looking all puffed up. "You'd be part of a program to combat the misunderstandings about vaccines. Measles has made a comeback, and potentially deadly diseases could do the same. So you'd be on the front lines, so to speak. You'd be trying to reach all the parents who believe, without any real scientific evidence, that vaccinations could cause autism and other problems."

"I'd be communicating about something that really matters," I say. I want to smile, but I'm afraid. It seems too good to be true.

"Exactly."

"And making real money to boot."

His grin broadens. "Exactly. I've already talked you up to the VP. All you need to do is get me your resume, I'll pass it along, and he'll schedule the interview."

"You really think I've got a shot at this?"

"You've got a great shot. I told him all about you."

Now I am smiling, bigger than I have in I don't know how long. "You don't know what this means to me. I've been so stressed out. Thank you so, so much!" I'd like to hug him but I don't want to give him the wrong idea. I'd hate to learn that there's a catch.

"You're very welcome." He stands up, glancing at his watch. I love this guy. Who actually wears a watch anymore? "Let's get to class."

I nearly dance out of the office, with Professor Myerson by my side.

A few minutes ago, I was afraid it was all over for me. Now I feel like it's just beginning.

40

Miranda

It was so good to meet you, Miranda! Just let me know if I can answer any questions for you. I've got a million ideas about your house. Really, I can think about nothing else. I'd make you my first priority.

Kimberly

Larry and I made it through a dinner of takeout Thai food without talking about Kimberly Zhou, though that meant we were nearly silent. Neither of us wanted to broach such an incendiary topic.

Larry and I have always had a very civil marriage. It was modeled by my parents, while Larry's parents illustrated the opposite. They used to have knock-down-drag-outs every few days, to hear him tell it. In contrast and sometimes through great effort (and fraught silence, like tonight), we've created a peaceful home. I think that's to our credit, given the strain of Thad's problems. A family member's addiction is a series of earthquakes, and marriages built on a fault line don't survive. Nar-Anon has certainly taught me that.

Larry scoops up one last mouthful of tofu and vegetables. "That hit the spot."

I was mostly pushing the food around my plate, too nervous to eat. I've lost five pounds over the past few weeks. "Do you want any dessert?"

He shakes his head, his expression turning grave. "You know we need to talk, right?"

"I'm afraid so." I try to smile.

"Selling's the only thing that makes sense. You must realize that."

"The market keeps going up. We could call Kimberly in a year." I'm fighting to sound as reasonable as he does.

He shakes his head again. "The bubble could pop, and Kimberly is excited now. She wants to take this on. Who knows how she'll feel in a year?"

"She'll feel like she can get five million."

"There are no guarantees."

"Right. She might not be able to get us the price she says she can. So why not let the house keep appreciating?" My reasonable tone is fast becoming whiny. I need to hold my own. Be a grown-up. "Larry, I want to keep the house."

"Why? You said yourself that you're tired of handling the rentals."

"It's not that."

"Then what is it?"

I'm trapping myself already. I'm not as good with words as other people. Larry, or even Dawn. What's she doing in this conversation? Rats and muddy shoes, that's what. They haven't been far from my thoughts, nor has Thad's blackmail. "I want to do a long-term rental. I'm not ready to let go of the house yet."

"It's just a house. It's not your father."

I flinch.

He extends his arm, like an olive branch. His fingers caress mine. I want to pull my hand away. He has no compassion, he's just learned the mannerisms. This is what he does with his patients. "What I mean is, all your memories will still be yours, whether we keep the house or not. It isn't going to bring him back."

"I never said it was. I thought it might bring us forward. You and me. That we could retire there."

He looks at me with astonishment. "Retire ten miles away?"

"It's a whole different way of life. You saw what it did for my father. He was like a new man. My parents were the best I'd ever seen them."

"You think it'll do that for us?" It's almost like he pities my naïveté.

"I'd hoped."

"We don't need to grow closer. I'm not the workaholic your father was." Only he's more like my father than he realizes.

I want to tell him it's not about his work, or about that California king bed, or the vacations I have to mandate, and maybe it's not even about Thad, not entirely. I don't have the words, just the feeling, but that feeling is strong. Something's not right with us. The house that is my life has dry rot; the foundation can't hold. I want to think Dawn is the dry rot. If I rid myself of her, once and for all, by whatever means necessary . . .

"I'm never going to want to retire to that house," Larry says. His tone is gentle, but it feels brutal nonetheless. "So if that's the sticking point, let's get unstuck."

"You haven't truly considered it! You're just dismissing the idea out of hand, like you do with all my ideas."

He gives my finger an extra placating stroke. "Don't get frustrated."

"I'm allowed to get frustrated!"

That headshake again. "Maybe we should table this discussion until you're calmer."

"I want to resolve it now. I don't need this hanging over my head anymore." I have to start eating and sleeping again. I can't take this another night. I won't. No defense anymore; it's time for offense. "It's my house, and I won't sell it."

His eyebrows rise. "I'm your husband. What's mine is yours, and vice versa."

"It was left to me. It's actually my house."

"I never insisted that you put my name on the deed because I trusted you. Was I wrong in that?" He's working hard to maintain his own calm.

I want him to fail for once. "It's my home. And I'm not going to sell it."

"It's a marital asset. We have to agree." I see by his face that he's not so sure of that. "This is a decision we need to make together."

"You mean you tell me what's going to happen, and I concede, no matter that I feel the opposite. That's what we call joint decision-making." My words are coming out clear and strong. For once, I'm saying just what I mean.

I've thrown him off-kilter, I can see it. I relish it.

"Let's talk again tomorrow," he says finally.

"We don't need to. I'm settling this tonight."

"You're being a child."

"No. I'm not." I look him straight in the eye. "I don't like Kimberly, I won't work with her, and I don't have to. I'm going to rent the house out, and we can revisit this next year."

He stands up, throwing his open paper napkin on the table. It flits down like a butterfly. Part of me wants to laugh. He just looks so helpless, which is how I've felt for weeks. Years.

I'm not ready to end the conversation. "You can't steamroll me anymore. Not with the house, and not with Thad."

His eyes widen. With surprise and, finally, anger. "You want to bring Thad into this? You want to go down that road?"

"I want him back in my life. He's my son. I want to support him. Emotionally, and maybe financially, if I see fit." I don't know why it didn't come to me before. I don't have to admit to helping Thad previously; I can pretend that it's just from now forward. From here on out, I can take the money from our joint checking account. No more lying. No more hiding. It's my money, too, and it's the perfect solution. Regardless, I don't want to sell that house. I won't.

I'm not sure what's come over me—who I'm channeling, by what spirit I've been possessed. Who is this Miranda?

I don't know, but I like her. More than that, I respect her.

"We agreed not to support Thad ever again," Larry says. "We AGREED!" It turns into a roar.

"I never agreed. I just did it."

"Then that's on you, isn't it?" Larry is beginning to huff. I want to ask if he's taken his blood pressure medicine, but I won't. I can't lose my newfound thunder by becoming a mealy-mouthed nurturer.

"Thad's an addict, and we made him."

Larry's face is vicious. "*You* made him."

"You think it's my fault that he's an addict?"

He refuses to answer.

"Addiction runs in families, Larry." I don't need to say any more. "You're a doctor. You know better than anyone that genes can be destiny."

"If you talk about the residency . . ." It's the most ominous I've ever heard him. Before I can respond, he's stalked out of the room.

For so long, I've been his puppet. I haven't talked about Thad, or the residency. I've tried not to even think of the residency, but it comes back up on me like reflux whenever Larry behaves coldly or cruelly. Then I think about what he's done, but more than that, what he's capable of forgetting. Joshua Stanwyck's death doesn't seem to affect him at all. For Larry, it's like it never happened.

But I suffer my own guilt. If I'd confronted Larry about what I'd observed sooner, Joshua might still be alive.

I learned from my mother that happiness comes from knowing what's best left unacknowledged, even to oneself, and it was during Larry's residency that I began to hone my overlooking skills. I got in the habit of denying my intuition. I told myself that young doctors had to blow off steam from time to time. Besides, Larry had always prided himself on self-control. On a night out, he never had more than two glasses of wine, or one mixed drink. I'd never seen him drunk.

But I'd sensed it. He never slurred, and vodka has no scent, yet more than once before he went to work, I recognized a certain blurriness around his edges, like a photo out of focus. I told myself that having a drink or two was essentially the same as sleep deprivation, and that's an ordinary part of medical training. Besides, Larry drunk would be better than a lot of other doctors sober. He was that far out of their league.

Then Joshua Stanwyck died, at Larry's hand.

Even then, I told myself that he couldn't have been that bad in the operating room or there would have been suspicion on the part of one of his colleagues. An OR nurse, or one of the senior doctors. Perhaps it was just a coincidence that Larry had imbibed and the patient died in surgery. After all, the man who died was almost seventy, with two previous heart attacks, so the family must have known it was inevitable. According to Larry, they never suspected anything. There was no autopsy, no lawsuit. Larry got away clean.

No one would have been served by Larry turning himself in. He wasn't planning to be a surgeon, and he had the makings of a good doctor. Everyone said so, and it's proven to be true. Besides, he was deeply remorseful. I watched him cry. No, not just cry. He wept.

I promised to never mention the incident again. It would go into the marital vault. But he had to stop. He couldn't drink before (or God forbid, during) work ever again. Whatever demons were plaguing him, he had to find another way to beat them back.

I didn't insist that he stop drinking wine with dinner. I never said anything about the occasional nightcap. There was no need to be punitive. He felt bad enough about what had happened, and resolved to change his behavior. I believed in his resolve. I colluded with him in pretending it had only been the one time. I was loyal. We never spoke of it again.

In our marital mythology, it goes like this: He kicked his habit, cold turkey, without a single relapse. He didn't need AA or any other treatment. All he needed was my faith.

He says that if he could do it, Thad could, too. Thad just doesn't want it enough, isn't willing to make the necessary sacrifices. He's weak.

But Thad isn't the one who killed someone; Larry is. Who is Larry to cast the first stone, to cast his own son out? He's quick to forget the sins of the past, when they're his.

Sometimes, when I hear Larry talking about his colleagues, especially The Ignoramus, I get a twinge. It can't be good to believe your own press and to ignore your own fallibility. But who among us is good, really?

41

Dawn

I'm not really an addict, you know. Not anymore.

I thought it's once an addict, always an addict.

That's what they want you to think.

Right now, I'm at my kitchen table with my textbook open before me. But instead of reading, instead of brainstorming for my final Ethics project, I'm going back and forth with Thad, the nonaddict. I guess I can't stay mad at him. I need him, I'm just not sure for what.

Who wants me to think that?

The addict-industrial complex.

What do you mean?

There are plenty of people who make a lot of money by spreading the word that once an addict, always an addict. They tell you that you're going to have this monkey on your back forever, and you need them to scare it off. But it's never gone for good so you need their rehabs, aftercare, IOP.

What's IOP?

Intensive outpatient program.

You've done all that stuff?

I had to. I was under 18. My parents controlled my life.

Do you talk to them now?

This is the hold he's got on me, part of it, anyway. I'm still pissed at his mother. "Pissed" is too mild a word, actually. I have a slow simmering hate toward that woman. She's made me feel small, and poor, and pathetic, which takes me back years. She's regressed me.

But all that's about to change. The VP has already set up my interview. I wouldn't have thought he'd be so quick to call, since I don't exactly have the most impressive resume, but I do have a high GPA and Professor Myerson's recommendation.

I'm on my way. I just have to keep telling myself that, as often as it takes.

I talk to my mother as little as possible. My dad, not at all.

How little?

Right now, it's none.

Even knowing that Miranda's life is far from perfect—that she has a son who avoids her—doesn't put out the fire. I'm not sure what will, but I hope it'll be getting that job. When I'm doing my share of good in the world and getting paid handsomely for it, I'll leave all the darkness behind, once and for all.

Can I tell you a secret?

Has anyone ever answered no to that question? But Thad doesn't even wait for the answer.

I haven't used in more than a year. Not meth, or pills. I barely even drink alcohol.

That's a pretty disappointing secret, Thad.

But he's not finished.

I just let my mother think that I'm in constant danger of relapsing. I text and tweet to keep her afraid. I keep her on the roller coaster.

I'd almost feel bad for her, getting manipulated that way by her own son. But then I think of how she tried to manipulate me with $400 and a feigned epiphany, and I know that he must have learned it somewhere. Thad's giving her a taste of her own medicine. How bad of a mother must she have been for him to be able to do this to her? It just confirms what I've been thinking about her all along.

You probably think I'm an asshole now, for real.

I think relationships are complicated. Especially with parents.

See, I knew you'd get it.

I don't get it. I'm just giving you the benefit of the doubt.

As in, tell me your story. The story of you and your mother.

I'm not saying I never had a problem with drugs. I did, when I was a teenager. Young, like 12, 13. But then I realized I could control it whenever I wanted.

Sounds like bullshit. Addicts lose all control, right? They throw their lives away, and they don't stop just because they want to; they can't.

But then, that really could just be what the media spoon-feeds us. Some communications majors out there are definitely working for the rehab-industrial complex, or whatever Thad called it. Spin's powerful.

I played this cat-and-mouse game through high school. I used to let them catch me so I'd get sent away. Then I'd get myself kicked out of the programs. I just couldn't sit still, was the problem. I got bored a lot. I needed to get away from her.

What was so bad about her?

She's distant. She's relentless. She was always spying and when she'd find something, she'd try to make me feel guilty about it. She'd talk about how I was killing her. Crocodile tears.

So she was a phony.

To the bone. Recently, I tried to give her another chance, to open up to her, and it didn't get me anywhere. You can't believe anything that woman says.

She must really love you, though, right, to put up with all your shit?

She says so, but like it's something she's cashing in on. A way to get me to do things. She never hugged me.

You've mentioned that.

She never wanted me close. When I was little, she tucked me in like I was a cyanide capsule. I was her job. She wanted to quit but couldn't. She was trying to get fired.

So you don't think she liked being a mom?

She didn't like me, that's all I know.

I've had that thought, too. That my parents would have liked another kid better. That maybe it was something about me that was bad or wrong. Something that my father could eventually use for his own ends.

That must have hurt. I know it does.

You hit me, I hit you back twice as hard. Ten times.

Is that from a rap song?

I'm just saying, she doesn't get to me now. I get to her.

How?

I let her chase me. She has to follow me on Twitter and Instagram. I only answer her texts when I need to.

When's that?

When there's money involved.

So your parents support you?

Not my dad. My mom. She hides it from him. It would destroy their marriage, if he knew. He cut me off, and she was supposed to do the same.

Pay dirt. I knew there was some serendipitous reason Thad had come into my life, something he was meant to tell me.

I won't do anything with it, not right now. But she'd better not push me. Ratting her out to the city attorney is nothing compared to ratting her out to her big-deal doctor husband. Yet for some reason, I find myself texting, *She must love you, if she keeps helping you.*

It's not love. It's fear.

What's she afraid of?

Right now, she's afraid I'll tell him.

Before that?

Here's the thing, Dawn. I'm not an addict, but I play one on Twitter because it's the best way to keep the money coming in. She pays so I won't rob people. So I won't fuck people for cash and drugs. That's how little she thinks of me.

Addicts do that kind of thing, though, right?

I never did. I only stole from her and my dad. I've got principles.

I'm not even going to touch that one.

Maybe she pays so you'll have someplace to live, and food to eat. Maybe she's trying to keep you alive.

Whose side am I on here? It's like I'm starting to feel for Miranda, just a little.

You don't give an addict money if you want him to stay alive. You know he'll spend it on drugs. You give him money if you want him dead.

Do you really think that?

She wants me to overdose. Then her problems would be over. Other than me, she's got a great life.

My mind reels. Would any mother do that? If so, I've encountered true evil. Miranda could make my mom look good.

But I don't even care. What I care about is my dad. He's what I miss.

What do you miss about him?

Sometimes late at night, he'd come into my room.

No happy story has ever followed a line like that.

We'd talk for hours. Those were some of my best memories. He was so

*honest. About his life, and about my mom. That's how I first learned what
she's really like.*

I'm about to ask more when I hear the front door open. Rob
didn't tell me he was coming home early, almost like he wanted to
catch me in the act.

42

Miranda

#happyfuckingmothersday

Thad is barely three. He wakes up crying—not screaming, as he often does, but a truly forlorn wail. He is plaintive, my little boy, and this is why you become a mother. So you can be needed in just this way. Not yelled at and kicked and told over and over again "Bad mommy," not like my usual days and nights. No, this is different.

I've made it a point never to go into his room when he's scream-ing, in an effort to break him of that habit. No reinforcement for that behavior. There's a lot of behavior that gets ignored in our house. But this is different.

I go into his room, and Thad is standing up in his bed, his arms outstretched, his butt thrust out. He needs me, there's no question, and my insides turn gooey. I am so full of love, just as I always meant to be.

I don't immediately lift him up. I proceed with caution, as if it might be a trick, a bomb about to detonate in my face. "Are you sick?" I ask. He nods. "Is it your tummy?"

He says yes in a small voice, a rare voice.

"Do you need to poop?" He doesn't think so. "Should I put you on the toilet?" He shakes his head no. "Would you like to sit in my lap and read a book?" I offer it hesitantly, afraid he'll snatch this moment away.

It would be a dream realized. Thad doesn't like books, and he doesn't like my lap, not normally. But perhaps this is a turning point, a chance to start over. I will be his new and better mommy, and he will be my new and better boy.

"Yes," he says, still so soft that I nearly moan with happiness. Yet I have to keep my face neutral. If I betray too much emotion, he can prey on it.

Do I really think this about my three-year-old? Yes, sadly, I do.

I pick him up and he smells so sweet, this boy of mine, and his body is relaxed, not rigid like usual, and he's leaning into me with all he has. I carry him over to the never-used rocking chair gingerly, not wanting to break the spell. I can reach the bookshelf from here—this was to be our reading corner—and I squint because the only illumination is the night-light. But I can't turn on the overhead, that would surely break the spell.

I can't really make out the words on each page of *The Cat in the Hat*, but it doesn't matter. Thad doesn't know them anyway. So I hold him close and I breathe him in and I make up rhymes to fit the illustrations. I approximate. Thing One and Thing Two don't want to be late for important dates; Sally says "no, no, I will not go"; and the Cat in the Hat says his tricks are not bad, though sometimes he's sad.

We read book after book this way, and Thad snuggles like he's wanted to do this his whole young life, and I think, Yes, it's all worth it, finally, it's all worth it. Then I think, Why hasn't this happened before? Isn't it this way for all the other mothers, all the time? Why is it always such a battle? I shouldn't think this, I can't squander my opportunity with bitterness. I need to just enjoy it, this moment, which is also a little creepy, enjoying a little boy's constipation-induced closeness, but it's not like I'm inducing it myself, or willing it into being.

So we read, and I'm as happy as I've ever been, and he's as content as I've ever seen him. Eventually, I ask if he wants to sit on the toilet. He says no, no, he wants to go back to bed. "With you," he says.

He's never wanted that before, and I've never even thought to suggest it. But I curl myself around him in his bed, and he stares into my face with the sort of love and wonder I've been dreaming about not just his whole life but my whole life, too.

"Try to close your eyes," I tell him, but neither of us does.

As soon as his eyelids droop, they open again, and he's smiling at me.

"Keep them closed," I say gently, "that's how sleep works."

He tries, he really does, and I do, too, but we can't sleep. I'm thinking what to do when Thad says, "I want a hug from Daddy. Then I can sleep."

I'm not sure Larry would want to be woken up; in fact, I'm pretty sure he wouldn't. But maybe he'd get to experience the kind of moment I just had, the connection with Thad that is so hard to attain, and I don't want to rob Larry or Thad of that, though a part of me doesn't want to share it either.

"Do you want to sleep in Mommy and Daddy's bed?" I ask Thad. He says yes.

We go into my room, and into bed. "Larry, Thad's here," I say.

"He wanted to be with us." Larry grunts in some sort of acknowledgment but without approval or engagement. I worry that Thad will feel rejected, but he's resilient. He climbs all over Larry, and eventually, Larry not only hugs him but wants to take care of him. He's vulnerable, this Thad, in a way that he isn't during daylight hours, and Larry responds to it, just as I did. We all try to sleep, snuggled up together, though none of us do. Larry tries to teach Thad how to slow his breathing and count in his head. We're all awake, and we'll pay for it tomorrow, but that's okay. More than okay.

Then I see that Thad has his eyes wide open, and he's staring right at me, differently than earlier. It's not love or wonder I see now. Just wide eyes, and a hand moving across his little thing, inside his pajama bottoms. He knows I don't like to see that. It disturbs me because he's so young; I've been too ashamed to even tell the pediatrician about my oversexed boy. I've told Thad not to do it around me, ever, and here he is, in my bed, staring right at me, and I'm sure that he's smirking.

I suddenly know that he's engineered this whole thing, lulled me into a false sense of security—no, worse, into a sense of love—so that he can mock me. So that he can defile my bed. So that he can humiliate me.

I'm filled with a fury I've never felt before. I haul him out of the bed, with him kicking and screaming as if at an injustice, and I throw him back into his own bed, not even caring if that thump is his head against the wall, I'm that angry. I don't give him one word of explanation, because he knows.

I slam the door behind me. I'm breathing heavily, leaning outside his door, and he's screaming bloody murder. I start to cry, because that's the Thad I've always known.

43

Dawn

I'm so lucky to have a mother-in-law like you!
Happy Mother's Day!
Love,
Dawn

I have to admit, Thad is on my mind. There were his revelations about Miranda, and about himself, and how could I forget that orgasm the other night? Still, I turned my phone off hours ago. I have, effectively, blocked him. For the night, I need to focus on Rob.

We walk, hand in hand, along Telegraph Avenue. Our apartment building is on a street that's safe but less than chichi, near the many Ethiopian restaurants. We head toward the gastropubs, tapas bar, and organic ice cream shop. Tonight, it's artisanal pizza and cocktails at one of our favorite spots.

The walls are brick, and the lighting is low, which I appreciate since my skin is horrific.

Rob looks good tonight. He's better looking than Thad, I remind myself. Just because he talked a little shit about me to his parents, that doesn't have to mean anything. He's a kind person, and he wants me to be kind to my mother, that's all. A life partner is supposed to improve you.

He reaches over and touches my cheek lightly, and what I'm thinking is, Germs. Oil. Now I'm going to break out even more.

"You look pretty," he says.

"Thanks."

"My mom had a really good time at brunch."

That makes one of us. Well, three of them. I faked my way through, saying as little as I thought I could get away with. At one point, "Mom" talked about how sorry she felt for my mother, being completely alone on Mother's Day, and we all had a little moment of silence. Then I said, "I texted her, she's doing okay," and there was another moment of silence, this one laced with Thiebold judgment. "I sent flowers," I added, which was a lie, but it did the trick. Everyone relaxed again.

Tonight, Rob and I are drinking gin with house-made tonic and eating fat green marinated olives. I find myself eavesdropping on the couple next to us. They're having one of those pseudo-fights, where you keep your voice light as you say something you mean heavily. She says gaily, "Next time, text me if you're going to be late!" and he responds, "It was only ten minutes, but sure," and she says, "Let's split the squid pizza," and he says, "*Squid* pizza?" and so on. There's an underlying tension between them, no doubt, but it occurs to me that they're actually talking, unlike Rob and me.

Rob must realize it, too, because he starts telling a story about some demanding customer from the shop. I try to get interested.

I've always wanted to find Rob funnier than I do. It's not that he's humorless; he can appreciate a joke. We laugh together, sometimes. Ours is not a grim marriage.

But we're in a sexy restaurant, with sexy cocktails and sexy lighting, and I don't want to talk about engraving.

What does that leave? My job interview tomorrow, which has me terrified. Miranda's manipulative refund. My father. My mother. Thad.

I don't know what Rob would do if he found out about Thad. Most likely, he'd decide it's another indication of my abnormal character.

I so wish I'd never overheard that conversation. All I want is for Rob and me to get back to normal, together.

So I let him talk, and I fill in the blanks with smiles and laughter, and I drink.

We split the squid pizza. I notice that the couple beside us is splitting it, too. They're whispering. Their laughter is low, guttural, and intimate. Whatever was between them earlier has evaporated now. Maybe their bickering is a sort of foreplay. They're going to have sex tonight, no question.

Rob and I walk home, hand in hand once again. As the pedestrians thin, I stumble into him in what I hope is a come-hither manner. Glancing at his face, at the set of his jaw, he doesn't look like a man who's about to get lucky. He looks like he's feeling anything but.

That's when it occurs to me: This is just as forced and effortful for him as it is for me. The storytelling, the hand-holding, the favorite bar.

Somehow, that makes me feel closer to him. We're in this together.

I squeeze his hand, and he looks down at me. His eyes shimmer, with moonlight or tears. "I love you," I say.

"I've always loved you," he answers, with great feeling. It's a strange sentiment, like a form of good-bye. But I could be misinterpreting him.

I reach up and hug him. In the middle of the sidewalk, he's clutching, I'm clinging, and we're both crying. Whatever illness exists between us, there's an antidote, and we'll find it, together.

When we start walking again, Rob's arm is tight around me. Once inside the apartment, I light upon him immediately, not so much seized by passion as determined to seal the deal.

Rob seems surprised but enthusiastic. We haven't done it outside of the bedroom in I don't know how long. We kiss up against the living room wall, his hands in my hair, my fingers clawing at the button of his jeans.

I turn around. "From behind," I grunt. Without even seeing his face, I can feel that he's surprised again. He normally looks into my eyes for much of the time. But this isn't making love; it's making a pact. Whatever it takes. For better or for worse.

He starts touching my clit, delicately. I'm already wet, and that kind of tentative touch is going to dry me out. "Inside," I tell him. "Now."

He thrusts, and I moan. I've always liked his girth. He's the perfect size for me. See, we fit. Different worlds, but this is what matters.

I can feel that he's caught up, too, and he has to still himself for a second so that he won't come. I reach around, toward his ass. "What the . . . ," he says, but I continue. He'll get into it. They always do.

"Stop," he commands, and with a wet reverse suction, he withdraws.

I spin around to face him. He's calling me a whore, with his eyes.

"Let's go to the bed," he says, like it's some sort of consolation prize.

Thad would have liked it. He would never have pulled out, not in a million years.

Rob takes my hand, and I let myself be led. I imagine what he must be thinking—*This woman can't be the mother of my child*—and while I've imagined it before, with fear and dread, this is the first time I think, Good.

44

Miranda

Dear Dawn,

You are a terrible young woman. To accept a refund but not an apology? That speaks to your profound lack of character. I will post on all the websites I can find and smear your name as you've smeared mine.

Yours,

Miranda

Delete.

She'll know I'm bluffing. I don't know websites where I can smear her name. I don't have a degree in advanced Internet harassment like she does.

Could I hire someone to do it for me? If so, it wouldn't have to be just in the virtual world. Someone could leave a dead animal in her apartment, a skunk, maybe? I just want to scare her, that's all. Scare her off for good. Make her feel what she's made me feel.

I like indulging in these kinds of angry thoughts. Fantasies, I suppose they are. I don't feel so frightened and lost when I do. I don't think about the fallout in my marriage now that I've overpowered Larry for the first time.

He went away to a last-minute conference in Palm Springs. Usually, he goes to conferences three to four times a year. It's a time for him to let loose with his fellow docs and learn a little something, too. Since he's already been to two and it's only May, I'd asked him to pass on this particular one. I suggested we could take a vacation together instead, wouldn't that be nice? He declined. I was hurt. What does he get out of those conferences that he can't get from time away with me? I fear that I know.

Now he's headed to Palm Springs anyway. "We could both use some space, and some time to think," he said. Time for me to change my mind, that's what he really means.

I'm sure he's arrived by now, but he hasn't texted to tell me. Normally, he'd let me know that he'd checked in, with a little aside about the accommodations or his colleagues. So he's freezing me out. It's a threat, or the promise of what's to come if I don't see things his way.

Dawn,

Delete the posts or I'll sue you for character defamation. Even if I lose, I'll drag it out for years. I have two multimillion-dollar houses. My funds are limitless. Meanwhile, you'll go bankrupt from the legal fees. How much do you think communications majors earn? I'll take every cent from you one way or another. I'll take your husband's store. Try me.

Miranda

P.S. If anything else shows up broken, dead, or dirty at either
of my homes, it'll be worse for you. I guarantee it.

It makes me smile a little, thinking of Dawn reading it, of her
quaking with fear, forced to realize that ultimately money is more
powerful than beauty.

"What do you think of that one, Mom?" I ask her after I've read
it from my phone.

The smile leaves my face as I look at my mother, staring off into
the garden as if I haven't spoken. See no evil, hear no evil. For a
second, I envy her.

"Do you think it's too much? She started it." No response. "Remember when George and I were little and we used to point to each
other and say that, and you'd tell us, 'Well, go finish it yourselves'?"
I have an impulse to reach for her hand, though we never did that,
not even when I was little. She was an excellent mother, but not a
touchy-feely type. "Do you remember George and me as children?"

She glances over, and I think she's going to answer, but then her
eyes go away. Back to nothing. She prefers nothing to me.

I don't know what I was thinking, telling her my problem. Maybe
I hoped that some maternal instinct from days gone by would reassert itself. She'd see how much I still need my mommy, and she
wouldn't be able to help herself. She would have to take care of me,
so much so that it would override whatever's misfiring in her brain.

But it doesn't work that way, of course not, and I was foolish for
ever thinking that it could. For thinking I wasn't alone.

"Bye, Mom," I tell her, and with anyone else, the suddenness
would seem rude. But she just lifts a hand in a vague wavelike gesture, the remnant of social conventions from long ago.

As I get in my car, I tell myself that it's not so bad, having the
house to myself for a few days, eating for one instead of cooking for

two. Normally, it's like I cook for one, for Larry, since it's all about his preferences and tastes. That's become automatic, unquestioned. What he wants is what goes. Until now.

I don't know if I can stay strong and hold the line with Larry. But better not to think about it. Better to drive to Whole Foods where I can buy for one, and talk back to Dawn in my head. The gall of that girl, telling me about consequences. She's going to be the one looking over her shoulder soon. I just have to figure out how to make that happen. Proactive, rather than reactive. Offense instead of defense.

At Whole Foods, I get a basket instead of a cart, which feels freeing in and of itself, and I actually start to have fun, browsing the refrigerated case and considering my true desires. Do I want the roasted golden beets and kale salad or do I just think that's what a woman of my age and midsection should eat? How about salmon cake? Or meat loaf? Green beans almondine or herb-roasted new potatoes? I imagine each bite passing my lips and hitting my palate. I can have anything I want. I am limitless, just like I tell the Dawn in my head.

If I get fat, what's Larry going to do, divorce me? If he does, I get half his money. Of course, he could battle me for the Santa Monica house. It is a marital asset, in a divorce proceeding. But until that time, if I stand firm, it's all mine. The decision to sell or not rests with me.

Larry's not going to divorce me. I arrange his life. I make things hum. This was the first trip he ever went on where I didn't pack for him. He's the one who's bluffing.

I have power. Over Dawn, over Larry. I. Have. Power.

I'm about to place the meat loaf in my basket when I hear my name. My good feeling evaporates instantly. I don't want to interact with anyone, to have to say how I'm doing, or worse, to answer any questions about my resignation from the board. For a few minutes, I'd managed to forget that my reputation's in shambles. Now I remember, like a splash of cold water to the face.

I force myself to smile. It's a woman from Nar-Anon, the one I recognized at the recent meeting, from the ones I attended years before. I can't recall her name, which is embarrassing since she remembered mine.

"Hello!" I say, with a cheer that sounds cringingly false and perhaps inappropriate, given our association.

"Gail," she says, pointing at her chest. She's dressed strangely for the warm spring weather—in a heavy gray sweater-coat that reaches her knees over black leggings and high black boots. Her hair is pulled back in a tight bun, and her face is makeupless, revealing large brown swaths of sun damage. "I wouldn't expect you to remember my name. It's overwhelming, coming back to meetings."

"No, I remembered. You have a daughter about my son's age."

She shakes her head. I can't even get that right? "Not anymore."

"Oh." I look down, absurdly, at the transparent plastic cube in my hand, as I realize what she's just said. "I'm so sorry."

"It was last year. The group helps."

I didn't know that anyone continued to attend the group once their primary reason for attending had ceased to exist, once the fight had been lost. The drugs won. How do the others feel about her presence? She's a walking reminder of the worst-case scenario.

"Yvonne went to rehab for the third time," Gail says, "and for the first time, it seemed to be working. She was finally taking it in, all the lessons they were trying to teach her. She moved into a sober living house and was working the program. She called me every day. I thought I had my daughter back—the sweet one, the honest one.

And then she relapsed. She didn't know how to gauge her tolerance anymore, it had been so long. She overdosed."

"I'm so sorry," I say again. It's as useless and as good as anything else. It adheres to the Hippocratic oath, and does no harm.

She nods, accepting my condolence. There are no tears, I notice. It makes me wonder if what I've suspected, in my darkest heart, is true: That some part of you is relieved that the whole bloody thing is over, and you're no longer imprisoned by love, hope, and fear. Now it's just loss, and humans are wired to handle that. What we're not equipped for is years and years of helpless uncertainty and baseless hope. Evolution didn't properly prepare us. Fight or flight is worthless in the face of a child's self-destruction.

"You should come back," Gail says. "It works if you work it."

"I've heard that somewhere." I don't mean it to be snotty, but I think that's how it comes out. I'm rusty in talking to people. My mother would be mortified, if she could still feel. She raised me to have social graces above all else. No, protect your family above all else, by any means necessary.

"The community is what's kept my head above water," Gail says. "I don't know what I would have done without them."

Involuntarily, I glance at her naked ring finger. "I appreciate what you're saying. I think I'm okay, for now."

"We're there if you need us." She smiles. "What helps me the most is that I have so much still to learn, and so much to teach."

This could be my fate. A dead child, a dead marriage, and desperate delusions. What is there to learn once your child is gone? What wisdom can you glean, or impart, once the worst has come to pass? The idea that Gail has anything to teach when she couldn't prevent her own child's death . . .

What she unwittingly teaches is that we are all powerless. While that is, in fact, the AA message, and the NA message, and the Nar-Anon message, it's one that I'm still not ready to embrace.

I have to cave. I have to sell the Santa Monica house. Because no matter what I do, even if I convince Thad to try rehab again, I may very well lose him, but I don't have to lose Larry, too. I can't find myself permanently alone, like Gail.

"I'll see you at a meeting soon," I say. It's the path of least resistance. Let Gail think she's converted me.

"See you soon." I can't tell if she believes me or not. But the conversation is over, and I abandon my basket by the sliding glass doors. I've lost my appetite.

Once in my car, I start to hyperventilate. What if Thad's dead? I didn't even check his Twitter feed yesterday, and the day before that, there was nothing. He hasn't texted me for two days, and I was relieved. After that tweet about Mother's Day, I didn't want to have anything to do with him.

I'm the monster. No matter what he's done, a mother should never feel that way about her own child. He has a disease, but I'm the one who's really sick.

I'm sweating as I scroll through my phone. Nothing so far today. *Just thinking of you. It's been a while. Do you need any money?*

It's the question that always gets a response.

As I wait, I turn the key in the ignition and put the AC on the highest setting. I take deep breaths and try to think of nothing but the artificial breeze on my face.

I'm not angry anymore, Thad. Just text back.

His synapses have been hijacked, his higher brain functioning corrupted. He's as much a victim as my mother is. Morality requires the highest brain function, which means that Thad's amoral right now, like a very small child. But just one year sober, and his brain can begin to reset. One year of one day at a time.

Larry and I can compromise. We sell the Santa Monica house, and I support Thad openly, with Larry's full knowledge. I could write this latest check to Thad out of the joint account. That would kill two birds with one stone. It would let Thad know he can't blackmail me, and let Larry know that I'm standing firm on the subject of Thad. It would say that I'm not under either of their thumbs.

I have a four-million-dollar bargaining chip. I'd even be willing to go with Kimberly Zhou. Maybe.

Yet every part of me is screaming in protest. I want to keep my ancestral home. That terminology might seem like a bit of a stretch to some people, but that's how it feels to me. It's been in my family for two generations—my parents' and mine—and I want it for Thad (if he's clean) and for his kids (if he has them). Before that, I want to live there with my husband. That doesn't seem like so much to ask.

Oh, please, God. Please, Thad. Can anyone hear me out there, up there? Or have I been forsaken?

45

Dawn

- Career Objective: To add my abilities, creativity, and passion for communication to a company that is actively making a difference in the world.

I'm remarkably relaxed. Sean Hayworth is a super-nice guy, and so easy to talk to. Somehow, I didn't expect that from a VP at Big Pharma. Maybe he's not that high up—there could be a million VPs—but he has a pretty big office on a high floor in downtown San Francisco. He doesn't look that much older than me and he was a communications major, too, from my university. "Professor Myerson was my favorite, too," he told me early on in the interview, which doesn't even feel like an interview. It just feels like a conversation, and a good one at that.

I didn't sleep last night, running over the most likely interview questions in my head as well as trying to commit all the relevant details about the company to memory. At the start of the interview, I'm sure my nerves showed. I wanted so much to pass. I need to be good enough, and classy enough, for this building, this company, this office, Sean.

But Sean really wants to know who I am and what I want out of life. He's telling me those kinds of things about himself, which again, I didn't see coming, but it's disarming.

"I'm from up north, too," he says. "Fort Bragg."

"I always meant to go to the botanical garden there."

"That's pretty much all we've got. Well, that and coast."

"You can't knock the coast."

He grins. "Maybe not," he concedes. "What brought you to the Bay Area?"

"It was a long-standing obsession. I thought I'd go to San Francisco, but I could barely afford Oakland, let alone SF."

"What were you leaving behind? You have family up there?"

"Not much. Just my parents." He raises an eyebrow, like he thinks there's more to the story. "It wasn't the easiest childhood, that's all."

"The mean streets of Eureka?" He grins again.

"You'd be surprised." I'm surprised by what comes out of my mouth next. "After you've been hungry, you stay hungry."

He nods slowly, like he's taking it in. Reassessing me, maybe. For a second, I think that I revealed too much and, in doing so, undermined my whole goal, which was to pass. Be middle class, be normal, be employable.

"I like that," he says. "You can't teach hunger."

He's wrong; it's practically the only thing my parents did teach me.

"Believe me," he says, "I didn't think I would end up in Big Pharma either."

"Really?" I appreciate the change of subject.

He shakes his handsome head, and a medium-brown forelock flops forward boyishly. "It doesn't have the best reputation, does it?"

"No, it doesn't."

"I was exploring a lot of different industries, and I didn't know which way to go. I had a chemistry minor, and someone knew someone, and I talked to this incredibly genuine guy who understood my reservations. He actually liked that I had reservations. He knew that I was like you, and that once I'm in, I'm in all the way, so I have to choose carefully. He liked that I think before I just drink the Kool-Aid. And what he said to me was, 'We make medicines that improve people's lives. Sometimes we even save them. Are we a charity? No. But we make a difference.'"

"That's just what I want! To make a difference."

"That's who we need around here." He leans in. "I don't actually do the hiring. That's for the district managers, and you'll still have to get the seal of approval from Artie, go out for dinner or a drink or something with him, but I know he's going to love you. Professor Myerson told me I ought to meet you, that you're special. I see what he means."

I find myself blushing, though there's no seduction in Sean's gaze. But it is direct. He's looking right at me, and still, I did it. I passed! He wants me!

So why is there this feeling in the pit of my stomach, like it's too good to be true?

Because I distrust happiness, I always have. For good reason.

"There's a lot of competition for these jobs," he says. "Mostly, it's because they pay well. Pretty girls want to memorize some drug data and bat their eyelashes at doctors. They think that's all there is to it." I don't love that he said "pretty girls" rather than women. It seems a touch sexist. "There's a lot more to it than that. You have to be a person of conviction. You have to believe in our products and what they can do, that they're going to help people, and that you're the one to get the doctor to see that. It's a mission."

"Get the doctor to see what?" I'm a little confused. Professor Myerson said that I would be educating the public on vaccines. I thought that was my mission.

"You're making sure the doctors are armed with the latest medical research so they can do the best for their patients."

"Don't doctors already know about vaccines?"

"Right, the vaccine project. That'll be about ten percent of your time. The rest, you'd be out in the field, building relationships with the docs. We've got a new antidepressant coming to market. It's going to be exciting. Transformative."

I stare at his widening smile and I get it. Sean's been selling me. On a sales job. But why? He already said pretty girls are lining up. "What would my job title be?"

He laughs. "You'd be a pharmaceutical sales representative. Is that title enough for you?"

"More than enough," I say quietly.

"Let's be real here. It helps that you look the way you do. Everyone likes to talk to attractive people. But you're more than that. There's a quality to you, an intangible, that's what Professor Myerson called it, and what it means is that doctors will also want to listen to you. They'll want to be persuaded. That's why I like a communications major more than a biology major. You're bright, you'll learn the science. But you can't teach hunger, right?"

I should be flattered. I've got a successful executive from one of the top five pharmaceutical companies in the world sweet-talking me. But going into doctors' offices to "educate" them, when I don't even have a science background myself . . . sounds like I'm going to be trying to persuade them with my intangible quality.

Sean thinks I'd make a great whore.

Is that what Professor Myerson sees, too? I know what my dad thought. So what about Rob? And Thad?

Maybe I haven't been passing at all.

46

Miranda

The Joshua Stanwyck Foundation exists to fight medical malpractice. It focuses on education, advocacy, resources, and lobbying, because the medical profession needs to be held accountable for its actions.

The foundation was started by Kevin and Martha Stanwyck after the tragic death of their son Joshua. He was a bright, beautiful seventeen-year-old who went into surgery for appendicitis and never woke up, due to the actions of an anesthesiologist who had been awake for twenty straight hours. Joshua was robbed of his future, and Kevin and Martha want to be sure this never happens to any other children, or their parents.

I have to fight to return my attention to Lex. His name is stitched on his pocket, orange thread on a brown canvas shirt. I just keep thinking of young Joshua Stanwyck, and his poor parents. Larry destroyed their family, and then he destroyed the reputation of an anesthesiologist to save himself. There's no other explanation, is there?

"The system is armed. Can you see the lights?" Lex is speaking slowly. He clearly thinks I'm a dotty old woman, still in my pajamas and robe at two P.M.

"It looks like it's armed," I say, "but someone's gotten in before. I don't have to remind you about the rat, do I?"

"Beverly Hills has a rat problem," he begins, but I cut him off.

"And in Santa Monica the rats wear muddy men's shoes?"

"I'll run some more tests," he says, resigned.

"I'd appreciate that."

I step back and let him work. I don't care if he's humoring me. Being alone in the house while Larry's away had the makings of a fun adventure, for about a half hour. Then I ran into Gail, and I was reminded that terrible things happen to good people all the time. During a long sleepless night, something possessed me to Google Joshua Stanwyck and I realized that sometimes people you thought were good have done terrible things, or maybe they're not good people at all. If Larry could lie to me about something like that— could turn a seventeen-year-old boy into a seventy-year-old man— then he could lie about anything. I'm truly and utterly alone.

Yet all day, I've had this feeling like I'm being watched, like Dawn's thugs are biding their time, waiting to pounce.

It sounds crazy, I know Lex thinks I am, but I can't shake it.

At least I heard back from Thad. The money smoked him out. He told me he's fine and I should stop "blowing up" his phone.

Meanwhile, I've been jumping at every noise and rechecking the alarm panel. But it's not helping. I can't relax.

I never did send Dawn that e-mail. Who am I kidding? I'm not about offense. Never have been. My entire life has been orchestrated around not giving offense, just as my mother taught me. What would she do in a situation like this, if she were pushed to her breaking point? Would even she have to push back, or would she just break?

I wish there were someone here with me, but it can't be Larry, not after what I've found out. I need to decide if I ever want him to come home again. Maybe I can go live in the Santa Monica house by myself.

The thought terrifies me. I went straight from my parents' house to a home with Larry. I've never been on my own, and I don't see how I can start now, when someone's after me, leaving their bathtub rings and muddy footprints.

I want to forgive Larry. I want him to explain it all away. But how can he? As much as I'd like to believe that Larry really didn't screw up that surgery, that it was the sleep-deprived anesthesiologist, in my heart, I know the truth. Larry must have framed that other doctor. He had the autopsy falsified or convinced someone they saw something other than what really happened or paid someone off, something. Because Larry was guilty. He killed that man— no, that boy. I saw it in his eyes, through his tears. Larry was truly remorseful, truly in pain. Yet it wasn't enough to make him take responsibility for his actions.

Larry's capable of framing someone because he could rationalize it. He'd think that he had more potential than the anesthesiologist and would ultimately help more patients. He's always looked down on his colleagues at least a little (sometimes more than a little, like The Ignoramus). He's always judged them and exalted his own medical acumen.

He probably decided that the anesthesiologist would eventually kill someone with his incompetence, it was just a matter of time, while he, Larry, would go on to do great things, to save many lives.

And he has, hasn't he? Or so I've thought. Are there others who've died at Larry's hands, other cover-ups?

No, that's not possible. He must have learned his lesson. He stopped drinking before work, I'm sure of that.

If he was just going to lie to me, why did he even tell me at the time? He must have been seeking absolution. Or no, he needed me to tell him how amazing and brilliant he is, what a great doctor he'd be, that the world needs men, needs doctors, like him. I said all those things, and I believed them. Perhaps he thought he might need me to stand by him if it didn't go his way, if the frame job didn't work, if he needed someone to lie for him. It could have been all of those.

When the incident happened—no, I need to call it what it is, when Larry killed that boy—I closed my eyes and ignored any inkling that something else might be going on. Sure, there was no Google, but there were other ways to gather information. I just preferred to take his word. Some part of me knew it was better not to ask too many questions. Not only to protect Larry, but to protect Thad, and myself, and our seemingly perfect family.

"It's working," Lex says, turning to me. "If anyone tries to breach your perimeter, our company will be here within five minutes. You've got nothing to worry about."

He can't begin to know my worries, but I thank him, profusely. I'm sorry to see him go. I'd let someone condescend to me all day, so long as they stayed. Officer Llewellyn didn't even return my last call.

I peer through the curtains out to the street. There are a few cars, unoccupied. I don't see any pedestrians. Yet I have the sensation that I'm being watched, that someone knows I'm all alone here and they're going to capitalize on it. I reset the alarm, just to be sure, staring at the pattern of lights, seeking reassurance.

Lex promised no one will breach my perimeter, but I no longer know if the greater danger is within or without.

47

Dawn

How'd the interview go?

Okay.

Do you think you got the job?

He pretty much offered it to me.

That's great! I'm proud of you, baby!

Thanks.

We should do a getaway to celebrate.

Maybe.

See you tonight! I love you.

I'm supposed to take a job I don't want, and have a baby I don't want, and the inducement is to go on a getaway that could very well be disastrous given the current state of our relationship?

My husband doesn't get me at all. I don't think he even wants to anymore.

I'm still in my interview clothes, marching across campus. I need to find Professor Myerson before I lose my nerve. I want to tell him what I think of him. No, I want to tell him what he thinks of me, and how that feels. I want to tell him he's wrong while I'm fired up enough to believe it.

I knock on his office door, and part of me is hoping he won't answer. Part of me just wants to go home and cry. But I drove all the way here for a reason. Because I still have my pride, if nothing else.

I looked up to Professor Myerson. I sought his recommendations, his contacts, and above all, his approval. Maybe the cliché is true, and I wanted a father figure. Unfortunately, he was a little too much like my real father.

Here he is, standing in front of me, smiling. "How did it go?" he asks.

"Sean's a nice guy." There's an edge to my voice that the professor either doesn't notice or pretends not to. "He thinks Big Pharma is God's work. I guess that's what his mentor told him back in the day to get him to drink the Kool-Aid."

Professor Myerson adopts a look of mystification. It could be genuine, I don't know anymore, about anyone.

"Do you think it's the best I can do?" I ask, and the edge is still there, but with an underlying plea. Please, think I'm worth something. Think more of me than my own father did.

"They pay a great starting salary. Great benefits, too. A lot of people are after those jobs."

"That's what Sean said." You didn't answer my question, Professor. Just tell me the truth.

"With the whole vaccine thing, I thought it might be right up your alley."

"The vaccine project is an afterthought. Ten percent of the job. The rest of the time I'm schmoozing doctors." Persuading them with my intangible quality. Does that quality smell like pussy?

He doesn't look as surprised as I would have liked about the 10 percent figure. He nods solemnly. "You can't get everything when you're first starting out."

"I'd be a sales rep. Did you realize that?"

"I don't think Sean said that."

"You don't think." I never expected anything of Dad. But Professor Myerson—he teaches ethics! Was it ethical for him to send me to a job interview knowing that I'd be getting 10 percent of what I asked for? Ten percent making a difference, 90 percent whoring myself. Again, is that the best he thinks I can do?

"Come in. Let's not talk about this in the hallway."

I shake my head. There are tears in my eyes.

He notices, and he reaches an arm toward me. I step back. "I was trying to help you. I thought it would be a great opportunity. You wanted money, above all, and then the chance to do something meaningful—"

"That wasn't my priority list!" But maybe I did say that. Maybe I do feel that. I didn't know I was so transparent, or that Professor Myerson knew I was so willing to sell out. The truth is, if Artie and I have that drink and then he offers me the position, I don't think I can say no. A lot of pretty girls would kill for this job. It probably is the best I can do, especially with my background.

I'm not even sure who I'm most disappointed in anymore.

"Thank you for this opportunity," I say. "I've learned a lot. I'll see you in class."

He doesn't have time to answer as I flee the scene. In my car, I'm deciding which man to text.

It's been one fucked-up day.

Tell me all about it, Beautiful.

No, you tell me something. Tell me a story. The kind of story that will take my mind off what's going on.

What is going on?

I don't want to talk about it. I want to listen.

Let me think.

More than a minute goes by.

Okay, here goes. It's about my dad. I've never told this to anyone.

That's a good start.

But before Thad can go on, I hear from Aunt Tanya:

WE NEED TO TALK ABOUT YOUR MOTHER.

I really hate those alarmist caps. My mother should not be my problem.

SHE JUST GOT AN EVICTION NOTICE. SHE NEEDS YOUR HELP.

I can't let that go unanswered, not today.

SHE NEEDS TO GET A JOB.

SHE'S NEVER HAD A JOB.

WALMART GREETER. SANDWICH MAKER. HOTEL MAID. DRIVE HER AROUND AND HELP HER FILL OUT APPLICATIONS.

THAT'S EASY FOR YOU TO SAY.

EVERYONE HAS TO DO THINGS THEY DON'T WANT TO IF THEY WANT TO SURVIVE.

SHE'S IN NO SHAPE TO GET A JOB.

SHE'LL GET IN SHAPE IF SHE'S DESPERATE ENOUGH.

YOU NEED TO STEP UP, DAWN.

I'VE BEEN TAKING CARE OF MYSELF MY WHOLE LIFE. SHE CAN DO THE SAME.

SHE'S YOUR MOTHER.

LATELY, SHE REMINDS ME OF THAT ALL THE TIME.

YOU CAN'T REALLY BE THIS WAY. STEP UP, DAWN. YOU'LL FEEL BETTER.

YOU LIVE IN HER TOWN. YOU HAVE ROOM FOR HER. YOU TAKE HER IN.

IT HAS TO BE YOU.

WHY?

BECAUSE SHE DOESN'T THINK YOU LOVE HER.

NOT MY PROBLEM.

I DON'T KNOW WHAT HAPPENED TO YOU, DAWN, THAT YOU CAN BE LIKE THIS.

MY PARENTS HAPPENED TO ME.

I'm always hungry because of them, and everyone can smell it on me.

I block Aunt Tanya.

The day just got worse.

You sure you don't want to talk about it?

Tell me your story, Thad. No, better yet, tell me a secret.

I already told you my biggest. That I'm not an addict, that I con my mother into thinking I am.

Miranda's been diminished by all that I have going on right now. Once I do my final presentation in Professor Myerson's class, I could exorcise her for good.

Yeah, I get it. You're a bad, bad boy who just wanted to be loved.

And what are you?

We're not talking about me. Are you going to tell me a secret or do I have to go somewhere else?

My father's an alcoholic.

As in, your father the doctor?

The very same. He goes on binges that last days. He plans them ahead of time. My mother thinks he's at medical conferences.

How do you know that?

I caught him once when I was in high school. Just ran into him on the street when my mother thought he was in Las Vegas. He was wrecked. Blacked out. He didn't even remember it later. Or he pretended he didn't.

You confronted him?

Yeah. It was the best talk we ever had. He gets it. The need for oblivion.

He said that?

He said that he gets so tired of being responsible, he likes not having to fulfill any expectations for a while. To be out of control. He said he envied me. That I got to shirk responsibility as a way of life.

He said THAT? It's almost like he was endorsing you being an addict.

He didn't mean to. It just slipped out. But after he confessed, he started to act like an even bigger hardass. Like it was a part he was playing in front of my mom so she wouldn't suspect.

Suspect what?

That my dad and me get each other. That we have what me and my mom don't. What he and my mom don't.

I had the impression you and your dad don't talk.

We don't anymore. And we never talked that much when he was sober.

All those nighttime talks, he was drunk?

That's when he was his real self. He'd tell me the truth about my mom. How she only cares about appearances, and how the world sees her, and she put all this pressure on him to be seen a certain way. Because if you let her down, she punishes you. She won't look at you the same, she won't love you the same, you can just feel it.

Your dad told you all that?

Yeah, he told the truth. With my mom, anything positive is just phony bullshit. I always knew she didn't like my art, that she was just humoring me. My dad confirmed that.

I could almost feel sorry for Miranda. I mean, who could like Thad's art? If his dad claimed to, then he was the liar.

My dad was just warning me. You can't believe anything good from her. All the bad is right there under the surface. She's just keeping up appearances.

But she's the one who's still in your life, right? Your dad isn't.

That's not exactly his fault.

What do you mean?

I blackmailed him, too.

Jesus, Thad.

It was after my dad had thrown me out and he said it was for good. I just needed him to listen to me. So I told him I'd tell Mom about his binges if he didn't help me, and I didn't mean with money. Or at least, not just money. My dad turned around and said he'd give me ten thousand dollars, but that would be the end. We'd never have a relationship again.

He was testing you.

He said that if I ever came back around, he would just tell my mom rather than let me have anything over him.

You chose the money.

Because it's what he wanted. He wanted to be rid of his addict son. I know because I offered to give the money back a week later if he'd have me in his life again. He never answered.

He didn't trust you.

Do you know how hard it is for an addict to give back money?

I thought you said you're not an addict.

I'm not anymore. I got clean for him. I'm going to show up soon and he won't be able to turn me away.

Sounds like someone's heading for a fall.

I have another secret. I've been pretending to be away in Arizona. I've been back in L.A. for a while.

Why have you been pretending?

My mother feels safer with me further away.

But why did you lie to me?

I thought you might feel safer, too.

48

Miranda

"This is Ed from Dunleavy Construction, just following up on that estimate we gave you. We could get started on the work next Wednesday . . ."

"Miranda, it's Vi. I want you to know I had nothing to do with that rumor. I never told anyone at the Association about you violating the ordinance . . ."

"The conference is going well. I hope the time apart is good for you, too. We need to let cooler heads prevail . . ."

"It's Officer Llewellyn. I've been busy with investigations so I haven't been able to call you back. What you described does not sound like cybercrime. There's nothing I can do for you . . ."

"Hi, Miranda. This is Kimberly Zhou. Larry thought we should get to know each other better. I have some time today, if you'd like to meet for coffee . . ."

"Hello, Miranda. It's Harriet. Calvin thought I should call. He saw a man who seemed to be skulking around your house, like he was checking *to see if it was occupied. He didn't go inside, but Calvin said that might be because he realized he was being watched. We're probably being overly cautious, I don't want to alarm you, but maybe your husband could drive over and make sure everything's okay? . . ."*

If that sequence of voicemails tells me anything, it's that I am fully alone, and I am under siege.

My reputation is the least of my problems. If Dawn's man was skulking outside the Santa Monica house, checking to see if I'm there, then how long will it be before he finds his way back to Beverly Hills? She's still after me, and I can't stop thinking about what comes after a dead rat.

Larry and I have never been gun people. I've never been touched by random crime, and until now, I've never been targeted specifically. The alarm used to feel more than sufficient. Superfluous, even. I'd forget to set it for days on end. That seems like a long, long time ago.

I'm on the living room couch with a twelve-inch chef's knife and a saw. I would have preferred an ax, but we don't have one. What we have is a saw that I can hopefully swing like an ax, with the knife for backup in case an intruder enters my immediate radius. It occurs to me that I could go out and buy an ax, but then it would seem like I should just be buying a gun, and it's all become so patently absurd that I can't move. Besides, I'm afraid to step outside; he could be waiting for me, whoever "he" is.

On what counts as a positive note, Thad's started tweeting up a storm. I have almost too much confirmation that he's alive.

It's painfully coincidental. He goes silent, I'm forced to pay money to confirm his continued existence, and then he's got loads to say. He's excited about some woman, probably a fellow addict. The rapid-fire tweeting makes me suspicious. It could be infatuation, or it could be meth talk. I transfer money into his account, and he goes on a binge. I'm financing my son's addiction. If he overdoses, it's on my head.

Maybe Larry was right. Total cutoff, black and white—it's the only way to go. Then you don't have to spend the rest of your life second-guessing. You can say that those were all Thad's choices, you had nothing to do with any of them. He knew what he needed to do to reenter your life, and he chose drugs instead. You wash your hands of all decisions. You're free and clean.

Not that Larry should ever feel clean again after what he did to the Stanwyck family, and to Tom Englander. He's the anesthesiologist who turned in his license rather than face the investigation into Joshua's death. Now he's a stockbroker. He might even be happier, who knows. Larry could have done him a favor.

That's just what Larry probably tells himself. I need to stop thinking like him.

Poor Tom Englander has been living his life believing that he killed a seventeen-year-old boy, and Larry has walked away without so much as a demerit on his record or a scratch on his conscience. Because after that initial weeping, I never saw much evidence that he was haunted by what he had done, which is all the more disturbing now that I know the extent of his crimes.

He's off in Palm Springs, and I'm barricaded in my own home, with a chair beneath the doorjamb, and an alarm system that I keep checking. In my bones, I'm sure that Dawn is coming for me. So, woozy as I am, I won't let my guard down.

I take a sip of strong coffee. It's my third cup in as many hours. First I couldn't sleep for reliving those voicemails, and seeing the smiling picture of Joshua Stanwyck, frozen at age seventeen. Now I won't sleep because it's too dangerous.

The TV is off, because I need to be able to hear every noise. That buys me the most time to react; it gives me a fighting chance. If someone tried to bust into the house, I'd sound the alarm and call the police, but what if that's not enough? If he forces his way inside with a gun, he could kill me instantly and be gone before help could arrive. Officer Llewellyn would finally have to take me seriously, but fat load of good it would do me then.

If I buy my own gun, I have to learn not only how to aim and fire, but how to do it under pressure. It seems more likely I'd shoot off my own foot than I'd harm any intruder.

I'm on my own. Up shit creek without a paddle would be a vast improvement. I'm on the ocean floor without an oxygen tank.

I remember that when Thad was about seven or eight months old, he stopped breathing. I didn't know infant CPR; I don't think they even offered the classes. Mothers back then weren't as braced for disaster as they are now, living in terror of autism and peanuts. We used to think it would all turn out for the best somehow.

Thad wasn't choking, but he was in paroxysms. He was turning blue. Panicked, I called 911.

The dispatcher asked me a series of questions, and the one that seemed most inane is the one that comes back to me now. "Is he holding his breath?" she said.

What baby would do that? And how would I know?

"He needs me," I wailed, "and I don't know how to help him."

She had missed her infant CPR class, too, apparently. She just kept telling me not to worry, the paramedics were almost there, and we'd stay on the phone until they arrived. I didn't touch Thad for fear that I'd make things worse. I'd impede his oxygen flow further. If I tried to pump his chest, I could break a rib. I could kill him with blunt force trauma.

Tears were streaming down my face, the dispatcher was reminding me to hang on, it would all be okay, and then the episode passed. Whatever was happening stopped. Thad drew in a sharp breath, and then another. There was a pounding on the door. Help had arrived. The paramedics listened to Thad's heart and lungs and declared him a very lucky, healthy baby.

Through it all, even when he hadn't appeared to be breathing, Thad watched me, impassively. It was like he wanted to see my reaction. His was the pitiless gaze of a future serial killer, one who had nothing to be afraid of himself because life is nothing to lose.

I can see it so vividly, it's like I feel his eyes on me now, though I know that's crazy. He was eight months old. The alarm system is working. There's no one here but me.

I pick up the knife with trembling fingers, and I ask myself the essential question.

Was it then?

49

Dawn

I know what you told Aunt Tanya.

I know you think you're so much better than me and your father.

Really? How are you different?

You live in a shitty apartment.

You don't work.

You're headed for a fall, Dawnie, and when it happens, I'll be here for you, because I'm your mother.

What, you're too good to answer me?

Does Rob know you're a whore

and not a very good one?

All this time, she knew.

I'm so stupid. That never once occurred to me. I thought I had to protect her from everything, even that knowledge, but of course, she was in on it.

This is why you should turn your phone off during class.

"Dawn," I hear Professor Myerson saying, from about a million miles away, "you're up."

My knees are shaking. With anger, hurt, and maybe the recognition of truth—that on some level, I've always thought I was a whore headed for a fall. I just didn't think my own mother would push me off the cliff.

I need to get through this presentation. It's the last one of the semester, and it's only fifteen minutes long. I'm good at public speaking. It must be my intangible quality.

So why hasn't Sean called me back about that job? I'm ready to whore myself, and now he doesn't want me?

"Dawn, are you ready?" Professor Myerson says, sounding concerned. He's in the back row, I'm in the front.

I force myself to my feet. It's not such a long distance to travel to the podium, and my first PowerPoint slide is on the screen behind me.

HOW TO RIGHT A WRONG: THE INTERNET AS AN ETHICAL EQUALIZER

A Final Project by Dawn Thiebold

I stand ramrod straight. In my public speaking class, I learned that with the right posture, confidence will follow.

Any second now, my confidence will kick in.

Any.

Second.

Now.

Professor Myerson has his face arranged in his usual mild listening expression. You wouldn't know that we'd had our confrontation just yesterday, though my damp armpits are well aware. I know what he thinks of me.

The rest of the class is watching me, the male students more avidly. I remind myself that oral presentations are my strength.

Don't think about Mom. She doesn't actually know anything about me. She never bothered to learn.

But she knew more than I ever guessed.

Some students are restless; others look more curious about my unraveling. I can't afford to wait for my confidence at this point. I just need to start talking. Get through it. Get out of here. But I don't even know where I'm headed anymore.

"There's an Adrienne Rich quote," I say, my voice trembling, "about how the political is personal, so I've decided to bring something personal into my final project. A few months back, I stayed in a house rental that I found on Getaway.com." I click the button in my hand, and the screen behind me changes. I wanted to show them Miranda's original listing, but of course, that's not available anymore. Instead, I exhibit a similar sample house. "Beautiful, right? Luxurious. It was a splurge for my husband and me, for sure, one of our only vacations this year."

I'm not going to tell them the haunted part, how it affected Rob and me, how it affects us still. The political is not *that* personal.

But my self-righteous fury is coming back to me. That's powered me through a lot in my life, and of late, it's what I look to Miranda for. It's going to get me through this.

I click again, and now the screen shows Miranda's e-mail, though today she'll be known as Marissa. "Then I receive this communication from the 'host,' Marissa." I can't resist the air quotes.

Please note: It is April 23, 2014. You'll have your deposit within seven business days, just like it says on Getaway.com. I've put through a refund to your credit card for the full amount, minus

$200 to replace the sheets. I couldn't get the stain out despite professional laundering and bleaching . . .

"You'll notice that there's no 'Dear Dawn.' Or 'I'm sorry you had to contact me repeatedly to get your deposit.' There's also no photographic evidence to support her contention of a stain. Quite clearly, there was no stain. The authoritative tone, the lack of personal touches—it's all intended to make me feel that she has the power in our exchange. This is a prime example of unethical communication."

My voice is stronger now. I see that my audience looks a little more engaged. Everyone loves a narrative thread instead of a dry presentation of an article, like the ones we've sat through so far today.

I click, and now it's my review from Getaway.com.

Beware of your "host"

THREE STARS

I wouldn't have left a review at all, if I didn't feel it was my civic duty to warn others . . .

I let them read the meat themselves, and finish with "This is an example of persuasive communication. I distinguish myself—an ethical consumer of goods and services—from Marissa. I demonstrate that I'm a trustworthy person and she is not. Then the site's users can draw their own conclusions." I glance at Professor Myerson. He's inscrutable. I look down at my notes, composing myself. Then I look up and smile. Somehow, against all odds, against my mother's prophecy, I'm pulling this off. I'm standing straight, and I won't let myself fall. Fuck her. And fuck Miranda. I click.

I'm shocked that you didn't address your issue with me first but instead chose to post a scathing review. Now people will be worried about their security deposit when they don't need to be. Look at my other reviews. No one else has had any problem with me. On the contrary, they rave about my hospitality . . .

You suggest in your review that I'm a liar. I can assure you I am not . . .

"Notice the condescending tone. And nothing suggests 'liar' like protesting that you're not a liar." I hear a few snickers. Professor Myerson is giving me nothing, but that's okay. I don't need a father anymore.

The fact that there are no other three-star reviews doesn't mean everyone has had positive dealings with you. . . . Maybe you're just in the habit of trying to bully people into taking their reviews down, and making them question their reality. Sorry it hasn't worked this time.

"Communications—and ethics—is about refusing to back down in the face of tyranny." I don't see any nods, so I clarify. "Just because one person has money and an expensive house doesn't mean they can force another person to do what they want."

Dawn,

Your review is based on miscommunication and inaccuracies. It is tantamount to character assassination, as it paints me as someone who would steal a security deposit.

My husband is a doctor. I do volunteer work. I have almost

all five-star reviews on my property because I treat people well.
That is my life.

Please call if you'd like to discuss this further . . .

"Would you call this woman?" A few people laugh. "Exactly. She could have responded with anything in this e-mail. She could have empathized with me. Instead, she chose to talk about her husband being a doctor, and her volunteer work. She tried to make me feel like she's better than me to get me to take down an honest review. It's poor communication, as well as unethical.

"Her only recourse—since I wouldn't take down the review—was to post a response on the website."

I've apologized repeatedly to the reviewer for any miscommunication but have only received hostility in return . . .

Some people want to find fault; they want to hate. That seems
to be the case here. Unfortunately, some people can't be pleased.

"Who's engaging in character assassination now?" I look around the room. They're just not getting it, they don't know why this is so utterly enraging. Do they have no sense of fairness, justice, and self-respect? Do young people today care about anything at all?

Professor Myerson seems slightly dyspeptic, like he's stifling a burp. I hadn't realized until just then how much I wanted them to get it, to see Miranda like I see her, and to see me like I need to see myself.

But I continue, because I have to.

I tell them about the Santa Monica ordinance and show my e-mail reporting Miranda to the city attorney. "While I never got a satisfactory response from them—they just told me they were 'looking into the matter'—the listing disappeared from Getaway.com. I had, effectively, put her out of business. And for someone like

Miran—Marissa, who's used to getting what she wants by virtue of her money and status, this was too much to take. She had to up the ante." I've got their attention again as I click.

> The police have advised me to block you. All further communications should cease.

"I followed her instructions. I ceased communicating with her. But that didn't stop me from communicating *about* her." This is the true heart of my presentation. I point out how I used the Internet to my full advantage, turning her own words against her by reposting our exchanges on multiple websites. The Bewarethisrental.com review is on the screen behind me. "This became her new Internet footprint. And as a result, I received this e-mail."

It's supposed to prove that I won. After all, Miranda begged for my forgiveness, pretended to be reformed, and refunded me double, while I did nothing for her. This should be my triumph.

"Notice the manipulative communication. There's the fake deference, the phony apology, the false flattery about me being a better writer than her, and her trying to buy me off for four hundred dollars."

I don't know how to interpret the look on Professor Myerson's face. It seems almost—pitying. He feels for me. He may even care for me. But he doesn't respect me. If he did, he would never have sent me on that interview.

"Needless to say, I'm not for sale, and I haven't deleted anything online. That, in conclusion, is how to right a wrong."

There's a round of halfhearted applause, though none of the other presentations so far have garnered anything more than that. Still, I didn't think it would be hard to top them. I have a sinking feeling in my chest as Professor Myerson clears his throat.

"Let me play devil's advocate," he says. "What if it's not manipulation? What if she had a sincere conversion?"

"Then why does she ask me to take everything down? She has an ulterior motive."

"Is it possible that both can be true? She can sincerely see your point of view, realize she's done wrong, but also want you to stop humiliating her?"

He's telling me to take her point of view, and it's not until that moment that I realize I never really have. Now I'm standing in front of a class and they can all see it. I was so obsessed that I forgot Communications 101: try on the other person's position; walk in their shoes.

On the screen behind me is the final image.

Thanks for the refund. Better late than never, I guess. And while I appreciate your epiphany, I'm standing by my reviews. You did what you did, and you can't undo it now. We all have to sit with the consequences of our actions.

"Class, do you have any questions?" Professor Myerson says.

"Isn't this actually an example of cyberbullying?" a girl asks from the front row. She's a chronic eye-roller.

"I never used that terminology for Marissa's actions," I reply, "but yes, it is."

Another eye roll. "No, *you* were bullying *her*."

"That had crossed my mind as well," Professor Myerson says. "Though I don't believe that was Dawn's intent, I do think her actions could be construed as such. That could be why Marissa visited the police."

I feel a rush of heat to my cheeks. I could possibly have been a bit off base in my communications, but a cyberbully?

All my actions were justified when it came to Miranda. Tit for tat, action and reaction. She started it. And continued it. She raised the stakes at every turn. Were these people even listening? Can't they read?

"Did you receive this woman's permission to use her communications?" Professor Myerson says.

"No," I say tightly, "it wasn't required by any of the websites where I posted."

"Ethics isn't about mere legality. That's the first thing I taught you."

"There was a greater good. I was reminding her that other people have feelings, regardless of their income level. They need to be treated with respect. She learned her lesson. You said it yourself."

"Did she? Or was she just telling you what you wanted to hear because you'd bullied her into submission? Because she was frightened? You can't teach through fear, or humiliation."

Ironic, since he's humiliating me right now. I was humiliated at the interview when I realized what the job really was, when I saw what my favorite professor really thought of me.

"I think," he says slowly, "that you felt you were communicating one thing and what we're all hearing is something else. We're seeing that the Internet can be used as a tool to exact vengeance, and sometimes we call that vengeance 'justice.' Really, it's something else entirely." His face has turned sympathetic by the end, or perhaps it was sympathetic the whole time. "Knowing ourselves and our own motivations is the source of all ethical—and unethical— behavior. It can be surprisingly easy to conflate the two. To rationalize, and to legitimize, and to think we're angry with one thing or person when maybe it's something or someone else. We've all, at one time or another, suffered from misplaced aggression. We've all lost people we love."

His eyes on mine are full of compassion, but he's wrong. This could not have less to do with my father's death. It's about justice, and holding people accountable. It's about consequences.

"Thank you, Dawn," he says, "for illustrating such an important point. For that reason, this was an extremely successful presentation." He begins a slow clap, and the roomful of bewildered students follow his example.

I make my shaky way to my seat. I've earned all my accolades since I started college here, except this one. This was pure pity.

Professor Myerson made me out to be misguided and vengeful. A cyberbully, of all things! No one's ever misunderstood me this badly, unless you count my husband.

Miranda was the bully. Stealing my money, belittling me, and then, when I used the Internet to call her on it, trying to manipulate me.

Is it really possible that I've been seeing this all wrong, that I've been the one bullying her? Professor Myerson is a smart man.

No. It's her. It's all her. She managed to trick them all, even Professor Myerson. Without even being here, she got them on her side. That's how good she is, how clever.

She'll get what's coming to her.

50

Miranda

Easy to create when you're inspired by a good woman.
#dawntbold

Dawntbold = Dawn Thiebold = Dawn and Thad know each other. She's his inspiration, which can only mean one thing. Dawn and Thad sitting in a tree, k-i-s-s-i-n-g. First comes love, then comes marriage . . .

Only she's already married.

What breaks my heart is that he has to know she has a husband. I raised the kind of man who wouldn't care.

He actually calls her a good woman. Like he'd recognize a good woman if she up and bit him. No, if she'd raised him.

How long has this been going on? Have they been in cahoots this whole time?

He always liked petite blondes. Not that he allowed me to meet his girlfriends, or (as he so charmingly called them) f— buddies. I caught a few of them leaving his room late at night when he was still in high school. All I could do was ground him, but it was after the fact. He'd already gotten what he wanted. His whole life, I've been playing catch-up. I wanted to get out in front of his problems but I was always trailing behind, mitigating the damage, cleaning up the messes, cutting my losses.

I could ask him how he met Dawn, but I'm fairly certain he wouldn't tell. Besides, I wouldn't believe any answer he gave.

I've been lying on my couch in the same clothes for two straight days, the knife and saw like extra appendages. I'm delirious from stress and lack of sleep, but I couldn't even make this stuff up: Thad and Dawn have formed some sort of unholy alliance.

I suppose I should be grateful. She's given him something to live for, the inspiration to create.

They deserve each other.

I'm shaking. In grief, and in rage.

No, they don't deserve each other. Dawn is a rotten person, and what she deserves is to be punished. She's come after me through Thad. Drugs have disabled his brain, and now she's using my hand-icapped son against me.

Hell hath no fury like a mother protecting her child.

Dawn T. Bold, you're going to learn your lesson. I will see to that.

51

Dawn

"Hi, Mr. Callahan. This is Dawn Thiebold. Sean said I'd be hearing from you to schedule dinner or a drink. I'm really excited to be a part of your team. I'll make myself available any time. Look forward to hearing from you!"

"Hi, Sean. This is Dawn Thiebold. Since I didn't hear from you, I decided to go ahead and leave a message for Mr. Callahan—for Artie—to schedule that drink but haven't heard back yet. I'm just wondering how everything's moving along in terms of my hiring? Please shoot me a text or an e-mail, whatever works. Thanks so much! I'm so excited about this opportunity!"

Maybe Sean got busy and never talked to Artie; maybe Artie's just having a hectic week. Or is it possible that Sean changed his mind? Or that Professor Myerson conveyed to Sean what I really thought of the job?

No, he wouldn't have done that. But just to cover my bases . . .

"Hi, Professor Myerson. It's Dawn. I've been thinking a lot, and I've realized how much I really do want that job. We can't have everything we want in life, but that job's a great start. I really appreciate you setting it all in motion. Maybe I could take you out for dinner or something to thank you? If you hear from Sean, please let him know how interested I am. I already left him a few voicemails but he must be in meetings or something. Thanks again! See you soon!"

I have to accept this job, and accept reality: I chose the broadest major but now I have fairly narrow prospects. What I can do is sell. Might as well sell myself to the highest bidder. That's if Big Pharma will still have me.

Rob said as much. He didn't even ask how I really felt, though I'm sure my reservations were written all over my face. I wanted him to say I was too good for that job, and that I should hold out for something better. Instead, he told me, "You've got to start somewhere, right? Pharmaceutical sales is lucrative, and it's competitive. And that VP wants you." He raised his glass in a toast. "Now you can support me for a while."

My mother's right. I thought I'd come so far, but I'm nowhere. My husband's a lousy provider, same as hers was. He doesn't care how I really feel, deep down, same as hers. But unlike her, I'm going to make my own opportunities.

Call back, Artie. Call back, Sean.

Fucking men. As soon as they can have you, they don't want you anymore.

Misplaced anger, that's what Professor Myerson said. That this hasn't been about Miranda at all, but about . . . ?

I orchestrated my whole life to avoid feeling powerless, dirty, and disposable, and here it is again. I'm back here, again.

I was sixteen, and yes, I'd had a lot of sex, but Planned Parenthood set me on a different path. I was rehabilitated. Then my father came home and told me he had a "business opportunity." Those were big words for him. He'd been working his temporary jobs through Manpower, a couple of days a week if we were lucky, and he sat on my bed and said, "Things are going to change around here."

He generally only spoke to me if it was absolutely necessary, and he never came into my room, so I knew something significant was under way. My mom was stressed out all the time, losing weight, with her hair coming out in clumps. When my father said that he was on the verge of a regular job, full-time, with good pay and benefits, I thought of her first.

"That's great, Dad," I said. "I'm proud of you."

"Don't jump the gun," he warned. "I don't have the job yet."

Then I asked the question that would haunt me for years: "What do you have to do to get it?"

"Do you remember Gary?" I shook my head. "He was over here last week. We were drinking beer on the front steps. You walked by in that white skirt."

I tried never to look at my father and his friends. They were a nasty bunch, and they'd been ogling me since I first filled out. "What about him?"

"Gary's a general contractor and he's looking for someone to work on houses with him full-time. Remodeling kitchens and bathrooms."

"Do you know how to do that?"

He made a face that told me he wanted out of this conversation ASAP. Which made me wonder why he'd ever gotten into it to begin with, but I was about to learn. He never said it directly but he made it clear that Gary was going to be over at the house the next day, and my mother would be out, and my father would take off for a little while, too, and then Gary just wanted to hang out with me, talk for a bit. "This job would change everything," my father concluded.

I wanted to think my dad didn't really know what he was asking of me, but neither of us could be that ignorant. Maybe he thought I was still giving it away for free all the time and what's one more, for the betterment of the family?

"I promise you, Dawn, I will not screw this job up. I'll treat your mom like she deserves to be treated."

That was what sealed the deal. I could turn things around for my whole family, but my mom needed it the most. She was the most fragile. And sure, I wasn't a slut anymore by then, but this wasn't like the other guys. I wasn't doing it to feel just a little better about myself; I was doing it for all of us.

So the next day, my father left me alone with Gary. He was about thirty and completely repugnant. He had one of those weird skin tags right between his eyebrows, and he made small talk while he chugged half a six-pack. I drank the other half just to get through. I insisted on a condom and he grumbled but agreed. I was grateful that he was doing it from behind so that I didn't have to kiss him and he couldn't see me choking back the bile. I was taking an hour-long shower when my father came back. He never said anything, not even thank you, but then, a thank-you might have made it all the grosser.

Days passed, and he still wasn't talking. Finally, I asked him when he was starting the job. He didn't want to meet my eyes and I couldn't tell if he was ashamed of himself or of me. He didn't even stop walking as he said, "It fell through."

So I wasn't the family protector; I was just a whore again. My father looked at me even less after that, if that's possible. I was so ashamed. Sex with me wasn't worth anything at all; it literally had no value. If I'd been better, my father would have gotten that job, and our lives would have turned around.

At first, I thought my father had been tricked, too, but a month later, he was sitting on the front steps drinking beer with Gary. They both acted like nothing had happened.

Then came the anger. At being duped, and used, and my father's complicity in it. He was the one who thought I had no value, right alongside Gary. I wanted to put them both in jail. But I didn't want the humiliation of going to the police and having to answer questions, and more than that, I didn't want my mother to know about any of it. She wasn't strong enough to handle it. She'd kept her head in the sand for years, and that's where it needed to stay.

I sometimes wondered if any of it was true, what he said to me. Had Gary really promised my father a job, or was that just a lie to get me to do what I would never have done otherwise? Was it a bet, or a debt between them? And if he had gotten that job, would he have kept his promise and worked hard and treated my mother right? Probably not. But while I was protecting my mother, she was gambling with my body and my sanity. I always knew my father didn't much care what happened to me, but I thought my mother was a different story, and not part of this one.

I get up and start making dinner. My mind continues to whir, but by the time Rob gets home, I'm not about to share my thoughts.

All I tell him is that I've made calls to take the pharmaceutical job. I'm rewarded with an approving smile.

I used to think he accepted me unconditionally. But now I have no way of knowing what he really thinks about me unless I eavesdrop on the next "family" dinner.

After a pro forma kiss on the cheek, he says, "It's been an exhausting day. I'm going to lie down. Just call me when dinner's ready, okay?"

I have to fight not to snort with derision. He had an exhausting day. There were probably ten customers, max, over eight hours.

I'm quiet all night, and if Rob remembers that today was my final project, he gives no indication. The fact that he doesn't even know the topic, hasn't even asked, speaks volumes.

Once we've climbed into bed, I'm all the way on my side, and he's all the way on his. It's been that way since I fingered his asshole. Sue me, I wanted to pleasure the guy. We did follow through on some missionary sex in our bed that night, as if he wanted to reassert our utter conventionality. I didn't come, and he didn't seem to care, which was pretty out of character. Or maybe it's evidence of the defective character that he's been concealing from me. They say cheaters are incredibly paranoid about being cheated on, so maybe it's the people most worried about normalcy who are the most deviant.

Rob says, without turning to me, "We have to start trying to have kids." It's in a tone I've never heard from him before—so absolute, so firm, that it's nearly mean. He's brooking no dissent.

I have to remind myself that I married him so I could have a normal family. So I could be a part of his normal family.

This isn't normal, though, this dictate of his. This is not how a couple decides to procreate, not in any world I want to inhabit, and when you think about it, marriage is really just an attempt to create your own world.

"Nobody has to have kids," I say, my back still to his.

He sits upright with such velocity and torque that the whole bed jerks. His anger is palpable in the room.

I don't move. I literally can't face this right now.

I'm not sure what provoked his sudden insistence. Maybe he's trying to rush the kid thing so that he doesn't change his mind about me. He won't have time to discover anything else that makes him so uncomfortable he'll have no choice but to walk away. A child would be an insurance policy against his own better judgment.

I could be flattered. He loves me that much. Or he really, really hates to be wrong.

He shakes my shoulder roughly. "I know you're not asleep. Talk to me."

"I don't want to."

"Don't act like a child. You're not your mother."

He's spoiling for a fight. I'm not going to give it to him.

"Get up, Dawn! This is our marriage here!"

I hug my pillow. "Then let's talk about it in the morning, when we're calm and rested."

"You can't control everything."

"I'm not trying to."

"You always do. Where we go for vacation, when we have a baby." I can tell he's struggling to find another example. "When we can have which conversation."

"I'm tired. You're tired. We both had long days. It's safer to just shut up."

For the moment, he prefers to live dangerously. "I need to know what you've got going on that's more important than being a mother," he says, ice dripping from each word, and I wonder if he finally knows about Thad. I told Thad to take down the tweet that mentioned me, and he did. But could Rob have already seen it by then?

No, Rob's not on Twitter. He and his dad talked about activating their social media presence, but I'm pretty sure it hasn't happened yet.

Could Rob have been checking my phone secretly?

"What are you saying?" I ask. "Don't speak in code. Come out with it."

"I want to know why you don't want to have our child. Is that clear and concise enough for you?"

"I want to have our child someday." When we're our old selves, the couple I thought we were.

"Which day? I want a date." I feel him bouncing up and down, full of furious energy. "Tell me the date when you'll get your IUD out."

"Or what?" I say softly.

"I just want a date."

"And if I can't give you one?"

He gets out of bed and walks over to my side, kneeling down so that we're eye level. "Do not fuck with me, Dawn."

I stare him down. "Or what?" I repeat.

He storms away and starts to get dressed. I'm supposed to ask him where he's going—no, I'm supposed to ask him not to go, but I don't have that in me. Instead, I lie motionless as he leaves the room, and then the apartment, with a ferocious door slam.

I clutch the pillow to me for a while, squeezing my eyes shut and willing sleep to come. I wish I were a little girl again, a different little girl, one whose mother held her and whispered, "Shh, it'll all be okay," instead of the other way around.

I reach my arm out for my phone and cradle it close. When he answers, all I can do is cry.

"Dawn? Dawn, what is it? What happened?"

"Everything is shit," I choke out. "The whole world is shit." People say they want you, but that's only when they don't know you, and when you don't need them. Life is desertion. Love is the big lie.

"I know that feeling. But I don't have it anymore. You know why? Because of you, Dawn T. Bold. Because you're—what's the opposite of shit?"

Despite everything, I have to laugh. "Piss?"

"No. You're gold. And I'm coming for you."

"No," I say weakly.

"You don't have to promise me anything. I'm going to promise you something, though. I'm going to take care of you. You won't cry on my watch. Okay?"

I nod.

"Okay?"

Oh, right, he can't see me. But it feels like he's right here. His voice is a caress.

"Okay," I tell him. I glance at the clock. If he left now from L.A., he'd be here at five A.M. Rob doesn't leave for work until eight. "You're still in L.A., right?"

"In Santa Monica."

Something's coming into focus. "Where in Santa Monica?"

"The best part. Right off the beach. My parents own a house."

"Do they know you stay there?"

"Hell no. I squat at the house between guests. It used to be easier when I could just check the Getaway.com availability calendar. Now I have to be more stealthy. I have a key that I copied years ago. She never changed the locks. Now I'm here more or less full-time, though I've had a few close calls. A Realtor's been sniffing around, so, you know, all good things must come to an end."

"Did you ever stay at the house after guests left, but before the cleaning crew got there?"

"That's a weird question."

"So I'm weird. Did you?"

"A few times."

Holy shit. It's all making sense now. "So you slept on someone else's sheets."

"The people who rent this house are top-notch. I'd rather sleep on their dirty sheets than the clean ones at some shitty motel."

Thad stained the sheets. Miranda didn't make it up after all.

I start to laugh and cry at the same time. Because it doesn't matter how it all started, not anymore. All that matters is what it's become—a tornado razing everything in its path. Miranda's lost her rental, and her son, and I'm losing my marriage, and my self-respect.

I actually feel a strange kinship with Miranda. Neither of us is cut out for motherhood. Is it better to try and fail than never to have tried at all?

My campaign against Miranda—whatever its true root cause, aggression that's misplaced or displaced or simply placed—is officially over.

I know that Miranda's life isn't perfect, and she knows it isn't perfect (Thad certainly reminds her of that), and isn't that what I was trying to establish all along? That money doesn't solve all your problems, or breed happiness? That we all bleed red?

Such deep revelations. I could have just read a book.

Thad must be thinking that I've truly lost it, but all that's left is to laugh and laugh and laugh.

52

Miranda

A stun gun is a device that is used or intended to be used as either an offensive or defensive weapon, which is capable of temporarily immobilizing a person by inflicting an electrical charge. (Ca. Pen. Code §§17230, 16780.)

In California, most people may purchase, possess, or use a stun gun, and they do not have to obtain a permit. However, you may not purchase, possess, or use a stun gun if you are:

- a convicted felon, someone convicted of an assault under federal or any state's laws or the laws of any country, or have a prior conviction for misusing a stun gun under Cal. Pen. Code §244.5, or
- addicted to any narcotic drug.

There really ought to be a weapons store. Of course I realize there are gun stores, but time is of the essence and I need something I can operate immediately. Besides, I don't trust myself with a gun right now. *Dawn and Thad sitting in a tree* rings in my head. I have to stop this before it goes any further. I have to stop her.

A self-defense store, that's what it should be called. Shelves full of Tasers, stun guns, knives, pepper sprays, and what have you. It'd be a haven for people like me, those who've been pushed too far, who've been forced into the conclusion that the only defense is a good offense.

Dawn's got more than twenty years on me, at least, but I work out. I have a strong core, and no health issues, and the element of surprise. She probably expects me to be some sitting duck. She wouldn't think some old lady from Beverly Hills would come for her.

It's not that I intend for things to get physical. I simply have no idea what to expect. This is uncharted territory. But I'll come prepared.

I haven't set foot in a Walmart since I don't know when. But for "personal security" on a moment's notice, it's my superstore.

The Walmart employee is so baby-faced that I suspect he doesn't yet have to shave. He looks surprised by my various requests, but he dutifully looks up each. "We don't carry Taser brand merchandise in-store, ma'am," he says. "It's online only. Here in the store, it's just the holster."

"What would I do with a holster and no Taser?"

He shrugs, managing to convey both apology and indifference. "We've got pepper spray and a stun gun in stock. Taser is just a kind of stun gun."

"Show me what you have, please."

"It's part of Home Improvement," he says, and leads me there. I never would have noticed on my own that near the lightbulbs and wall sconces, there are two different pepper sprays and one type of

Mace. And—I almost laugh out loud—a pink stun gun/flashlight combo disguised as a lipstick.

"That's the only one?" I ask, pointing to it.

"Yep." He grins back uneasily.

"I guess I'll have to get the matching pink pepper spray, the one that supports breast cancer awareness." There really is a pink ribbon on that package. What will they think of next? I would never normally carry anything in candy pink, it's so déclassé, but I'll make it work.

"Do you need anything else?"

"You carry axes, right?" It would be a last resort, but an ax with a good swinging radius could potentially come in handy. The Dawn I know is capable of anything, and I won't be the one surprised anymore.

His eyes widen.

By the time I leave, loaded down with my purchases, I am, genuinely, feeling a greater sense of personal security. Thank you, Walmart.

After days of cowering in my house, I'm walking straight and tall. It's good to feel something other than fear. I'm coasting on pure venomous rage. Larry has been trying to get ahold of me, but he's irrelevant right now. This is about Thad and Dawn. Thad, most of all. He's always needed to be saved from himself.

With my weapons locked in the trunk of my car, I drive to see my mother.

I feel transformed in some way that should be visible, but as I check in with the staff, I'm greeted in the usual way. No one gives me a second's pause. I should be glad I'm not setting off any alarm bells. Yet I want to be seen. For better or worse, let me register, with someone.

Let it be her. My mother. She's walking toward me now, neatly dressed and hair brushed, with the same erect posture I've inherited. No shuffling gait here. She doesn't set off any alarm bells either, until you sit and talk with her. Then you're treated to blank stares, non sequiturs and rambles, confusion, memory failures, and, on rare occasions, screaming, arm-wheeling agitation.

"Let's go to the garden," I say, as usual.

"That sounds lovely," she replies, as if it's a delightful idea that has never occurred to her. She's in hostess mode. She doesn't remember me; she's just been briefed on who I am. I wonder if she's been talking to my father today.

"Has Dad been in to see you?" I ask her. I'm trying something new.

"My husband?" She smiles. "He comes every day. He brings smoothies."

She lets me take her arm and lead her outside. She generally starts out pliable. She's a people pleaser by nature, and LBD can't steal that away entirely. The conditioning remains. It occurs to me that the same would be true of me, if I were to suffer from LBD someday. Everything would be stripped away but my basic desire to be what everyone else wants.

We take our seats at a table among the purple and white of the lavender, daisies, and hydrangea. "Tell me how Dad's doing," I say.

She casts me a quick uncertain glance, as if it might be a trick question. She doesn't trust me, and I have no idea why. Who does she take me for? "Well, you know your father." It's the light response of a born hostess.

"Some days it's hard for me to remember him," I say.

"Why is that?" This, for her, is an incredibly lucid, responsive state. It's the longest conversation we've had in months, an actual duet.

"I think I'm losing myself. Do you know what that's like?"

"No, I don't." She stares out at the garden. It's never before occurred to me that she wills the blankness into being, that she wants to escape her time with a person she's been told is her daughter. Catatonia might be her preferred state.

Well, I'm not going to let her go. Not this time. "I have to tell you something that no one else knows."

She glances at me, then straight ahead. She's not gone yet.

"I'm about to take a little trip. To Oakland. Do you know where that is?" I think I see her shake her head no, so slight it could be a passing palsy. "Remember that woman I told you about, the one who's been harassing me?" No headshake. She's drifting. "Dawn Thiebold. Dawn Thiebold. Dawn Thiebold. You have to remember that name, okay? Are you listening?" Nothing. "Dawn has made my life hell. She's taken away an important source of income, the rental income from the Santa Monica house. You do remember the Santa Monica house? You and Dad spent your last years there together. They were happy years. Your happiest. It's where he makes smoothies." My mother blinks rapidly. She's back, almost. "You and Dad left that house to me, so I could make my own happy memories there, and Dawn's ruining it for me, Mom. She's hurt my reputation. Her lies are all over the Internet. I had to resign from the board. She left a rat in my pool, and muddy footprints in my house. She's got someone skulking around, threatening my safety.

"But that's not the worst of it, Mom. The worst is that she's a married woman, and she's having some sort of relationship with Thad. An affair." I see the bafflement in my mother's face. "Thad, Mom. Thad's my son."

"Your son," she echoes.

"Yes, my son!" I feel excited. She's never before spoken when she's in this state. Once I've lost her, it's over for the day. But to be able to bring her back . . . My eyes fill with tears. "So I have a choice. I can go to Oakland and I can tell this woman's husband who she really is. I can confront her. Or I can stay here and hope that she leaves me alone. I can hope that it all blows over. Thad's relationships never last long."

I study her face. She's listening, I'm almost sure of it. She's raised me to turn the other cheek, to never behave rashly. If she loves me at all, she'll stop me. I can carry my new lipstick/stun gun/flashlight in my purse for self-protection, and go about my business.

"He's not a good boy," she says.

"You remember Thad?"

She shakes her head. "He's a no-good alcoholic, just like your father."

"Thad isn't an alcoholic. He's a drug addict."

"Not Thad. Thad is a good boy. I'm talking about your husband. Your husband's just like your father."

"You're confused. Dad wasn't an alcoholic."

She purses her lips and shakes her head again stubbornly. That look says *I know what I know.*

"You're confused," I say again.

More head shaking. She's blocking me out. She's done with me.

"Do you even know who I am?" I'm on my feet. She needs to see me, all of me. "I'm your daughter! I'm here, asking for your help! Your advice! I need you! Do you get that? Do you get what I need? I come here all the time! I bring you flowers! Do you want me to go to Oakland? Just answer that! Should I go to Oakland?!"

I want her to be as agitated as I am. She needs to react to me. Your bond with your children is stronger than any other; it's the true for-better-or-for-worse. If she remembers my father the alcoholic, she should remember her own child.

Not that my father was an alcoholic. He was a workaholic. She's confusing her -holics.

She's escaped into her catatonia, and all I can do is yell for her to come back, come back.

The next thing I know, there's a nurse at my side, one I've never seen before, with fire-engine hair and equally clownish makeup. "You need to leave!" she says sternly. "Now."

A large orderly appears, and I figure out his role. He's supposed to escort me out, if necessary. I'm being kicked out of my mother's facility.

"You're upsetting your mother," the nurse says.

"You're wrong about that." I gesture toward my mother, who is stock-still. "She couldn't care less."

"Please leave."

Is there any lower moment than being kicked out of my mother's facility and returning to my car with its trunk full of weapons and a GPS set for an engraving store in Oakland?

I haven't got a thing left to lose.

53

Dawn

I'm in front of your house.

Thad and I stare at each other across the threshold, boldly, nakedly, mutually . . . disappointed. That's the best word for it.

It was inevitable. Buildup leads to letdown. Also, we're two people who are better looking in selfies than in the flesh.

I've always been photogenic, and I know how to tilt my head to camouflage my flaws. My skin is a certified disaster area right now, with all the stress. *War and Peace* is written across my forehead, cheeks, and chin in Braille. Then there are the dark parabolas beneath my eyes. My body looks good, in a tight black tank top and jeans, but he may have been expecting someone taller. In pictures, I can give the impression of height.

As for Thad, he's no Justin Theroux or Joaquin Phoenix, unless one of them was cast to play a junkie. His teeth appear shadowed, and not well fixed in his mouth. It seems like one good chomp on

an almond could send them hurtling in my direction. I never noticed before that all his selfies involve sexy half smiles, with a closed
mouth. He's sickly-skinny. His clothes are ill-fitting and threadbare,
thrift store rather than vintage. My consolation is that he only looks
homeless, rather than smelling it.

He wasn't playing an addict on Twitter; he clearly is one, in real
life.

What have I gotten myself into?

He reaches out and grabs me somewhat roughly into an embrace.
He says into my hair, "It's good to finally meet you, in person." He
holds on, too long. Maybe my first impression was wrong, and he's
not disappointed at all.

What have I gotten myself into?

There's no way around inviting him in. He drove here from South-
ern California, knocking on the door fifteen minutes after Rob left
for work. He was sitting out front. For some reason, the thought
that he knows what my husband looks like unnerves me.

He could be dangerous. Miranda obviously thinks he is. She's
been paying him a monthly stipend to keep him from breaking into
people's houses, and who knows what else. This is her son. She must
have insider information.

What would she think if I texted her and said, *I have your son in
my house, come and pick him up?* If I said, *Thad's here, how do I get rid
of him?* It's almost comical.

Almost.

No one knows he's here. No one knows we're linked. He could
do anything to me. He's a liar who let me think he was in Arizona
rather than six hours away. He's a bad seed who'd blackmail his own
parents.

"Come in," I say. The sooner he comes in, the sooner I can get
him out. I hope.

He follows me inside. As he glances around, I can see what he's thinking: *This is a shithole.* I feel like punching him. Yes, he was raised in Beverly Hills, but still. He's a junkie squatter.

"Do you have anything to drink?" he asks.

I walk into the kitchen. It's the room closest to the street, with the window open. People would hear me if I screamed. "Water. Orange juice."

"Put some vodka in the OJ and you made a sale."

"It's not even nine A.M." I'm facing away as I reach into the refrigerator. That's probably a mistake. I shouldn't turn my back on him.

"It's not like you have anywhere to be, right? You're playing hooky today."

I pivot back, the juice in my hand. He's lounging in a chair at my kitchen table, his spindly arachnid legs stretched out in front of him. I have to step over them to get to the cupboard for glasses. I'm repulsed.

But he's given me an out. "I have a class in an hour, actually."

"That you're going to miss." He has an insouciance that would have captivated me years ago. Nice to realize that I'm all grown up now.

"I shouldn't skip this close to the end of the semester. I don't want to blow it now."

"Come here." He gives me a smile. Those teeth—it's like he's permanently leering. "Sit with me."

I put two glasses on the table and take the seat across from him, the farthest possible diametric distance. "Did you want some juice?"

"So no vodka, that's what you're saying?"

"I'm saying it's eight thirty in the morning."

He laughs like I'm full of charming peccadilloes. "Okay, Dawn, you win. OJ at the kitchen table it is." So he's picking up on my vibe, after all. What's creepy is that it doesn't seem to faze him at all.

Is it because he doesn't care what I want? Because he's going to take what he needs?

I'm getting ahead of myself. This guy could be completely harmless. I've had the upper hand since we met.

Or he's allowed me to think so.

"It's time for us to really get to know each other," he says.

My stomach drops, though I'm not going to show fear. "We already know plenty."

"I've told you my secrets. Now I want to know yours. I figure you're the kind of woman who has to be face-to-face. You have to see what you're dealing with before you give it up. I can respect that." He leans forward slightly. "I respect you, Dawn. I might even love you." Then he sits back, satisfied with his almost-declaration.

Does he know he's scaring me? Is that the point?

Miranda could have been behind this the whole time. She sent her son to do her dirty work.

No, that's ridiculous. I'm just freaking myself out here. He's harmless. A harmless thieving, blackmailing junkie. You know, one of those.

"I was a mess last night," I say carefully. "I thought I needed someone other than my husband. But it turns out, I don't." I'm sitting as far back as I possibly can, the chair digging into my spinal column. "I owe you an apology. I shouldn't have wasted your time. I shouldn't have let you come here."

"Let me? You were begging me."

"I don't think you're remembering right. Were you on something last night, when we talked?"

"On something?" His tone is mocking. "What something do you mean?"

"Meth? Pills? I don't know, just something that would make you remember differently."

"You mean make me remember wrong. Sorry, Dawn, I was stone-cold sober. You're the one who's confused. You've been begging me to come here for months."

"Wrong again."

He moves his chair closer to mine, with a loud scraping sound. Both the sound and his nearness make me want to flinch, but I know better than to show fear. He grabs my hand. "I'm here now, Dawn. I'm not going to let anyone hurt you."

"You can't stay. You know that, right?"

"I'm not staying. You're leaving with me."

Either he's nuts or I've been leading him on way more than I ever realized. "No one's hurting me. Rob is a good husband. I need to be a better wife."

He laughs. "Is this the 1950s?" He releases my hand, and it pulses with gratitude. "I'm not saying you have to be an artist like me, but you've got to be free, Dawn. You're not some hausfrau in the hood."

"This isn't a hood. Temescal is—"

"I don't know what Temescal even is. I don't care. You belong in L.A., with me."

"Squatting in your mother's house until she sells it?"

"I'm about to get a show. Do you know how much money you can make in one night at a good gallery?" He's so confident, I could almost believe him. "Besides, I'm not going to take care of you in terms of money. That might be how you and your husband do it, but you and me, we're going to be fifty-fifty. True partners, in love and work. You'll have your degree soon, and then you'll get a job in L.A. I'll bring you home to meet my parents, and they'll love you. They'll see I've finally got it together. Beautiful woman, art show, a house in Los Feliz or maybe Silver Lake."

I can't keep the bemusement from my face at the idea of him bringing me home to meet Miranda. We've crossed over into total lunacy.

He grins. "You like me. I know you do. Let's have that drink, Dawn. What do you say?"

54

Miranda

20% off all commemorative items. #engravingisthenewblack

Under other circumstances, I would really enjoy walking around this neighborhood. There's an old-time movie theater, al fresco dining at bistros, boutiques, ice cream and gelato shops, chocolatiers, even an apothecary that makes its own personalized fragrances.

But Thiebold's Engraving doesn't really belong. Where the other places have a self-aware retro quality, Thiebold's just feels dated. I don't see any dust on the shelves, but there should be. Pocket watches and silver trays behind glass, and figurines in curio cabinets—who would shop here? No one, based on the tumbleweed blowing along the worn taupe carpeting, stained in some spots, actually threadbare in others.

I recognize Dawn's husband, Rob, from the Internet. He's behind the counter, and he doesn't belong here either. He's a handsome man, with a plaid button-down tucked in neatly, sleeves rolled up, oozing affability. Good things could happen to him, if he weren't saddled with this dying cow of a business. But maybe he's the type who can't actually make good things happen; he takes what comes. That could be how he wound up with Dawn for a wife. She bowled him over.

"What's the event?" he asks with an easy smile. "Anniversary? Graduation? It's that time of year."

"It is." I smile back. My social graces reassert themselves in the face of his. If the stars had aligned differently, correctly, this would be my son. I feel a sudden ache keeping time alongside the anger that has ticked inside me all day, a constant companion during the six-hour drive. I was speeding along with my internal metronome. I never speed.

I'd be lying if I said there wasn't some exhilaration as I hurtled toward Oakland, coasting on fury, throwing off the yoke I've experienced my whole life. I'm almost sixty years old, and I've remained a good little girl, my mother's daughter. But she doesn't remember who I am, so what am I trying to prove? Maybe all these years, I've been no one at all, just a voiceless automaton, going through the motions, pretending to be a good mother.

Thad could tell, though, couldn't he?

I'm not a good little girl anymore, I'm an angry old woman. To hell with all of them.

"So? What can I do for you?" Rob leans on his forearms across the glass case, an acceptable form of flirting between younger and elder. "We have some rings over here. Gold. Platinum." He gestures toward a different case. He's going to try to upsell me, and I can't blame him. This should be peak time, with all the graduations and anniversaries, and yet, here we are, just the two of us. But he's barking up the wrong tree.

"I'm not here to make a purchase," I say. "This is awkward, so I'll just introduce myself. My name is Miranda Feldt. You're Rob Thiebold, correct?"

His expression changes instantly. Gone is your friendly neighborhood salesman, and in its place, a fire-breathing dragon. *"You're Miranda?"*

"I don't know what you've heard about me, but I have some information for you."

"I don't want to hear anything from you. You've been harassing my wife."

"It's most certainly the other way around."

His lip curls in disgust. "You need to leave my store."

"It's natural that you'd want to side with your wife. But there are some things you don't know about her. There are some things I could tell you that might change the way you feel about the situation, and her."

"You've already done enough damage."

Damage? To Dawn or to him? To their marriage?

Good.

"She's done far more damage to me, I can assure you," I say. "And, potentially, to my son."

"I don't know anything about your son, and I don't want to. I'm asking you to leave. If you don't, I'll call the police."

The idea that he would need the police against me is so outrageous that something inside me snaps. "You need to hear the truth! Your wife has been lying to you! About me, and my supposed harassment of her! And about her extracurricular activities!"

Suddenly, I can see it so clearly. Dawn's henchman was Thad. That's who Calvin saw skulking. That's who put the rat in my pool. Is that who soiled my sheets?

"She's been with my son," I say. "He's been doing her dirty work."

"Get out of my store, *now*!"

"No!" Getting thrown out of two places in one day—I'd thought I couldn't sink any lower. But I will not be silenced. "You're going to hear the truth! Your wife is having an affair with my son! His name is Thad Feldt. Find him on Twitter. Your wife, Dawn T. Bold, is *inspiring* him!"

Rob storms around the counter, and I feel a twinge of fear. He's not a small man, and he's as fired up as I am. Dawn doesn't deserve him and his loyalty, his defense of her honor. Her honor. What a joke.

"Leave my wife alone, and leave me alone." He grabs my arm and begins to yank me toward the door.

"Take your hands off me," I shout. Then I yell out Thad's Twitter handle, but by then, he's hustled me out on the street. I'm still yelling, and pedestrians are shooting me quick glances and then averting their eyes, the way you would from some crazy homeless woman making a spectacle.

I ignore them, trying to catch my breath as I decide what to do next. A part of me wants to call the police myself. A man should not lay his hands on a woman, under any circumstances. He's a business owner, or at least, his family is. I could do him harm.

But I don't want to. None of this is his fault. It's hers. He's just a fool in love. Like Thad.

Rob isn't willing to listen, not yet. But I've planted the seed, and it could grow fruit. In the meantime, I know her address.

She's not just messing with me anymore. I'm a mama bear, and she's threatening my cub. He might be a grown man, but he's stalled out emotionally, like all addicts. He's so susceptible to her wiles that he would attack his own mother. That's the behavior of an adolescent, someone who can't see until tomorrow and the next day. A foreshortened future, that's addiction in a nutshell. They used that phrase a bunch in Nar-Anon.

I feel unadulterated rage. At Larry, and at Thad, and at a life that's spinning out of my control. But really, it comes down to Dawn. She's the one threatening to destroy me, and Thad, and I have to get to her first.

I'm not going to leave Dawn alone, no matter what Rob says. On the contrary, I'm going right for her. She'll never see me coming.

For some strange reason, I find myself smiling. She won't see me coming, but ultimately, she will see me and she'll hear me, clear as bells.

55

Dawn

Don't let your grad be forgotten #engravingisthenewblack

I don't know how it happened, how the vodka got into the orange juice, but I'm feeling a whole lot better about everything now. Thad would never hurt me. He's here for the opposite reason.

I'm feeling good, actually, sitting here on the couch with Thad, buzzed, not drunk. At the moment, Thad seems neither ominous nor ridiculous but nearly attractive. He probably has a trust fund coming to him at some point, and an inheritance. There are worse horses to bet on.

He still wants me to tell him my secrets, but now he says it lightly, teasingly, and honestly, I can't seem to keep track of what I've said. Sometimes he's nodding with his eyebrows knitted together like I'm revealing something deep as the cosmos, and then seconds later we're both laughing, our heads lolling back on the cushions.

I've gotten past the cadaverous appearance and the teeth. It's like I'm looking through some kind of digital enhancement, a blue screen of sorts, and his teeth have lost that jack-o'-lantern quality and he's put on twenty pounds. He's the Thad I first saw on the Internet, the one at his high school graduation, flanked by his well-heeled parents, full of promise, headed to UC Santa Barbara.

I'm not sure what the segue is, but Thad has gotten serious. He's talking about his parents, and part of me wants to stop him because I'm just not interested in Miranda anymore. I finally am letting go of all that, but it seems like he really needs to talk.

I'm not catching every single word through my buzz but I do get this: The good doctor is actually a Dr. Jekyll and Mr. Hyde, and he has screwed Miranda's relationship with Thad big-time. When he was drunk, Mr. Hyde came out. He would go into Thad's room for their late-night chats and he'd poison Thad against his mom. It went on for years and years, so long that it seemed like Thad didn't know where his dad's version of Miranda ended and his own experiences began. It was stressful, being fed all these stories about his mother, and it might have even been part of why Thad started using drugs, so he could be elated instead of confused, at least for a little while.

"I wanted to be perfect myself," he says. "I wanted my mother to love me like I was but she never could. It was all an act."

"How do you know it was an act?"

"I could feel it."

"But did you feel it because you took your dad's word for it?"

"I'll tell you a story," he says, "and at the end of it, you'll see."

I take a swig and get ready to listen.

Thad tells me that when he was fourteen, his father came into his room, sobbing. He'd killed somebody on the operating table, an old guy who was probably going to die soon anyway, but his dad was such a good person that he was still royally torn up. "I'd had one drink," he cried to Thad, "to take the edge off. To deal with the pressure your mom was always putting on me. I never should have done it."

Thad said his dad was obviously tormented, crying and shaking. What he'd wanted was for his wife to tell him it was okay that he'd made a mistake. He wanted her to tell him that he didn't need to be perfect, that he should own up and take responsibility, which was what he really wanted. He wanted to make things right with the hospital, and with the family. But of course, she'd never tell him that. She didn't want a black mark on him, and on her. So he had to cover it up.

Over the coming months, he cried other times, too. He always felt so bad about it, but there was no way to make it right now, was there? He had to live with it.

"I said to my dad that he couldn't admit that he'd lied, after the fact. It would ruin him, and my dad said exactly, he was trapped. That fucking bitch. She trapped him. She destroyed my dad."

"He doesn't sound so destroyed when you talk about him," I say. What he sounds is evil. He kills someone while he's drunk but he can't come clean because his wife won't let him?

"That's because he's strong. He found a way to deal with it."

Poor Miranda. Her whole relationship with her son's been hijacked by Mr. Hyde, and I bet she doesn't even know it. Thad clearly doesn't get it. I'm trying to think how to break the news when the front door flies open.

My reflexes have been substantially slowed by my buzz. Before I can even register what's happening, Rob's standing in front of the couch, his chest heaving. He looks massive, like Thor. It must be the contrast with Thad. My vodka goggles disappear instantly, and I see Thad as he in fact is, as Rob must.

I stand up. "It's not what it looks like." Oldest line in the book. Alcohol has never sparked my creativity. If only Thad had brought some meth.

Rob ignores me. He's focused on Thad. "Get up."

Thad puts his hands in the air. "I come in peace."

"You came to fuck my wife."

He shakes his head. "Like she said, it's not what it looks like. She needed a friend, I was in the area."

"I bet you were!" Rob roars. I didn't even know he could access that decibel. No, wait, I heard it once before. The road rage incident. Rob, my protector. "Get up!" Wait, wasn't he screaming that at me last night? He was spoiling for a fight then, too.

"Let's talk this over, man." I imagine Thad's been in situations far more dangerous than this one. Maybe you stay seated so that you're nonthreatening. It's zoo rules: You don't taunt the gorilla. Or you stay low to the ground and sweep the leg, like in *The Karate Kid*.

Thad could have tricks up his sleeve, though. He must go to all sorts of shady places to buy drugs. He has to know how to defend himself when he spots trouble. Rob went to a Christian college full of rich preps. He's the one in over his head. Whatever the state of our marriage, I don't want to see him hurt.

"Rob," I say, "Thad was just leaving."

"Thad." Rob nods briskly. "Of course. This is Thad."

"She's talked about me?" Thad queries.

"I just met your mother."

"My mother?" Thad glances at me, like we're on *Candid Camera*.

His mother? Rob met Miranda? So Miranda's in Oakland, trailing her son like a bloodhound? I know I'm a little slow on the uptake, but this is a lot to process.

"She said her son, Thad, was fucking my wife. I told her she was crazy." Now Rob's glaring at me. "I told her to get out of my store."

"You kicked my mother out of a store? Awesome!" Thad claps his hands together with a childish glee.

Rob turns back to Thad. "You're a real piece of work." Disrespecting mothers is definitely not the way to Rob's heart. His face has hardened to pure hatred. He advances, grabs Thad by the throat, and lifts him. I've never seen a maneuver like that in real life, and I wouldn't have expected my first time would be with Rob. Thad is dangling like a skeleton, and Rob actually hurls him toward the front door, then advances again. I think it has to be the adrenaline, the same thing that allows moms to lift cars off kids. Dads must be able to lift cars off kids, too, but you never hear about that.

Thad is scrambling backward, still on the floor. Rob is walking slowly, like he's relishing this moment, and that lets Thad get to his feet and sprint out the door. Rob looks back at me, like he's debating whether to chase Thad, and I say, "Let him go. We just texted sometimes, that's all."

Rob is looking back and forth, between the door and me, considering his next move. By now, Thad's got a head start. I hear the outer door to the building slamming shut downstairs.

The hatred is still on Rob's face, and now it's directed at me. "Lift your shirt."

Is he saying he wants to have sex? Now? I don't know what I feel. His anger doesn't seem so attractive at the moment, but I know I need to do penance for Thad. "Nothing happened with Thad."

"Lift your shirt." Each word is guttural, through gritted teeth.

I find myself complying.

"I knew it," he spits out in disgust. "I knew you'd be wearing that bra."

It's not my workaday seamless T-shirt bra with the racerback; it's the one with the lacy cutouts around my nipples. Now, it's evidence. I wore it for Thad. Just in case.

"You would have fucked him if I hadn't come home."

"I wouldn't have." I'm pretty sure I wouldn't. "Did you see his teeth?"

"You would have fucked that nasty track-marked piece of shit in the apartment I pay for. On my couch, or in my bed?" He looks like he still wants to hit someone. "My father was right. You're a gold digger."

"You see any gold around here?"

"I'm going to inherit the business."

I guess we're all delusional in our own ways. "A business that's worthless."

"We're tweeting now." There it is, that Thiebold optimism. I never stood a fighting chance at becoming one of them. "You don't know anything about the business."

"I know you have almost no customers. I know you lived in this apartment for three years before me, and we've been here more than three years together. That's not exactly upward mobility."

He looks away, like he's fighting for control. His fists clench and unclench. "We're not talking about me. We're talking about you."

"About me being a gold digger. Which I'm not. I've just been unhappy. My father pimped me out, my mother's a waste of space, I'm begging Big Pharma for a job I don't even want, I'm texting a junkie, I've been harassing his mother for weeks. I've got to figure my shit out, I know that. But I'm not normal, and I never will be, and that needs to be okay with you. It needs to be okay with me. Can it ever be okay with you?"

I see the answer in his eyes at the same time that I hear a male scream of agony from the street below. It's followed by a door opening and slamming, and a woman yelling, "Oh my God, help!" Then there are only wails.

56

Miranda

I don't know what happened. I was sitting in my car outside Dawn's house, boiling for a confrontation, and a voice inside told me to wait. I thought it was some kind of guardian angel, or my mother coming through at last (maybe my mother died after I left and she *was* the guardian angel), and I trusted that voice.

I was parked there, and then Thad came running out of the building. A scarecrow of Thad, but a mother can always recognize her son, no matter how much he's deteriorated.

There he was, running, and my first thought was not, Someone's chasing him, or, Is he okay? No, it's, Oh my God, he's robbed someone. He's hurt someone. It was a robbery gone wrong. Do I cover for him? Do I turn him in? For years, I've expected it to come to this. I should have had a plan.

Is Dawn dead? It would be so like the universe to solve one of my problems while creating an entirely worse one.

So I decide that I need to follow him. He doesn't even notice the car trailing him, he's in full flight. One block, then two, then he stops. He bends over, out of breath, and when he looks up, I duck down. He wouldn't necessarily recognize my car. Then I realize he's not looking in my direction at all. He's looking back the way he came, and a certain resolve comes over his face, and he's headed back. Back to the scene of the crime, perhaps. This time, he's walking instead of running.

These are residential blocks in midmorning in what looks to be a depressed area. I bet no one goes anywhere in midmorning. This place comes alive at night, with drug deals, probably. This is just the kind of neighborhood Thad should be avoiding. It's a trigger.

But he clearly hasn't been avoiding anything that's bad for him. I know that look. He's emaciated. He's been lying to me about being clean these past months.

He'll never be clean. Never.

I'm filled with a hopelessness and fury that can't even be expressed as I follow him back toward Dawn's apartment. I'm wondering if the meth has done something to his hearing because he never turns toward the car, and while it's a luxury machine, it's not soundless.

We're almost there, and that's when he spins and sees me. I slam my brakes, and he narrows his eyes. He doesn't look entirely surprised, is the strange thing. But he does look hateful.

He hates me. After all he's put me through and everything I've sacrificed—even right now, I'm here for him, to pry him from Dawn's clutches—and still, *he* hates *me*.

He steps out in front of my car, and he bangs on the hood. He's yelling that I need to get out of here, that I don't belong, not here, and not in his life. He's cursing prolifically, even though he knows I abhor that. It's *because* I abhor it. Another slam on the hood.

He'll never be clean. The addiction is a monster that's devoured my Thaddeus, my little boy, the one who had dreams and potential and a heart. This is the monster he will always be.

That's what I'm thinking, but what I'm not thinking is: Reverse. Then put your foot on the gas.

I swear, I never once thought that.

57

Dawn

I'm chasing after Rob, down the flight of steps, and he stops so suddenly that I nearly run into him. "Oh my God," he says.

Thad is half-under a large Audi sedan, and he's not moving. Miranda is kneeling on the ground by the front tire, her hands over her face, genuflecting. Sobs escape from between her fingers.

"Did you already call 911?" Rob asks Miranda. She shakes her head, panicked. That's my first clue.

Miranda is not what I expected. She's wearing a long-sleeved T-shirt, jeans, and sneakers. Her hair looks like it hasn't been washed or brushed today or maybe yesterday either, and she's wearing no makeup. I was sure she'd be Botoxed to within an inch of her life, but she's got deep frown lines beside her mouth and pleats in her forehead.

"It's you," she says.

"And you," I say.

Rob ducks under the car and reports, "He's breathing."

"Thank God," Miranda says. But there's something in her tone . . . that's my second clue.

Having met Thad, I get it. I really do. I feel like I get her. Yes, her grief is real, but there's nothing simple about it, or about her. I've misjudged her all this time, same as Thad has. Miranda has layers. She's more conflicted than I could ever be, until I have kids of my own.

Now that I'm looking at her, I can see so clearly that she's not the one I've been mad at all along.

The one I've been mad at is me. I married Rob to become someone else, and I did the getaways for the same reason, and here I am, still me. All that darkness insisted on coming out anyway. In fact, I don't see how I can be any brighter until I'm on my own. I can't be a good person by osmosis. It'll never work.

Rob is talking to the dispatcher now, describing the situation. "An ambulance is on the way," he mouths to Miranda.

"I don't know if I should touch him," she says to me. "Should I hold his hand? You know him. Would he want me to?"

I say, with full compassion, "Probably not."

"Would he want you to?"

"Maybe. But I can't." I indicate Rob with my eyes. Just because my marriage is ending, that doesn't mean I need to hurt him any more than I already have. I married him under false pretenses, even if I didn't know it at the time. I *was* digging for gold, of a sort. I wanted the Thiebold golden aura, the one bred of years of care and love. But instead of absorbing those rays, after a time I seemed to refract them. Rob has begun to take on my worst qualities, and while they were the very qualities I'd hoped to eradicate by marrying him, they've actually grown stronger. We've begun to make each other worse instead of better.

"If this is it," Miranda says, her eyes glistening, "if these are his last minutes, he needs to know he's not alone. Doesn't he?"

"He's still breathing. He'll be okay. Thad's the type with nine lives."

Miranda begins to shake. "I don't know what happened. How did all this happen?" I can see she doesn't just mean hitting Thad with her car. That's the culmination. I feel her pain, and her bewilderment. Neither of us meant to get here. We'll be intertwined, forever.

"It was an accident," I say. "I saw the whole thing from my kitchen window. He ran in front of your car. I'll tell the police."

The look on Miranda's face—that's the third clue. She meant to do it, and she didn't. I'm intimately familiar with that. We're more the same than we are different. Otherwise, it would never have come to this. One of us would have turned back long ago, given in, but instead, we kept driving right for each other.

She wants him to wake up and be okay, and she wants this to be the end of the whole ordeal of having been his mother.

"If he wakes up," I say, "I'll tell them to check his blood alcohol level. They should screen for other drugs, too. He's an unreliable witness under the best circumstances." I catch her eye meaningfully. "Not like you and me."

I'm going to lie for Miranda, because it's the right thing to do. I owe her that much.

Miranda's been set up her whole marriage by her husband, Mr. Hyde. Her relationship with her son was doomed to fail. Perhaps Dr. Jekyll doesn't know about Mr. Hyde, and all the sabotage occurred during blackouts. He might not have any memory, but Thad sure does.

Poor Thad. Poor Miranda.

I know that no matter how I explained it to Rob, he would never understand my decision to lie to the police. He'll never understand me, and if we stay together, I'll keep trying to be someone else for him. We have different moralities, Rob and me, but I do have morality. I do.

58

Miranda

I'm in the surgical waiting room, all alone. There are a few blue pleather recliners, though I opt to sit in one of the matching straight-backed blue chairs that skirt the perimeter. The TV is tuned to a cartoon network, and there's a beautiful, sparkly princess of indeterminate race having adventures. I can't bring myself to look for the remote control; my legs wouldn't support me if I tried to stand up. Besides, what do you watch while the son you ran over with your car is in surgery? It's too late for Dr. Phil.

Thad has a closed head injury. That means I didn't crack his skull, which is good, but they need to put a bolt inside to monitor pressure in his brain cavity. They'll also drain some of the intracranial bleeding. "We'll do our best," the surgeon assured me. I can only hope he hasn't been drinking, and the anesthesiologist is well rested.

Thad can't die. He just can't. There's simply no way. I will not even entertain the thought.

But as soon as you try not to think something, you can think nothing else.

"I thought you might need this." I look up to see Dawn proffering my purse. "You left it behind in your car."

I leaped into the ambulance, and since then, I've been so beside myself, I didn't even realize . . .

I left my car in the middle of the street, keys still inside. Purse, too, apparently. Right next to the police, who were at the scene of what was presumed to be an accident.

If the police run any tests on the Audi, they'll see how fast I was moving at the time of the collision. There may be marks on the street to show that I backed up before I went forward, producing additional velocity. There must be forensic evidence, if they look for it.

They've had more than enough time to examine the Audi's exterior closely. Are they legally allowed to look inside? What would happen if they found an ax, stun gun, and pepper spray?

It's all for self-defense. That's what the man said at Walmart. It was in the Personal Safety department, a subsection of Home Improvement. A very small department, but they call it that for a reason. All it suggests is that I feared for my own safety, going into a neighborhood like Dawn's to retrieve my wayward son. That explains everything, except the ax.

Do not let Dawn see you panic.

"Thank you," I say, accepting the purse. I don't meet her eyes. I want to riffle through the contents, making sure everything's as it should be—nothing taken, nothing planted. This is, after all, the infamous Dawn Thiebold.

She must realize what I'm thinking. I've always been transparent. "Everything's in there. I'm not the type to take anything, contrary to what you might think." Her tone has no sharp edges.

She seems at peace. Maybe she and Thad were doing drugs together.

This is neither here nor there, but Dawn's not as beautiful as I'd made her out to be. She's attractive, yes, but she has a lot of acne, and wears heavy makeup in order to (unsuccessfully) conceal it. She's trashy, in that tank top and skintight jeans. Well-proportioned, but short.

She takes the seat next to me, and I tense up. "I owe you an apology," she says. I keep my eyes on the floor and my shock to myself. "I should never have taken it to that level. I'll delete everything online."

I want to ask why the change of heart, what's in it for her, but I remain silent. It's probably good practice for me.

"You might not believe me, but I'm going to prove it to you. I told the police that I saw the accident. I said that Thad was behaving erratically, that he was drunk and probably high, and he ran out of my apartment when Rob came home." Now I have to glance at her, and what I see is a lot of pimples and an equivalent amount of sincerity. "I said you were here to help him, but he wasn't ready to accept help."

"Why would you do that?"

"Because it's true. Right? You've always meant to help him." Her blue eyes are peculiarly kind. This is not the woman I've come to know. This is not a woman I'm prepared to trust.

She's willing to lie for me, but it can't be out of the goodness of her heart. Not Dawn Thiebold.

There will be strings, probably expensive ones, and now that I've seen her husband's store and her neighborhood, I understand a little better. She didn't have an extra two hundred lying around to replace those sheets. She never had any business renting the Santa Monica house.

If I pay her off, I'm as bad as her, and as bad as Larry. No, I'm nothing like either one of them.

Whatever I've done, it was because I felt too much. I loved too much. That is surely not Dawn's problem, or Larry's.

I'm getting ahead of myself here. There's no reason to believe I'm even a suspect. A documented drug addict ran in front of my car while inebriated. It's a much more plausible story than "Pillar of the Community Mows Down Addict Son." The former wouldn't even be a headline, only the latter.

I can hold my own with the police, if it comes to that. I'm a respectable citizen, a concerned mother. I would never try to kill my son. That isn't me. It's someone else. "Temporary insanity" is entirely apt.

This could be it, my fork in the road. Sell the Santa Monica house, start over somewhere new. I'm leaving Larry behind, that feels like a given.

He is still Thad's father, which means I should call and say that Thad's in surgery.

"Where's your husband?" I ask Dawn.

"I don't know. He's pretty upset with me right now."

Well, no wonder. But I'm not about to jab at her, not when she's managed to get the ultimate upper hand.

"There's something you should know," she says. "This wasn't your fault."

"That's what you told the police."

"No, I mean from way back. Thad held you responsible but he was wrong. He was responsible for his own actions, with an assist from your husband."

"Larry?" I can't even muster surprise, and that seems to surprise her.

"Ever since Thad was a little kid, Larry would go into his room late at night for drunken confessions."

"Which one was drunk?"

"Larry. But his confessions were more like complaints about you. About how you were impossible to please, and the only love you showed was fake, and how"—she lowers her voice—"you wouldn't let him admit that he killed that guy on the operating table. You wouldn't let him own up to it."

"What!" I exclaim.

She nods. "See, I knew that was crap. But Thad totally believed it. I guess the conversations went on for years, and Thad came to really trust this dad who came to see him at night."

"But then ignored him pretty much the rest of the time." My head is spinning. I never saw this coming.

"Larry undermined your whole relationship with Thad. Any nice thing you did was chalked up to being fake, and any time you showed something negative, Thad thought that was the real you. You pretty much couldn't win. Mr. Hyde saw to that. You know, like Dr. Jekyll and Mr. Hyde?"

I'm speechless.

"And just so you know, Thad's been squatting in the Santa Monica house. He was behind the stained sheets."

"I figured," I say faintly.

"I think either you and Thad were both pawns in some master chess game that Larry was playing, or he was just a really, really mean drunk who couldn't remember anything in the morning."

I'm angry for what Larry's done to me, yes, but more than that, I'm sad. For the relationship Thad and I might have had without interference, and what Thad could have been without the burden of being turned against his own mother.

"I'm sure you made mistakes, but a lot of it's not your fault," Dawn says. "That deck was stacked. I wanted to tell you that."

"Thank you," I say. "It's good to hear." Larry has never told me that, I realize. Thad would never.

How did Larry get his drinking past me all these years? Because during the residency, I knew. My instincts told me, unequivocally, even as I tried to tamp them down. Maybe after the residency I learned to turn them off completely. It was in my genes, after all, a family trait I'd inherited from my mother.

I remember being a little girl and trying to shake my father awake. I remember my fright, and the smell of him high in my nostrils. Running downstairs, I told my mother we needed to call 911, and she said, without turning away from the counter she was scrubbing, "He needs sleep. And he needs you to forget, and to never mention this again. Love gives a wide berth."

Translation: You don't shake people awake; you learn to sleepwalk.

I'm awake now.

The doctor comes out and he looks from Dawn to me and back again, questioningly. "She can stay," I say. "She can hear."

We're in this together, after all.

"Thad's alive," the doctor tells us. Now, for the bad news (or what he clearly thinks is the bad news): there's brain damage; Thad is like a five-year-old who'll need to relearn everything.

He might not remember that he loved meth. He might think he loves me. The two of us could start over together, far away from Larry's influence.

I'm going to have another chance, a clean slate, a fresh start. I'll be free of all the old expectations, all the lies, all the encumbrances of convention. No more social graces. No more husband. It'll be the real me, and the real Thad, in a grand do-over.

This time, I'll do it better. This time, I'll get it right.

Perhaps all of this was the universe's way of telling me I was meant to be a single mother.

"Where there's life," I tell Dawn, "there's hope." She nods, like she gets me completely.

Thad needs this second chance more than anyone, and however it's come about, it's here now.

This is not over, not at all.

About the author

About the book

Insights,
Interviews
& More . . .

Meet Holly Brown

Photo by Yanina Gotsulsky

HOLLY BROWN lives with her husband and toddler daughter in the San Francisco Bay Area, where she's a practicing marriage and family therapist. Her blog, *Bonding Time,* is featured on PsychCentral.com. ∾

Reading Group Discussion Questions

1. Dawn and Miranda initially come into contact through an Airbnb/VRBO-type rental. Do you think they would have had the same fiery outcome if they'd connected by other means, or is there something about the intimacy of a home rental that predisposed them to what followed?

2. The women escalate in their outrage with each other. Did you find one of them to be more reasonable—and more sympathetic—in her outrage, given either the provocation or the circumstances of their lives?

3. Miranda is struggling with a drug-addicted son. Is this a situation that you related to? Is it generalizable to other types of issues with children, in that a child's issues can become consuming for a parent and the parent can lose perspective along the way?

4. Both women want desperately to be validated, for the other woman to just say, "You're right and I'm wrong." Why do you think that is so important to each of them? Have you ever experienced a similar need for validation, with either a stranger, a friend, or a loved one?

5. Miranda and Dawn have misperceptions about each other. Specifically, each imagines the other's life to have what hers lacks: Miranda envies Dawn's youth and beauty and that Dawn is just starting out with her handsome, adoring husband; Dawn envies Miranda's money, stability, and certainty, assuming these bring peace of mind. How do these misperceptions fuel their interactions?

6. How does social media play into people's misperceptions of one another? ▶

Reading Group Discussion Questions *(continued)*

7. What did you think of their marriages and their husbands? Were you surprised by what's revealed about each as the novel progresses?

8. Is Thad a pawn, a victim, or a villain? Or is he something else entirely?

9. The book begins with the image of stained sheets—which is particularly enraging for Dawn, as it reflects her fear that the damage that's been done to her is irreparable and she can never be clean again, no matter what she does. For Miranda, given her son's addiction, the idea of "coming clean" has a different meaning. What does it mean to you? What do you believe about human potential?

10. The women come together in the end, under unusual circumstances. Does that feel satisfying for you as a reader? If not, what had you hoped would happen? Share your alternate ending. ∽

The Story Behind the Book

THE IDEA for my third novel found me close to home. Well, close to someone else's home.

While it's not unusual for strangers to offend one another, sometimes the irritation lingers just a little longer than you'd expect. That's how I felt after I stayed in a rental in a coastal California town and, a week later, received an e-mail from the owner accusing me of leaving soiled sheets. To be more specific, I was told that I'd left a "child-sized gray stain." My toddler daughter wasn't filthy, and I wasn't blind, so I became convinced the owner was scamming my security deposit.

We went back and forth a number of times, a thrust-and-parry between two people who were each convinced of their own correctness. I found myself almost looking forward to the owner's next e-mail so that I'd have another opportunity to refute her, and I had the distinct impression she was doing the same with me. She wanted me to know she was a pillar of her community, and I wanted her to know that my child wasn't made of ash. She told me never to stay at one of her rentals again, and I responded, "Gladly." Ultimately, I left a review on the rental website that was as much about her as it was about her property; she left a rebuttal; and we went on with our lives.

But if I'm honest with myself, there was something in me that welcomed our exchanges, that liked feeling self-righteous toward a stranger. It allowed me to vent and to purge, to displace other daily frustrations onto a target. She served a psychological purpose for me, as I must have for her. Otherwise, we wouldn't have been vying for the last word.

The novelist in me thought, *What if we'd kept going? What if we had painful histories and present truths that we wanted to avoid at all costs, even if it led to a slow-motion, head-on collision?* So my "host" and I became Miranda and Dawn. ▶

The Story Behind the Book (*continued*)

The Airbnb/HomeAway/VRBO world intrigues me, because there's a certain psychology embedded within it. When we choose to stay in someone else's home rather than a hotel, we're making an emotional as well as a financial decision. Being surrounded by someone else's taste (and in some cases, their actual possessions) impacts the kind of trip we intend to have. It might mean we want to feel like locals rather than tourists. Or it might mean we want to play an adult version of pretend. We want to feel how the other half lives, just for a little while.

In Dawn's case, she scrolled through many properties looking for just the right one, seeking a certain luxury that was very distinct from her real life. She wants to escape and to inhabit someone else's life, kind of like playing dress-up. On the other hand, Miranda's motivation is purely mercenary. She likes that people appreciate the house, but really, she needs the income for a reason that becomes clear as the novel unfolds. So there's a certain conflict set up right from the start that fuels the rest of the book. Dawn wants what (she thinks) Miranda has; Miranda just wants Dawn's money.

But that begins to change. While Dawn dreams of the happiness that she imagines is derived from financial security, Miranda becomes envious of Dawn's youth and beauty. Miranda yearns for a do-over, while Dawn desires to arrive at a higher station than the one she was born into. Then they Google each other, and that adds more fuel to the fire. Online footprints can easily feed misperceptions. On social media, people curate themselves for the world, creating a persona to show to others. It can be something of a double life. Unfortunately for Miranda and Dawn, they're a little too convincing.

As a writer, I tend to be inspired by contemporary events and phenomena. With my first novel, *Don't Try to Find Me*, I was intrigued by a real-life story about how a parent's use of social media helped find a runaway daughter. In *A Necessary End,* I was compelled by all the maddening hoops that people have to jump through in order to adopt a newborn. I like to take an emotionally charged situation and then imagine the people within it. I build the kindling, psychologically and dynamically speaking, and then I light the match. For *This Is Not Over,* I loved combining the aspirational psychology of Getaway.com with the personal psychologies of these two women who seem very different at the outset but grow more alike as the book progresses. Or perhaps they were alike all along; they just had to strip away the trappings.

Since I'm a practicing marriage and family therapist as well as a writer, I take my psychological fiction very seriously. I know I have to raise the stakes, since it is suspense after all, but it's important for the plot twists to derive from who these characters are. That's how it'll feel credible and real. I want readers to consider what they'd do if they were presented with a series of choices always escalating in complexity. The fatal flaws of the characters consistently push them closer to an edge they never saw coming but that feels inevitable to the reader. And who among us is without flaws? Who doesn't occasionally need a vacation from their real lives? Who doesn't, every now and again, want what they can't have? ◦⌣

Q&A with Holly Brown

Where did the idea of two women squabbling over an Airbnb-esque vacation rental property initially come from?

From my own vacation gone wrong, of course! (I'm only partially kidding.) I did stay in a rental with my family and was subsequently accused of leaving a "child-sized gray stain" on the sheets. I felt pretty offended, since my daughter was two at the time and being bathed regularly. The "host" and I went back and forth a few times, each of us increasingly aggravated with the other's failure to see her point of view. Then she kept part of my security deposit, I left a nasty review, and that was the end of that. Until, that is, I had the idea about what kind of women would keep going, past the point of no return.

How did your profession as a marriage and family therapist influence the characters' home and family life?

While I don't provide substance abuse treatment to those who are addicted, I do work with their families. I counsel around enabling and codependency issues, and how to hold boundaries. There's no way a parent can truly prepare for that most extreme scenario: having to cut off a child. It's very much like cutting off a limb. You feel the phantom pain always. So I didn't base Miranda on any specific client, but my professional immersion in the experience of family members was very much with me when I created her.

As for Dawn, she's the victim of childhood trauma that has shaped the way she relates to other people and the man she's chosen for her husband. She sees the world through a certain ▶

lens because of what she's been through. That's something I often see in my clinical work. As a therapist, my job is to supportively help correct the distortions. As a writer, my job is to create drama. Same knowledge base, very different objectives!

A recurring theme in the book is the notion that the two main characters, Miranda and Dawn, each believe the other to be living a life very different from her actual one. How does this idea relate to our cultural aspirations, and how is it exacerbated by social media?

I think staying in a VRBO or an Airbnb rental is often about wanting to feel like a local and not a tourist; it relates to the cultural ideal of authenticity. But paradoxically, it's also about trying on someone else's neighborhood, trying on their life. It's a very intimate thing to stay in another person's home, surrounded by their taste if not their actual possessions, and we form all kinds of impressions.

Dawn browsed all the listings and then chose to stay in Miranda's home. She wanted to live like Miranda for a long weekend. On the other hand, Miranda never really chose Dawn.

Their status imbalance quickly comes to the forefront once they start sparring. Then they look at each other's social media, and—surprise, surprise—it seems to confirm their biases about one another. So often, we find what we're looking for because we create it in our own minds. We turn our own perceived deficits into someone else's strengths.

Social media perpetuates this. People are curating the reality they want to present, and if you forget this, you can really wind up feeling inferior. I have a number of clients who've benefited from the intervention of just getting off every social media site so that they're not constantly interfacing with the supposed perfection of other people's lives. Then they can just focus on improving their own reality.

A lot of the exchanges between Miranda and Dawn are via e-mail and text. In this day and age, what are the risks and consequences of communicating behind a screen instead of face to face?

Face to face, we have to deal—in real time—with the consequences of our actions. We say something hurtful, we see someone flinch. Witnessing another person's reactions creates a layer of civility. It's at the heart of etiquette.

It's also at the heart of empathy. Humans are wired to empathize based on facial expressions and vocal cadences. We see that someone is sad or about to cry, or we hear a choked-back sob, and it'll inspire compassion. Or we can tell that someone is sincere when we might have thought they were false if we'd had only the written word, devoid of nuance.

Think of Internet trolls and cyberbullies. They don't have to see their victims, and it leads to a very dangerous sort of liberation, to an aggression that's unchecked by empathy.

If Miranda and Dawn had met earlier in the book, if they'd actually met, they could have defused the situation with relative ease. The events of this novel could happen only because of the dehumanizing channels by which the women communicate.

There are a lot of "little" details that both Miranda and Dawn don't tell their husbands that eventually snowball into major events within the book. Why would you say the women are so reluctant to communicate honestly with their husbands? Do you think this reflects a trend in marriages today?

I wouldn't say all women are reluctant to communicate honestly with their husbands, but ▶

telling the whole truth is as fraught now as it's
ever been. When we share absolutely
everything, we risk hurting or alienating our
partner; we risk exposing ourselves, maybe the
parts we feel are undesirable. While we may
have more honest marriages now than in the
past (or at least there's a lot more talk about
intimacy than ever before), I think the
fundamental insecurities and vulnerabilities are
the same as always. The impulse to withhold a
small detail or tell a white lie is just part of
human nature. We all want to be loved, and
once we are, we don't want to risk losing that
love by exposing ourselves, especially when we
can just rationalize our omissions. One thing I
know for sure from therapy is that people have
an infinite capacity for justification.

*In the book, Miranda has a drug-addicted son,
and a lot of her actions and decisions are
influenced by this fact. In your opinion, what are
some healthy ways to support but not encourage
someone who may be struggling with similar
issues?*

If someone you love has truly committed to their
recovery and taken the crucial steps to remain
sober, then the best way to support that person is
with acceptance and patience. It's going to take a
long time to learn a new, chemical-free way of
being in the world. There may be relapses. But it's
about commitment to the process. You need to
let them know you believe they can stay clean
and that it's worth doing, and insist that they
continue to engage in that process.

However, if the person you love refuses to get
help, or seems to be manipulating you (as is the
case with Miranda's son), it's important to stand
firm on what you know to be true. Confront in a
supportive way. Hold your ground. Enabling is
about going against your gut instincts and

supporting the addiction by pretending to believe the lies and/or providing practical and financial support. I tell clients to think of it this way: you hate the addiction; why enable it to flourish?

You've written two books prior to This Is Not Over. What did you learn from writing those two that helped shape this one?

With each book, I come up with the idea for a situation, and then I figure out what type of people would inhabit that situation. I think: *What characteristics, personality traits, and psychologies will propel the narrative forward?* That's because it's really important to me that all the plot twists feel like they derive organically from who the characters are, when placed inside a pressure cooker. My job as a writer is to turn up the heat.

While my method was the same for *This Is Not Over* as for the other books, I feel like it flows more with each effort. I could visualize the characters with a lot of clarity right from the start. I always had the image of Miranda and Dawn playing this game of chicken, poised for a head-on collision that I could see coming but they couldn't.

What's next for you, writing-wise?

I enjoy writing a hybrid of women's fiction and domestic suspense. I have a true interest in the psychological underpinnings of everyday life, because often, there's a lot there that's combustible. There's a lot of kindling waiting for a match.

With my next novel, I don't want to give too much away yet. Let's say I'm broadening the canvas. My first three novels were fairly different from one another in terms of plot, but they had in common that they were about just a few ▶

people and their loved ones. It was a fairly intimate setting. This time, I'm going to have a much bigger cast, and a lot of red herrings. It's a whodunit. And a who-keeps-on-doing-it and what-will-they-do-next.

Sorry to keep you in suspense! (Or maybe I'm not.) ⌒